ABOUT THE AUTH

◉

Charles Fernyhough is a writer and psychologist. His first novel, *The Auctioneer*, was widely praised. *The Baby in the Mirror*, his book about the first three years of his daughter's psychological development, was translated into seven languages. His most recent non-fiction book, *Pieces of Light*, is about the science and stories of autobiographical memory. He divides his time between London and County Durham.

A BOX OF BIRDS

◉

CHARLES FERNYHOUGH

◉

A Box Of Birds

unbound

This edition first published in 2012

Unbound
4–7 Manchester Street   Marylebone   London   W1U 2AE
www.unbound.co.uk

A CIP record for this book is available from the British Library

ISBN 978-1-908717-57-3

Typesetting by Bracketpress
Cover design by Dan Mogford

Printed in England by Clays Ltd, Bungay, Suffolk

For Valerie and her grandchildren

When you begin to study the warblers you will probably conclude that you know nothing about birds, and can never learn. But if you begin by recognizing their common traits, and then study a few of the easiest, and those that nest in your locality, you will be less discouraged; and when flocks come back at the next migration you will be able to master the oddities of a larger number.

– Florence Merriam,
  Birds Through an Opera Glass, 1889

Tit lark —
I dont know it

Red Lark —
never seen it

Great Lark —
dont know it

– John Clare,
  Bird List of 1825–26

PART ONE

◉

Gareth

The Thought Show

◉

They turn up in fancy dress, expecting a party. They can arrive at my lab done up like naughty French maids, jolly pirates still drunk from the sea, or maybe a pair of gorillas with realistic flaring nostrils. Once, they broke into someone's amateur dramatics costume cupboard and came straight here with the spoils, and I spent an hour teaching the essentials of synaptic signalling to both ends of a moth-eaten pantomime horse. I tell them that neuroscience is a serious business, but it's hard to be serious about anything when you've chosen your third-year options and there's no coursework due this side of Easter. Gareth shows up first, glancing around at the framed photographs of professors on the corridor walls, wondering which door is my lab and what he would have to do to get in there. James swaggers on behind, carrying his public-school confidence like a bulky parcel on a busy street, expecting people to get out of his way. They're not meant to be up here on the research floors at all, given the security situation, but this is the only part of the Institute where I can hide their threadbare costume dramas from fellow scientists' eyes. Besides, I have to get some facts down them if they're going to have a chance of passing anything this year. At least if they come up here to my office, they can't attract any attention. Persuade them to keep the noise down, and no one will have to know they're here.

'I'm going to need a volunteer,' I tell them.

Gareth dumps his file onto one of the comfy chairs and offers himself uncertainly. Today he's turned up as a Franciscan nun, complete with black veil, polyester tunic and clunky plastic neck-cross. His eyes are anxious and shadowy, and can't stand anything for long. He gives the constant impression that someone is shooting at him.

'I'm going to need you to sign a consent form. What we're doing involves pretty harmless magnetic fields, but we need to get the paper-work right.'

3

James finally gives up on trying to read the secrets of my desktop and settles down in the other chair. 'She's going to experiment on your brain, Gaz. She's going to wire you up to her machines and find out what makes you tick.'

'Am I wearing *that*?' Gareth says.

I grapple with the box. I come up holding an aluminium-cased helmet padded thickly with foam. A spacesuit visor slots over integrated goggles. A spinal column of processors and cables hangs down from the back.

'For a little while,' I say. 'Just long enough for us to find out what you're thinking.'

'Better take your wimple off, Sister,' James says.

I've pulled the blinds down in the office. The one-way glass of the observation window looks out onto the black emptiness of the lab. Outside it's daylight, a bright March afternoon in the heart of the Forest Campus. James and I are perched on the workbench by the door, separated by a pile of research papers. Gareth is sitting in the comfy chair with his head inside the helmet, which is feeding real-time outputs to a desktop machine linked to a distant mainframe. The output of the software is going to a series of floor-mounted projectors planted in a fairy ring on the carpet. The space between us is filled with a huge 3-D hologram of Gareth's brain.

'What does it look like?' Gareth says.

'Colourful,' James replies. 'I'd say the rude thoughts are the pink ones.'

Gareth makes a snorting sound behind the visor, and a blob of brilliant yellow shoots out from the centre of the light-show and dissolves into the rose-threaded haze of his frontal lobe.

'Can you actually tell what I'm thinking?'

I laugh, and realise I shouldn't. 'This isn't the movies, Gareth. You can't read someone's thoughts like you read a computer file. You can see which brain areas are active, but that's pretty much all. It's a toy, really. Something to keep my brightest students interested.'

'Think of something pleasant, Gaz,' James says.

His friend's lips move behind the visor. Blue streaks of neural activity

4

loop from front to back of the brilliant ghost-brain, and a warm red glow swells in his limbic system, that blurred loop of nuclei lodged between the two hemispheres.

'Not *that* pleasant, perv-features ...'

I'm wondering how far back this friendship goes. The fancy-dress thing, the nerdy jargon, this shared certainty about what's funny and not funny. It suggests a schoolboy closeness. A history.

'Have a look,' I say.

Gareth lifts the visor. As soon as the light sparks on his retinas you can see a smudge of activity way over in his visual cortex, on the far right from where we're looking.

'That's you seeing. The bit at the back is where you process visual information.'

'So you could download this stuff ... you could put all my thoughts and memories onto some massive hard drive and have a virtual Gareth Buckle sitting there on your computer?'

'Like I say, this isn't Hollywood.' I click on the remote and zoom in on an amethyst flashpoint in his frontal lobe. 'Even if you had the best resolution in the world, you would only be able to see which neurones were working. You wouldn't be able to see *inside* that neural activity—what it means to the person who's having it.'

In the gloom next to me, James sounds unimpressed. 'It's not *him*, though, is it? It's just biological jazz. Stuff going on in his brain.'

'It's all him, and none of it is him. What's *him* is the way all the different bits work together. Consciousness is probably just a lucky by-product of the brain's enormous complexity.'

'You don't get out much, do you, Miss?'

I pretend not to hear.

'OK, so can it work the other way round?' Gareth flips the visor shut and disappears into the helmet again. 'Can you give a person thoughts and memories they didn't have before? I saw this film with Arnie Schwarzenegger ...'

'You've never watched a film that *didn't* star Arnie Schwarzenegger.'

'Sorry,' I breeze, 'but it doesn't work that way. A memory isn't a chunk of data you can just plug in like a game cartridge. That makes for great TV, but it has nothing to do with real science. You want me to point to what makes Gareth the person he is. I can't do it. *You* — that consciousness, that self, that body of memories — is only possible because of lots of different parts of the brain working together. Memory implants are another one of your science fiction myths, I'm afraid.'

The nun in the helmet makes a disappointed groan.

'Anyway,' I say, thumbing the remote and quitting the software. 'We're only allowed to zap you for a couple of minutes at a time. Sorry.'

I reach behind me and undim the lights.

'So this is what you do in your top-secret research centre? You experiment on people's brains?'

Gareth is keeping the helmet on, like a kid who won't get out of a fairground ride, thinking he'll spot the silent secret of its magic.

'Not people,' James says. 'Animals. The kind of considerate volunteers who keep their outrage to themselves.'

'No wonder they've been round here breaking your windows.'

I think of the circular email that went round after the latest attacks on the East Wing. Professor Gillian Sleet, the lithe and permatanned Director of the Institute, reminding us of the need to maintain vigilance in light of the new security situation. No one knows if those Conscience activists were students or not. The trouble is, we don't know who's a danger and who isn't. Just be careful, they tell us, and trust nobody. Which is precisely why these two are not supposed to be here.

'Look at this scan.' I dim the lights again. 'This isn't you, Gareth; this is a composite made up of images from hundreds of different volunteers. Same technology, just a much more powerful system.'

I touch the remote. Another holographic brain ghosts up in front of our eyes, its shapes made perfect by countless superimposed iterations. Running through it, like the root system of some supernatural orchid, is the vermilion net of the Lorenzo Circuit. I'm always stunned by it, humbled and threatened by its beauty, by the ambition of the thing as much as anything. It leaves nothing out: the control systems of the frontal lobe, the emotion circuits of the limbic system, all the linked factories of meaning that patch the human cortex. That swirl of self shows me a dream of connectedness, challenges me to be more whole than I am.

'Hey,' James says. 'Who's good-looking?'

'As I say, this isn't any one person's brain. It's too perfect. It's been morphed together from lots of different scans, and a fair bit of artistic impression. But it shows the circuit we're interested in.'

Gareth tips up the visor to look.

'You can see how it runs through just about every major brain area: the prefrontal cortex, the limbic system, the memory circuits of the temporal lobe, the visual and auditory areas. We understood what these different parts do, but we didn't understand how they all fit together. This is the Lorenzo Circuit: the connections that make us what we are. The deep root-system of the self. The basis of memory, emotion and consciousness in the human brain. And we're trying to map it.'

Gareth is distracted by the activity on my terminal. The scan is drawing data from my own hard disc, which has blown the screensaver and revealed my desktop. A lilac banner stares back at us, displaying another paragon of connectedness, the virtual universe of the networking game we call Des✲re. I feel dangerously exposed, witnessing this public demonstration of my obsession.

'Cool,' he says, his eyes still gravitating to my screen.

I wish I'd had the sense to log off before they arrived. A few minutes rooting around on there and he would think he knew me inside out. With a twitch of panic, I wonder whether anything new has come through for me.

'Why would you want to do that?' James is saying. 'Map it or whatever?'

'Because this circuit is the answer to your question. It's what makes you *you*. The work we're doing here is going to tell us how a brain comes to have a sense of itself, how it gets a view of its own past and future, how it situates itself in the present. Some people doubt whether this circuit even exists. They say you'll never be able to trace human consciousness back to any single immensely complex system. But we don't doubt it. This whole Institute, all these different research teams, are dedicated to it. We've got the world experts on these techniques, supported by very substantial international funding. We're trying to map the Lorenzo Circuit in more detail than has ever been done before.'

I hear the sound of my own enthusiasm, and respond with a little internal shiver. It's probably dangerous to care too much about this stuff, at least while people are watching.

'But why are you using animals? Why don't you just zap a load of humans?'

I sigh, recognising the complaint from a hundred tutorials before this one. 'Some of these processes are very basic. They work pretty much the same way in mice as they do in people. The human brain has vastly more complexity, but we can't do the experiments we would like to do with people. It's like trying to map a city. Brain scanning gives you a rough street atlas, but we need to understand these pathways brick by brick, stone by stone.'

'Neurone by neurone,' Gareth muses.

'So to do that you've got to chop up a load of monkeys?'

'Not monkeys,' Gareth says. 'You'd never get permission for that.'

He shoots a glance at his partner, which is returned with a look of mock surprise. There's a joke here, something they're not sharing with me.

'OK, so you torture a few rats. What does that tell you?'

I hesitate, wondering how much to tell them. All the answers are there in the holding-room across the corridor, locked away in the terabytes of data that are my experiment on amyloid plaque formation. I feel a sudden pang for my ninety-nine mice, born by mail-order, raised under artificial light, just so I can find out whether an overdose of protein in their brains sends them drooling into dementia. It's the same guilty dread I feel at the thought that it might not work, that they will have lived and run their mazes and died for nothing. But you don't let yourself have that thought. Wherever you go, as a scientist, you don't go there.

'The research we're doing here is part of this bigger project. Up here on the fourth floor we're using animal models to work out why certain bits of the Lorenzo Circuit start malfunctioning. My particular interest is in dementia. Profound, pathological forgetfulness. We manipulate the gene which controls the formation of a certain protein. We think it's the build-up of this protein, in certain key regions along the course of the Circuit, that causes dementia.'

My screensaver blooms, saving my secrets from Gareth's stare. If I've had another gift from my mystery trader, somewhere far away in cyberspace, it will have to wait until these two have gone.

'So that's why memories can't be implanted? Because it's this massively complex circuit, passing through all these different brain areas? You can't just implant a memory; you'd effectively have to implant a whole new brain?'

'Exactly.'

Gareth finally extracts himself from the helmet and holds it out to me.

'*You* put it on, Miss. We want to see what makes *you* tick.'

My skin prickles. I light up with a blush. All my life I've been dodging this, hiding my doubt behind determined smiles, hoping the question would never come. But then something happens that throws you wide open, and you sense people looking in on the shattered illusion of you, marvelling at the workings. I tell myself it's just the hangover of another late night at the computer, silently communicating with people who are as lost to themselves as I am. But it's more than that. It's the woozy, broken-up feeling of being in a million places at once, watching that mysterious circuit trying to pull it all together, and yet somehow failing to feel it. They're looking at me, interested. I made out that I didn't question it, didn't doubt that that swirl of connectivity on the screen actually added up to a person. But maybe I do.

'Nothing ticking,' I tell them, as casually as I can. 'There's nothing ticking in here.'

James gets up from the bench and goes over to the one-way mirror. I follow him and reach over my desk to release the blinds. It's still light outside, and the room takes shape with startling clarity, exposing me with a sharpness that feels like guilt. James stands there looking into the blackness of my closed-down lab, one hand shading his eyes.

'So what exactly do your demented mice do in there? What's the big paddling-pool thing?'

'Flotation tank,' Gareth quips. 'It's very stressful being a scientist.'

'Water maze,' I say, calmly searching my desk for their essays. 'The big paddling-pool thing is basically a big paddling-pool. You add some milky stuff to the water so that it becomes opaque. You put a mouse in somewhere around the edge and see if it can find its way to a submerged platform. That way you can test the animal's spatial memory.'

James is looking at the paddling-pool, trying to decide if it's cruel to make a humanely-reared mouse swim through milky water. He takes his essay without even glancing at the mark. Gareth is trying to disturb my desktop again, to see what lies behind the branching-neurone screensaver. My late night comes back to me in yawning colour. The human clutter of the gaming rooms, the movie clips gifted from faraway traders, the network of linked webcams that creates the virtual universe of Des✳re. Hours of poring over that brilliant ribbon of streaming video, probing its anonymity settings, trying to decode the when and the where of it. And, through it all, this nagging certainty that I've found him, or that he's found me.

'Do you get out into the forest much, Miss?' Gareth is saying.

He's standing at the window, looking down at the burn that flows round the back of the Institute.

'Of course she does,' James says. 'She works here.'

'Have you ever seen McQueen out there? You know, when you're walking to work and stuff?'

'I don't know. What does he look like?'

Gareth makes a simian chatter and chucks at his armpits.

'Sort of chimpanzee-ish.'

I shake my head wearily. 'There can't be a chimp living wild in Wenderley Forest, James. It's not possible.'

Both seem convinced. 'It belongs to that biotech company, Sansom. Your rivals. We reckon it escaped from their lab and it's now roaming free with the squirrels. The word is that it's surviving on scraps from the kitchens. Sansom are getting in a real state about it. They're trying to find it and shoot it before anyone finds out the truth about their research.'

'I've heard rumours like that before. It will have been some bored student, dressed up for a prank.'

'No, Miss. It's a real chimp. One of our mates has seen it.'

'Chimps are practically human, Gareth. You'd never get ethical approval to work with them.'

'Sansom don't worry about ethical approval,' James says. 'They're the third biggest biotech on the planet. They do what they want. Anyway, I assumed you'd know about McQueen. I thought all you vivisectionists stuck together.'

The label stings. I'm too aware of how it sounds, to people who don't actually understand what this work involves.

'Don't worry about him, Miss,' Gareth says. 'His lot say *all* of it is wrong. Ethical approval or not. Experimenting on animals can have no justification, whatever the potential benefits to the experimenters.'

'Who are "his lot"?' I ask, with a feeling that I'm breaking in halfway through an argument.

'Conscience. The radical animal rights group.'

Gareth looks at me, enjoying my unease. James' eyes are turned down, gazing past a smile. He's shaking his head gently. My heart goes flat and stiff in my chest. The last thing I need is a Conscience activist in my tutorial group.

'I'm not with Conscience,' he says. 'I'm nothing. I'm not anything.'

'You were on that demo! At Sansom. You're there every week. It's either you or it's your twin brother. You made the local news, humanoid.'

James yawns extravagantly, dismissing the argument as easily as he started it. He doesn't really care what happens in that lab next door. He just wants to win something, some game of his own making, beat someone, it doesn't matter who.

'Well, save it for the debate,' Gareth says. 'I might let James ask a question if he's lucky. Are you coming, Miss? Tonight, at the Priors' Hall.'

I glance at the invitation card pinned to my corkboard. Gareth has invited me to something, a college debate on issues arising from the East Wing attacks. Motion: a species that wants cures for its own diseases should not test them out on its inferior cousins. Just what you need, when thousands of dollars' worth of damage has been done to your world-class research centre: a bunch of students talking about it. But Gareth is scheduled to be speaking. I'm his tutor; I'm supposed to be supportive about this kind of thing.

'I don't know. Won't I be at home marking your essay?'

He lifts his file onto his lap and starts scribbling in it. The label says GAZ'S RANDOM NOTES ON NEUROSCIENCE.

'Just applying the finishing touches, Miss.'

'You'll have to read it really carefully,' James says. 'He's not letting anyone else see it.'

'What's the big secret?'

'It'll all be in the essay.' James taps his nose confidentially. 'He won't tell anyone until he's absolutely ready to go public. He'll get in trouble again.'

'I didn't get in trouble because of my foolproof scheme for getting rich. I got in trouble because I hadn't satisfied my slave-masters.'

'You mean, you hadn't handed in any work?'

Gareth looks up at my computer, seized by an idea.

'Can you access my college record on that thing?'

'That's for me to know.'

'I'll have to hack into your account, then.'

'You could try. After recent events, they've gone a bit tight on security.'

'He can handle security,' James says, with a sly wink at me. 'You know he hacked into the Pentagon? He was, like, *twelve*.'

I think of the new bank of firewalls they put in after the latest attacks on the East Wing. You now have to enter a daily-changing security code just to get on to the networked computers. I remember the Executive's hurried press release in the hours after the last attack, about the importance of scientific work being allowed to continue while we strive to find alternatives to experimental research with animals. That doesn't help this feeling of dread. They look harmless enough, with their big smiles and prankish undergraduate humour, but I'm still going to find myself in desperate amounts of trouble if anyone catches them up here. I want them out of here, I want my house in the trees, a large Jack Daniels and my own company until bedtime. Not the thought of some uniformed thug walking past at any moment, pushing the door open on this flagrant breach of security.

'If you come to the debate, Miss, you can give the scientist's point of view. Set the record straight.'

'Yeah. You can tell us what your mice are thinking about while you're fiddling around with their brains.'

I watch James slump back into the chair and push off his trainers. He's wearing a Fred Flintstone hairpiece and a tee-shirt that says BIG IN NORWICH. His lips are dry, and there's a tender colour in his cheeks that hints at childhood embarrassments. His eyelashes are long and dark. A mole on his right cheek is the mark of a perfect arrogant beauty. I've heard this tone of voice before, of course: the slick automaticity of the outrage, the wince in his cheeks as he hurts himself on the words. No doubt the people who firebombed an empty storage room in the East Wing had it, took it with them to their Conscience meetings to argue for a better world without cruelty to animals. But James doesn't seem the sort who would act on his convictions. He's just testing me, pushing on the edifice to see if it'll break. He wants the easy kick at the cruelty of animal research, but he hasn't the heart, or the arguments, to see it through.

'Like I say, in this lab we're mostly using transgenics. We don't have to tamper with their brains at all: we let their genes do it for us.'

'Don't you have any doubts about that?'

He stares at me, sensing a weakness I didn't know about.

'Sometimes,' I say.

'So are they conscious when you're fiddling around with their transgenics or whatever?'

'That depends on what you mean by conscious.'

I wish he'd look away now. I like to think I can hide it, by speaking when I'm spoken to, smiling back when people smile at me, and maybe giving a little obligatory blush when it's a man. But then, out of nowhere, someone sees right through me, notices how I stumble over a response to a question, or leave a glance out of a window hanging a half-second too long. That feeling of being centred, that X that's supposed to mark the spot of the soul: it gets shown up as the nothing it is. James has scented it, the doubt that's at the heart of me. It's like I've thrown open a door onto a party you can hear from the street, only to show that there's nothing there.

'I mean what *you* mean, Dr Churcher. I mean what it feels like to be alive. To experience the amazing qualities of existence. I'm not talking about neural pathways or bits of the brain working together in harmony. I mean what it feels like to be *you*, Dr Yvonne Churcher. Age thirty-something. Possibly single. To be that person, in this room, right now.'

I redden, and hate myself for it.

'Here, in this room, is not really the place to discuss this, James.'

He holds the gaze. It's too determined; its need to embarrass me is too much on show. But I find myself yielding to it, in a kind of admiration for his guessing the truth about me. He has me in his gaze, that cool, fascinating fixedness: not fighting me now, more like what comes after fighting.

'You take it to pieces, Dr Churcher, and then you can't put the pieces back together again.'

I laugh. I know I shouldn't, but I can't help it. It's a mid-brain reflex, some neural cluster buzzing some other neural cluster, and going nowhere near that mythical centre, whatever it is that's supposed to be *me*. He's blushing now, scorched by an older woman's mockery, and I can feel the tingling dread that tells me that I've gone too far. He's hauling up the smile, hardening it, putting a bit of menace into it, a clench of anger. It's too hot in here. All the doors and windows sealed, and electronic locks on all the doors, and just the two of us trapped in this moment, fighting for air.

It's true: I do doubt myself. Not in the way that I would doubt whether I could climb that hill or make that person fall in love with me; it's more like doubting the 'I' that's supposed to be doing the doubting. I use this word, this feathery personal pronoun, like you might say the name of a foreign town you're headed for but have never actually seen, hoping the act of utterance might bring it closer. But I don't believe in that town. I never did. That feeling of centredness, of me-ness, that is supposed to keep you rooted in your life: well, it passed me by. I have this fantasy that I'll do what Gareth wants me to do, I'll take the thought-helmet and put it on, dim the lights and let everyone see what's going on inside. There'll be the low-level buzz of life-or-death routines, the reflexes that keep the machine working. The Lorenzo Circuit will be flickering, knitting together my past and future selves. As I turn around to see James sitting there, there'll be the swirl in the back of my brain corresponding to the sight of him. But then he'll ask me again, 'How does it feel to be *you, here, now*?' And suddenly the evidence of my existence will be gone. I'll be back to being a network of activity, one neural cluster buzzing another neural cluster, one lot of bio-electrical traffic taking the ring-road around the soul; one deluded meat puppet sizing up another deluded meat puppet and wanting to fight it or fuck it or whatever. 'What about how it *feels*?' James will ask me. 'There must be something that it feels like to be you.' I'll shrug and say that it feels like this. You sitting there with your fading blushes and your day-old stubble, wanting to fight me or fuck me, both, I don't know. Knocking at the door, trying to work out why there's no answer.

Calling my name.

Wondering why there's no one at home.

CHAPTER TWO

Forest Glade 7

◉

He's on the stairs ahead of me. Gareth left ten minutes ago, saying he needed to slip away early so that he could get his speech ready for the debate. There's no one else on the stairwell. I see James on the third-floor landing, peering at the iris scanner that controls access to the maximum-security areas. He flips out his phone and films the scanner for a few seconds, and then glances up at the CCTV camera which eyes him from a safer reality. He pushes on the door, recoils from its solidity, and frowns at it as if it had broken a promise. I'm watching him from one flight above. It feels wrong to be spying on him, but I was the one who let him up here. If I've got a Conscience activist in my tutorial group, I need to know.

He carries on down the stairs. The lift doesn't even stop at this third floor, unless your access privileges reveal it for you on the control panel. You wouldn't know that this research floor existed unless you'd worked out the architecture from the outside. This is where the Lorenzo Circuit is being pieced together, neurone cluster by neurone cluster, to make a map worth — to our rivals at least — a price that goes beyond money. If James were with Conscience, this honeycomb of sealed rooms would be top of his target list. As I pass the iris scanner, walking fast to keep him in sight, I feel the hum of the secrets it is protecting, its silent, massively automated efforts to stop certain facts from becoming known. At the second-floor landing, James increases his pace, all at once in a hurry. By now, the grey stairwell holds a wash of daylight from the windows on the lower floors. I can hear his feet clattering as he skips down the last flights of stairs and through the door into the atrium. If I run, he will hear me. Betas buzz around, yabbering into mobile phones. I have to push through the queue for the coffee cart. Someone stops me with a question about an assignment, and by the time I've shaken her off James is already out of the building and crossing the concourse by the boarded-up windows of the East Wing.

Outside it's the slanting light of late afternoon. A couple of contractors' vans are crash-parked on the kerb outside the East Wing. A radio blares, but no one is working. James walks past the scene with his Fred Flintstone mask jacked up on top of his head, his gaze set dead ahead, oblivious to the damage his fellow protestors have caused. I watch him catch up with a crowd of betas heading for a session in the Peer Review. He'll have to do his drinking quickly if he wants to catch the heritage steam service to Fulling, where the students have their colleges, in time for the debate. I'm tempted to follow him, but I'd rather make sure I'm there to watch him tonight, when positions have been stated and I can see which cause he's fighting for. *I'm nothing*, he told me. *I'm not anything*. If I want to know what that means, I'll have to be there when the shouting starts.

One of the contractors' vans is blocking the access to Libet Avenue, which is the way I go when I'm on my bike. The surface is compacted grit, fine for cycling, and at night there are lights in little ground-level turrets, security points every fifty metres. Then there's a maze of narrower footpaths that trace different routes back to Forest Glade, and less chance of being mown down by some proto-scientist on a thirty-speed racer. Down this way, gorse prickles your shoulders and red squirrels play pirates overhead. From odd clearings you can look up at the treehouses at the top of the rise, paused like tripod aliens taking a break from conquering the earth.

Today I'm walking. This morning I stood on the roof of my treehouse and realised that I needed to pace it out, leave these jittery thoughts scattered among the undergrowth, and feel the certainty that only the footsore rhythms of a long walk can give you. A feeling is in me, a conflux of internal states that I call a feeling, and at a certain point it'll turn into a thought, and the conscious machine will start believing. Something has already tipped off my endocrine system; I can already feel the panic that will ripple out. What surprises me is the lovesick feeling that drags it here, a soft buzzing nervousness, all that adrenaline and noradrenaline licking at my insides and twisting me out of shape. Thinking's a gut reaction, rooted in the heart, the large intestine, the adrenal cortex, and only doing its conscious work in the brain. Hot intelligence, Mateus used to call it. His excuse for never losing an argument. If you went against his theory, you went against him.

Come to Florida. Whether it's golf, fishing, or old-fashioned sunshine and beaches, we can help you to find the new life you've been looking for.

Hot intelligence. That's what was bothering me last night, when this video message came through. Alone in my treehouse, curtains open to the blackness over the forest. The wind tongueing the flue of the stove, a reddish glow from a hollow stash of embers as fragile as a house of cards. I logged on and saw the shimmering lilac banner of Des✶re, flickering like a flag in a virtual breeze. Another mouse-click or two and I'd be getting a detailed rundown on the items traded, the webcam trails to obscure locations, all the clues and red herrings of this obsessive networking game. The welcome banner gave way to a night sky. Each new message twinkled in the firmament like a star. Some people think I overdo the graphics, but I want the full experience, especially when the rest of me is falling apart. There was one new star, brighter than the rest. The sign of a new trader, travelling under maximum anonymity. Once I'd started trading with him I would get to see his icon, details of his avatars and perhaps even a clue to the flesh-and-blood gamer behind the mask. But for now he was a stranger, casually setting my heart on fire.

I clicked on the new star. It exploded into a cam-feed of a windy beach under a grey sky. A self-conscious black woman, clearly doing a favour for a friend, was explaining why she was glad she'd picked a realtor to manage the purchase of her condo on Anna Maria Island. Then the movie had been edited, and another voice dubbed onto the soundtrack, speaking through her lips. *Even if you lost it in the dark, you could try looking where the light is.*

I only know one person who talks like that. At least, I used to know.

I looked away from my wallscreen. I saw the cream sofa with chocolate stains on the cushions, stacked with essays waiting to be marked. His photograph on the bookcase, his Sansom car park swipecard and ID badge. That pile of dog-eared journal articles which he never wanted anyone to see. How had he tracked me down? He had his settings configured for maximum privacy, but he must have known that I would see through them. I made myself visible. I could see his icon now, coyly shaded to grey. A Portuguese guitar trapped behind the bars of a cage. It was Mateus alright. My gorgeous, suffering fadista. He tore my heart out, but it was he who sang the sad songs. Mateus who thought he had a monopoly on hurt.

I went to bed shaking. Why had he bothered to come looking for me? This morning, as sleep and not-knowing poured off me, it made no more sense than it had last night. Which is why I'm out here now, on my own two feet, hoping that this fresh March air will shape some common sense. Trusting that my footsteps will dislodge something, set the thought free.

Even if you lost it in the dark, you could try looking where the light is. But where is the light? Where is he hiding?

The spruces reach up into the blueness, scaly branches still rimed with frost. Needles sag, too heavy for this altitude.

He wants me back. Or else he wants me to hurt me all over again.

It's been two years. In all that time I didn't know if he was alive or dead. He never had the courtesy to tell me.

Oh, my dark man. It takes its time but it breaks eventually, and something in the heart region shifts bluntly to one side, and the thought is conscious, here to stay.

He's back. Mateus is back.

Florida is where the biennial meeting of the Association is going to be held. The first chance I'll have had to see him for two years. Since the last meeting of the Association, in fact, the hell of Quebec City. He's inviting me, the arrogant bastard, as though a meeting of eight thousand neuroscientists was somehow going to be Mateus Pereira's own show. The Pereira Effect was big, but it wasn't that big. I'm supposed to be presenting a poster about my research. He'll know by now whether his own submission has been accepted. The business of neuroscience has arranged it that I'll see him there. All that stuff about buying a condo and setting up life together is purely his sick joke. I'll be in Tampa for five days, and then I'm coming back home to my lonely life.

The thought bounces and shatters, shedding more of its mortal heaviness, and I can hear my own voice in the silence.

Try looking where the light is. If only it were that simple.

I wonder what he's working on now. No doubt he's still toying around with his human–machine interface. Trying to persuade silicon chip to speak unto neurone, that kind of thing. It wouldn't be Mateus if it wasn't breathtakingly ambitious. But if anyone could make the impossible happen, it would be him. With a little help from his employers, perhaps. He was already busy with the interface when he was working for Sansom, back when we were together. Is he still on their payroll? I could never find a trace of him, not anywhere. Last night, after his message came through, I sat and called up the citation record for his famous paper, "Anomalous conductivity responses in non-organic tissue", which he published in *Neuroscience* a few years before we met. The article that first described the effect that took his name, and cleared the way for technological advances in everything from sensory enhancements for the blind to control of prosthetic limbs. Referenced in just about every article published on the topic in the last decade. I was going to print out the full list of citations and scrutinise it for evidence that he still loves me, that he's trying to communicate with me through the chain of influence the Pereira Effect has left behind, like you might track down a film star at a party just by following the trail of starstrucks who are still whispering his name. But there was nothing. If he's still in the business, he hasn't been publishing. Sansom have research centres all over the world. He could be holed up somewhere in the tropics, working on a project they don't want anyone to know about. He could have planned the whole thing. Disappear for a couple of years, make out that you're dead, and then jump out to give the grieving ex the fright of her life.

There's a crashing sound in the bushes to my right, and I startle, my heart in flames.

Sansom want the map of the Lorenzo Circuit. The knowledge of what goes on in my building would be a gift beyond price. The Executive keep telling us that we cannot trust anyone. And that, if he really is back on the scene, means Mateus as well.

I stand, halted, watching for where the noise came from. My head is spinning from the climb and the oxygen that's been forced through me. The undergrowth keeps its counsel. The ferns swirl, set spinning by motion after-effects. I must have startled a pheasant or something. But nothing flew up; whatever it was, it's still in there. Shapeless, nameless, whatever my fear wants to make it. Thinking is a rush of blood, a panicked jumping to conclusions. Not a person, though, not this far out. Just let it not be a person.

Up ahead, the trees shrink back from the path. As I hurry around a corner I can see the massive steel supports of the first of the Forest Glade treehouses. They trudge in pairs up the slope; mine is Number Seven. I can see that they've delivered my firewood and left it next to my winch. No neighbours for me since the woman in No. 8 failed her PhD, so my comings and goings are nobody's business but mine. But that also means that I'm alone out here. Right now, that isn't the comfort it would usually be.

I pull on the heavy beech door and drag the boxes of firewood into the winch. I tap in my passcode and feel the solar-powered motor jolt into action. Everyone has their ritual of homecoming; mine is this smooth electric ascent. They've fixed the problem with the elevator transport. We might be one of the more distant outposts of the Lycee, but they try to keep this particular social experiment running smoothly. There's a special division dedicated to the treehouses, to prove that their commitment to the project is still strong. See, say the animated graphics of the Forest Glade website, these fourteen huts on stilts ('built in 1999 to demonstrate the Lycee's commitment to sustainable twenty-first-century living') haven't been a complete waste of Federation grant-money. Half of them are empty now: people couldn't stand the height, the morning bird-din, or the way the treehouses were designed to sway in the wind like streetlamps — an essential safety feature, of course, but disconcerting when you're on your own in your first week of occupancy and the storm is roaring down the dale like the end of the world. One careless post-doc actually managed to fall out of his — pissed after a Sunday session at the Peer Review, and lucky to be in one of the little fifteen-metre ones and have his fall broken by a forgiving rhododendron. Mine is the grown-up version, though: if you fell from here it would be like one of those dreams you're never meant to be woken from, a down-the-rabbit-hole flypast of your life's unfinished business, with the things that really matter to you ranged like lost treasures on unreachable shelves, safe from your dreamy grasping.

I need to get this firewood in before it gets dark. I ride the winch all the way to the roof, propped up awkwardly in the narrow floor-space left by the boxes. When I push open the door and step out into the cold air, it's like emerging from the roof of a submarine, surfacing onto a sea of brightness, one brave survivor inheriting the world. The silence is total, the kind of stillness that makes your own thoughts audible, and the view breaks your heart. I'm thirty metres off the ground, on top of the capsule of larch and Douglas fir that houses me and everything I own, pretty much the last thing to break the forest canopy until it reaches the fine print of the Eskdale moors, that visible blueness on the forty-mile horizon.

The bunker is in the corner under the wind turbine. For the moment the white sails are motionless, frozen in a turn. There's not a breath of wind. Right now my treehouse is draining power from the earth, the back-up grid under the forest soil, thirty metres below. At the same time the solar cells are heating water, the idea being that all these sources of energy will provide enough hot water later for a bath. I'll need this firewood in the morning, when I awake in the fog and the whiteness outside the windows will make me think I've died and gone to heaven. I can see that they've sent some good stuff. I like these hard bits of ash, the historic feel of them, as though they'd witnessed things in their lives. Split one and you'll see how its heart is pinky-brown, like it once had blood flowing through it.

In the shadow of the rail, some apple bits I left out for the squirrels have all been eaten. They are ravenous this year; I can't feed them fast enough.

When I straighten up from the bunker with a basket full of ash bits, I can see Sansom's European headquarters laid out under the eastern sky, five miles away as the crow flies. I can make out fifteen or twenty low-slung bunkers each a quarter-mile wide, the whole thing like a little American city, gridded and freewayed. They say it's got its own airport, hospital, TV station, police force. *Strong enough to care*: just on the funny side of understatement, when you're talking about the third biggest biotech in the world. To the south, directly below me, a gap in the canopy displays the forty-acre plot of the Lycee's Forest Campus, where I've just walked from. To the right and west, a road takes you higher and higher into the valley, past that indiscernible boundary where the land starts to crowd out the people: slow them, quieten them, make them mythically robust and self-reliant. It runs through the Saxon villages of Scarf and Winning, those high gold gleams that are just visible on a sunset evening, and on into the dale, through the last sheep-bitten straggles of forest and up towards the mining country.

Mateus and I used to go cycling up there. Two centuries ago there were a quarter of a million men working those hills, chasing lead, iron and fluorspar through tunnels you couldn't stand up in. The pits are abandoned now, shafts lying open to the wind. They say there are still people up there — Sansom has an outpost, apparently, a research team and a couple of labs, some classified project to kill the years. It's bleak up there, anyway; as soon as you get past Winning the cold gets under your skin, the wind starts to howl inside you, and you long for your treehouse in the valley, that large-whisky/hot-bath kind of daydream.

I let myself in through the trap door and take the back stairs down to my living floor. Only when I'm inside, with the front door locked behind me, do I feel comfortably invisible again. I glance into my bathroom and the corners of my white bedroom, just to reassure myself, although the unease I'm feeling is something more than the fear that I might have been followed here. I grab some clothes and carry them back into the living room with me. I need to hurry if I'm going to make it to Fulling in time for the debate. Mateus' face stares down at me from a beechwood frame high on the bookcase. I should have got rid of him by now. I thought that moving him up there would be a kind of statement for myself, a sign that I'm pulling through. By the time he's relegated to the hallway I'll know I don't love him any more. I stand in front of him, caught between the window and his big eyes. Nothing happens. I pull the bobble out of my hair and feel its unglossy waves frame my paleness. I ought to wash it, but I wonder what's the point. Mateus would see through it, anyway: he always could. If I could have him back for a day, I'd ask him how he managed to get into me like this, why I can't even get dressed to go out in the evening without wondering what he'd think of me. That's the problem. He can hurt me but I can't hurt him. And the one weapon I have against him, I can't use. Unless Florida gives me an opportunity. The thought makes me pause, and I stare at the pile of papers on the bookcase with a slow, unreeling fascination. That obscure journal article from the 1980s, written in Portuguese, which no one but me was ever allowed to know about. I look back at his image with a nervy sense of possibilities unfolding. You think you know things about me, Mateus Pereira. But I also know things about you.

His eyes follow me out of the room. In the kitchen I neck a solpadeine

23

and wash it down with a slug of tapwater. The light on my messaging system is flashing. For a moment I wonder whether it could be Mateus, calling to explain. But then the beep goes and the line clears and I hear an uncertain, old-lady voice, strangely formal, committing her words to digital memory as though dictating a telegram. My heart dives for cover. Effi. I was supposed to call her today. She chatters on about her washing machine and the wonderful view she has from her ugly new apartment. Today she is fluent, remembering the names of things and the basic details of the world around her, or at least the gloomy few square metres that her world has shrunk to. Then Daren, her nurse, takes the phone and reminds me that I'm supposed to go over there tonight, to cover for him while he's at the football. I knew there was a reason why I couldn't go to Gareth's debate. I press the button to return the call and listen for the guilty silence to break, for Effi's worn-out voice to croak softly into my ear, my fairy godmother, my milk-and-two-sugars friend.

'Yvonne,' she mumbles. 'Thank God for you.'

She still recognises me, then. Dementia has not cast her adrift so completely.

'I'm sorry I haven't called. I've been really busy.'

'I know. You live out in the country. It's hard for you to get in to Pelton, what with petrol and everything.'

'Even so. I shouldn't be letting you down like this.'

She doesn't understand what I'm saying. My voice is unsteady. I want to turn the clock back, edit our recent lives so that we had this conversation long ago.

'I can't make it tonight. Something's come up. I'm really sorry.'

'What is it, Yvonne?' Effi says.

There's that faraway tone to her voice, and the question splinters into a million different requests for certainty. The doubt of Alzheimer's. What is it? What is *any* of it?

'I can't make it tonight. Can you manage your dinner and everything?'

'Of course I can. My dishy nurse has it sorted out. Tell me, have you ever heard that boy sing?'

I tuck her back into her reverie, unclip the French windows and step out onto the balcony. I'm still gripping the phone, dimly conscious that there are more calls I need to make. Home, that pebble-dashed house of science and faith, would be top of my list of neglect. I dial my parents' number at the vicarage, looking out over the detailed stillness of the forest. The distant sheen of Sansom's headquarters is the only sign that any human being was ever out there. I remember Mateus setting off for work from here, on those drowsy mornings we shared as lovers. He would cycle the five miles and then cycle back to me again at night, only slightly less radiant than his morning self had been. All the long nights of that summer, up on the roof of my treehouse, cupped in love's warm fingers. I told him I had this fantasy: me, standing on my balcony in front of the forest. Hearing, feeling, a man behind me, but never getting to see his face. He told me he wanted to be that man; he wanted to love me without me knowing it was him. Why? I asked him. Because then you'll never know who to start hating.

Someone is cycling along the path beneath my treehouse. I wonder how long he's been visible for; whether he has only just come into view, or whether I have only just noticed him. He's riding a mountain bike and carrying something strapped lengthwise across his back. He's wearing the grey uniform of the Lycee's security team. His head is shaved, and he's bare-armed in a polo shirt despite the cold. His arms are dark with tattoos. I recognise him as the security officer who comes to the Institute to lecture us about the risk of terrorist attack. He came to talk to us after the firebombing of the East Wing, promising the wrath of the Executive, the police and every other law-enforcement agency in the country to anyone who breached the new security code.

The security guy disappears beneath the platform. I hear my doorbell ring. I realise that the vicarage phone is still ringing, and cancel the call. Then I see him again, walking around the base of my treehouse to the north side. He's pushing the bike and holding the implement, the length and rigidity of a golf club, in one hand. I'm still holding the phone, and I think vaguely for a moment about calling for help. But I don't yet know what I'm afraid of. I'm guessing that my visitor is circling the treehouse. I pull back from the rail, abuzz with instinct. If he catches sight of me up here, he'll know I'm deliberately not answering the door. I cross to the eastern end of the balcony and look out towards where I think the security man will be coming round. It's a mistake, because I've walked straight into his line of sight. He is standing astraddle his bike, pointing his golf club at the space I've just moved into. But it is not a golf club. I can see its polished wood and black metal, how his hand at the trigger looks as though it were cupping something precious, easily spilled. The frail life of something; maybe even mine. When he sees me he swings the barrel wildly, as though parting a curtain. Then he hesitates, realising that my presence up here is a problem that cannot be waved away. He lowers the gun, glares at me blackly and hooks the weapon back over his shoulder. He barks an order into his ultra-thin mobile, wrenches his mountain bike through a tight circle and sets off again the way he came.

I watch him vanish around the bend in the path, breathing hard with the aftershock. I can't get past his embarrassed expression, his look of offended apology. Whatever he was meant to be taking aim at on this winter's afternoon, it shouldn't have been a member of the Lycee's research staff. Something is happening here, and people like me are not supposed to know anything about it. I can see I'm not alone in hearing rustlings in the undergrowth. But no one else has come at the problem with a rifle.

There's a noise from the rooftop terrace above me. I'm used to the squirrels that gather up there, but this is different. An impression of restless weight, a shuffling of heavy feet on the wooden platform. A shot of adrenaline spurts from my chest and tingles in my fingertips. The security man could have seen something up on my roof, and this was what he was aiming at when he accidentally took aim at me. I pull the balcony door shut, absurdly fastidious about keeping unwanted wildlife away from my living floor. I start up the ladder steps that connect my first-floor balcony to the rooftop. The air is thin and dizzying. My fingers stick to the cold metal rails. At the top, I look out from the cover of the fuel bunker and halt on an in-breath. A black shape is hunched in the corner, picking over the remnants of my fruit offerings. The animal turns suddenly, hearing me, and I'm looking into the eyes of an adult chimpanzee.

I freeze on the ladder, calculating distances. This is no student in a monkey suit. The animal looks frightened. A grown chimp can do a lot of damage to a person. I have to control his fear as well as my own. That means no sudden movements, and as little eye contact as I can get away with.

'McQueen,' I say softly. 'That's what they call you, isn't it?'

The chimp climbs up onto the rail and looks back at me. A spruce branch that overhangs my rooftop will give him an easy escape. He chatters loudly at me, peeling open his tennis-ball mouth and showing his pink gums and gappy teeth. It's a show; there's no real aggression there. If he's come from a lab, he must be used to humans. He probably understands who, in her ignorance, has been feeding him all this time.

I watch him lope up into the tree and vanish into the canopy below my platform. I'm shaken and cold, and this high in the winter sky I feel like a disaster victim awaiting rescue. To the west, the sun is setting over a bristling range of evergreens. In the other direction, Sansom's metallic expanse is tinged with orange. Somewhere in that gleaming complex is the unwanted home that McQueen has escaped from. But what is a huge corporation like Sansom doing with a colony of chimpanzees? I told Gareth and James that the story of the escaped chimp was just a rumour, but the rumour is true. And if I'm the only person who appreciates that, things are going to start getting difficult for me.

CHAPTER THREE

This House Would Suffer Alone

◎

In the train on the way to the debate, I toy with the idea of reporting what I've seen. The night through the carriage windows is black, fields of moonlight laid over a landscape starred with farm lights. Over towards the university town of Fulling, a sky-hoarding flashes out the name of a property company scattering dream homes all over the countryside of UK-D. Another thirty miles to the east, a column of laser-smoke climbs over the high-rises of the city of Pelton, ready to splash its brand on any lingering patch of cirrus.

I see a man running down a lane, scrambling over a stile and cutting across a bare field. Sprouts of winter corn squish into mud where his feet land. I wonder if he's a migrant, heading back to the new four-hundred-bed reception centre of Dartford 17, whose night-lit hulk just shot past me on the edge of the forest. He reaches the embankment, fingertips up the slope and falls in alongside the railway line, then there's a blast of iron and coal-smoke and he's gone and wet fields gleam. Rain scores the windows, etching obscure diagrams onto the glass, cross-hatching areas of substance and uncertainty. There's a window open somewhere, a wind coming off the North Sea that smells of Siberia. Way over to the right, Sansom squats like a radioactive retail park, suffusing the night with its halogen-blue glow.

The chimp's flared features haunt my brain. McQueen, the mythical runaway. Escaping from Sansom's labs must have been quite an adventure. It had a reason to look frightened. Sansom's people are trying to recapture it before anyone can link it to them. But the man with the gun was from the Lycee. Whatever Sansom knew about the runaway chimp, their biggest rivals knew it too. I'm trying to fit the pieces together, but they resist. James insists that he works alone, but that only makes me more certain that he's a member of Conscience. According to Gareth, he and his activist friends are demonstrating at Sansom all the time.

Which means he must have some idea of what goes on there. What kind of wildlife the biotech is interested in, and why.

The medieval town of Fulling appears from behind a billboarded hillside, and clouds flash past a heavy moon.

I sit alone by a window, shivering inside my military coat. There are four or five other people in the carriage. They are all betas, or maybe young-looking postgrads. The light is strange, that odd panicky surrealness of a railway carriage at night, and I have a sense that this sudden jolt into focus needs to be turned back on itself, scrutinised in some way. It's not clairvoyance, that feeling you sometimes get of being a second or two ahead of yourself; it's maybe just the particular patterning of the sensations, an interplay of light and colour that you haven't experienced before. Anyway, there is no *you*. There are just fragments: the buffed mahogany of the train seats, the crimson swoosh on that girl's trainers. The pieces glow brighter the further you get from the centre. It's an ordinary moment, but it says everything about who I am, why I choose to do one thing rather than another. Maybe this is the hint that gets thrown my way, the nervous system's anonymous tip-off, warning me that even this brief glimpse of consciousness is out of date, and I'm already someone else.

I force my attention back onto Gareth's essay. It came through just before I left, while I was scouring for new messages about Florida. I printed it out, thinking I might get a chance to read it on the train. He's gone way over the word limit, and hardly paid any attention at all to the title. He must have written most of it in the hours since he left this afternoon, as there are garbled references to the Lorenzo Circuit and the possibility of the artificial stimulation of memory. We never talked about any of this before today. I should be pleased that I've made an impression, but the manic onrush of his argument, sustained over pages of single-spaced text, is unsettling me. *It's not that plug-in memory implants are impossible,* he has written, *but that they are unnecessary. You don't _need_ to implant memories when you have a brain which constructs them out of their raw materials, every single time that it needs to remember. All the information is in there, tangled up in the Lorenzo Circuit. The million-dollar problem is how to put it all together.*

For my eyes only, James said. Gareth reveals the first details of his get-rich scheme, and no one but his tutor gets to see them. I suspect that he's unsure about his ideas and has come to me for approval. But I'm hardly going to be encouraging him to exploit the commercial value of the Lorenzo Circuit, even if I knew how it could be done. There's a second attachment, entitled GAZ'S RANDOM NOTES ON NEUROSCIENCE. I skim through the few pages that printed before my paper ran out. There are notes on philosophical zombies, neurogenesis, phenomenal consciousness, all the gleaming factoids that have taken his fancy over the course of our wide-ranging second-year neuroscience class. They are a snapshot of his obsessions, and they alarm me. If there's a message here, I'm not getting it. He'll have to explain it to me himself, in all the detail he needs.

The train takes us to within a hundred metres of Sansom's perimeter fence. Rail tracks snake away into a floodlit diorama of containers and low-slung storage units. The flagship buildings at the north end are swathed in forest. The biotech is known for its eclectic tastes, and that means limitless space to create different experimental habitats. The great escapee had a hell of a prison to break out from. I always knew that Mateus' human–machine interface was only a fraction of what Sansom were interested in. But chimps? There's no other way of explaining what I saw. There's not a zoo within a hundred miles. You couldn't keep one of these animals in captivity unless you had an enclosure the size of a small house. If Sansom have the will to do it, they have the space to hide it away.

The point is, Miss, that if you could map the Lorenzo Circuit then you would have the foundations of a system for enhancing human memory. This is the basis of my proposition for you.

The students get louder as we reach the outskirts of Fulling. As the train pulls into the station they stand up and fetch down banners and oversized teddy-bear mascots, and for a moment we're a freeze-frame of awkwardness, half-standing, overbalancing with the weight of things and the slowing jolt, jolt of the train. As we step out into the cold, the floodlit abbey soars into the blackness, brilliant with amber light. The Norman stonework seems melted into the rock. It's a sheer drop on this south side. In front of it, the market square is full of circus grotesques: fire-eaters, stilt-walkers, geeky betas on great tall unicycles, costumed girls milling about with buckets of money. There are some middle-aged tourist couples watching from a safe distance, measuring off non-lethal doses of excitement, counting the seconds before they can scurry back to their hotels. Students dressed as rival sandwich-chain mascots are handing leaflets into thin air. This year's Charity Week debate is brought to you by PowerServe Technologies.

Inside, the Priors' Hall is heaving. Betas in drag-queen wigs are crushing forward out of the lobby clutching flutes of complimentary bubbly. Who's paying for all this? PowerServe, I guess. That girl with the trainers sees someone she knows and squeals to be hugged. I watch the security guy run his scanner over my pigskin satchel, wondering whether his terrorist-sniffing software will detect signs of imminent attack in Gareth's unmarkable essay. I can see its author over by the bar, happy, a glass in each hand. A college rowing eight have already necked the free stuff and are getting the beers in. I wouldn't let students into a place like this. The floor tiles are two hundred years old. Someone carved their name into the oak panelling way back in the seventeenth century. The gold-plated lettering over the fireplace says FLOREAT DOMUS.

Let this house flourish. I think the Executive's offshore investments will have seen to that.

'ATTENTION, VERMIN!' squeaks a voice through the PA. A nervous compère pulls a face for the cameraman, who is filming it all for a live webcast. A girl with silver pigtails jumps up and down as her pills kick in. I can smell kebabs. Someone prods me in the back. I turn. Just faces inclined to the light. The spotlight swerves around in time to catch the compère vanishing stage left. There's a commotion behind the curtain. The compère backs out again onto the stage, followed by two female betas wheeling a huge high-backed armchair. Fixed in oils on the walls, long-dead churchmen avoid each other's stares.

'This house wants to know if there is any justification for using non-human species to improve the human condition.' There are cheers and jeers. 'So, to tell us why animals are still suffering in the name of science, I give you... our first speaker!'

The noise drops a notch or two. A few people clap. Gareth climbs up onto the stage and looks at the compère, who is slouched on a sofa at the side holding a control box in one hand. Gareth pulls an expression of mock shock, jerking his head back and unscrolling his eyebrows for the audience, then takes his seat on the throne. The compère's finger hovers over the punishment button. Gareth pulls a piece of paper from his trouser pocket, reads something and folds it away.

'Gareth Buckle,' he says, shrinking from the brashness of the microphone. 'Opposing the motion. But that's just a name, isn't it? A label for the humanoid. Who am I *really*?'

There's laughter. Someone quips that he should get his crib-sheet out again.

'No, I mean: *why* am I who I am? What makes me the person I am rather than someone else?'

We hear an opinion about a genetic accident. Gareth gazes blankly out at the crowd, his face a wet moon in a puddle.

'All right then, what makes you *you*? When you wake up in the morning, how can you be sure you are the same person who went to sleep last night? How do any of you know that you are the same people you were thirty-seven minutes ago, when you walked into this building? The answer is: because you possess an amazingly complex neural system which can integrate facts about your past history, your emotional memories, and the quality of how every single moment of your life looked and felt.'

Familiar themes, then. Whatever interests him about the Lorenzo Circuit, it's still doing so. But this is the public version. The version in my satchel is meant for me alone.

'But how are we going to find out more about these incredibly important brain systems? We can't study them in human beings. The techniques are too invasive. Computer simulations can only give us a small part of the picture. We need animal research. We need researchers, I mean, who can do carefully controlled, completely humane studies of all the different branches of these pathways, and put them together into a complete map of the system.'

That's enough detail, I want to say. I'm pleased he's got the hang of this so quickly, but I don't want to be hearing a précis of my own research in front of a gathering of animal rights campaigners. I'm not ashamed of what I do, but I am careful. Thankfully, there's no mention of my ninety-nine mice or their tests of spatial memory. Gareth is just gearing up for a standard defence of regulated animal experimentation.

I could have written it myself. The benefits of mapping the Lorenzo Circuit are going to be huge, but we can't map the circuit without getting close enough to the brain to see how it operates. And that's where my mice come in.

'Take Alzheimer's Disease.' The crowd are agitated, but Gareth's voice struggles through. 'The average life expectancy in this part of the Federation is now into the nineties. Intelligent toilet-paper and networked early-diagnosis expert systems mean we can catch most cancers early enough now. These ninety-year-olds are healthy old birds. But their brains are degenerating as fast as before. We've got a dementia situation which is impairing the bingo-playing efficiency of half the population of UK-D. Social insurance spending is running at over thirty percent of GDP. This work will benefit the millions who suffer with the enforced zombie-hood of this crippling disease. We will be able to find out why the build-up of a certain protein, at specific points in the circuit, leads to Alzheimer's. We are all, in this room, lucky enough to know who we are. With this research, we will be able to help some people who aren't so lucky.'

'And how many monkeys have got to be tortured before that happens?' some well-spoken Conscience sympathiser whines.

'Not monkeys!' Gareth shouts. 'At least, the *good* guys aren't doing that ...'

There's uproar in the Priors' Hall. The compère leaps up from his sofa and does his pushing-down-on-the-volume thing. Half of the audience are screaming about what the other half are shouting. Gareth looks as though he wants to continue, but the compère has already hit the punishment button, sending yellow holographic flame spouting out of the microphone. I wonder what Effi would say if she was here. If she understood enough about what was happening to her, I would ask her. *Are my ninety-nine mice worth your sanity?* I suspect she would say no. She could never dream of doing harm to anything, even humane, government-licensed harm. In her heart, there is no weighing of moral imperatives. She would take all the pain for herself, before she would even think of sharing it around.

At the interval Gareth is back on the champagne. I think about going over, but decide against it. He's got his mates with him, some of whom seem to be the same beer-monsters who were heckling him a minute ago. I swear I'm the only person here old enough to be a tutor. I hang around in the passageway for a bit, watching them muscle past with slopping plastic glasses, faces glistening with the unanswerable joke of being young. There's still no sign of James. Maybe he's not coming. Maybe, I don't know, that actually bothers me. The emotion catches me out, as though it only became possible to understand it when I felt it, deeply and heart-lurchingly, in that throb of anxiety inside. He's sensed something about me, that's obvious. In my office, this afternoon, he looked right through me. And I want him to do it again, if only so I can tell him that he's wrong: he doesn't know the truth about me, he can't just hassle me into believing so. That's why I'll be disappointed if he doesn't turn up. I dread a confrontation about his allegiances, but it's more than that. He seems to think he can talk me out of this doubt I feel about myself. Through sheer bullying enthusiasm, he thinks he can make me share his certainty.

The compère takes the mike again. There's a table covered with leaflets at the back of the hall: Conscience propaganda, spun from shoddy paper and worse information. *Lycee scientists conduct brain research on transgenic capuchin monkeys* ... You can't genetically modify capuchins, even if there was any point in doing so. *Researchers at the Institute for Research into Neuronal Death and Regeneration, at the Lycee's high-tech Forest Campus, today denied that* ... It's wrong, but the sight of my own institute's name is still too close for comfort. I remember the day I spent trying to clean a tin of pink paint off my car at Warwick, and have the dread sense of something starting up again. And worse: that I might know the people who are doing it.

I've just binned the last of the leaflets when James gets to his feet.

'We all know what causes Alzheimer's. It's the build-up of a particular protein, known as beta-amyloid, at certain key locations in the parts of the brain that control memory. The biotech company, Sansom, is trying to find a way of reversing the damage caused by these amyloid plaques. To do that, it needs a map of those memory systems — the same map that researchers here at the Lycee are working on. Now, I'm not going to tell you about all the ways in which Sansom are trying to get their hands on the Lycee's mapping data. Instead, I want to tell you about Sansom's own research, conducted at their European headquarters, not five miles from here.'

Boos rise from the body of the hall. James raises his hand meekly and flashes his shatterproof smile. He hasn't shaved. He's wearing grey joggers and a green rower's hoodie. His right-hand fingers palp the bulb of an old motor-car horn bracketed to the arm of the throne. He doesn't need to hoot: the waves of sound part for him.

'Sansom was founded in 1904 as a manufacturer of hair oil. Since then it has grown into one of the top three biotechnology companies, with research centres in France, Germany, Australia, Taiwan, as well as the US. As a private company, Sansom's business is to conduct research and exploit the fruits of that research commercially. The Lycee, in contrast, is a national seat of learning, its endowment supplemented by funds from the regional assembly and the Northern Federation. It therefore has a responsibility to make the outcomes of its research public, according to the most ancient traditions of academia.'

'Get on with it!' yells one of the beer-monsters.

'Which is just a way of saying that Sansom and the Lycee want different things for the mapping data. The Lycee's team will soon be ready to assemble this data into a complete map of the memory circuit. If Sansom could get hold of it, they would be well on their way to an effective treament for dementia.'

I thought I was invisible. I'm at the back of the hall, barely out of the foyer. There are students all around me. But somehow it's me James is looking at, as though the bodies in between us were just the medium that made my awkwardness all the more visible — as if he could see me *because* I'm hidden, and that very effort gives me away.

'And who are they going to test their new Alzheimer's drugs on?'

A roar goes up at the front of the hall. A shaggy black figure lopes onto the stage, and my first thought is that it is another runaway chimp, stumbling on into a benevolent limelight. Then I recognise the prank of a beta in a gorilla suit. There's a slowly dawning familiarity to those realistic flaring nostrils: this is one of the outfits Gareth and James tried to embarrass me with, back when the world was straightforward.

'Apes,' James says. 'Apes is who. Dudes, let me tell you about Sansom's chimp model of Alzheimer's Disease.'

The gorilla waddles over and slumps down next to the compère on the sofa. So this is what Conscience are planning. They're going to accuse Sansom of conducting secret experiments on primates. Earlier today, the idea would have seemed ridiculous. But then I made the acquaintance of McQueen.

'Sansom are buying in enculturated chimpanzees that have outgrown their usefulness at American primate research stations. These are chimps that have been brought up as humans to see if they can learn language and stuff. Back in the nineties, every tenure-fixated grad student was trying to teach chimps language. What no one ever considered was what would happen to these guys once they'd claimed their subject expenses. They've been brought up as humans, and so they now expect human company, human privileges. They're so human it's not true. You can't just return them to the wild: they'd be bushmeat before sundown. So Sansom have bribed their way to getting an import licence, and they're shipping them over here. They've got themselves a subject pool of little hairy human-substitutes who, conveniently, can't make much of a noise about how they're treated. Result: Sansom can try out various manipulations to mimic the effects of Alzheimer's. Because most of these chimps and bonobos know sign language, you could argue that they provide a plausible model of human dementia.'

The Conscience contingent whoop it up. The scientists in the audience groan at the absurdity of it all.

'So this is the truth behind Sansom's research on Alzheimer's. Chimps that have been reared like American children are being shipped over here and kept in the animal equivalent of a Victorian lunatic asylum. They're given none of the social contact or intellectual stimulation they've been used to all their lives. They're fed on a special protein drink rich in amyloid precursors and aluminium, to encourage the build-up of plaques. On their last day on earth they do a bunch of psychological tests and are then killed so the scientists can see how much damage this amyloid cocktail has actually done to their brains. The whole thing happens a few miles away at Sansom's European headquarters. No doubt they think they can get away with this because they're only using dumb animals. Dumb animals who chat to each other in sign language. Whose favourite TV programme is *Sesame Street*. As dumb as you are, in other words.'

The crowd roars. A drunken boatie climbs up onto the stage and starts wrestling with the gorilla. The two stagehands try to pull them apart. James hasn't moved. He's still settled on the throne, staring out over the audience towards the portrait of Bishop Walden, as though waiting for a harmless fire to burn itself out, and prove a point about the transience of small disturbances, the all-conquering power of patience.

Night rain has flushed out the market square. Streetlight buzzes and expires on a wide curve of cobblestones. The rain has stopped now, but there's still that bitter wind. I'm hugging myself inside my military coat. The crowd disperses noisily, with nothing particular in mind. The shops keep on selling. Plasma screens in the window of a bank give details on a range of tax-efficient investments; a DNA nanoprocessor laptop above the doorway of a computer shop rotates slowly inside a glass case. I've only had two glasses of champagne but still the façades seem to lean and totter. Alnwick Street feels narrow and sepulchral. I can hear them up ahead, the little crowd we're following. They're drunk and happy. The townies have gone home, leaving the ancient city to the occupying force of term-time. My satchel is pulled tight over my shoulder. It's as if I'm dragging something, a weight I've been hitched to while I slept, but if I look around there'll be nothing there.

James hasn't said a word.

We're walking side by side. He slows with quaint chivalry to let me go first down a narrow bit of pavement, even though there are no cars. He's come out without a coat. His face is red with cold. He looks heavy, bear-like. I have a wild urge to push on him, shove him as hard as I can, see if he wobbles. All that mass of meat and bone.

'I didn't know you were going to be speaking.'

My tone alarms me. I should get to know him better before I start nagging him. He looks up, frosts up his lungs with a gallon of night air, and contemplates the wet trail of cobblestones leading up to the abbey.

'Last minute thing. The main speaker dropped out.'

He doesn't look around.

'That's why you were giving me such a hard time this afternoon. I thought it was a bit suspicious that you were suddenly so interested in my research.'

Not just *my* research, I want to say. He can't know that I watched him earlier, as he filmed the iris scanner on the third-floor landing. He's a Conscience activist, sizing up our institute as a possible target. He demonstrates at Sansom every week, and now the Lycee is going to start getting the same attention as the biotech. At least I know now what side he's on.

'I thought that was the point of tutorials. To challenge the received view.'

His privileged accent. The carefully insinuated hurt.

'You're Conscience, aren't you?'

The idea makes him wince. 'I think for myself.'

'But you agree with all that stuff.' I brush the green ribbon on his chest, the badge of the animal rights activist. My touch is firmer on him than I meant it to be, and he smiles.

'Of course I agree with it. It's common sense. The lines we draw between humans and animals are entirely arbitrary. They're based on bad, out-of-date theology. You're a scientist. You should understand that.'

We pass a seventeenth-century estate agent's clad in scaffolding, and James scans rows of little dream houses, seeing nothing he likes.

'You've been going on demos at Sansom.'

He takes it calmly. His lips are in motion again, wrestling with a smile.

'I'm there all the time. The guards call me Fred.'

'Fred?'

'The mask. Fred Flintstone. It's pretty unnecessary. They all know who I am.'

'I thought you might have told me.'

'I didn't lie to you, Dr Churcher.'

'You didn't tell me you were going on demos.'

'Should I?'

'It might have been polite to declare an interest. Given the nature of our relationship.'

'Do we have a relationship?'

'I'm your tutor. You're my student. Which is pretty relevant, given the kind of things I was going to be teaching you about.'

'Surely none of *that* involves hurting animals?'

I don't give him the pleasure. 'And given recent events at Forest Campus. The security situation. There are guidelines, James, judgements to be made. I need to know what my students are up to.'

'Don't worry,' he says. 'I'm not that kind of activist.'

His hands make deep nests in the pockets of his boatie top. The poor boy is shivering.

'Anyway,' he says, 'I couldn't tell you.'

'Why not?'

'Because if I'd told you, I couldn't have been in your group.'

That throws me. My cheeks start to burn, and I'm sure he's noticing. I'm too bothered by this. Whatever's happening, it should not be happening with one of my second-year students. I can feel myself walking faster, trying to outstrip it. I need to stand my ground.

'You could have let me decide that.'

He frowns, perhaps regretting his confession.

'All right then. It didn't seem relevant. We're not interested in you lot. Those break-ins you've been having? Just kids. It's Sansom we're targeting, not this place.'

He gestures vaguely at the college buildings that dwarf us. Medieval sandstone has been worn away into deep concavities, leaving bas-reliefs of harder mortar. You see faces in the contours, accidental gargoyles. This place looks after its own, even those who would try to destroy it. I remember the leaflets I saw stacked up on the table at the back of the Priors' Hall.

'So what about the animals we're supposed to be torturing at the Institute?'

He's seen the leaflets too. He shakes his head, and it almost looks like regret.

'We can't control that stuff. This movement attracts idiots, like any high-profile thing. You're not going to feel any pressure. The big guys are not going to bother with a few loony mice in a paddling pool.'

'The big guys?'

'You know what I mean.'

'Are you a big guy?'

'I told you. I think for myself.'

His pace slows again, for whatever invisible traffic.

'Anyway, James, you're going to have to get your facts right. What you

39

said about the chimps at Sansom. There's not an ethics committee in the Federation that would give permission for that kind of research.'

'OK, so they just do it without permission. That's why they're trying to keep it quiet.'

'And how do you know that?'

'We've got evidence. Photos. Memos rescued from the shredder. A very graphic video smuggled out by an ex-member of staff.'

I run my gloved thumb along the strap of the satchel. It feels soft and sticky, and clings to the suede even in this cold.

'And you think that's enough basis for you to start taking action against Sansom?'

'It's plenty. Have you seen the railway track that goes through their land? It carries supplies for their experiments. Some of us were up there last week, after dark. They were taking a delivery. Suddenly the guards were not so tolerant. This lorry drives in with its headlights off. Our guys were watching from the trees. Saw them pulling out huge crates of tomatoes and fork-lifting them into this great big hangar thing. Our guys tried to get in for a closer look but the grunts were getting intense. It was pretty obvious the attention wasn't welcome.'

'Tomatoes?'

'For the chimps. You've got hundreds of chimps in there. Fruit-eaters, yeah? They need feeding. Tomato salad and then brain surgery.'

'Well, that's one interpretation.'

He gives a showy, thrown-back laugh. 'You can interpret all you like, it won't change the truth about Sansom.'

I let the satchel swing out on my hip. Eclectic tastes, maybe, but Sansom surely don't think they can get away with illegal experiments on primates. Whatever Conscience think they've got on the world's third biggest biotech, I hope they've bothered to check their facts.

'Sansom are going to claim that they're the victim of a smear campaign. They'll say all that evidence was planted by Conscience.'

'Of course they will. But then there's the kind of evidence you couldn't fake. Like the fact that there's an adult chimpanzee roaming wild in Wenderley Forest. How's that got there, if it hasn't escaped from Sansom's labs? One of these days someone's going to get a good look at this chimp they call McQueen. Then Sansom's PR people will be busy. Unless, of course, Sansom get to him first.'

'What do you mean?'

'They've got men going after him with guns. They're brutal. They have people working for them who will stop at nothing. They'll shoot him. Do whatever it takes to dispose of the evidence.'

I feel a shiver. He flashes his knowing look. But he can't know. Only I know what I saw on my rooftop this afternoon.

'How could a chimp be surviving in Wenderley Forest?'

'He'll have a food supply. Fruit or whatever. And he's probably living close to people. Buildings where there's a heat source.'

The treehouses. Half of them are unoccupied. I don't go up to the boiler housing in my own stairwell from one year to the next. It's possible.

'So what are you going to do?'

'We're going to put this video out there. This time next week, the whole world's going to know about it. Keep the telly on. You'll probably see it on *All Points North*.'

The crowd has stopped at the kebab van at the top of Alnwick Street. I can see Gareth at the front, joking with the serving woman. James has already joined the queue and is inspecting some change in the palm of his hand.

'James, I don't know what this evidence is that you think you've got. But I know what sort of research they're doing at Sansom. A friend of mine used to work there. They're working on interface systems, developing biocompatible electrodes. They take incredible care when they work with animals. Do you know what sort of hoops you have to jump through to get a licence to do animal research these days? This is not some evil biotech trying to take over the world.'

'They're doing a lot of stuff. You don't know *what* they're doing. Anyway, my job is not to understand how Sansom's different interests interconnect. My job is to stop them.'

We look across the river to where the Memory Centre is already dominating the skyline. This is how the Executive will celebrate the publication of the map of the Lorenzo Circuit, with a monument to the modern understanding of human memory. It will be an international research centre, a temple to neuroscience, a memorial to achievements and atrocities, a museum of forgetting. Some dismiss it as an empty gesture, the kind of overhyped public engagement shop-front that passes for a research institute these days. Others wonder what the Executive will do to fill it. But it looks impressive there on the northern bank, a bright space-park of arc-lights. Beyond it, the sky-hoardings over Pelton burn the edge of the darkness.

'This is how I see it,' James says. 'Sansom want to get their hands on the mapping data. With the layout of the Lorenzo Circuit, they'll be able to take their research to a new level. They'll be able to develop treatments that are tailored specifically for these pathways, and test them out on their Alzheimer's chimps. Have you any idea how much money's going to be made out of this? Within three years they'll have cleaned up.'

A flush of cortisol tickles the lining of my skin. What he's saying is uncomfortably plausible. A dietary supplement could fill you with enough amyloid precursor to trigger the build-up of the plaques that cause Alzheimer's. If that's what they're doing to chimps, they're going to have cases of dementia. Maybe that explains McQueen. Too confused to find his way home, he followed his instincts: a warm boiler room, a ready source of food. In which case, the dementia that Sansom gave him might have saved him from being tracked down.

'They won't get those mapping data,' I say. 'They're safe.'

'Any encryption system can be broken.'

'It's not about encryption. Trust me. They're as safe as any data could ever be.'

The next thing James does is order a steak sandwich from a woman who looks like she's been handling meat too long. I think my surprise has lights on it.

'What?' he says, hatching the burger's insides with mustard.

'I just assumed you animal rights campaigners were vegetarians.'

'Don't worry. This stuff has never been anywhere near a cow.'

He hears shouts from the footbridge and turns to look. People are crowded at the far end by the arts centre, looking up at the parapet of the rooftop terrace. Someone has climbed up onto the parapet and is trying to mount a unicycle while drinks-traying a kebab in one hand. The white paper bustles, a greasy flag in the wind. The parapet must be a couple of feet wide at the most. A hundred feet below, the dug-up collapse of the riverbank sinks into black water. The prankster seems to glance down, and then has to grab the unicycle to keep it from toppling into the drop. The Churl slides by, massive and sequinned. People have died falling from here. James has wandered down to the foot of the steps, already certain of what I'm still just realising. Now he breaks into a run.

'Go on, Gaz! Go on, my son!'

I'm running too, breath rasping at my throat. Red fleece, black woolly coalman's hat. It's him.

'Jesus ... you've got to get him down!'

'Don't worry, he's brilliant on those things. They made him secretary of the One-Wheeled Bicycle Society.'

We reach the rearguard of jeering students. James seems hardly out of breath.

'He's going to get killed.'

I grab at my satchel, wondering what I've done with my phone. He grins, retrieves an old-fashioned button-phone and starts dialling for himself. Up on the parapet, Gareth has climbed up onto the unicycle and is pedalling a couple of very quick turns, and then one foot jerks backwards and he loses it and seems to panic. The kebab swings out of his hand and flies out in an arc over the river, shedding shreds of lettuce, loops of onion and sopping meat. A couple of figures appear behind him on the terrace, apparently sent up there to talk him down. Gareth has caught himself again, seesaws his feet on the pedals, and then with a yell he topples, someone grabs the unicycle, arms reach up and drag him to safety and he's lost behind the parapet. A gas heater topples over, and I can hear the scrape of beer tables. After a moment I see Gareth surging to his feet, raising a pale hand in triumph at the gathered crowd, beatified by his brush with death, still drunk, still happy.

The talk-down squad shepherd him down the fire escape. Gareth seems to have lost the ability to walk and see where he's going at the same time. His coalman's hat isn't anywhere. One of the beer-monsters has climbed up on to the terrace and is trying to repeat the stunt. But the crowd has lost heart, and no one cheers the latecomer. I watch them disperse, seeing a younger me in a few fresh faces; convinced, as I was, that this is just the giddy start of a blissful immortality. If I could tell them the truth, I wouldn't even bother. I'm thirty. This isn't the time to start feeling old.

The last of them haul up over the steps on the other side. We're alone on the bridge. This is me, and that's James.

'Actually, that was fucking stupid,' he says.

He takes a hipflask from his pocket and hands it to me. The whisky is fiery, warmed by his body.

'I read his essay. It's pretty bizarre.'

'He won't show it to me.' He presses his mouth to the steel lips of the flask, still wet from my own mouth. 'I've asked him. I've watched him work so hard on it, and I want to know what he's doing. He's my friend. I want to share this with him. But he's obsessed. Completely adamant. You're the only person who's allowed to know about it.'

'Why the secrecy? What's he afraid of?'

'Everyone. He's totally paranoid. He thinks this thing he's working on is so big, people are going to do anything to steal it from him.'

'Well, if he's trying to give me a clue, it hasn't worked. I'll have to ask him about it tomorrow.'

'You're seeing him?'

'We're meeting to talk about his essay. Perhaps I can get him to explain his suicidal behaviour as well.'

James props himself against the parapet. 'It was like this last time. One minute he's pushing the pranks a bit too far, and the next he's attracting the interest of the sanity police.'

'Last time? What happened last time?'

'You know Gaz missed a semester?'

I didn't, but maybe I should. 'Is that why he was going on about his college record?'

He passes the flask again and watches me drink. 'He was obsessed with these philosophical thought experiments. Pure rationality. He was totally in his own head. Reading like a fanatic, all this stuff about the mind and the brain. First it was the idea of an artificial consciousness. The brain is just a machine, and the brain is conscious, so machines should be able to become conscious too. He got this idea that if he could connect up enough second-hand computers he could create conscious-ness in an artificial system. You know, like a network that would become aware of itself. It all went over my head. Then there was some other thing which was like an art performance. He sat in this box in the middle of Monastery Green and got people to pass bits of paper to him through a slot in the side. And then he'd pass them back with other stuff written on them. The writing was all in Chinese. What's that about?'

I try to recall the details. 'It's to do with how you can have a material mind. If you go by the scientific description, we're just a complex system of connections. How does that come to have experience, to feel pain and joy and all the rest of it?'

To be that person, in this room, right now. James put it pretty well. I think of the attachment that came with Gareth's essay. His notes were full of these kinds of musing on the philosophy of consciousness. They might be a better guide to his obsessions than I imagined.

'Anyway, that got him in enough trouble to start with. He got on to one of the networks and tried to get all the accounts talking to each other. Like the network itself could become conscious. Then he just vanished.'

'Vanished?'

He tosses up his hands, scattering imaginary cards. 'This hacking stuff he's into? Normally, when you're online, you leave a trail: sites you've been to, messages you've sent. Gaz knows how to cover the tracks. He knows how to make himself disappear. I mean *completely.* Without a trace.'

'So how did they find him?'

'They didn't. Not until he was ready. He just turned up. Suddenly he's in New York and he's trying to get a meeting with the CEO of PowerServe. You know, the software corporation? Says he has a deal to offer them which will make them both rich. He gets about eight seconds into his spiel, they call Security and he's escorted off the premises.'

'Into the arms of the psychiatrists?'

He nods. 'Diagnosis: bipolar disorder. Manic phase.'

'You say he's planning something. You think he's trying to make money out of this?'

'I don't think it's about money for Gaz. It's about the ideas. You tell me. What does it say in his essay?'

I hold my satchel close. Gareth has entrusted me with this, and I'm not sure I'm ready to pass that trust on, even if James is an old friend.

'Not much. Some weird stuff about enhancing human memory. It's manic alright. I think he's got fixated on what we were talking about today. I'm going to have to talk to him.'

Some postgrads wheel past, heading for the same late-night bar. James' whisky is tugging at my sense of balance. The thought almost shames me, but an obscure regret is tingling in me, a feeling that Gareth's attention-grabbing has spoiled something.

'I'd better be getting back.'

'Wait.'

He's leaning on the rail, reading his future in the exposed workings of the Churl.

'If you want an extension on your coursework, forget it.'

'I want to know what you think.'

'About what?'

'About me.'

'I'm thinking that I ought to report you.'

'Why don't you?'

'Because sometimes I'm not sure if it really matters. Whether I do the thing or don't do the thing.'

'What do you mean?'

'You want to know what I think, James. I *don't* think. That's the problem.'

He turns around to face me. I appear to amuse him.

'I'm empty,' I say. 'There's no "me" to do the thinking. I'm an illusion. The confection of a restless, pattern-seeking brain.'

Fuck, it's cold. I wish we could go somewhere warmer. I don't know what I'm saying any more.

'I'm sorry. You don't really want to know all this.'

'I like learning from you, Dr Churcher.'

I stand next to him at the rail. His body makes a faint shield from the wind.

'You think you're in control of your actions. You think that just by deciding to do something, that makes you do it. But it doesn't. Something makes it happen, but it's not anything that corresponds to "you". You might feel you're in control, but that's just because you're taken in by the illusion. I'm not saying there's anything *wrong* with me. I'm not different to you. I've just stopped believing in the illusion.'

'And this illusion … That's just because we're all made of molecules and connections and there's nothing else?'

'Basically, yes. I'm not saying it because I want to be different. I'm saying it because the neuroscience proves it.'

'Weird. You're some kind of zombie, Dr Churcher.'

'Well, I have perceptions and everything. My input systems are working. I can tell you that my knee is aching and I've got a shiver down my back, and the little toe on my right foot has died and gone to heaven. But it doesn't have any centre to it. Maybe it's a bit like being mildly drunk all the time, except it's not like that because you feel like it *all* the time. You have this onrush of sensations and somehow they don't all fit together.'

'I'm a student: I know about being mildly drunk all the time. But how come you don't fall over?'

'Because the individual systems work well. My visual system sees an obstacle coming and patches the information straight through to my motor cortex. All you need are close linkages between input and output, more-or-less autonomous subsystems doing what they do. The neuroscience has moved on. We haven't got a Mr Spock up there, working through everything coolly and logically and omnisciently. We've got a ragtag collection of self-obsessed processors, each of which is mostly blissfully unaware of what the others are doing. We think we're steering this thing, but we're not. There's no one in control. There's not even a centre of consciousness. Half of the time you don't *need* consciousness. You'd get along fine without it.'

'Because there isn't a *you*.'

'Exactly.'

'I don't see how you can deny consciousness, Dr Churcher. What about love? What about ecstasy? Don't they make you feel complete?'

Was I there, when Mateus was there? I remember his weight, his garlic sweetness. That summer night we lay on the roof of my tree-house, our bodies warm chocolate, held in the sticky hand of love. He *thought* he was there. He *thought* he was inside me. But he wasn't anywhere near. I was just a figment of his higher-level visual processes,

47

a brilliant illusion. I was in pieces, and all he saw were fragments. His zombie girl.

'I wouldn't know.'

'Well, maybe when you meet someone you really like, it will feel different.'

'I'll let you know.'

Is that why Mateus is getting back in touch? Because he wants more of that emptiness, pushing back against him?

'Don't worry about me,' I say. 'I've just read too much neuroscience.'

'But listen to what you're saying. You're talking about *me*. What's *me* if not a single, indivisible self?'

'It's a word. A word for a thing. However fragmentary my experience is, it's tied to a particular body, a particular pair of eyes and ears, the biological machine that runs all these separate systems. I'm not one of these people who'll doubt the existence of the bridge I'm standing on. I'm here, I'm real. I can't doubt that.'

He turns to me, rubbing his raw red hands, leaning with one hip propped against the rail. There goes my windshield. In the lensy cold I see him blurred against the union buildings, the millionaire town-houses, masses of piled-up land waiting for snow. My gloves are lined suede, but I can distinctly feel his hand pressing down on mine, squeezing the fingers into each other then slowly letting go. This word comes into my head — *whoosh*, just *whoosh* — and I feel a warm, throbbing amazement, and I wonder what happened to that girl who was loved for her emptiness, that zombie girl. Whoosh. Just whoosh. He turns me around and closes his hands behind my back. I look up, wanting to say something. Then he kisses me, fleetingly and insubstantially, like divers must kiss, when they're buoyed up by something heavier than air. All my life's been like this, a richly-detailed sleepwalk, a being caught off-guard by the passing of important things, so that none of the importance could stick to them, they would all be forgotten in the morning. He tastes of blood. I could conk out in his arms. A woman clicks past in expensive heels, and with her goes the vague idea that she might be my boss, Gillian Sleet. But I take no notice, because I'm nothing but the trembling object of James' kiss, which isn't ending, because I don't want it to.

'You're here,' he says.

CHAPTER FOUR

How To Get Rich Without Really Trying

◉

I've arranged to see Gareth the next day. I want to talk to him about his essay, and find out more about this scheme he's trying to convince me of. But last night has given us other things to talk about. His performance on the footbridge could have been the first sign of something serious. James seems to be half-expecting another breakdown, and this is how it would begin. I'm Gareth's tutor; I have a duty to keep him out of trouble. And if that means arranging to see him on a Saturday, when the Institute is supposed to be closed to all but essential research staff, then that's what I'll have to do.

He's five minutes early. He's standing next to the water maze in my lab, watching a mouse sink to its ears in the milky water and paddle out from the side of the pool. I reboot the tracker and watch the icon nibble its way across the monitor screen. You'd never have thought a mouse could be a good swimmer until you saw one in the water maze. At first it's going wrong by about forty-five degrees, heading straight for the middle instead of the south-west quadrant, but then it finds its bearings and starts closing in on the platform. The plastic disc it's looking for is submerged fifteen millimetres below the surface, invisible until you're right on top of it. I haven't moved it since the last block of trials. We watch the mouse scrabble up onto the platform and sit there, flicking at its whiskers in quiet triumph.

'He's done that before,' Gareth says.

'Only once. But the tracking's playing up so I need to give someone an extra trial.'

'*Someone*?' He sounds amused. 'Does he have a name?'

'There's ninety-nine of them. I can't give them all names. Now, you've had your treat. You're not supposed to be here.'

Gareth seems quite convinced that he should be here. He's leaning with both arms stretched out along the rim of the pool, as if he were the owner of this thing and he didn't quite like where it had been planted. It's warm in here, but he's still wearing his coalman's hat. I thought that had gone in the river last night.

'You said you wanted to see me. I'm just doing what I'm told.'

The tracker monitor blanks out. I turn the light down over the pool, hoping it's just a reflection confusing the sensor. The screen stays blank. I reboot the tracker, fish the mouse out of the pool and dab at it with a towel. A few years ago they found that half the mice trialled on the water maze were suffering from hypothermia. My little chat with Gareth can wait: I have to get these two back into their room across the corridor before they catch my cold.

'That was a normal mouse,' I tell him, trying to asphyxiate a sneeze. 'This next one's been transgenically modified to produce too much amyloid precursor. That's the thing that makes beta-amyloid, which is the protein that forms the plaques in Alzheimer's. James got that bit right, at least. We genetically programme the mice to produce too much precursor, so they end up with brains full of the same kind of plaques. So we've got a mouse model of Alzheimer's.'

I put the second mouse down at the same starting point. It starts paddling even before it hits the water, hugging the wall like a drunk then striking out blindly for the dead centre. The monitor tracks it for a while and then flickers into blankness. The mouse reaches the far wall and starts swimming back in the direction it came from. I watch it struggle back to where it started, then reach in and pluck it to safety.

'That's the transgenic one. Classic Alzheimer's features: memory loss, behavioural inflexibility, impaired learning. This mouse has got what your granny will probably have by the time she hits eighty-five.'

'Cool,' Gareth says. 'So you've cracked the mystery of Alzheimer's Disease.'

'I wish. This is quite exciting because we can now directly connect these mental problems with the formation of amyloid plaques. What we still don't understand is where the critical points for plaque formation are. You've seen how complex these memory circuits are. We need to know where the amyloid is building up, and how it's having the effect it's having.'

'That's why you need the map of the Lorenzo Circuit.'

'Exactly. Once we know where the pathways run, we can work out how the system goes wrong in Alzheimer's. That's what they're working on downstairs. Charting the Lorenzo Circuit, neurone cluster by neurone cluster.'

'Is that the floor the lift doesn't stop at?'

I get the mouse into its cage and start hunting for a tissue for myself. 'You noticed.'

He starts pressing buttons on the tracker. 'Don't you need huge scanners to do all that brain-mapping stuff?'

'They've got huge scanners. They've got optical imaging scopes and lightweight headcoils of a power I could only have dreamt of when I was a student. The main cooling problems were solved ages ago. They run computer simulations using linked mainframes spread across the Lycee. They're not short of ways of getting this mapping information.'

'But they analyse it all downstairs. All the top-secret data which the evil biotech Sansom is desperate to get its hands on.'

I smile, and sneeze violently. 'James is a romantic. He has his ideas.'

'But it *is* hot stuff.'

'It sure is. Everyone's desperate to get hold of it. But they won't.'

I remember the one time I got let on to the third floor. I was trailing along with the head of the Institute, Gillian Sleet's puppy for the day. Even the great scientist had to press her manicured fingers against a bioscanner before they would let us through. Combination-locked doors, screened-out windows. They didn't let us through for long.

'How come they won't get it?'

'Because it's safe.'

He looks awestruck. 'Have you got FGP? Is that how you're protecting it?'

'Safer than that.'

'Cool,' he says, in a different voice.

I start trying to recalibrate the two infrared sensors. My eyes are streaming and I can't make out the markings on the fiddly little dials. I undim the light over the pool and a headache comes sirening into earshot.

'So you take security pretty seriously. I had to give my life story before the defenders of science would let me up here.'

'We have to. You've seen what some people want to try and do to this place.'

'I thought Conscience were going after Sansom. Because of what they're supposed to be doing with chimps...'

I swallow painfully as one of the calibration thumbwheels starts to loosen between my fingers. Too long standing out in the cold last night: it's left me open to infection. I've seen my own evidence of Sansom's chimp experiments, and it has to be more convincing than any of the video footage that James and his Conscience friends have dredged up. Our moment on the footbridge is not going to change any of that. It's the sort of fact that's dead before it has even finished happening, because the world is how it is, the size and the shape that it is, and there's no room in it for students to go around stealing kisses from their sad and lonely tutors. Moments on dark bridges don't fit anyone's reality. The world spins on without them. It's probably better that way.

'Look,' I tell Gareth, 'no one can get the mapping data. They're not on any one computer. People sign up to this particular top-secret server, and they get an account name and a password. It's set up so that everyone who has an account on this server can dump data onto there. But it doesn't actually go onto one hard disc. It gets hidden around all over the place. And the really important thing is that you can't get anything *off* this special server unless you've got all the passwords. Everyone's working on different fragments of the map and filing them on the mainframe as they go. When they've got all the fragments together, they'll access all the separate accounts and put the whole map together. As soon as they're ready to do that, they're ready to publish.'

'So, in order to get the map, you'd need to have all the passwords?'

'Exactly. It's like the sum total of human knowledge. There's no one part of the brain where we store the knowledge that we know. It's diffuse, scattered all over the place.'

'Distributed representations. The basic principle of how the brain stores knowledge.'

'You *have* learned something. And in case you're wondering, I haven't got an account on this... *Fuck!*'

The thumbwheel comes off in my hand and plops into the water before I can catch it. I start to regret that there are over five hundred litres in this thing, and that every one of them has been carefully made opaque. Gareth stops what he was saying and stands there in shock.

'It's all right. I'll have to drain the pool. The water needed changing anyway.'

'Might find some drowned mice in there.'

'No. Drowned ones rise to the surface after a few days.'

'Like drowned students.'

He's smiling. He follows me through into the office and watches me run through a couple of routines on the computer. He knows we're talking about his high-wire act above the Churl last night.

'You could have been killed, Gareth.'

'Were you there?'

I park the cursor in the corner of the screen and the screensaver dances into view. I have to be careful how I talk to him about this. I need to keep him trusting me.

'I was never in any danger, Miss. I worked out the mechanics very carefully.'

'Not how it looked to me.'

'How did it look to James?'

'I don't know. Was James there?'

'You know he's putting it on, don't you? This month it's animal rights. Last month it was veganism. Next month it'll be something else.'

'So you know all about James, do you?'

'Everything,' he says, smugly. 'All there is to know.'

I pick up his essay, prickling, and flick through it. I realise I haven't written anything on it.

'I've read your assignment, Gareth. Do you really think you're going to be able to find a way of stimulating people's memories?'

'I got it wrong about memory implants. I can see that now. You can't plug in a complete set of memories like you plug in a new DVD. Memories aren't DVDs. They're made in the brain. They're a cocktail of impressions and feelings and bits of knowledge you hardly knew you had, all mixed up together in the Lorenzo Circuit. What I'm planning, Miss, is about stimulating what's already there, rather than plugging in something new.'

Nerdy accent on the last two words. A whiff of Suffolk in his voice. He's still showing this ironic deference, addressing me like I'm a primary school teacher. I need to go online. There's a discussion group somewhere that might help me solve this problem. People around the world are using this thing: maybe some other clumsy twit has lost their thumbwheel at the bottom of the pool. I bash in my password and see the icon for Dougal appear bottom-left. Once onto Dougal, I can access all my discussion groups, closed email lists, the contents of any number of virtual libraries. From Dougal I can go anywhere. Except onto Ermintrude.

'But how on earth,' I find the discussion group and start scrolling down, 'are you going to stimulate what's in the Lorenzo Circuit? You've got a neural system that obeys its own laws. It speaks its own language. How are you going to get your computers or whatever to talk to that?'

'That's exactly why I've got to break into Sansom.'

I look at him, checking for signs that he's joking. He has the brain chemistry to make this a possibility. Talking to the nervous system was exactly what Mateus was trying to do. All at once, it doesn't seem such a coincidence that he's getting in touch with me now.

'I see.' I hit LOGOUT, clumsy with frustration. 'That's all it's going to take, is it?'

'Not exactly. Once I've got the technology, I've then got to implement it.'

His hands fly up above his head, fending off imaginary blows. There's something ancient, Laurel-and-Hardyish, about the gesture.

'Is this the thing you were trying to sell to PowerServe?'

He grins. 'You could come in on it.'

'I don't think so.'

'Give the project some proper academic credentials. And whilst you're at it, make yourself enough money to retire.'

'I don't want money.'

'Think of all the mice you'll be able to buy with five million dollars.'

The mice. Christ almighty. They'll freeze to death if they're not rinsed and heat-lamped and put back in their thermocontrolled maisonettes. I leave Gareth looking over his essay and go back into the lab. They're shivering, poor things, huddled together in the corner of the holding cage. I take one in each hand, cross the corridor and tap in the combination with one free knuckle. Something nags at me, a dense unease, like sick can't-face-the-world depression, hanging from my gut like a stone. But my mind is blank, swept clear for an emergency that never comes. The streptococci have scrubbed my voicebox raw. I'm going home after this and pouring myself the mother of all Jack Daniels. Declaring war on my colony of microbes. Napalming them all.

When I get back the desktop is showing. My screensaver is set to come on after three minutes. I must have been away that long, and yet it hasn't tripped. Has he touched my machine? Maybe the mouse got jogged accidentally. Gareth doesn't seem to have moved. I sit down at the computer and check for signs that any of my folders have been opened. Dougal's face has a red cross through it, showing that the connection has timed itself out. Which means I was still online when I left the room. Gareth is sitting with his essay squared neatly on his lap. He looks even more wired than usual.

'Panic over,' I say, panic screeching through me.

'Five million dollars.' He squeezes out a quiz-show smile.

'No.'

'All right, then. I suppose I'll just have to spend it myself.'

I'm tired. I really wish he'd go.

'What are you going to spend it on?'

I try not to make it sound like a question. I start working through my unopened mail, hoping he'll take the hint.

'Birds,' he says.

This is what Gareth tells me. I sense him slowing it down, wrapping it up with quiet emphasis. Memory, he seems to be saying: let me celebrate it with you.

'We were in Verona. This was back in the days of childhood, when foreign countries were still foreign countries. There was me, the mother object, the father object and the brother-shaped humanoid. The mother object wanted to go there before she got the divorce. We stayed in a hotel full of cockroaches near the old town. The concept in that sector was basically medieval. Winding alleyways, squares that jumped out at you from behind churches. Laundry trying to escape across the roof-tops. One morning me and the brother object were exploring. I was x years, he was x plus 2. We were in this narrow lane somewhere in the twelfth century when we heard it. It was like a million referees at the world's biggest football match all blowing their whistles at the same time. It took us a while to find it because the lane kept swallowing us up and then expelling us the same distance away. We knew the thing was there because it kept squawking. This was not a squawking noise I had any experience of.

'We turned a corner and the whole square was full of birds, millions of birds in wooden cages with wire mesh sides, one cage stacked on top of another, higher than a lorry, millions of caged birds all singing and chirping away.

'I looked more closely. They were all European songbirds. Nothing tropical, no cockatoos or rainbow lorikeets or macaws. Some of them were rare, though. You couldn't buy them in this country. I went up and asked the guy how much. One thousand euros, he said. I thought how cool it would be to be unfeasibly rich and spend all your money on expensive, rare European songbirds. Some of them were really colourful. Standing there listening to them chirp away, I realised the potential. Imagine if you could take a few hundred of them home with you. You could keep them in a huge aviary at the back of your house and they could decide your life for you. Say you wake up one morning and you can't quite decide what you want to think about that day. You go out to your aviary, stand there looking appealing but not too desperate and see what bird comes to you first. A small, slender-billed warbler might signify a morning spent in calm reflection. The dazzling wing patches of a White-Winged Lark might promise a day of slightly nihilistic thrill-seeking. All you have to do is stand there and wait for your thoughts and memories to come to you. After that, your day seems a bit less complicated. The birds get you started. There's a little less responsibility on *you*.'

'You were a smart ten-year-old. You pretty much foresaw modern neuroscience.'

'If you want to put it that way,' he grins. 'Like you said yesterday, it's *all* you, and *none* of it is you. *You* is just the sum totality of the system you make.'

I remember my conversation with James last night. If he had been Gareth, I wouldn't have had to explain a thing.

'Plato said the mind is like an aviary full of birds, one for every thought or memory you've ever had. They're all there, all these thoughts and bits of knowledge: the problem is *catching* them. I like that. Somehow I don't think thoughts: they just come to me.'

'Exactly,' he says. 'Respect to the old Greek guy. You could absolve yourself of all freewill and responsibility. You could let your life be entirely controlled by the collective behaviour of creatures who hadn't the slightest interest in that life. All *their* world consists of is bird-stuff: inconceivably erotic behavioural displays, flight patterns and wing markings, atmospheric conditions signifying the presence of particular kinds of flying foodstuffs. You would enter a universe ruled by completely different laws, where your every movement would be determined by the decision-making powers of fundamentally different life forms. Instead of thinking a thought or making a decision, you could just wait for a bird. I was ten. I thought that was a pretty good definition of happiness.'

'You and Plato. You both foresaw the Lorenzo Circuit.'

'This is what I mean. I need you to help me to tell people about this. The bloke in the street thinks there's someone in control up there, making the decisions. But all he really is is a flock of birds, a vast collection of inscrutable life forms flitting around in these amazingly complicated patterns. If people only allowed themselves to believe that properly, it would change their lives. Understand your aviary, man! Take control of your life, just by letting go of this ridiculous idea of *you*.'

I spin my eyeballs and let out an almighty sneeze. Gareth finally realises how I'm suffering, and gets up to go.

'It's okay. We still have time.'

'You want to stimulate the Lorenzo Circuit? And that's why you want to get into Sansom?'

'Get to know your birds. Your thoughts, your memories, the bioelectrical happenings that make you what you are. Learn how to make them come to you. It'll be simple. All you have to do is say yes.'

I watch him through methylated eyes.

'You've never told anyone this stuff before, have you?'

He looks stung, remembering past ridicule.

'The brain doctors wouldn't listen. Which is kind of ironic, since the whole point of their happiness drugs is to send the birds to sleep so they can't be any bother to anyone.'

57

'Well, let's keep it that way. Think it through. We'll talk about it some more.'

He needs to trust me. And I need to keep him from doing anything stupid.

'I've already done the thinking, Miss. But you're right. We need to keep this secure.'

He looks impatiently at me. A frown sharpens the angles of his face. His skin looks tanned, but it is an indoor, milk-fed complexion that bears the marks of his anxiety. His ears look capable of catching any sound. I can see how much this matters to him, and it scares me. He has trusted me with his secrets, believing in my loyalty before he has really seen evidence for it. And somewhere, somehow, I feel as though I've already let him down.

CHAPTER FIVE

After-Image

◉

I'm here. James kissed me and told me that.

But that's my body. I know I'm in a body. I'm single, indivisible, can't be two places at once.

I lie awake, fizzing with sleeplessness. The last two days have filled me up, and now bits of what I've heard, seen and felt keep seeping out of me. Insomnia floats me like a kite, tethered to one fixed point and free to blow in all directions. And while I blow, I can be anywhere.

Then thoughts happen to me.

I'm standing on my balcony on a summer night. The trees are cracking in the heat. Owl-hoots lob back and forwards in the moonlight. I don't know how long I've been talking. I'm telling the story of my first love affair, in the South of France, my last summer before university. I'm wearing a red dress hemmed above the knee. My legs are bare and the breeze is running warm fingers all over. I can hear his voice behind me, agreeing, gently questioning. For a long time he is just sounds: his breathing, the faint tunneling roar of his listening. But then I'll feel his hand on the back of my knee, brushing up over the little downward-pointing hairs on the backs of my thighs. I'll keep telling my story. I'll feel his thumb nosing between my buttocks, pushing deep. I'll feel it in my toes, in a twinge in my arm. Connections: that's all I am now. I'll flinch as his thumb pushes in deeper, but I won't hesitate, I'll keep on talking. His other hand will have my dress up around my waist. He'll reach under, between my legs, and I'll feel myself breaking like a fruit, coming to pieces along lines of segmentation. I'll hear his chair scrape as he stands up, working my circumference, easing my pants down. I'll slide my feet apart on the deck and lean right forward on the rail, opening up to him without even missing a breath, waiting for the heat of him, still talking, still waiting

Fuck, fuck, fuck.

I open my eyes. The room is full of moonlight. On the roof, the wind turbine ticks like a bicycle. Clouds scud across a plutonium moon.

'Weird,' James says. 'My lover is some kind of zombie.'

'*Lover*? Give it a chance.'

'Does he want you back?'

'Who, Mateus? I don't know.'

'Self-abuse won't help,' says my mother, dressed as a vicar.

She's right. It doesn't help. The battery is dead. Someone is ringing a doorbell in my head. *Dring-dring! Dring-dring!*

Mateus answers. The chimps bounce screaming off the walls.

Sometimes, when I'm in a state like this, I have a vision that scares me. It's like I get into an extremity of tiredness which takes me beyond normal perception — door-shapes and furniture details, the moonlight in the room — and I can actually see the random firings of my cortex, sparking a kaleidoscope of object shapes, a strange neural light-show. My eyes are closed, but still it feels as though I'm staring straight ahead, at the degraded photograph of the bedroom scene. Everything is nauseous and pale. Then suddenly there'll be a flash of bright light, half-obscured, like sunlight behind clouds, so much brighter than the twilight inside my sleepless brain. A brief powerful flash, and then it's gone, like a searchlight swinging around. It has made me cry before now, waking in the morning, wretched, alone. It has a kindness behind it, an ineffable gentleness. The light of God, perhaps, shining into my soul.

This light is not like that. It's small, yellow, battery-powered. A rod of torchlight, bouncing across my room.

I open my eyes. The light is coming from the window by the stairs. It flits across the bedroom, seems to settle, and goes out again.

If this was sleep, it wouldn't matter. But after that moment on the footbridge, after that kiss, I haven't been sleeping.

Slowly I steer the thought into shape. The light is torchlight. There is someone clinging to the window ledge. Someone who doesn't care if they live or die. Someone whose idea of a joke is to hang thirty metres off the ground, spying into a young woman's bedroom.

'Thanks,' he says, when I finally get the window open.

'Jesus Christ, Gareth.'

'The epithet is unnecessary. Just call me Beta Registration Number X001678D.'

He slots his head sideways through the gap and looks up at me with a skullish grin. The cold night rushes in. I peer out at the narrow wooden ledge he's standing on. He must have shuffled along here for ten feet at least. I wonder if he's thought to look down.

'Couldn't you have knocked?'

'I couldn't find the doorbell.'

He gives an effortful grunt and tips forward through the window. His rucksack snags on the overhang. I grab the strap of it and jerk it sideways to free its passage through. He slides down over the radiator, arms stretched forward like a sky-diver, and coils into a broken crouch on the floor. One leg crumples painfully beneath him. I help him to his feet. His hands are so cold.

'Do they know you're here?'

'Who? The sanity police?'

He puffs out breathlessness through a round O of a mouth, then pins it out into a smile.

'I needed to see you.'

We're upstairs in my living room. He's sitting on my cream sofa, clutching his rucksack on his lap. I've made him some tea but he seems to have forgotten about it. I crouch next to him in my dressing gown, trying to resurrect the stove.

'I need you,' he's saying. 'It won't work without you.'

I sigh, or perhaps it's a yawn. 'You think I'm a competent person, Gareth. I'm not. I'm useless.'

'Ah,' he says. 'You just don't yet know what the organism is capable of, Dr Churcher.'

'Gareth…' I break up some kindling and poke it into a complex of glowing coals. 'How did you get up here?'

I sense him turning on the cushions, watching me. I blow gently on the glow, trying not to disturb the warm powder that's sitting there. A skinny ghost of flame uncurls from the ash-speckled black.

'I climbed up the fire escape. I reversed the evacuation procedure. Pretending there *wasn't* a fire made it much easier.'

'You could have been killed.'

He seems to take it as a compliment. I catch him looking out towards the balcony, trying to work out if anyone else is here.

'Have you seen James?' he says.

The question throws me. I punt the stove door shut and crouch there, watching the brand-new flame.

'What, since yesterday afternoon?'

He looks at me, eyebrows raised. I'm trying to work out whether he could have seen us together on the bridge last night.

'Has he invited you over to meet the storytellers yet?'

'Who?'

'He lives in a squat in Pelton. When he's not living it up in college, that is. There's no mum or dad on the scene. His family is a bunch of militants with an unhealthy interest in this guru called David Overstrand.'

'I don't know much about James,' I breeze. 'You might have noticed, I have quite a few students to keep track of.'

He scans the interior of my treehouse suspiciously. He's wearing a white shirt unbuttoned at the neck. It has a faint nylony translucence, like fish-skin, an almost-wetness that clings and makes his nipples visible. It's come untucked at the waist, and there's a long rip running upwards from one corner. He must have snagged it on a bush or something on his way through the forest. On top of the shirt is a thin grey anorak, the sort that elderly men go shopping in. He's shivering. That sweat smell must be old. He perches forward on the sofa with his elbows on his knees, ready for an escape, fire or no fire.

'So why did you need to see me?'

I stand up from the stove, still wobbly with sleep. He glances at me, looking pained. I go and sit down on the other sofa, facing him, tightening the dressing gown over my knees.

'I've been thinking about what you said, Miss. It's all starting to make sense.'

His sticky-out ears turn forward like an owl's. He seems attuned to sounds as much as anything. For a weird moment I wonder if he uses those thyroid eyes at all.

'What is?'

'Sansom. What they're up to.'

I catch him glancing over towards the kitchenette. It seems to have struck him that I actually live up here.

'And what *are* they up to?'

'Actually, it's pretty obvious. It just took a few lucky accidents for me to see it clearly. Have you ever had the feeling that something strange is going on, that you've got access to knowledge you shouldn't possibly have? That's the tip. I'm offering you the iceberg.'

I think of McQueen. The iceberg chills, right through to the heart.

'Go on.'

'It's about Ermintrude. The Lycee's top-secret server. And what's on it that Sansom want so much.'

I told him about the server myself, in my lab this afternoon. But I'm certain I never referred to it by name.

'What do you know about Ermintrude?'

'I went on to the network when you were out of the room. I saw the icon on your desktop and I knew it was the big one. I couldn't get on to it. It's really secure.'

'It needs to be. With those mapping data, you could be marketing an effective treatment for dementia within three years.'

'Exactly. Which is why Sansom want it so badly.'

'And which is why they're not getting it. I told you about the pass-words. To get anything off Ermintrude you'd need to know every single one. That's a lot of heads you'd have to hold a gun to.'

He stands up suddenly.

'Have you got a car?'

'You could hardly call it a car.'

He looks around for the door, and then turns back to me, flustered.

'Look, Miss, Sansom are smart. They've spotted something that no one else has spotted. If you're going to stimulate the Lorenzo Circuit, you've got to speak its language. Even if we knew exactly where the pathways run, how are we going to get information into them in the right format? There's a system incompatibility. An assumption that silicon chip cannot speak unto neurone. Which is true, if you want to look at it that way.'

He's going too fast. But mania *is* fast. Fast is the point.

'What other way is there of looking at it?'

'It's simple. There needs to be a solution that will make the stuff that a computer does directly intelligible to a human nervous system.'

'Is this the idea you were trying to sell in New York?'

'Yes. And it's the reason you're going to give me a lift to Sansom.'

My laugh alarms me. I must sound as demented as he does.

'When?'

'Now.'

'We've obviously got a hijack situation here, but I can't see a gun.'

He grins. 'Not hijack. Just blackmail.'

'What do you mean?'

'I don't need a gun, Miss. I've got the fact that you allowed me to get within sniffing distance of Ermintrude. The Lycee's most important and secret mainframe computer. I'm sure Security would like to get their hands on that particular narrative.'

'Are you threatening me?'

'I'm trying to persuade you. It's for your own good. This is going to make you a very rich humanoid.'

My heart thumps, a sucker for the adrenaline rush. If he blabs to Security that I let him onto the network, I'll lose my access privileges. I can't make sense of my data without access to Dougal. A fierce burning breaks out on my neck, metastasizes to my armpits, and then fades to a fizzy calm.

'What do you want me to do?'

'You only have to get me into the car park. You don't have to show your face. You can wait for me in the car.'

'What makes you think I can get you through the Sansom barriers?'

'You've got a pass card. I've done my homework, Miss. I've been looking at all the published articles on human–machine interfaces. Checking the acknowledgements sections very carefully. You know, the bits where people thank their mums and their girlfriends for making them all those cups of tea? I'd say that a certain ex-boyfriend of yours used to work at Sansom on exactly this same topic.'

He's bluffing. Even if he's found out about the Pereira Effect, he can't know that I've still got Mateus' swipecard.

'If I did have a pass card, it would be years out of date. They change the codes every day.'

'Not necessarily. Sansom suffers from a worrying complacency about security. The new iris scanners have made the buildings so secure, they've let other things lapse. The car park security system was due to be upgraded last year. They got the new server in place but it didn't work. For about three weeks people could come and go as they pleased. Then Conscience got a bit too excited one day and a couple of them got into the main compound. The Sansom bosses thought: We can't have this, so they just went back to the old system and seemed to forget about it. They never updated it. The old cards still work.'

'How do you know this?'

'*He* said.' He jerks a thumb over his shoulder, meaning James. 'All the Conscience people know the loopholes in Sansom security. They don't want to use them until they're ready for something big. The buildings are safe, sure. But the main compound: it's not the fortress you think it is.'

'And you can get all you need just from looking around the car park?'

He nods. 'You don't even have to get out of the car.'

I want him out of here. I want to go back to bed and forget this ever happened.

'If I drive you to Sansom and let you have a look around, will you go straight home afterwards?'

'After fast food,' he says.

CHAPTER SIX

Sansom

◉

A car is not a self-portrait. Just because my vehicle is falling apart, it doesn't mean my life is.

'*Kyrie eleison*,' Gareth says. 'What do you call this?'

'It's a Shanghai-VW Santana. Chinese thing. Built by communists for communists.'

'What's a communist?'

I think for a moment. 'It's a sort of dreamer.'

'How can you afford to run it?'

'I can't. You're paying for the petrol.'

I have to dismantle his door from the inside. He climbs in and settles down with both hands folded in his lap, as if afraid of touching anything.

'I can't believe I'm doing this. It's the middle of the night.'

'Don't worry. It won't take long.'

I have to reach down to put my driving shoes on. He finds this funny, that I have special shoes for driving.

'Wait ...'

He reaches into his rucksack and pulls out a tiny camcorder. He flicks the screen out and starts filming my shoes as I drive. I can't stand people watching me drive. All that handbrake and checking mirror stuff. Especially when you're in a communist-era Santana which stalls every time you apply the brakes.

'There you are,' he says, turning the camera up over my mud-spattered jeans. 'Documentation. Proof that all of this happened.'

'I could live without that.'

My Lycee pass card gets me out of the Forest Campus and onto the empty road east towards Sansom. The night has a broken, unreal feel about it, as if only the flaring nets of streetlight were holding it together. Thankfully we have this cat-eyed blacktop to ourselves. The streetlights drop away and we're lost in the darkness of open countryside. It's ten minutes before we pass another car.

'You'd better not be long,' I tell him. 'The place is going to have security all over it.'

'Unlikely. It's Sunday morning. They'll all be tucked up in bed with their heated wife-systems.'

'There's going to be a man on the barrier. He'll want to see some ID.'

'Every door will open,' he says, 'if you know where to put the explosive.'

The turn-off to Sansom is marked by a discreet green-and-gold plaque. It's the sort of poised understatement that only the world's top corporations can afford. From here to the West Gate there's half a mile of evergreen forest. Half a mile of disorienting blackness: Sansom's first line of defence. The darkness is studded with tiny red diodes, unsleeping camera lenses. The forest films itself; owls and badgers star.

'There's the barrier,' Gareth says. 'This is where you're glad you brought your pass card.'

I drop to third. The Santana moans, slowed by its own racing engine. Second. I need to keep the revs up to stop the thing from stalling. The booth is lit, and occupied. We're close enough to see the dismaying silhouette of a man.

'Shit. I told you...'

Gareth hangs the camcorder around his neck and starts rummaging in his rucksack. I pull up alongside the window and wait for the guard to raise his eyes from the Italian football. His voice crackles from a speaker on the sealed glass.

'Bat,' he says.

I gawp at him like a tourist.

'Bat,' he repeats. '*Bat.*'

At which point my passenger is reaching across me, holding what looks like a small black metallic butterfly. He's filming the booth-man, and the booth-man is getting camera-shy. I take the thing and display it coolly on the dip-moulded dashboard.

'Go on,' the man says, glancing at the bat and triggering some event on his console. The barrier goes up. I don't even need Mateus' pass card.

We're through. The five-metre chain-link fence rattles shut behind us. Sansom spreads out before us, glass-walled and light-studded, a Manhattan of the mind.

'So where did you get that?'

The illuminations scan across the close-shaved knots in his cheeks. He picks the bat up from the dashboard and tries to unscrew the end.

'Conscience. They've all got them. To one of those bunny-lovers, a Sansom ID bat is as much a fashion accessory as the elegant green lapel-ribbon. You're only as good as your Sansom access privileges.'

'But won't the guard know it's stolen?'

'He would, if he'd been wearing his virtual lights. He's supposed to have them glued to his face. Our friend was slacking, having a footie break. That's why he didn't like me filming him.'

'I see what you mean about security.'

'Like I say, it's not actually that hard to get into the compound. It's so tight inside, they don't really bother.'

We cross the light railway track. The camcorder fills the car with turquoise reef-light.

'So if you had that thing all the time, why did you need me?'

'I needed your opinion. I need to know what you think.'

We're headed north, towards the biggest of the glass-fronted buildings, whose shopping-centre-in-space dome I can just see from my rooftop. I came here with Mateus once, a few months before our disastrous trip to Quebec. He was giving a promotion talk to some of his colleagues. The thing I remember most about the interior was the complete absence of any corporate ID. They'll splash their logo across the façade of a twelfth-century abbey, but they wanted no trace of it in their European headquarters. After his talk they called him upstairs for further discussions, and I sat in the car park with the radio on, waiting for him to come down. At least I know there's a car park. Gareth is filming a low bunker unscrolling on our right. The architecture is bomb-shelter. Strength, maybe, but Sansom doesn't do beauty.

'Animal wing,' Gareth says. 'They've made it student-proof.'

'I don't think so.'

'You don't think what?'

I can feel the Santana losing it. I have to jam it into second and rev like mad.

'Wind your window down.'

He gets it half-way and then the handle comes off in his hand.

'It's the smell. There isn't one. Whatever your security systems, you can't lock in the stink of five thousand experimental mice.'

'Maybe enculturated chimps don't smell. They take showers and stuff.'

I shake my head. 'Look. There are windows. Daylight. You couldn't maintain an artificial light routine in there. It's the little things, Gareth: the fact that there are no anonymous-looking feed sacks piled up by the back door. No furnace chimney, so nowhere to burn dead bodies. Trust me. There are no animals in there.'

We round the corner of the main building and clatter across the empty car park. I pull up facing the dome. The entire building is see-through, the guts of it detailed by the blue light of low-energy screen-savers. The huge entrance atrium is boutique-bright. Three guards are at the desk, talking.

'So what's the plan?' I say.

'I'm just going to have a look round. You wait here.'

'You're not going in. That bat will be useless. They change the codes every day.'

'If you're worried, I'll leave it with you.'

He reaches over and clips the bat to my lapel. His hand seems to linger, and for a moment I think this student–teacher thing is going to turn awkward. But then he's palming his camcorder and banging the door open, and I'm watching him cut across the front of the car, heading back the way we came.

My heart climbs the ladder of my ribs. If he tries to get in there, we're in real trouble.

He reaches the corner of the main building just as a security Land Cruiser is swinging into view. His pace doesn't change. The Cruiser slows as Gareth passes. He's headed around the back of the building, towards the place he thought was the animal wing. A mock antique street sign reads FLUORSPAR ROAD. There's an exchange of words that has my heart lodging in the back of my throat. Satisfied, Security crawls on.

Then I can't see Gareth any more.

Over in the atrium the guards are finding a joke in something. Two perch high up behind the bleached-wood counter, while the other, the storyteller, leans on it like a drunk in a bar. They're all wearing virtual lights. Anyone who hisses through that electronic door will have their name, title and affiliation flashed up instantly on the inside of those goggles. The virtual lights know everything because the bat knows everything: access privileges, personal details, even how many credits you've got left in your refectory account. I touch the black metal with the tip of a finger, trying to imagine the volumes of information micro-chipped away in there. I wonder which poor Sansom lab rat this one codes for.

They didn't fit clocks in the communist-era Santana, so I fitted one myself: an old strapless fake Rolex from Kuala Lumpur, stuck to the dashboard with Blutack. It says 01:32 a.m. The temperature inside the Santana nudges lower. I realise how much I depend on this communist-era heater. Tiredness weighs in my stomach, adds its millisecond-drag to my eyes. I close them, wanting the comfort of darkness, but then I feel too vulnerable. Until Gareth is back in this car with me, I need to stay awake.

I waited here for an hour and a half that day. It was early spring, before the clocks went forward, and no warmer than this. The lights were burning on the second floor. I assumed they were asking Mateus if he felt ready to take on a new challenge. Looking back, the portents seem more sinister. Should I have noticed the signs of his disappear-ance in those unblinking second-floor lights? Could that even have been the moment when he accepted whatever deal was on the table and committed to going to work for Sansom overseas? I call up the list of countries where Sansom has headquarters: Taiwan, Germany, Australia, America ... A global network of massive corporate understatements, where staff are bussed in and out in secure convoys. When you want to start up a new life, useful places to hide away.

Even if you lost it in the dark, you could try looking where the light is. He's playing with me, and I hate him for it.

Gareth reappears at 01:40. He's been all the way around the back of the main building and is returning from the eastern side. I start the car and reach both hands under the dashboard to the heating vent, waiting for the warmth. Gareth gazes up at a high window, turns on his heels and walks all the way back to the perimeter fence. He turns again and looks back at the coloured diodes of Sansom Central, flickering like a server in a smoked-glass cabinet. The wind blows scatterings of pre-drizzle across the car park, and cones of floodlight stand exposed. After a while he extends the index finger of one hand and holds it horizontally, like a painter measuring the proportions of a scene.

'Come on, Gaz,' I mutter shiverishly, toeing the throttle up a semitone or two.

I see him glancing back at the car. He seems to remember that I'm waiting for him, and starts moving this way. Then he stops and swings the camcorder to his eye. For a few seconds he films me in the car, the guards in the atrium, then that high eastern corner of the building he's just been studying. Rain supernovas on the windscreen in front of me. When he starts walking again, he's headed for the main entrance of Sansom's headquarters.

Christ. He's not stopping.

A jerk of panic sets the throttle growling under my foot. I watch him climb the steps to the atrium, steadying the swing of the camcorder against his hip. He's still metres away when the door hisses open. The guards glance up and move hands to their tasers. Their virtual lights will have labelled him already. Intruder. No access privileges. If I leave him to the guards he'll be sectioned again. But if I go in there after him, I'll get my own taste of Sansom's displeasure.

I kill the engine and get out of the car, just as the night explodes with rain.

I can see Gareth inside, talking to one of the guards. The storyteller has gone behind the desk and is working at a keyboard. The third has disappeared. I start running. They're not giving him a hard time, not yet — they're still working through the possibilities, flicking through a memorised training manual for clues to whether this is a harmless crank or a terrorist attack in the making. Their manner is conciliatory, but they're a quarter-second from triggering a major alarm. Gareth is probably telling them his plans, trying to sell them his dreams of manipulating the Lorenzo Circuit. They're long dreams. That gives me time. If I could just tell them that he's crazy, that he has a history of mania which has sadly just started repeating itself. Then only Gareth's camcorder will prove that my second visit to Sansom ever happened.

The door hisses open, and I step through into the glow.

'Morning, Dr Bonham.'

The bat. It's still pinned to my coat. But what did he call me?

'Morning,' I try and breeze.

Gareth is grinning at the electronic door that leads through into the rest of the building. He seems not to have noticed that the guard has just called me by James' surname. I can see the spooky optician's apparatus of the iris scanner.

'I have unusual eyes,' he's saying to the guard. 'I have total control over my iris muscles. As far as your scanner is concerned, I can be anyone I want to be.'

'*Tom!*' I say, scrabbling for big-sister authority. 'I told you to wait in the car.'

Gareth looks shocked, and then twigs, painfully slowly. He winks at me and starts jiggling about as though his shoes were on fire.

'My brother,' I tell them. 'He's got … *challenges.*'

I twirl an imaginary forelock. The guard lets down a seen-it-all sigh. On the inner screens of his virtual lights I'm labelled as Dr J Bonham, access code blah blah blah. He can't yet see a photo, and he can't know that J Bonham is actually one of his employer's most vociferous opponents, a veteran of animal rights demos at the West Gate and now, apparently, a would-be infiltrator.

'Just step up to the scanner, Doctor, and we'll get you through.'

'It's OK. We're not stopping.'

I grab Gareth's arm and pull him towards the door. Then I turn back to the uniform, waylaid by an idea.

'Have you sorted out my second-floor access yet?'

It's a dangerous bluff, and I regret it immediately. The guard moves behind the desk and pulls forward the screen, where the full security details of Dr James Bonham are about to be displayed.

'I'll just check that for you, Doctor …'

'No. Don't bother. I have to get him home. Mother's going to be worried *sick …*'

'Is this the mother I dream about?' Gareth says.

*

Alnwick Street is deserted. From the footbridge you can see the glowing shell of the Memory Centre, spotlit while its builders sleep. Forty-five kilometres away, fantastic constellations writhe over the city of Pelton. These days the denizens of the sky are animated: the scorpions crawl and the fish shimmer, and they're each trying to sell you something. Effi is under there somewhere, high in the neglected tower of Millennium Heights. The thought comes with a pang of guilt. I was meant to go over there today.

'That's the railway line,' Gareth says. 'I'm round the back.'

He's back in my passenger seat, showing me his home movie of the east wing of Sansom Central. He's pulled the viewscreen flat so we can both see.

'This building here. The one I thought was the animal wing.' The viewscreen freezes on a two-storey hump on the back of Gareth's bunker. 'It's housing something.'

'Like what?'

'That's the interesting bit. Come on …'

He gets out and starts walking fast across the footbridge. I can hardly summon the energy to follow him, but I need to get him back home before he can get in any more trouble.

'So how come that bat thing had James' name on it?'

'I told you, they're always looking for new ways to get at Sansom. They had this plan to infiltrate the building using fake IDs. Someone managed to hack into the security system and change some of the user details. They're taking a risk. Sansom play hard. You get on the wrong side of them, you know about it.'

'I'm glad you're telling me that *after* we tried to break in there …'

He's heading for the Memory Centre. The entire site is surrounded by a yellow hoarding, three metres high. The four-storey skeleton of the building gleams under the floodlights.

'Come on. Let's get in there before the place opens.'

He pushes on a small door in the hoarding and ducks through. There's no sign of any security, although a plaque promises 24-hour video surveillance. The Lycee's gate-keepers are obviously not the insomniacs that Sansom's are.

'It's OK,' he says, leading me through a tunnel of scaffolding. 'I come here all the time.'

'You promised me you'd let me take you back home. I don't even know where you live.'

'I just wanted to show you something.'

We're inside the circular shell of the building, looking up at the shadows of its insides. Steel girders are threaded with cables awaiting connection. Furls of silvery insulating material gleam in the faint light. Gareth is just a silhouette in the overspill of arc-light from outside.

'This is it,' he says. 'This is how they're going to celebrate the publication of the map of the Lorenzo Circuit.'

'It's going to be a kind of museum. That's what they're telling us. You'll come here, you'll look around, and you'll remember.'

He steps over a low foundation wall and walks out into the centre of the circle. I follow him, sensing a mind returning to its obsessions.

'It's an empty system. It hasn't learned anything yet.'

'It needs some birds,' I say.

He looks up, his eyes moving intently across the space between the girders. I wonder what he can see up there.

'Come on,' he says. 'We've done enough trespassing for one day.'

He's silent for the journey out to his hall of residence. As he sees the low buildings exposed by the moon, he starts moaning a line from The Smiths. I pull in at the side of the empty road, and he gets out and stands there in the open door. His thin body shivers under the grey jacket. He's understood something about what we've seen tonight, but he's not telling me yet. His big eyes are wet with anxiety. Perhaps he's trying to say goodbye. I feel like a furred-up disaster of a mother dropping her kid off at boarding school, barely able to wait for the moment when I can go home and drown myself in gin and tears. He slams the door and watches me go; for a moment his white shirt flickers in the corner of my rearview mirror, and then there's just open road.

CHAPTER SEVEN

Long-Distance

◉

The phone rings.

'Dr Churcher?'

Four days have gone by. It's a bright March morning, crisp with fresh snow. Tons of it are snagged in the treetops and plastered to exposed trunk-sides, and now parcel-sized lumps are breaking off in soft small avalanches as the sun gets to work. I'm sitting in my dressing gown on my sofa, waiting for a piece of ash-heart to catch.

'Gareth? Where are you?'

I can hear traffic. He can't be at his hall of residence.

'Somewhere very expensive. They've got a whole suite of hi-tech conference rooms. We need to get going.'

'I'm not going into business with you, Gareth. Have you told anyone where you are?'

'Of course not. I'm just starting to understand how this all fits together. The trouble is, I think Sansom understand it too.'

'What do you mean?'

'I mean, they seem interested in what I've found out. I'm sure they'll be back. And this time they'll have an offer I *can't* refuse.'

'What are you talking about? How do Sansom know about you?'

'Simple. They have security cameras. I hacked into their network. There are cameras on the gate, in the car park, everywhere. The coverage is impressive.'

My heart goes into a dive. 'Are we on there?'

'I could only get their output in real time. I have yet to tap in to the megalith's memory. But we'll be on their hard drive somewhere, doing our "Dr Bonham and her demented brother" routine.'

'Don't remind me. Did you tell James that we went there?'

He doesn't answer. He doesn't seem able to say his old friend's name. James and I haven't spoken since that night on the footbridge a week ago. I haven't been in to the lab in all that time. I've been walking in the forest, looking for chimpanzee tracks in the snow, wondering whether, in my drunkenness, I gave James my phone number. And if I didn't, what stopped me.

'I told him,' Gareth says. 'By the way, he says he's got something for you. But you'll have to go and pick it up. He's lazy like that.'

At least I know now that I didn't give James my number. Which might explain why he hasn't called.

'Hang on …'

There's a pause. The traffic surges. I can hear Gareth talking to someone in the background, his voice muffledly imperious, the other faint and accented. I'm trying to work out if this is a satellite link. When Gareth vanishes, James told me, he vanishes completely. He could be anywhere.

'Room service,' he explains, returning. 'I've got a lobster, possibly radioactive, seven slices of synthetic cucumber, and an ice-cold bottle of either liquid nitrogen or champagne.'

'How do you intend on paying for all this?'

'The company is paying. Don't worry, it's tax-deductable.'

A siren wails below his window. Is he back in New York, trying to sell his ideas to PowerServe again?

'So what are you going to do?'

'Well, at some point I realise we're going to have to go down there and see for ourselves.'

'Down where?'

He pauses. I can hear the cracking of a lobster shell.

'Fluorspar Road. Lead Street. Tin Chare.'

'What are you talking about?'

'The names of the access roads at Sansom. I thought, Shall I tell her this? and then I thought, Well, I'm going to be lying low for a while so I'd better get things straight now.'

'I'm sorry, Gareth. You've lost me.'

'They paid them to leave.'

'Who?'

'The villagers. Sansom came along with a ton of cash and bought the village up house by house, street by street. There weren't that many of them left anyway. It was a Category D village, earmarked for demolition. The place was a ghost town.'

'What place? What are you talking about?'

The earpiece fills with eating sounds. I hear the pop of a champagne cork, the sound of pouring.

'The names of the access roads. They're the names of the streets in a mining village called Echofield. Thousands of people were employed there in the nineteenth century. That land your treehouse stands on is a honeycomb. They found lead, iron, fluorspar, you name it. The mines stretched twenty, thirty kilometres, right up into the dale. I went to County Hall and found the old maps. In 1851 the biggest employer in the area was a mining village called Echofield. Sansom is built on the site where Echofield used to stand.'

'So those streets are the original streets?'

'You learn fast, Agent Churcher. And the railway line is the original mineral line.'

'But those lines are all new...'

'So I thought. When I was round the back I had a good look at the trees. There are oaks there, growing into the sides of the cutting. They have to be at least a hundred units old.'

I remember James talking about this the other night. The Conscience theory is that Sansom are using the light railway for clandestine deliveries. But any huge corporation needs a transport system, for deliveries of all kinds. I don't see what Gareth's trainspotting tells me.

'And that proves what, exactly?'

'I don't think I should tell you. This is a business secret. You haven't told me if you're in or not in.'

'Tell me, and then maybe I can decide.'

He sighs. There's a rustling sound as he shifts position on his executive bed. I hope he's got some clothes on.

'Do you remember that hump on the back of the animal wing?'

'On your video?'

'Yes.'

'But it wasn't the animal wing...'

'It was a motor housing. For a lift shaft. For a lift mechanism, capable of raising huge weights from many hundreds of metres underground.'

I hear him sipping his liquid nitrogen.

'All right. I give up.'

'Agent Churcher. What was the prosperity of your region founded upon?'

'Minerals? Zinc, tin, lead, whatever...'

'Precisely. And where do minerals come from?'

'They come from the earth. From mines.'

'Then at last we understand. You've got a lift shaft going hundreds of metres underground. The tunnels are still there and the lift is still working. Trains are coming in and out, loading and unloading. They're moving unfeasibly heavy objects up and down this lift shaft every day. They're doing something down there, something they don't want anyone to know about. I guessed it, and now I've seen it for myself. They've kept the layout of the village, the railway line, the entire structure. Sansom's European headquarters is built slap-bang on top of the Echofield mines.'

Clairvaux College is deserted. The lawn in the centre of Old Court is trimmed with a pristine carpet of snow. Not a soul walks in the cloister. I feel I should be paying an entrance fee. A hypothermic-looking porter watches me as I clonk through the gatehouse in my non-medieval shoes. I study the wall-mounted map for a moment, and catch sight of the sign for D staircase on a diagonal across the court. James' room is 5, on the second floor. The names of the inmates are displayed on a board on the landing. James' slide is flicked to OUT, but I go up anyway. The stairs are wooden, the landing dark and narrow. I smell vacuum-cleaner bags and desiccated wax. This afterthought of a staircase must lead to a place that's hardly used, where time hasn't passed properly, so it can curse entire lifetimes with an agony of still-happening. James hasn't even started to tell me about his past. Reminders of his presence keep squeezing me inside, and yet I still don't know the first thing about him.

That's not what I'm going to ask him about, though. I'm going to ask if he knows about Sansom being built on the site of the Echofield mines. And I'm going to find out whether that kiss was the beginning of something, or the end.

After that, who knows.

There's no answer from Room 5. I wait, full of lovesick butterflies, and knock again. A radio is playing in the room across the landing.

Someone's left a message on the corkboard next to James' door, saying they'll meet him at the Bankstown Odeon at nine. Signed *B*. Bankstown is in Pelton. The message is undated. I forbid myself to ask the question, but my heart answers it anyway. It's a girl's handwriting. He's not been alone up here.

The handle to James' door is cool, brushed steel. It turns easily in my hand.

Behind it are sunlight and emptiness. If James was ever here, he's long gone. The bed has been stripped, the bookshelves cleared. If there were once movie posters, pin-ups of women, cars or bands, they were taken down long ago. Somehow I'm surprised that his room looks so ordinary. When I was an undergraduate, this was how they left the room of a girl who hanged herself. Hoovered it, dusted it and shunted it into a siding of time. The residence indicator permanently flipped to OUT. An agony of still-happening.

I knock on the door opposite. When a voice calls out, I go in. A beta crouches on the floor in his underpants, assembling the pieces of a human skeleton. He's taking leg-bones and arm-bones from a big wooden box and putting them together on the floor. The radio is telling him what to do. *Position the head of the femur between the ischial spine and the sacrum. Ensure that the greater trochanter is aligned with the posterior superior iliac spine.* The lesson is intoned softly by a physician with an Australian accent, over a soundtrack of ambient electronica. It's learning by relaxation tape. My death-black business skirt suddenly seems to put too much on show.

'Sorry. I was looking for James.'

The medic slumps back into a bony lotus and draws poignantly on a cold spliff.

'You should get together,' he says. 'You and all them what is looking.'

'How do you mean?'

He blanks me contentedly. *Observe how the head of the tibia sits within the intercondylar notch to form the knee joint.* The half-legged skeleton on the floor grins up at me, enjoying its own careful reconstruction.

'Are you going to be a doctor?'

'Someone's got to do it, angel.'

I hate it, but I need to get something out of this guy.

'Did James go home early?'

He puts on a thoughtful face and relights his spliff. The barrel of his lighter says IT'S MINE!

'Two months, yeah, that's early. They had to stop his sponsorship because he wasn't turning up to anything. I reckon he's been thrown off the course. They shouldn't let time-wasters in here. Spoils it for the rest of us.'

He's been gone for two months. Since almost the start of the Lent term. So who was that who kissed me? Whose call have I been waiting for?

'But I saw him last week. We've been having tutorials...'

Your final task is to tackle the complex anatomy of the human foot. It's tricky, but fun!

'Hey,' the guy says, dropping some metatarsals back into the box. 'Are you his tutor?'

'I used to be...'

He puts a finger to his lips, hushing me. I watch him stretch, repack his underpants and rise to his feet. He pads over to a shelf and comes back holding a silver soundpod.

'He says this is yours. He says if you ever show up looking for him, you have to have it back.'

I stare at the gadget in my hand. The young medic puts his hand up on the door, inviting a continuation I don't want to think about. I back out through the door before he can say anything. The latch clicks shut, and I can hear the anatomy lesson starting up again. In the gloom of the corridor I turn the soundpod over, looking for an inscription, anything that might explain this strange inheritance. When I turn it face up again, I see that it has switched itself on. I choose PLAYLISTS. There's only one: THE TRAVELS OF DAVID OVERSTRAND. I lean back against James' door, plug the phones into my ears and set the thing playing. A man is talking, a voice I don't recognise. I can hear the background hubbub of an audience, light traffic on a residential street. There's an atmosphere of performance, as though I were eavesdropping on some theatrical game. The speaker is telling the story of a young woman roaming the city on a summer's afternoon. Something is not as it should be, and she is distressed. People in the background keep mentioning Pelton landmarks: Bankstown Underpass, the Stadium of

Northern Electricity. He lives in a squat in the city, Gareth told me, with a guru called David Overstrand and his disciples. I wonder if these are the people I am listening to.

Then the voice stops. The microphone keeps recording a hushed room. A motorbike goes past on the street outside. I can hear the clinking of wine glasses. The people in the room seem to be expecting something. I can feel the weight of James' door pressing on my shoulder-blades, but the proof of this physical reality doesn't convince me. I'm no more in this corridor than I am there in that room, in the recorded silence in my earphones. Gareth asked if I had been invited back there yet, to meet David Overstrand and the storytellers. I have a strange feeling that it's me they're waiting for.

I hear the purr of a ringtone, and it takes me a moment to understand in which of these two realities a mobile phone is ringing. When I realise that it's my own, I almost drop the soundpod in fright.

'Yvonne?' says Gillian Sleet's voice. 'We need to talk.'

CHAPTER EIGHT

Pleasure Systems Of The Brain

◉

The Institute is deserted. Only the diehards are in today: people with animals to run, technicians who have to be here because the animals are. My lab is dark and airless, windows blinded against the late afternoon sun. The water maze lies empty, its plastic liner gleaming palely in the gloom, as forlorn as a drained swimming pool. I never found the missing thumbwheel.

Gillian is at her desk, studying a student file. It has James' photograph on the inside cover.

'This place is quiet,' I say.

'It's spooky. Science must be the only human endeavour that makes no noise at all. Except when it's going wrong.'

She looks anxious. Whatever's bothering her, she blinks it away, and fixes her priceless agate stare onto me.

'This James Bonham,' she says, waving the file at me. 'He's a student of yours?'

'He was. I think he's quit.'

'Can you think of any reason why he might have quit? Like the fact that he was having an inappropriate relationship with a member of staff?'

I let her savour my dismay. Gillian is getting ahead of herself. That is, unless I was right, and she did see me and James together the other night.

'He's a little young.'

She halts, half-risen from her chair. I watch her losing momentum, and then sinking back and staring at her screen. I can feel the heat of the sun through her smoked-glass windows.

'Well, I hope he knows how to look after you. Anyway, your sex life is not top of my list of problems. I've got the slightly bigger headache of having this Process Nine to deal with.'

I feel a clamping dread, oxygen shut-offs to my heart. 'What do you mean?'

'The place is quiet because they've sent everyone home. Process Nine is the Lycee's highest security alert. It can only be triggered in the event of a catastrophic attack on our data. Right now, it's making our recent problems with Conscience look like a break-in at the Allotment Association.'

'Someone's got at our data? How?'

'With a very clever bit of hacking. They used a thing called a sniffer program. That's a bit of software designed to pick up on the information flowing through a network. Let's imagine that the Lycee had some top-secret passwords which only an elite group of its network users knew. The sniffer would sit there, wait for those users to log on, then copy their passwords and file them away. Post them to some remote server, if that's what the hacker wanted. It turns out that you only need to be logged on to a terminal and you can lay one of these things in three minutes, if you know what you're doing. Which our intruder obviously did.'

'So what's been sniffed?' I say, trying to sound calm.

'Ermintrude. The gateway to all our mapping data. The data that were supposed to be safer than any data could ever be. Someone got onto the network and managed to lay one of these sniffers. It's too late to change the passwords. The whole point about Ermintrude was that you had to know all the passwords to get anything off there. But if you had all the passwords, you could do it.'

'So someone hacked into it for fun. That doesn't mean the data are lost.'

'They didn't just hack into it, Yvonne. They encrypted what was on there into some format we can't identify. They've surrounded it with firewalls we've never seen before. We now can't get anything off Ermintrude. We think the data may still be on there in some form, but we can't unlock them. On top of that, the hacker thought he'd have a laugh at our misfortune. He's uploaded a bunch of bizarre documents, rambling stuff about the artificial stimulation of the Lorenzo Circuit. The real problem is that this joker has now got our mapping data and will be hawking it around town. We're talking about informational meltdown. On the Richter scale of security earthquakes, this is total destruction.'

Gareth. I left him alone in the office with an open network connection. He had at least three minutes while I was tending to my mice. According to James, he once hacked into the Pentagon. No one else would have the imagination for a stunt like this.

'You don't know who did it?'

She flicks her luscious bob in denial. 'The police are looking for a Lycee student. They can't see that anyone else could have had the access or the technical know-how. Whoever it is, he's got himself some hot property.'

If Sansom have got wind of this, it explains why they're interested in what Gareth has found out. They'll be back, he told me. And this time he might not be able to resist their overtures.

'So what do we do?'

'No one has the first idea. Council has been meeting practically 24/7. The Executive have gone into end-of-the-world mode. It's a PR disaster. If this is how we're seen to handle our research, we can kiss goodbye to any future funding. Oh, and the other news is that our head of Security has been relieved of his post under suspicion of having been spying for Sansom. That's how bad things have gotten.'

Somewhere, the man with the tattoos is still pointing his rifle at me. I thought it was strange that the Lycee's chief security officer would be roaming alone so far out in the forest. I was right about him looking for the escaped chimp. But I was wrong about which side he was working for.

'The guy's a thug. He sends himself over to lecture us sometimes. Are you saying he's been sacked?'

'I'm saying the Lycee couldn't pay him as much as Sansom were obviously paying him. You see our problem, Yvonne. We simply cannot let on how devastating this has been.'

'So we carry on as normal?'

She does that smiling-wincing kind of thing.

'*Normal* is a loaded concept, Yvonne. We carry on.'

*

The spookiest thing about Gillian Sleet's office is her floor. You can see it. It isn't ankle-deep in papers, books, notes, student essays. I'm not sure I've ever seen an academic's floor before.

'Do you know what pleasure is, Yvonne?'

She stands up, adjusting the strap of her bra through the strap of her black sun vest. The skin on her shoulders has been buffed to bronze by a portable Australian summer. In her microzipped hipster jeans she has the figure of one of her students. I swear she has fewer wrinkles than I have. The only exceptions are the laughter-lines that fan out around her eyes, quote marks around each smile. Don't trust it, they say: this is my sense of irony writ large. But then again, they're marks she has worked for, the proof of years spent creasing up at the jokes of better men, a career spent playing the game.

'Pleasure?'

The laughter-lines net out.

'It's a state of heightened activity in the mesolimbic dopamine system.'

'I pity *your* boyfriend,' quips Gillian.

We laugh. It's neuroscience laughter. And for me, at least, it hurts.

'So how do we know all this?' she says.

'Because animals will work for electrical stimulation to those bits of the brain. You put a rat in a Skinner box with an electrode in its septum, and it'll keep pressing the lever until it drops dead from exhaustion.'

She's making coffee. She never makes me coffee. I'm evidently going to be here for a while.

'Does that mean it's pleasurable? All the lever-pressing?'

'Not necessarily. It could be triggering some awful craving which can only be reduced by yet more stimulation. But the few times it's been done with human subjects, there have been some reports of pleasurable sensations.'

I give a weak, deoxygenated smile. It's weird enough to be called in for special treatment like this; I didn't think I'd be getting grilled on animal learning theory as well.

'OK. So we're talking about animals who'll learn to press a button, pull a lever or whatever in order to electrically stimulate their own brains. And yet the evidence on human self-stimulation is contradictory, to say the least. Why's that?'

'Because real human pleasure is more than just pressing a button. There's no simple pleasure centre that can be switched on or off. It's about pressing all the right buttons at the right time. It's about connections.'

'What if I told you that there is a way of pressing all the right buttons?'

'I'd say I'd get rid of my boyfriend.'

Sleet and the coffee machine laugh in synchrony. We're so cool, sisters talking sexy. She comes and parks her perfect arse on the desk opposite me, hands clasped over her knee.

'I've just got a feeling that this is what they're trying to do.'

'Who? Sansom?'

'I'm not saying that they've stolen our data. But I'm saying that they're going to be interested in it, whoever it is that's got it now.'

'If you had the mapping data, you'd know where to put the electrodes...'

'Exactly. Deep brain stimulation in humans is a hit-and-miss affair. So far, they've never been able to go near the really interesting circuits because they run too close to vital pathways. Get your placing of electrodes wrong in the hypothalamus, say, and it's goodnight Irene. The problem has always been that we didn't know where to put the damn wires. We didn't understand the pathways well enough. But we do now, with this map of the Lorenzo Circuit.'

'You think Sansom are working on deep brain stimulation? Putting electrodes directly into the brain and trying to stimulate the neural circuits like that?'

'Of course they are. Your ex-boyfriend was working on it. The Pereira Effect and all that. That work he did on human–computer interfaces made him pretty famous. With his help, Sansom were developing a new kind of ultra-reliable electrode. It was an open secret. Are you still in touch with him?'

'On and off. He'll be at the conference in Florida.'

'Sounds like you and he might have some things to discuss.'

If I can bring myself to speak to Mateus, I won't be discussing anomalous conductivity responses in human–machine interfaces. I'll be asking what he did with my heart, where he buried it after he ripped it out and stole it away.

'So what are Sansom using? A rat model?'

'If you believe the rumours, they're using something bigger than that.'

'You mean this thing about chimps?' I hesitate, wondering how much knowledge to own up to. 'You believe that?'

She nods. 'I'll believe anything these days. Apparently one got away. It's roaming wild in Wenderley Forest.'

'I know. I saw it.'

She looks at me, fingering the hem of her suntop. The nervousness of it is not her. Directness is her. Speaking her mind is her. That's why I like her as a boss: she's not afraid to stamp and shout.

'Of course. You live out there, don't you? If anyone's going to catch sight of that thing, it's going to be you.'

'I'd have reported it but ... I think they're trying to shoot it.'

'An aroused chimp can do a lot of damage to a person. You just saw it the once?'

I nod. 'I've been leaving food out for it. I've been trying to work out where it's living. I don't want them to kill it.'

She sighs and shakes her head. Then she frowns, remembering something.

'This chimp. Did it look ... I don't know. *Demented*?'

'I only caught a glimpse of it. To me, it just looked scared.'

'It would do. It's had quite an adventure.'

And so will Gareth, if he tries to get down to where the chimp came from. But I'm getting ahead of myself. Gillian doesn't seem to know about the mines.

'How do they think they're going to get away with it?' she is saying.

'I don't think they are going to get away with it. Conscience are planning an exposé. They've got videos. They're getting them shown on TV.'

'And James Bonham told you this?'

'Yes.'

She blinks it away.

'The trouble is, is anyone going to believe James' story? Look, Yvonne, this institute is in the shit. We have been well and truly fucked over and there was no pleasure involved. We've lost the mapping data, and Christ knows how many zillion man-hours of research. We were a few months away from understanding exactly how amyloid plaque build-up causes dementia. That would have been the biggest breakthrough in understanding this disease in twenty years. We can reconstruct the fragments of the map from our back-ups, sure, but we've lost time. Sansom, or whoever else gets their hands on it, will publish and patent and take all the credit. Not to mention the money.'

'So what do we do?'

'We do what Sansom will obviously be doing. We try to find out who stole our data and we try and get them back. Whoever's got that map of the Lorenzo Circuit is in real trouble.'

She picks up James' file, scowls at the photograph and drops it back onto her desk.

'You think Conscience might be involved in this?'

'For what possible reason? Conscience are a bunch of animal rights activists campaigning against the use of animals in research. What do they want with a load of brain mapping data?'

'They've attacked us before. They were spreading rumours about us using genetically modified capuchins, for God's sake.'

'Well, perhaps you'd better talk to your boyfriend about that.'

'James Bonham is a long way from being my boyfriend.'

I didn't expect that this would be easy. And still Gillian only knows half of the trouble I'm in.

'Whatever. I just know you're taking a big risk with your career, getting mixed up with people like him.'

It's not James who's got the Lycee into this mess, I want to tell her.

'Gillian?'

She gets up, stretching her body wearily. 'Yes?'

'If you had the right electrodes, and the right mapping data, you'd effectively have a way of manipulating a person's memory?'

She nods. 'That's what the Lorenzo Circuit's there for. It's the material basis of memory and consciousness. The matrix of who we are.'

And if you could only find a way of speaking their language, the birds will come when you call.

'So there are obvious therapeutic benefits. For Alzheimer's.'

'Absolutely. Think about what we're dealing with here. These are people who have lost their most basic sense of identity, every flicker of memory that made them what they were. Their Lorenzo Circuits are a mess of tau and amyloid. Put a nice safe electrode in, stimulate a bit of temporal cortex and — who knows? Maybe Grandma will remember something.'

I say nothing. For the first time since he walked into my lab, I think I'm beginning to understand what Gareth is trying to do.

◉

PART TWO

The City

CHAPTER NINE

All Stories Are True

◉

Effi says I can stay with her in Pelton for a few days while I try to find James. I don't want to hang around in the forest any longer than I have to. The daily reminders of the security breach are bad enough; the thought that my own carelessness has caused a Process Nine to happen is stopping me from sleeping. Gareth had the technical ability to hack the Lorenzo Circuit data, but I gave him the opportunity. I left him alone in my office with a live connection, which was all the opening he needed to get on to the network and lay the sniffer. Reconstructing the map from the backed-up fragments will take time. I couldn't have caused more trouble if I'd been spying for Sansom myself.

At least I understand now what Gareth meant about lying low for a while. If he's got hold of the mapping data, then Sansom are going to be interested. From what he told me on the phone, I know that someone from the biotech has already approached him. The police are looking for a Lycee student, someone with the access and the know-how. If Gareth can keep himself out of danger, I might be able to find him before this goes any further. If not, then I'll have more trouble to feel responsible for.

That's why I need James. He knows Gareth; he knows why his friend went off the rails last time. And he knows how Sansom operates; he's there every week, demonstrating against their research. He might know something about the mines, and he might have some idea why Gareth is so interested in what Sansom are doing down there. He's not been straight with me about packing in his studies, but for all I know his vanishing from college was just some misguided effort to protect me. He knew it would be a problem for me, having an animal rights campaigner in my tutor group. It all fits with the idea that, when he kissed me on the footbridge that night, he was kissing me goodbye.

I pack for Florida and move my bags to Effi's. I listen to *The Travels of David Overstrand* again, hearing the story of the woman roaming the city, joining up the landmarks of Pelton as though they might reveal some carefully obscured message. The Stadium of Northern Electricity. The twenty-four-hour markets of Star City. From Effi's flat in Millennium Heights, these are visible landmarks. Gareth has already mentioned David Overstrand's name to me. They live together in a squat, he told me, James and his activist friends. I printed out the address from Academic Records. The street name looks harmlessly suburban, and yet there's something going on there, enough to make James lie to me and throw away the prize of a Lycee degree. He wants me to go there, that's obvious. The mysterious recording, this self-conscious effort to intrigue me: it's James down to the ground. But, then again, it isn't James on the recording. Whatever game he's playing there, he isn't playing it alone.

I try to explain to Daren, Effi's nurse, that I can't help him out today.

'But I need you, Yvonne. These days, bathing your mum is a two-man job.'

'My mum?'

Effi left India for England sixty years ago. This morning we did what we always do in the hour or so before Daren shows up: we got out the old Bombay street map and looked at it together, tracing routes through the post-war city along streets that still had their imperial names. I always want to hurry to the beaches. I want to imagine her in an impossible bikini, busty and lithe, the talk of the subcontinent. Now, at eighty-five, her skin has the powdery wrinklings of a nutmeg. Daren's is a different kind of blackness, glossy and sullen. If he's making any joke about Effi being my mother, he isn't showing it. A mosaic of sweat gleams out from under his stubble. There's a transparency around his eyes, a frailness there.

'Yeah. She's no skinny disco dancer.'

I hear her coughing in the living room across the landing. The TV drones. She hears the man on the mid-morning cookery show, can't tell if he's black or white. It doesn't matter any more.

'Is she all right? Apart from the dementia?'

'I don't know. She's losing weight. They're running some tests. When you've been around as long as she has...'

I watch him washing cups at the sink. The kitchen window is open, and I can see the twisted floodlights of the football ground, the parks and galleries of the new docks, then the dismal sprawl of Northside. The city lays itself out for me like the forest used to, eight storeys of distance and solitude. All of yesterday I was poring over a battered *A–Z* of Pelton, trying to work out which of the grey blocks that mark St. Lawrence Road is James' house. The church is visible from here, a sad relic of old England above the slate tiles of the refurbished terraces. Maybe, if I knew where to look, I would even see the squat that James calls home.

'Come on,' Daren says. 'Let's do those obs. Blood pressure, blood sugar, all the rest of it. You get to her age, you need a daily MOT.'

I follow him through into the living room. The dual carriageway reaches us with a steady ripping sound. Daren dumps his medical bag onto the table and checks his blue plastic smock for breakfast stains. Effi thumbs off the TV and looks up at her young saviour. He's been coming here for months now, smelling of sports fragrance and the optimism of youth, and he's already one of the certainties she clings to, proof that, amid the unravelling of every thread of selfhood, there's a human link back to health and happiness. He rewinds the clock for her, undoes the ravages of time. She sees through him into a past no one else can see, smarting with wedding-night nerves, the jangle of wirelesses.

'Sing to me,' she says.

Daren shoots a look at me and puffs out a sigh. What was a joke when he first started coming here has become a comforting routine. He picks up a hairbrush from the side and twirls it in his hand. He goes over to the old one-piece stereo, exclaims silently in mock surprise and lifts the arm onto the vinyl. Cliff Richard croons into the room. The ancient amplifier is turned up full against the traffic, and the edges tear. The nurse grips the hairbrush like a microphone and sways from one foot to the other, mouthing the words silently, rock-and-softly-rolling then giving it a bit of pelvis when the drums come in. Effi smiles and drifts away. She's twenty-four again. England is new. The Shadows cruise down the dual carriageway under our window, quiffs a-tremble, Strats zinging in the breeze. And on the back seat of their convertible Rolls, a young immigrant bride cannot think about dying, can't see into that distance, cannot even frame the thought.

I wait for him to rock past me, then catch his eye.

'Daren, I've got to go somewhere.'

'Florida,' he says. 'Have a nice time.'

'No. Before that. I've got to go out for a while. There's someone I have to see.'

Effi is asleep. He tosses the hairbrush onto the sofa and grins at me.

'Take your time. I've got my mates from the five-a-side coming round. We're going to have a party, aren't we, Mum?'

Outside I find a grey spring afternoon, bleak with sea fret. The flagship redevelopments around the waterfronts are half erased by low cloud. I feel like some off-duty public-school sixth-former among the beautiful young things who are throbbing out of Bankstown metro. This place has become fashionable since I first came here as a student, visiting Effi as part of our community action scheme. There are trendy coffee dives where there used to be charity shops. The bingo halls are full of body-pierced couples making ironic statements. Even the graffiti on the boarded-up church halls is now done with aching poise, suggesting night-time streets thronging with art students. AGATHA, IF YOU DON'T BRING MY SOUNDPOD BACK YOU'RE GOING TO GET YOUR FACE SPLIT OPEN. I don't mind graffiti, as long as it's spelt correctly.

They're selling God outside St. Lawrence's. A Chinese migrant is pulling pamphlets from a Morrisons bag and slotting them into invisible hands. Out of pity I take a few. Further down, St. Lawrence Road is getting a makeover. The first stretch of houses seem to have their contents in their front gardens: mattresses, washing machines, ripped-out kitchen units piled to the height of a man. Through dusty windows you can see the gleam of undercoated doors closed on emptiness. These are the lucky ones, the ones that are attracting investment. Others are simply giving in to decay, opening rotting doors to walk-in claims of ownership by whoever takes a fancy to their derelict charms. Old Union Jacks hang, curtain-wise, over glass taped up from the inside. Halfway down it all changes: the townhouses get their top coats of blue or purple paint and rise to untouchable heights on flights of grey granite steps. Affluence is creeping down the street, a house at a time. Whoever lives in the ruins of Victoriana, they won't be here for long.

Number 76 is one of the squats. A banner in the downstairs window says YOU'LL MISS US WHEN WE'RE GONE. As I wait to cross the road I can see a man eating chips in a car outside the house, his driver's door open and one foot rooted to the kerb. His car is even older than mine. He's kept the engine running, possibly for heat, possibly just for the rare olfactory pleasure of petrol fumes. It's the smell of my child-hood, a Victorian townhouse in Bristol, traffic jams on summer days. The chips guy has a Greek policeman's moustache, a blue tracksuit, white socks and loafers. He watches me go up the steps to the house, and then throws his chips into a skip and comes up after me, making screwing movements with a little key.

'They're wasted,' he says. 'They won't hear you.'

His accent is estuary. He opens the door and stands there beside me, waiting. A thick sift of dinosaur metal is filtering down through the floorboards.

'I was looking for James,' I say.

'JAMES!' he yells up the stairs.

There's a thud, like something falling, and I hear a woman's laughter.

'Go on up,' the man says.

The staircase has other ideas. Some half-hearted renovator has ripped out all the carpets, leaving broken gripper bars like arrays of shark-teeth. Several of the steps have come loose and the rest are spongy with woodworm. There are no banisters. Maybe James' animal rights friends get around by levitation. I can sense the moustache guy watching me as I pick my way up, thinking weightless thoughts. The music is coming from behind the second door on the landing. BEWARE THE HARSH REALITY is scratched into the maroon paintwork. I knock twice, try-ing to cut across the machine-gunning bass drum. I think how easy it would be to give up on this, take Gillian's advice about the danger of getting mixed up with these people, turn on my heels and walk away. But Gillian doesn't know the half of it. Gareth is out there, lost in some neon-crazed downtown, and Sansom will be trying to find him. I can't let that happen. I have to get to him first, and for that I need James. He knows what happened the last time his friend lost control. I might need that information.

I realise that I'm taking his bait, though. He left the soundpod for me for a reason. Perhaps he thinks David Overstrand can work the same magic on me as he did on him. In which case, there's more to this than the story of the woman in the recording. There's the story of me, the real Yvonne Churcher, the true self under all those layers of illusion and habit and biology. Who knows: maybe it's a love story. And this is where it starts: with a lonely woman in drab mufti, heart in her mouth, knocking patiently on a door.

'Go on in,' comes the moustache voice from downstairs.

Maybe James calls out the moment he sees me, and maybe what he says is my name. Maybe he's never stopped saying it since we parted on the footbridge, our lips still zinging with each other. Whatever he says, I don't hear it. I'm too cut up by the sight of him, standing in the corner of the room in black jeans and a paisley shirt, striding across a double bed to get to the sound system, turning the music down. There's a girl on the bed, younger than me, who tries to bite his leg as he climbs over her. She has blonde hair tied up, a face stretched between cheek-bones and nose-bridge, a thin mouth that looks as though it's tasting tin. She's wearing combat trousers and a faded tee-shirt saying 2010 ADULT MOVIE OSCARS: BEST SUPPORTING ACTRESS. Her fingers are busy with a magazine. I can smell dope, toast, old dust-engrained floorboards, chocolate and possibly sex. A guy in a suit is scanning some photos onto a hard disc at a desk under the window. There are body parts and hairy bits, gleams of animal flesh under studio lights. A colour printer is churning out glossy repetitions of his work. In the time it takes the spill of blue scanner-light to work its way up the page, the suit guy is folding up the printouts and stuffing them into envelopes, and then writing addresses on that I can't see.

'Yvonne,' James says, stepping down off the bed.

'James,' I feel myself saying, 'I know you think it's funny to keep turning up to my tutorials when you're not even a student any more, and then getting me drunk and coming on to me in the middle of the foot-bridge when my *boss* was quite possibly walking past,' I'm saying the words, can't stop them, this embarrassing leakage, this flow of thought made flesh, 'but now Gareth has got the mapping data and Sansom are already on his back, and you send me this recording like it's some big mystery, like this is all an experiment to see if I'll fall for your story, like ...'

'Yvonne,' he says. But really I haven't said a word.

*

'Wait…'

'Where are we starting?'

'*Listen.*'

We're in the living room downstairs, looking out over the wasteland of No. 76's garden. The guy in the suit tongs another lump of coal onto the fire, and then begins.

'A young woman is roaming the city in the heat of summer. She has blonde hair held up with a tortoiseshell slide, and pale, reclusive skin. She is dressed lightly in a sundress with big yellow flowers, but she walks as though she were being dragged down by tremendous weights. She makes her way through the shopping district as far as the river, where she stops. She looks westwards along the embankment, searching for a crossing, and then turns to the east. A river is the only true absence in a city. You can't build on it, fill it with rubbish, park your car there. You need that connection with nothingness in the midst of all the chaos. So observed David Overstrand.'

'Nice,' James says, jotting something down in an exercise book.

'Soon enough, by straight routes and crooked ones, the young woman comes to the Half-Span Bridge.' It's the blonde girl, picking up on the suit guy's opening. 'There's a walkway where pedestrians can cross, with cars rushing by on one side. On the other side is a steep drop into the river. For a while the woman stands there on the walkway, leaning on the parapet, looking down through the girders at the water. The traffic goes by behind her, but nobody takes any notice.'

The guy with the moustache makes to protest, but he is silenced by the suit.

'It's OK. That's pukkah.'

The girl — Bridge? — sits back, satisfied, in her corner of the sofa.

'Second verse, same as the first.'

'What are the young woman's precise coordinates at this point?'

The guy in the suit starts sketching something on a piece of paper.

'Start at the Persian buffet on Spring Gardens.'

The group nods in agreement.

'Chuck a lefty down Westwood Road and proceed towards the city centre through Bankstown Underpass.'

'Not at night…'

'David Overstrand only saves the souls of the damned by daylight.'

'It *is* daylight. Shopping time in the cool west end of the city. You have to fight your way through the crowds at Bankstown Market. Then you branch northwards off Westwood Road and cut along Summerhill until you reach the Royal Infirmary…'

'You can't do that,' Bridge says, shaking her head.

'That's a Leipzig Transgression,' James says.

He glances across, sending me a grin I don't need. A motorbike goes by on the street outside. It's all right, I want to tell him; I know what this is. It's the story of the young woman roaming the city in a mysterious state of distress, wandering the streets on a summer's afternoon against the backdrop of Pelton landmarks. I could be back in James' corridor, listening to the recording on his soundpod. I'm none the wiser, though, about why they have invited me here. If I twist around in my seat I can see through a knocked-through wall into the next room. It looks like a studio of some kind: there's a photocopier, video equipment and several TVs.

'Come on, Yvonne,' says the suit guy, whom they're calling Level Ten. 'We want to hear from you.'

'Is that a structural wall?' I say, still staring at the hole.

'We don't know. Grandstand decided he wanted open-plan living so he took a sledgehammer to it. Just start where you like.'

'But no one's explained the rules.'

'Don't worry about the rules,' Bridge says kindly. 'Just be yourself.'

She stretches out on the sofa like a kid in sand. She's beautiful, in a fierce sort of way, but she seems bunged up, cut off from the world. It takes her a second or two to respond, as though the words were coming to her through water. Perhaps she's a mermaid, who's lost the shell-encrusted mirror that will get her home. Grandstand, the moustache guy, is filthy with her. But she only has eyes for James.

'OK.' I take the coal tongs Level Ten is offering me. 'What you didn't mention is that they're doing roadworks on the bridge. The traffic lights are turning red, and the cars are stopping. That's all it takes for someone to finally notice the distressed woman.'

'Fuck me,' Grandstand says. 'She's a natural.'

'You can't have traffic lights,' Bridge complains, as Level Ten waves her quiet. 'That's a transgression…'

'A man gets out of one of the stopped cars.' It's James, picking up on my opening. 'He glances back at the red traffic light, and then cautiously approaches the railing. They both seem oblivious to the traffic piling up around them. She's a thin woman, nothing on her, and for a moment it seems like she could just slip through the railings like a set of car keys...'

Grandstand raises his thumb in approval. Bridge starts up a solitary applause.

'David Overstrand, for it is he, has to lead her to the railing and guide her hands and feet up onto it. If you want to jump, you can jump, he says.'

'The traffic lights turn green.'

'The woman jumps.'

'The lights stay red.'

'The woman is saved.'

We break for food. Kitchen sounds have been hinting at it for an hour or more, and now Grandstand and Bridge are trudging in and out of the back room with trays of Turkish pide and black bottles of beer. Level Ten is browsing on a tablet, looking through recordings of the first game. James is leafing back through his exercise book.

'You started in a named location,' Grandstand says. 'That's a violation of the assumptions of quantum entanglement.'

James catches my expression. I need to talk to him about Gareth. But first I have to get him alone.

'Quantum entanglement,' he explains. 'The ability of events in one universe to influence those going on millions of light-years away. It's a genuine scientific phenomenon.'

He climbs through the hole in the wall behind me and starts rooting around in the other room. He comes back with a pile of hardback notebooks. Grandstand and Level Ten get busy flicking through them, checking labels and turning pages.

'And you shouldn't have tried to take that short-cut along Summerhill,' Bridge observes.

'Why not?' I say, eating like a god.

'Because it's a transgression. It's an A-lapse.'

'You mean your game has rules?'

'Of course it has rules. You can't have a game without rules.'

'But what's the point of it? Is it some sort of art project? Are you like art students or something?'

'Sorry,' Level Ten says, 'what's this one's name again?'

'Yvonne.' It's Bridge who answers. 'She used to be Jim's tutor. The *scientist.*'

'I get it. You're the ones who left all your data in the back of a taxi?'

'They didn't leave it in the back of a taxi. It got hacked. Jim says he knows the guy who did it.'

A spliff goes round, and I wave it through. James watches me with an incipient smile. It seems he's already jumped to his own conclusions about Gareth and the mapping data.

'I thought you were all Conscience supporters,' I say. 'I assumed you'd be more, I don't know, rooted in reality.'

'Reality?' Level Ten says. 'The objective truth about the world that only science can deliver? Nice one, Yvonne: you just told a really good story.'

'Reality is not a story. Science is not a story.'

'It's *your* story. It's no better than anyone else's.'

'I'll tell you a story,' Bridge says. 'The supposedly scientific arguments they use to justify the torture of animals. The myth that animals are not conscious in the way that humans are conscious. They're stories, Yvonne, stories the vivisectionists tell themselves when they can't get to sleep at night.'

It's not an accusation. It's laced with vitriol, but that's meant for all the other vivisectionists in the world.

'Think of it as part of the protest.' This is James now. 'We're sick of science being elevated above all other ways of knowing. We want to give people their truth back.'

'I just don't see how it fits with what you're doing. If reality is just a story, why do you need to blockade biotech companies? Why do you have to dress up and spend all your weekends hassling security guards? Why don't you just tell a story about the way you want the world to be?'

'We take action,' Bridge answers, 'because *they* take action. They keep macaques in cages so small they end up ripping out clumps of their own fur. We're just trying to reflect that horror back at people. I don't see how you can have a problem with that. When you look at what your "truth" has given us. Your science and its ... *atrocities*.'

I feel faint. The sugar rush has worn off, and so has the comfortable feeling that I'm among friends. It's getting dark out there. I have the vague, dragging sense that I'm needed somewhere.

'Well, my reality is more real than this.' I flick a gesture at the piles of exercise books in front of me. 'It's more real than what you're doing here. Creating myths about your favourite therapist? Telling stories around the fire?'

'Stories *are* truth,' Level Ten says. 'Stories are the truest truth.'

I feel their eyes on me, and hold the smile. They've been here before. A new face turns up in the gaming room and you spend a little time finding out about her, testing her, seeing what she'll believe and what she won't believe. I wonder how deeply you have to test me before you find out that I'm a vivisectionist; that, from their point of view, I have blood on my hands. I'm the worst you can get, and they invited me here. What happens when they find out? Am I still going to get my love story?

It's time to get back to Effi.

CHAPTER TEN

Sleepwalking

◉

His accent is bothering me. Most of the time he's just another well-spoken beta, with that flat way of talking which is a sure sign that there's something he's trying to hide: a privileged background, a dad with a title, one of those bonuses of birth that do so much to smooth the transition into Lycee life. But then he'll get excited and harden a vowel, and I'll remember that he was born in a mining village in Cumbria — and then, seeing that I've noticed, he'll do a snatch of the pub-talk for my benefit, and for some reason I'll find that funny. 'Actually,' he'll say, enjoying the slideshow of his blurring identities, 'I grew up in Africa' — and then you'll get him shouting abuse at some imaginary farm worker, just like Daddy used to do. After that he travelled: on a banana plantation in Queensland he picked up his fondness for the terminal rise, so that every sentence comes out like a question about your understanding of it, an affectation that usually makes me want to kill people. But he's too gauche and playground-fresh, too certain that he's already conquered the world, to pick a fight with. I love the way he'll avoid making eye contact with you while you're talking, and then, just as you have given up and are looking elsewhere, you'll catch him staring straight at you, willing you to return his gaze, let the battle begin again.

'You really believe this David Overstrand guy, don't you? Everything comes back to him.'

'David showed us the truth. He showed us what was really going on. We were all in trouble, in our different ways, and he got us through.'

We're in his room at the squat. James is sitting with his back to the window, lit by the deteriorating light from outside. There's a silvery sheen to his hair, as if it were close to going grey. Watching him, I sometimes get a feeling that he's been caught out of time, snagged on the past. He looks at you with a certainty that seems inherited, not learned. You could cut yourself on those blue eyes.

'In trouble? In what way?'

'David showed me that I was carrying this weight, and it was killing me. He said there was a way I could be free of it. He told me that I've got to understand Bankstown Underpass if I'm going to understand now.'

'Bankstown Underpass? What happened at Bankstown Underpass?'

'Everything.'

'That sounds a bit dramatic.'

He hasn't forgotten how to smile. We spent the afternoon at an achingly fashionable arts pub on Westwood Road. Grandstand stood at the door and handed out photographs of naked people in cages. The others were playing their storytelling game. James spent most of the time quizzing me about the security breach at the Institute. Neither of us needed any convincing that it was Gareth who took the data, even if we couldn't guess at his reasons for doing so. Now it's getting dark, and we can hear the occasional bit of pre-pub shouting, a forewind of Friday night turbulence on the streets of Pelton.

'So when's David coming? When do I get to meet him?'

'He's not coming.'

'Why? What's happened to him?'

He's silent. I try to catch his gaze, but he's unavailable, shut away in a place I'm not invited to. I suddenly feel quite drunk, and the fact that it's twilight outside only makes it worse. I feel a crashing regret for all the hours I've spent in dingy bedsit rooms, waiting for the door to open and a new life to walk in. And then, when the thing turns up, it's never quite the thing I was hoping for. All the times I thought I was equipped for the big surprise, when actually I was nowhere near.

'You talk about him like he's something from your past. Where is he now?'

He gives a sad, defeated smile.

'David was a prophet. He was a freedom fighter. In this world we've made, these people are vulnerable. They can't survive.'

'Are you saying he's dead?'

'He's not dead. I don't think. No one really knows. We just wait here, trying to fulfil our tasks, and hoping. He had to leave. He had to vanish. We don't know where he is.'

I think of the playlist on the soundpod.

'He's on his travels … That's the idea? And one day he'll return?'

'David wanted us to carry on with the work he started. Keep up the pressure on the biotechs and everyone else who tries to impose their order on a beautiful world. Anyone who wants to claim a truth they don't have.'

'And you're going to do that by telling stories?'

'People have always fought for their freedom, Yvonne. Some use guns and hand grenades. We use truth.'

He's rolling again. If I smoke any more I'm going to be in trouble. I'm being stared at accusingly by an underwear mannequin in dark glasses and a white furry bra. She has her hand held out, like she's just sung a song and now wants paying. James' house-keys hang from one of her fingers. I didn't know squats had house-keys. I thought people just came and went as they pleased.

'How long has David been gone?'

'Years. There's a lot of people like us out there, spread across the planet. He moves among them. They protect him from the people who want to destroy him. He's far away. Last I heard he was helping to stop a dam being built in India. But that could just have been a rumour.'

'Why do people want to destroy him?'

'Because of what he's done. He tells things as he sees them. That's made him a lot of enemies.'

'So what's he going to say when he comes back and finds a vivisectionist in his house?'

'He's not coming back, Yvonne. Not any time soon. We'll get word. We'll have time to get ready. I don't know how, but we will.'

'So it wasn't him on that recording?'

James takes a moment to make the connection. 'That was Level Ten.'

'And all the storytelling? The game by the fireside. Was that David's thing?'

'We talked about this already, Yvonne. You want to deny the truest truth about yourself. You can't see how you've been shaped by the things that have happened to you. You want to deny your own story.'

'That's therapy bullshit, James.'

'Sure, you think it's all neurotransmitters and chemical imbalances. But what about your soul? Why do you do anything if you don't have that truth at the heart of you? Where does your sense of morality come from, if you're just a bundle of nerves? Why did you want to come here today, if you didn't have a self to do your wanting with?'

What about love? he once asked me. *What about ecstasy?* He knows about Mateus now, anyway. He'd bought me two pints of some medal-winning beer, and I was well past my irretrievable blab point. But today is not about the tragedy of me and Mateus. It's about James and his humanity, his common touch, his endless capacity for listening. It's about the voice that he's deliberately pitching lower, his clear forced eye contact, even the slight trace of affected lisp he's putting on, that extra sibilant polish that he puts on each word.

'So do they hate me?'

'Who?'

'The others. Grandstand. Bridge. Level Ten.'

'Why should they hate you?'

'Because I'm a vivisectionist. I torture animals. I fuck up their brains and then appear surprised when they don't behave normally. I'm one of the people that David Overstrand is trying to punish.'

'They don't know that. They want you to join us. They haven't a clue what you do.'

'Are they going to know?' I ask.

'Depends if you put your lab coat on.'

'Be serious, James. This is serious. Our biggest rivals have got their hands on our most precious data. It's probably my fault. I can't tell you how much shit that has put me in.'

'Don't worry. Sansom won't get the data. Gaz will want to hide it, and he's had time to do a good job of it. He'll have hacked into the website of some lads-and-dads soccer team in Malaysia and stashed it away there. No one, not even Sansom, is going to find this stuff unless Gaz tells them where it is.'

'He said they'd already been in touch with him.'

'He doesn't want their money. If Sansom were able to get to him before, they won't be able to get to him now. I told you. He's a magician. He can make himself disappear.'

He sways, or the room does. Next to the mannequin is a black data projector. It's pointing at the blank wall above his bed, as though set in place for some kind of slideshow.

'Do you know what he's trying to do, James?'

He shakes his head. 'He won't tell anyone. If he had told me, I wouldn't have understood it. He's obsessed with you. You're the only person he would have given any clue to. That's why it's so important that you tell me everything he said. Everything you remember. No matter how trivial.'

He finishes the spliff and sets it going. He's sitting in the seat he's made for himself in the window, with one bare foot up on the sill and the other resting on the desk below him. The light from his bedside lamp is gilding the arches of his insteps. I'm lying on his bed, his pillow fragrant against my cheek. Something is being asked of me, and I can't deliver. The feeling is a hollow disappointment, like having to turn down a plea for help you could easily have afforded. If only Gareth could have made it clearer. Or if only I'd listened to him better.

'He's got some idea about stimulating the Lorenzo Circuit. For that, he needs a way of talking directly to the nervous system. Sansom have been working on a new kind of electrode. The kind of thing you could harness to stimulate memory. I don't know what he's trying to do. All I know is that he shares quite a few interests with Sansom.'

'And that's it? You really can't remember anything more?'

'I wish I could, James. Then we might have a chance of working out what he's up to …'

The door opens. Maybe it's the fact that Bridge doesn't bother knocking that irritates me. Or maybe it's the way she's started claiming James for herself before she's even through the door.

'Oh,' she says, noticing me. 'I didn't realise you were here.'

It's a squat, I tell myself. People come and go.

'I need a hand to shift the photocopier,' she says, waiting for the dimness to reveal my exact position on James' bed. 'But I can see you're busy…'

The door clicks shut again. Just being splashed by Bridge's mermaid smile has sobered me up a little. There's an intimacy here, a taking for granted, that I don't want to think about.

'Is she *B*.?' I say, staring after her.

'Who's *B*.?'

'On your door. In college.'

He makes a show of trying to think. Like there are so many girls leaving notes on his door.

'I don't know. Probably.'

'Bridge is short for Bridget, yeah?'

I see him grappling with something, the aftermath of a confession he was never brave enough to make. Then, whatever it is, he stamps on it, and he's acting again.

'Why didn't you tell me you'd packed in your degree?'

He turns his eyes away and down, to the black street below the window.

'College was getting me down. It was full of really safe people who just wanted the dream home and the dream holidays and the whole vacuous affluence deal. They thought having money would give them freedom to make choices. Yeah, choices between this kind of soulless shit and that kind of soulless shit. That medic guy you met, across the corridor from me. On the outside he seemed OK. Inside, he just wanted to get his consultant job and have the freedom to choose to spend his days on the golf course. I couldn't find anyone who wanted to use their education. I couldn't find anyone who wanted to *think*.'

'So you just quit? Without telling anyone?'

'It was complicated. Sponsorship and that. There'd have been questions.'

'So why did you keep turning up to tutorials?'

'Because I wanted to see you.'

Maybe I just wanted to hear him say it.

'You seemed to want to think about stuff. You weren't just going through the motions.'

'I think I've spent my entire life going through the motions.'

He turns around in the window seat and plants both bare feet on the desk. He shrugs, inviting an explanation. Come here, I want to say. And I'll explain.

'It's a sham, James. I've got to fly to Florida tomorrow for an international conference. I have to stand there in front of my poster and pretend to care what ninety-nine mice do when you fuck up a gene which controls the production of amyloid precursor.'

'I thought you were going to find a cure for Alzheimer's ...'

'Oh yeah. We're going to learn a lot about human dementia from studying an animal that's been genetically tampered with so much it has to be taught how to feed.'

He finally gets around to handing me the spliff, and I suck on it like a builder.

'So mice aren't a good model of human dementia?'

'Of course they're not. The mouse brain is separated from the human one by about a hundred million years. It's like trying to get around Pelton with a map of Fulling.'

'You should have come on our demo. That's what we were saying. The myth of the mouse model. It's like the myth of the macaque model. The chimp model.'

'I don't know what I should have done. Right now, I don't know anything.'

I'm such a cliché. One look from him and whatever illusion of self-belief I still hold scatters into thin air.

'Will Mateus be there?'

'In Florida? I don't know.'

'You say he used to work on these human–machine interfaces. Maybe he'll know something about Sansom's special electrodes. At least if you go to Florida you can talk to him and find out more. That's our best chance of finding Gareth.'

I feel the agony of the thought, in every part of me.

'Alternatively, don't go to Florida. Stay here. Join the team. We need someone who knows what they're talking about. I don't know one end of a mouse from the other.'

'That would mean making a decision, James. I don't do decisions. I just take in information and produce a response. I've sleepwalked through my whole life and I can't see myself stopping now.'

It's over. I've said too much. I'm standing up, putting on my coat, looking for my gloves, looking for something I can't find.

'Stay,' he says. 'Don't go.'

I look at him sadly. 'I was never even here.'

CHAPTER ELEVEN

The Pereira Effect

◉

I fly to Florida with my head full of James. Along with everything else he's done to me, he's made me feel differently about the prospect of seeing Mateus again. I knew I was going to have to do it — go to the convention in Tampa and lay myself open — but I don't feel it can hurt me as much as it would once have done. James might be a sworn enemy of what I do for a living, but he is on my side. I can't help but be infected by his certainty, his confidence that the world has been put together in a particular way. His boyish contradictions are part of the appeal. If there's a reason to be wary of them, I'm blind to it for now.

He's right about one thing. Talking to Mateus has to be our best chance of finding Gareth. If he can let us into the secret of what Sansom are up to in the mines, we might be able to understand what Gareth is trying to do. I need that information, but I also need to understand what Gareth was trying to tell me. Perhaps talking to Mateus will jog my memory as well as jumpstarting my heart. The grand scheme to stimulate the Lorenzo Circuit, using Sansom's new electrodes to talk directly to the nervous system. If I could work that out, I could go back to James with a plan.

At the immigration desk I get the international terrorist treatment. They've stood me on a duct-taped cross on the floor and made me gaze into their camera, and now they're trying to tell me that my retinas are identical. Left and right, mirror images. It's a biological impossibility. The genius from US Immigration is just about to whisk me into a side-room for further interrogation when the bug fixes itself and the display recomputes my security risk as zero. America is safe. 'Purpose in visiting the US,' he inquires, disappointment smarting in his inhumanly blue eyes. 'Academic conference,' I reply. 'As in Section 3.17.' I point to my immigration document, where it's all down in black and white. I ought to be terrified of these guys. They do nothing all day except make towelette-fragrant travellers gaze into a convex mirror while a laser plays over their optic nerves. They don't even use ink stamps any more. No way at all to get out that aggression.

At the baggage reclaim I catch sight of Simon Weatherall, an old face from my postgrad days at Warwick. He's surprised that I've been on the same flight all this time. He kisses me, awkwardly trying to grasp my shoulders and hold me still, and suggests we share a cab to the hotel. I can trust him not to talk about science all the way so I say yes. He's sallow and nervous, the redness of his hair leaking into his face, his freckled complexion ravaged by a lab rat's diet. No doubts about that grin, though. The next four days are about nothing but pleasure for Simon. Everyone knows about his conference flings, his late-night movements along hotel corridors, at play in the fields of neuroscience women. They don't mind his bad skin and his faltering conversation; they don't find it sad that he's got his extra-marital excitement compartmentalised like his PowerPoint presentations and business cards. The neuroscience women have their own pressure valves and tacit understandings. They're doing it too.

America. When I was a kid and it only existed on TV, I thought it was made of a different substance to the world I knew, each granule somehow minutely hallmarked with Americanness, microscopically starred and striped. Now it's just bigger, wider, shinier, an upgrade you can barely afford, and it runs so quiet I can hardly hear it coming — it creeps up on me from behind the doors of mega-chain hotel rooms, through the ventilation ducts of air-conditioned conference halls, and its otherness does nothing but weary me, make me think I should be working. We whoosh out of Tampa International in a tinted-windowed peoplemover, Simon beside me clutching his laptop and gazing out at the unpeeling landscape of palm trees and flimsy wooden homes, and then the traffic on the freeway slows to a halt and our driver, a politely humourless Latino, actually starts talking. A car is on fire just up ahead. He's heard it on his radio. We join the queue and crawl past, gawping at this urban prodigy of white steel, smoke and flame. I'm deaf from the flight and dazzled by the Florida sunshine, but still I'm hypnotised, compelled by the vision of the blazing car. Even America blows up sometimes, it says; even the dream is flammable. 'First time in Florida?' our driver asks, as the mirrored towers of downtown wheel into view.

We both shout yes and he grins, our best friend in America, proud that he himself is taxiing us into this gleaming, blue-skied world.

The convention centre and conference hotel are the last stops before the waterfront. MARRIOTT WATERSIDE WELCOMES THE XXXIIND BIENNIAL MEETING OF THE ASSOCIATION FOR RESEARCH IN BEHAVIORAL NEUROSCIENCE. Those Roman numerals kill me. Simon pays the driver and presses a tip into his hand with a blundered handshake. Our best friend in America re-evaluates his worth. Inside, Reception is carved from marble. I'm on the XIVth floor. I resist the advances of a bellboy and haul my flightcase over to the lift, which servoes me up through the floors at a speed that makes the Roman numerals blur. I'm probably being scanned for tumours at the same time. I'm expelled onto logo'd carpet and directed by neat arrows to Room 1411. I love these American hotel rooms. The way they light up when you slot your keycard into the holster and an electronic voice welcomes you by your first name. The bathrooms are the best. You sit there and stare at the still life of the sink top, the millimetre-perfect arrangement of conditioner and shower gel, the pyramidal sculptures of white face-flannels. I want to hug the poor Latina woman who did all this. She's given me four tiny glasses for water, individually wrapped in polythene for the comfort and hygiene of each of my guests. It's all mine, for the next seventy-two hours.

I strip off and lie back on the bed until we're both as cool and neat as stationery. The air-con exfoliates my skin. I could unflap that fake mahogany box and watch five channels of weather or porn, but for the moment I want silence, time to savour the dull tug of my jetlag. A dead red LED on the console tells me that no messages are waiting. No one is paging Dr Churcher, no one wants to know if I've arrived yet. The air-con makes it sounds as though it's raining outside, but the Florida sky is clear and blue. A sprinkler crouches above my head like an ornate robot spider that's crawled through the skin of the room from another world. I unzip my flightcase and pull out a dog-eared journal article and a Portuguese dictionary. If I'm going to do this, I need to be sure of my facts. This is all I have on him. I just need to make sure I spend it wisely.

*

If I want to know if Mateus is here, I'm going to have to go and register. According to the events screen in the foyer, the desk has been open since early this morning. In my delegate's pack there'll be an up-to-date attendance list. He wasn't on the draft programme, but he might have got his proposal in late. All I have to do is go across to the convention centre and queue up for my pack, and then find a quiet place to go through it. I wouldn't want an audience if I had to read his name.

I've searched for him, obviously. For a year I was going on to *Web of Science* twice a day, to see if the latest update showed his name on any new publications. The fact that it didn't was my strongest proof that he was dead: Mateus would never have allowed this much of a gap in his CV. I tried all the general search engines. I couldn't work out how to stop my new browser remembering the search details, so every time I typed in an *M* it came up with his name. *Mouse, memory, Morris water maze*: they all turned into *Mateus*. At last I found something. A paper had come out in *Neuron*, with M. Pereira as fourth author. It was something on anomalous conductivity in a titanium–neurone interface, another potentially momentous application of the Pereira Effect. His affiliation was still down as Sansom Europe, which meant it was old stuff, research he must have done when we were still together. I scrolled down to the end of the paper, where they give current contact details. Only the first author was listed. I checked the Acknowledgements. *Thanks to Yvonne Churcher for all her support, encouragement, love, great sex while this paper was in preparation.* Nothing, actually. If Mateus was still in academia, his new work had not yet shown up in print. The thought that he might have lost his inspiration when he left my bed set my heart sparkling with guilty thrills.

I have to spell my name out for the woman at Registration. She trots over to the back of the booth and comes back with a monogrammed canvas bag. I can't wait. People are queueing around me, sidestepping. The attendance book is green, sick with anxiety. *A, D, M, P.* Paddy, Panic, Petrified, Pereira. Mateus Pereira. He's here.

*

Simon's got a paper into *Nature*. He came all this way with me in a taxi and he didn't say a word. This is like saying, I'm so unfazed by getting an article into the leading scientific journal that I'm actually going to neglect to tell you, even though we're sitting together on a gridlocked freeway and we've completely run out of things to say. I'm being told this by an irrepressible blonde from Bundaberg. I can't remember where I've met her before, but I know she's called Alyssa because her name badge tells me so. Usually you hear news like Simon's and you go straight back to spend an hour at your laptop, too drunk to do anything useful, probably, but still fired up with blurry possibilities. Tonight, it just feels like further proof of my failure. Alyssa asks me about my research and I lie and say it's going OK. The Grand Ballroom of the Tampa Marriott Waterside is athrob with rumours, greetings, important news, all of which are conspiring to make me feel small. People mill past, glance at my name badge and hurry on. I feel like a bargain basement offer, condemned to a thousand iterations of conference indifference, of being picked up, examined briefly under chandelier light, and then dropped, world without end. I can see Simon over by a publisher's stand, already smooth-talking a post-doc from Yale. I don't imagine they're discussing the impact factor of *Nature*, either. I'm trying to scan the room while still listening to Alyssa, which unfortunately means not looking at her. She'll drift away eventually and hate me for ever, but I need to know which of these eight thousand delegates is Mateus Pereira, once of Portugal, probably of somewhere else by now. Simon comes over and asks us if we want to come out to dinner with a big bunch of them, and I can see that the girl from Yale is invited because he's got her cellphone number written on his hand.

'Can't,' I say, with a genuine yawn. 'I've got to conserve my energy.'

He winks. 'Who's the lucky guy?'

'I'll tell you, once I've found him.'

'Well, take your pick. There are eight thousand hot neuroscientists here.'

I smile. 'That's just going to make him harder to find.'

*

I dream of Sansom. Chimps are being unloaded from cattle-trucks at the light railway depot and herded into the mine-shaft, where an elevator takes them down. Mateus leads me underground. Carbide lamps make everything the colour of video. Behind one glass-panelled door a chimp is undergoing surgery. Its scalp gleams white with analgesic cream. 'These experiments are being done for the benefit of mankind,' Mateus is telling me. 'I don't need to tell you the attractions of that argument.'

I wake up in a buzz of sleepy certainty, because I know I am close. Somewhere on one of these twenty-one floors, Mateus Pereira is looking out on the same untroubled dawn.

It's true: I needed an early night. I have to be up at six to get my poster up by 7:45. American conferences don't schedule sleep. But jetlag has kept me awake since four, watching CNN and the build of traffic on the freeway. At six a computer named Sally telephones me and invites me to enjoy my day. I'm reaching for a tissue in the bathroom when the metal dispenser falls out and bangs me hard on the toe. America is attacking me. The shower is so powerful that I come out expecting to see hail-damage on my skin.

There's no sign of him at breakfast, nor at the queue for velcro tags in the poster hall. I stand in the thousand-voice roar and watch the crowds file past, glancing at the banner of my poster and then down at my name badge and then, occasionally, at me. A conference is supposed to be about talking, but with eight thousand delegates the real communication is visual: the skimming of name badges and poster abstracts, the placing of business cards to request offprints. By nine o'clock I've made eye contact with precisely three people and actually spoken to two. A few more have glanced at my title banner, looked puzzled, and then excused themselves by leaving a card or a mailing address label. They'll never read what I send them. They're just marking out their territory, the eager puppies of the scientific frontier, showing the big wide world where they've been.

A guy called William T. Daniell comes up to me. His name badge says he's from Wayne State. I've never heard of him, but he's heard of me. He's surprised to see me doing this stuff. It seems he's been doing the same thing for a couple of years now, but using a rat model instead of my less satisfactory mouse one. I ask him how he has managed to breed transgenic rats to show signs of behavioural inflexibility when several groups around the world have already tried and failed, and he refers me to his recent paper on the subject. Even in my own field there's stuff I haven't managed to keep up with. The hall is resonating like a hellish cocktail party. Huge grey serpents hang from the roof, processing the air. I look at William T. Daniell's pewterish hair and hothouse complexion and realise that he has been sent here from my future to scare me away. He proves that there is a hell specifically for academics, that you can spend your whole life banging away at a problem and there can be people on the other side, banging away at the same rock, whom you've never even seen. It shouldn't surprise me: we're looking at big problems, big rocks. I'm just not sure I want to be banging any more.

A collaborator from Ohio State drops by, wanting to talk about the paper we've been writing together. Doug is in his element, scanning the whole bright hall and keeping track of who's who, who's coming, who's been. There are diamonds of sweat in his fastidious goatee. He says he's forwarded me the reviewers' reports from some journal we apparently sent our paper to, but I don't remember seeing them. I can't tell him that I haven't been back to my lab in two weeks. I feel like my career is over and I missed the announcement. I've let him down. I've let everyone down.

'That's Mapsy Panij,' he says. 'I've cited her three times this year and the bitch still hasn't returned the favour.'

What am I doing here?

'Alyssa says she saw Remko Kamlic,' he continues, staring at my name badge as though even he needed reminding of who I am. 'He's on his way down here.'

'Kamlic,' I say. 'Great.'

'It certainly is great. The genius of animal learning theory is gonna see your poster, Yvonne.'

'No, he's not.'

Surprise, or this industrial lighting, gives his face a sickly gleam.

'Why not?'

'Because I'm taking it down.'

The title banner comes away quite easily.

'Are you crazy?'

The laminated paper coils like a spring. It doesn't want to be here any more than I do.

'What's the point? No one's looking at it. It's an unimaginative answer to an impossible question.'

'Remko Kamlic is going to look at it. He's going to dig your funky transgenics shit.'

'Then he's as stupid as the rest of them.' I've got the velcro off the bottom now. 'There's more to life than the neuroscience of spatial memory.'

'But not much more. C'mon, Yvonne, people's careers are made at this convention. People get tenure from sucking cock with these guys.'

'I don't want tenure. I'm quitting.'

'You're quitting? You are fucking insane.'

I stare at him, his open logger's shirt and chinos, his safely dated academic's beard.

'Just slowly coming round,' I say.

I go back to the room and call Effi. The poster tube rolls, defeated, onto the abstract carpet. As I'm awaiting my turn for the satellite, I flick the TV on, mute it quickly and surf through to the adult channel. Then I turn it off again, because watching porn seems offensive when the person I'm about to speak to is trapped, body and soul, in the nineteen-fifties. She comes on to the line, giggly and panting, and tells me she's feeling fine. Her long-lost son has finally come up from Brighton to visit her and is already getting on her nerves. I wonder whether to tell her. She's never needed to be told anything before.

'Where are you?' she asks.

'Tampa. Florida.'

'How is it?'

'Crap. I'm giving up.'

'You need to get a new job, Yvonne. All this brainology can't be good for you.'

'I mean it. I'm quitting. I'm going to hand my notice in as soon as I get back.'

'I think I guessed that.'

'How? I've only just decided.'

'Maybe you do your deciding noisily,' she says.

I go online and check for messages. The video about the condo on Anna Maria Island is still playing. There's nothing new. If Mateus wants me to come and find him, he's not making it easy. I flick through the Portuguese dictionary again, trying to pick out a few more words from the well-thumbed photocopy I picked up from the bookcase in my tree-house. Probably the only such copy in existence, he used to boast. I can decipher enough of this obscure European natural history journal to confirm everything I ever suspected about the Pereira Effect. This is all I have on him. But, for the moment, it's all I need.

I pick up the programme book and turn to tomorrow's presentations. Mateus' symposium is scheduled for 10 a.m. If I have the courage to see it through, tomorrow might bring some answers. If not, then I'll always have the memory of a plan.

I dream of Sansom again. This time it's Gareth who follows me there. He's eating lobster with an elderly chimp while another in a maid's uniform pours champagne. 'Connections,' he's telling the chimp. 'It's all about making the right connections. If you can just find a way to talk to them, the birds will come when you call.'

The phone drills me back into the world.

9:50 a.m. is dead time in the Tampa International Convention Centre. In all the meeting rooms on this floor, symposia are winding down, final questions are being picked out from the floor, conveners are checking their watches and sorting their index cards. In five minutes these glitzy salons will be turning themselves inside out, floods of wan and yawning delegates clattering through huge double doors, checking their programme books for details on their next two-hour session in a tube-lit, fake-flowered meeting room. For now, though, it's as quiet as cyberspace. I shuffle past the elaborate coach lanterns that mark the entrance to the Clinton Room, trying to gauge the size of it from the spacing between the two sets of doors. I hope it's a big one. I could do without him knowing I'm here.

As I round the corner I can hear the first people coming out of the Clinton Room behind me, the doors opening and shutting on the polite applause of an academic audience. Here, though, there's no one. I move silently over the floral Versailles-effect carpet tiles, trying not to look as though I'm trying to hide. Plastic mock-skylights cruise by over my head. The air-con purrs out the sound of deep space. Around one corner I come across a toy-sized Latino going at the floor with a carpet-sweeper. There is no dirt to sweep up. It feels like a terrible injustice, that this harmless man should be made to waste his time on an utterly clean corridor. He's the human slave in some apocalyptic future's robot world, dwarfed by space-station architecture. I want to talk to him, ask how you can have your pointless tasks set out for you in the minutest detail and still manage to go about them with dignity. But his secret is safe. Behind me, the audiences are changing over. The Clinton Room is emptying and refilling. It's time to go.

When I was revising for my finals, I had my own table in the library. I'd be there every morning at nine and stay there until my eyes were dry and my notes were a lurching blur. I knew the precise width of the table, the exact position my chair had to be in if I was to escape the late-afternoon sun. When the exams were over and I no longer had to spend days huddled over my files, I missed it like some people would miss a childhood home. I was less of a person when I was away from it. I'd left something of my strength, my certainty, there.

Science, for me, has always been a place like that: a room you could walk into and quietly occupy without anyone noticing, a place with reliable light and unchanging dimensions, to which no one ever questioned that you belonged. It was like one of these slowly filling meeting rooms, in fact: familiar, polite, unshowily welcoming. Taking your seat among all those eminent names was always going to be a test of nerves, but you knew that, in the end, you'd be OK.

When I see Mateus sitting there with his shaved-off goatee and his pony tail cropped to nothing, I wonder if I know this place at all.

But this surprise shouldn't surprise me. If science is a place, then it's never the same place for long. Ten years from now, most of the findings presented on this third day of the Biennial Meeting will be obsolete. In ten years, Sansom or someone will probably have found a cure for Alzheimer's. My ninety-nine mice will have long gone up in smoke. No one will care that I sat here today, my heart thumping as its greatest tormenter was introduced by the symposium chair in the most flattering of terms. It won't matter that I did what I did, that I couldn't stop myself doing it, because science moves on. It's far greater than the sum of its parts. It will forget us, and our false theories, as soon as reality proves them wrong.

Fuck it. I'm still going to do it.

The first speaker is one of Mateus' old colleagues from Lisbon. He has fifteen minutes, plus five for questions. Mateus is on third, which puts him forty minutes away. I can wait. There must be five hundred of us in here, and only the symposiasts have lights on them. Occasionally I see Mateus tapping at his laptop, making a few last-minute changes to his presentation. He always got nervous before these big shows. Only once do I see him glance out anxiously at the room.

The second speaker is the most famous of the four of them. He got a paper into *Science* in the early nineties which, Mateus once told me, went on to become the most widely cited paper in its field. You can tell he's done nothing interesting since then. These are old data he's presenting, maybe even offcuts from that one famous study, the royalties he's still living off. He's proof that you can get to the top without talent, without ideas, just by plugging away and being careful who you love. If science is just a story, as James likes to say, then this one is a fairy tale.

The guy finishes early and no one has any questions. There's an awkward moment and then Mateus puts up his hand. The audience will remember his generosity, his concern for his fellow-symposiast's awkwardness, and his own talk will be the more brilliant for the contrast. I don't understand the question, which is probably because I'm falling apart, but the speaker doesn't appear to understand it either. Remembering the etiquette of the situation, Mateus just nods and smiles. Wherever he's been, he's learned some manners. Or maybe he's simply learned how to be afraid.

Then he's standing, my dark man, picking his way through the chairs to the empty lectern, and the lights go down and the first slide of his presentation ghosts up onto the back wall of the room.

'I'm going to talk today about an aspect of neurone–silicon connectivity that has interested me now for several years. At UCSD we've been developing a model that tries to account for...'

So he's at San Diego. I can live with that.

'With this new model we've tried to make sense of anomalous conductivity in the mammalian nervous system by considering...'

It isn't a new model. He presented this at Quebec and it was old then. But science moves on. For Mateus, Quebec never happened.

'We hope that this effect we've been studying will allow us to make some real progress towards exploiting deep brain stimulation in the creation of effective therapeutic strategies...'

I can see it clearly now. He's cheating, like he cheated me, like he's been cheating all these people for all these years. And yet, as scientists, we have to take our orders from reality. If the truth about his little secret is out there, it's only a matter of time before it gets known.

The chair asks if there are any questions. Three hands go up. Not mine: I can wait my turn. Mateus sees them off easily, flattering the questioners that their comments are both apt and smart, while at the same time showing how far he is from being stumped by any of this. The chair is nosing the air, scanning the room for further questions. Mateus follows his gaze, bestowing a smile that's pitched just this side of arrogance.

To me it's just arrogance. I put up my hand.

'Mateus,' I say, 'I was looking again at the 1983 article by Pinheiro and I wonder if you could explain how your model differs. He seems to be describing the same basic effect, even down to the size of the action potentials that he was trying to transmit, and what he says about the importance of a steady voltage supply is very similar. I'm assuming you're aware of Pinheiro's paper, as it was originally published in your native Portuguese.'

Five hundred neuroscientists look at me, and then at Mateus. Mateus just looks at me. He recognises me now, I hope. I haven't aged that much in two years. He didn't destroy me just by walking out on me; I'm alive and kicking, and briefly enjoying the kicking part. He's still smiling that politician's smile, but it's edged with white now, hardened by embarrassment and, very gradually, anger. My voice came out calm enough, but it's the only part of me that isn't shaking. I've got the sick aftertaste of bad sex, of something that's supposed to be enjoyable only making me feel cheap and empty. Revenge doesn't agree with me. I'd rather just let the thing go.

So I'm getting up calmly, waiting for the people in my row to clear bags, knees and programme books from the passageway, and then, without even glancing at the podium, I'm out of there.

A minibar is a beautiful thing. It gives you no anxiety of choice. You start with the ready-mixed cocktails, move on to the beer and macadamia nuts, and finish with Toblerone and whisky.

Effi's number is just beeping at me.

I get pissed and fall asleep in my clothes. I get up and take my clothes off. I can't get warm and I can't cool down. Butt-naked and shivering under the ruthlessly efficient air-con, I order a Marriottburger with onion rings and eat half of it. I drink one more beer then turn the air-con off. I sit in the armchair by the window and let the reflux heat of the building rise around me like a lover's smell. The sky looks crisp and beautiful. I stare out of the sealed fourteenth-floor window, watching the through-traffic of Tampa International take off into the late afternoon sky. At the edges of the window, patches of tinting material have peeled away, and you can see the true colour of the world, the real-life, carcinogenic glare that the hotel authorities want to protect you from. It's shocking and satisfying, the glimpse of that chink in the façade that could bring the whole illusion down.

There's still no answer from Effi.

It's dark when I'm woken by a knock at the door. I wrap a towel around myself and put my eye to the little viewing hole. He floats past like a goldfish, absurdly magnified. A troubled goldfish, on his fifth divorce. The loss of his goatee reveals more of his face; more of him, you might say. I wouldn't say. His face was always the biggest liar of all. I let him in, anyway.

*

He stands at the window, looking out over the rooftop pipework of the building next door.

'Stay away from the window,' I quip. 'This is a dangerous city.'

'Don't worry. You don't get bad guys this high.'

He sits down on the sofa, leaving me standing there in the towel. I'm trying to pretend that I've just had a shower. But I probably look too dry.

'I'm going to put some clothes on,' I say after a bit.

'Clothes are good,' he says, lifting his hand and turning his face away.

This concern for my modesty amuses me. I go into the bathroom and come back in an embroidered Marriott robe.

'You're not angry with me?'

He laughs. 'You got your revenge, Yvonne. I just hope you enjoyed it.'

So it was just a game. He hits me and I hit him. If only I'd known.

'It was OK. Anyway, you don't have to worry. No one will have read that obscure Portuguese thing.'

'They will now. Ten years of my life have been based on trying to explain that effect. I'll have to publish a clarification.'

'That's easy enough to do.'

'Maybe. I knew this would happen one day. But things get their own momentum. Maybe somehow I wanted to take the fall.'

He takes the hand from his face and turns to the window. He looks younger now than when he first fixed my bike in the rain on Libet Avenue. I used to tie his hair up in bunches, for a joke; now it sits in an inoffensive trim, neatly tapered to the collar of his regulation denim shirt. I can't resist a secret smile: my dark man has turned into Doug. For all his strutting bravado, his only real concern is to please the boss, impress the editors, be patted on the head and told he's a good boy. I think of the list we drew up, all the things we would do together before we settled down. I wonder if he's managed one of them.

'Your work is still valid,' I tell him, doubting the reassuring tone. 'It's just that you can't claim the effect for yourself.'

'Yeah.' He manages a weak smile. 'I'll publish the clarification in *Neuroscience*. I'll still be famous before you.'

I sit down on the chair opposite him, but feel too exposed. I get up and put the air-con back on, and then try the chair again.

'I'm not going to be famous at all. I'm packing it in.'

He doesn't revise his expression. I can't expect him to start caring, just because I'm selfish enough to start having a life.

'Why did you just fuck off like that? I didn't know if you were alive or dead.'

'Dead,' he says quietly. 'Without you.'

He stares at me with those huge wounded eyes. I'm not even sure he's putting it on. He's a stranger, a face from the year before last; I can't judge him any more. For a moment I think he's going to get up and do something dramatic, but he thinks better of it. This is drama enough for me: the too-late heart-spilling, the against-all-odds declaration of undying things. It's fantastic that this is what we've sunk to: a tea-time tearjerker, tugging the usual heart-strings in all the usual ways.

'I'm sorry, Yvonne. I can never even begin to explain it to you.'

'Come on. You could explain the Pereira Effect.'

He gets up and goes over to the window. I see him holding the curtain aside and staring out like a stake-out victim.

'I was afraid,' he says. 'I know that's what everyone says, but it's true.'

'You're right. Everyone says that.'

'But it's true.'

'Remember, a theory has to account for the evidence. How about the month I was in such a state about you that I couldn't be bothered to wash my hair?'

I catch him looking down at my phone, which I must have left on the windowsill after calling Effi. He turns back from the window and stares at the desolation of my executive room.

'Do you remember what I told you that one time? About fear?'

I remember it. That summer night, on the roof of my treehouse, the warm hand of love. I could feel his heat inside me, still taste him in my mouth. I'd just told him about my balcony fantasy. Me, standing at the rail in a red dress, telling my story to the dark forest. A man behind me, whose face I would never see.

'Tell me again,' I say.

He glances at me. I can sense something shifting. The memory has laid me open. He remembers that night too.

'I was trying to explain to you how a person gets to be afraid. You didn't want to hear this, but I had to tell you. You had this amazing sense of *loyalty* to your ideas. It was a moral position, not a scientific

125

one. But you were so gorgeously unknowing. Almost gauche, I would say.'

'Yes, well. It was a long time ago.'

'I know you, Yvonne. Nothing you do surprises me. Not even today.'

'You *used* to know me. Then you lost interest.'

He shakes his head, eyes closed, smiling.

'So this is what I told you. This is how I tried to tackle your certainty. You didn't want abstract theorising. That used to drive you crazy. You wanted examples, illustrations, some facts you could put your finger on. So I asked you to think about fear. I asked you to imagine being out there, alone, in that forest. Just you and the noises of the night. Every cracking twig or rustling leaf would have your heart leaping. There's nothing you can do to stop your brain from making its hypotheses. But you can be aware of how that three-pound lump of nervous tissue is processing your experience for you. Even as you feel yourself jumping at these tiny sounds, these little signals of danger, you can imagine all this going on in your limbic system. If you could visualise it, you could control it. I was trying to tell you that fear was a material response, a neural circuit. It could be brought under control like any other bodily activity.'

'Never a good theory,' I say. 'The fear circuit's out of bounds to consciousness. It's on a floor the lift doesn't stop at. The lizard brain, millions of years old.'

And my lizard heart remembers the night he told me that, flat on our backs on the roof of my treehouse, the sky sticky with stars.

'Maybe,' he says. 'But this philosophy seemed to work for me. I'm asking you to remember what we were like, what *I* was like, back then. I had gone through my life afraid of nothing. I was a straight-A student, my teeth were perfect, I knew how to make *cozido*. I knew I was good, and I could get anything I wanted. Then you came along, and I began to learn what fear really was.'

'Fear of what?'

'Fear of losing you. Losing the thing I loved so much.'

I ought to resist the smile. 'Go on.'

'I could see what was happening to me. All the mind games were useless. It had got bigger than me. This was one fear I couldn't control.'

'But you still believed in it, that night? You still thought your method could work?'

I hate it, but somehow I'm anxious about the answer. That night from my memory: it was the beginning of the end.

'No. I don't think I did believe it. Even as I was telling you, I was doubting it. I think that could have been the moment it all changed.'

'So was that when you stopped loving me? Or did you never actually love me? Was that all just another great effort of will?'

'No. I never stopped loving you, Yvonne. I just became too afraid.'

'Don't tell me. You were so in love with me you had to disappear to California without telling me.'

He shakes his head. 'Not California. I went around the world. I couldn't sleep. I couldn't eat. I couldn't get in touch. I couldn't tell you.'

He looks like he wants to sit down. So would I, after spouting bullshit like that. I hope he picks the sofa. Mateus on my bed is not an arrangement I could cope with.

'Is that why you tracked me down? All that *Come to Florida* stuff. The video about the condo on Anna Maria Island. That was a good joke, wasn't it?'

'I needed to find you. I knew that what I had done was wrong. Anyway, it's too late now. You've probably found someone else.'

I say nothing. If he's fishing for information about me, he'll have to get used to ignorance. I'm not telling him anything. I'm not telling him how I was afraid of my dreams, just because Mateus might be there and I'd have to wake up from that dream and lose him all over again. I'm not telling him about the letters I wrote, scratching around in clumsy, unpractised handwriting for an answer to the question he left me with. Saying this stuff would be like selling my own blood. It's mine, not his. That matters.

'You gave me uncertainty. I don't know how you could do that to a scientist.'

'I was always planning to get in touch, Yvonne. When things had had a chance to calm down. But the moment never came.'

I wish I'd brought those letters I wrote him. He could have had something to laugh about on the plane.

'Maybe that's because they never calmed down. You didn't even know

127

if I was still alive.'

'I did. I had your research articles. Your institute's website. And you know that my old employers are interested in everything that the Lycee do.'

I look at him, shading to anger. He raises his hand and nuzzles it absent-mindedly, where the wedding ring would be.

'You and your Sansom friends know about us losing our mapping data, don't you?'

'In our little world it's headline news. By the way, Sansom were not behind this security breach. They're as astonished as anyone.'

Astonished perhaps, but they will almost certainly know by now that Gareth has got the data.

'Do you know what they're doing in the mines?'

He's probably never spoken about the mines. He knows, of course: you couldn't work there and not know. There's an instant of surprise, and then Mateus refixes his stare. He looks flushed, a little irritable, and very sure of the beauty of what he has in mind. I recognise this look. The look that comes before the touch that comes before the sigh that leads to the fumbled shedding which is the precursor to the same old gorgeous thing. He's going to try it on. But first, there are things I need to know.

'Have they got chimps down there? Enculturated chimps?'

He nods, eager to please me on this and then get on with pleasing himself. 'They've got enculturated chimps, bonobos, any language-trained primates they could get their hands on. They're working on a new kind of electrode which can be implanted deep into the brain to stimulate the relevant neural areas. The basic technology's been around since the late 1990s. The difficulty is in finding a biocompatible material for making the implants from. Something the body doesn't reject as soon as it's gone in. These new electrodes have got a special kind of titanium casing which means the body won't reject them. They're smaller, safer, easier to place and more accurate. Absolutely perfect for self-stimulation. And you don't have to carry a battery the size of a cow to power them.'   ———

'Self-stimulation?'

'Of course. That's what this research is all about. They've been using deep brain stimulation for years. They had a lot of success in treating

Parkinson's. But these other diseases are a different matter. The pathways of the Lorenzo Circuit run too close to vital areas. You need to know exactly where to put the electrodes, and you need to be able to control the way the current is distributed across them. The problem with deep brain stimulation techniques is that they have been scattergun. They have only been able to produce a steady current which you can't even switch on and off. With this system, users can both vary the strength of the stimulus and control which electrodes are active.'

'That's why Sansom want the map of the Lorenzo Circuit. So that people with dementia can control their own memories?'

'Exactly. A safe, painless operation, over and done with in half an hour, and the patient has her own electronic box of memories. When she wants to remember who she is, she presses any one of a number of buttons corresponding to the different electrodes she's had installed. And the good times come flooding back.'

This is what Gareth was talking to me about. It's all about the control of memory. But there's something else I'm not remembering. Some detail he entrusted to me, which could explain everything.

'What would someone do if they wanted to get hold of these implants?'

'They'd have to find their way into the mines. And be very persuasive when they got down there.'

He pauses, watching the effect of his words. I have an image of Gareth, alone, far away, walking a long distance in the dark. While these thoughts hold me off guard, Mateus takes a step towards me, holding out both hands.

'Now let me tell *you* a story.'

'You're on a balcony on a summer night. You're wearing a red dress which reaches to just above your knees. You're talking, telling the story of the first time you made love. He sits on a chair behind you, listening. You don't turn around. All you need to know is scattered between those black trees. You smell the endless millions of pine trees standing dead still under the stars. Underneath that you smell your own smell, perfume and sweat and longing. It's been a hot, amazing day.'

He's moved behind me, to the chair I was sitting on. I haven't flinched, haven't moved away. He knows what he's saying. It fills me with a deep, fiery satisfaction, the thought that he remembers my fantasy, assumes it has kept its power. I'm standing by the sealed glass, the net curtain pulled wide. Planes rise from one end of the horizon and stroke upwards across the night, blinking. I'm on them, every one of them. They carry me off in pieces. Far below, a police light strobes along a freeway. All over the city, traffic lights are turning green then red, holding up the traffic on empty roads.

'The first thing you feel is a finger at your ankle, brushing at the skin. Your voice is still speaking but you have no consciousness of the words. It doesn't matter. There is no *you*. You're nothing but connections, accidents, illusions of control. The finger brushes upwards over your calf and turns into a hand. Now there are two hands, one on each knee. You feel your stomach tighten. His wrists nudge upwards on your hem, raising the fabric over your skin, exposing you to the air. The hands reach up over your hips and hook the elastic of your panties. You feel them being pulled down gently over your hips, their astonishing new wetness turning cold against your thighs. The breeze on your skin makes you gasp, and you lean forward further over the balcony rail, opening yourself up to the night. You feel something warm and wet, a tongue, licking at the crack of your buttocks. His hair tickling your skin. He parts your buttocks with his thumbs and sinks his tongue into you. What does that feel like to the man? What does it taste like? You'll never know. His consciousness is unknowable, a star you can never reach ... '

'Wait ... ' I push his hand away and jerk my body upright, bumping my cheek against the window. 'That's you. It's not me.'

He is there behind me, hard, ready. I feel him brush uselessly at the folds of my dressing gown, not knowing what to do with his hands. This is the closest I come to completeness, this twitch of lust and grief that catches sight of itself just as it dissolves. I stare up at a passenger jet slicing through the still-blue horizon, amazed that there are people up there inhabiting lives they never question, never doubting the illusion of themselves.

'Yvonne, you've got to trust me. I can make you whole.'

I don't answer. I don't turn around. He can do anything he wants to me but he can't make me look at him — he can't make me *attend*. My consciousness is unknowable; it's the floor the lift doesn't stop at, the uninhabited planet. I can hear him breathing, waiting for an answer. The answer doesn't come. I sense him wondering what to do, how to get me to look at him. The silence stretches into embarrassment, into shame. Then zipping, rustling, a human body moving.

The quiet closing of a door.

CHAPTER TWELVE

Be My Cinema

◎

The night Mateus came to my room, Effi collapsed at Millennium Heights. The nurse found her when he turned up for his morning visit. I'd become fond of Daren, but it still felt odd to be discussing Effi's life and death with him down the hotel phone.

'She's had a stroke,' he told me. 'Not the first one, neither.'

'What happened to her son?'

'He went home. Saw she was getting her dinner down and thought she was OK.'

I packed in a hurry and took the hotel shuttle to the airport. I was at the front of the queue for security when I realised I didn't have my phone with me. It was too late to go back to the hotel. I remembered Mateus' curiosity about seeing it on the windowsill in my room, the reason it evaded my last-minute look-around. It would have been out of charge, which was probably why Daren had called the hotel. I sat on the plane, watching its cartoon image crawl pixel by pixel across my in-seat movie screen, and thought about upgrades. At Pelton Airport I picked up my flightcase and poster tube from the baggage carousel and got a cab straight to the hospital. I found Effi sitting up in a corner of a mixed ward, trying to peel a banana.

'Yvonne,' she said. 'Thank God for you.'

The neurologist took me into a side-room.

'We gave her a thorough scan after this stroke. We found evidence of numerous small lesions in her temporal cortex. About here,' he put a hand to his own head, 'on the left hand side. It explains why she's been forgetful, not recognising people.'

'I thought it was Alzheimer's. You're saying it's the strokes that have been doing this to her?'

'It could be either. It could be both. Hers is an old brain, a tired one. It's under attack from all sides.'

Effi watched me come back into the ward.

'You look shattered,' she said. 'You should go home, get some sleep.'

Her hair was unpinned from its bun and hung loosely on her shoulders. She hadn't dyed it in weeks and now it was clouding to white. Even in the hell of this hospital ward she'd managed to put her lipstick on.

'I'm sorry, Effi. I shouldn't have left you.'

'Of course you should have left me. You don't have to worry. I'm a creaky gate. I go on for years.'

I leave her and hurry back along the peach-hued, endlessly replicating corridor, with a vanishing hope that I somehow remembered to pack my phone in my hold baggage. I spend ten minutes rummaging through my flightcase on the hospital forecourt, then go back inside and find a card-phone on the corridor.

'I seem to have lost my phone,' I tell James. 'In America.'

He wants to come and pick me up. You don't drive, I say. Grandstand can drive, he says. I'll borrow Grandstand's car.

I don't know what happens now. He swings onto the hospital forecourt with the visor down and a Brisbane Lions baseball cap pulled down over his eyes. It's black night, gone nine, and Westwood Road is a long fluorescent-lit hangover, kebab joints and shuttered shops and plasma screens advertising a life that is going on elsewhere. He was having me on, telling me that he couldn't drive: he cuts through these dead streets like he's been doing it all his life, carves pieces off this city till there's just me, him and the big old house he calls home.

The place is deserted. They're on an action somewhere, projecting cinema-sized images of experimental marmosets onto the walls of Bankstown Underpass, and then lying down in the traffic and drawing chalk outlines around each other, conjuring the images of the slain. Bridge and Level Ten are going to be playing sounds on a portable PA to the cars at the traffic lights, distortion-level recordings of a dawn rainforest, a hospital respirator. This is the Atrocity Exhibition, James explains: any means necessary to show the world the reality about what is done in its name. Last week Grandstand smashed up two brand-new plasma screens and thus saved a small sector of downtown Pelton from three days of pharmaceuticals advertising. Where does it end? I ask James. He glances up at the sky, which tonight is sponsored by TransGen Technologies. There, he tells me.

'My friend's had a stroke. I don't need to be reminded of reality.'

'You've spoken to a doctor, Yvonne. He's shown you the world through a stained-glass window. Come back when the glass is broken. Then you'll see what's really going on with Effi.'

'I saw Mateus,' I tell him, as he tries to get the fire going in his room. 'Was he just a story as well?'

'Did he try it on? That's the best way of telling.'

'He tried it on. But I wasn't interested.'

Maybe there's a longer silence than usual.

'Are you going to see him again?'

'No.' I'll tell him this, and no more. 'He wants to.'

He turns away from the grate and looks darkly at me. 'That guy's a fool. For letting you go.'

He's lit a good fire. He knows how to give it structure, how to let the thing breathe. He drapes a piece of newspaper over the grate and there's a roar, a blazing suction, like a door to hell blowing open.

Then the gorgeous sight of James' stash-box.

'Anyway,' he says, unfurling papers. 'You say there is no *you*. No centre of rational choice. Just inputs and outputs, stimuli and responses.'

I wonder if Mateus could feel that, as he tried to make me look at him. My absence. That was all he loved, after all, all that was available for him to love. The ghostlessness of my flesh. His zombie girl.

'Maybe that's why I feel I've been sleepwalking through my whole life. I've managed OK. I just haven't been *there*.'

'But you do make decisions. You decided to phone me.'

'I *said* I'd phone you.'

'You decided to say it.'

'I just speak,' I tell him. 'I never think first.'

'Is there anything else you do without thinking?'

'I don't know. My mind's a blank on that one.'

He smiles and starts breaking tobacco into the papers he has stuck together. I like watching him work. His dark, thickly waved hair needs a cut, or at least a good comb. I can't guess when he last shaved. The sight of his stubble sparks ghost-burns on my skin, the bleeding of a signal between areas of cortex, the memory of a touch that hasn't yet come. Sometimes, when I'm driving, I'll pull out from a junction with the certainty that I've misjudged the manoeuvre, and that truck I saw in the distance has, without my brain having yet caught up with the fact, slammed into my side; there's a half-second of heart-in-mouth waiting that makes fools of my senses, until my brain catches up and I see that I'm OK. This is like that feeling. It's the impossible foreknowledge of having had this face next to mine, of having stared into it in my absence, woken up next to it when I couldn't conceivably have been there. Whatever's going to happen has already happened. I've crashed in flames; I just haven't yet heard the news.

'Anyway, we talked about Sansom. We were right about the mines. They're using these implants to try to manipulate the Lorenzo Circuit. That's their big idea. Their cure for Alzheimer's. Allow people to control their own memories, and so reverse the effects of the disease.'

He twists up the spliff and comes over to the sofa. Our bodies sink down together on the old springs.

'So that's what Gareth's interested in. That's why he took the data, and why he'll now be trying to get into the mines.'

'You think that's what he's doing?'

'I don't know. Until you can remember what he told you, we're just guessing. I've been asking around. No one's heard from him. He doesn't have any friends. That's why you're so critical in this, Yvonne.'

Movement starts up on his terminal, some sort of still-image slide-show. The data projector, its guts lit with the restlessness of stand-by mode, points darkly at the wall above his bed.

'You're going to have to talk to Gillian,' he says.

I shake my head. 'And tell her that I'm the cause of her losing all her data? No way, James. I'm not going back there. I'm quitting.'

'You can't quit. We need you. You've got to help us to nail Sansom.'

'You've got your videos. They're all the proof you need that they've got chimps down there.'

'We need more. What you were saying the other night about animal models of Alzheimer's being a waste of time. We need someone who can explain that.'

I stare at the poster tube propped up in the corner. I was tempted to leave it revolving on the baggage carousel, as a somehow apt valediction to my old career. But it's followed me here, to this nerve centre of anti-vivisectionism.

'You don't need me. Your friends don't want me here. Bridge wants me dead.'

'All right, then. *I* need you.'

He glances at me and reaches into the pocket of his jacket. He opens my hand and fills it with something warm and metallic. A golden amulet. It's the figure of a woman, of Asiatic features, her curves exaggerated like a fertility goddess.

'A friend of mine made it. I wanted you to have it. Forget about the others. Do this for me.'

He takes the amulet from me and lifts it to my throat. I feel his fingers at the back of my neck, tracing the soft hair in front of my ear.

'Sounds like I don't have a choice,' I say.

I hear his voice from the bathroom. I turn off the taps and the backflow starts to sing in the pipes, and I can hear James above the clatter of the Edwardian plumbing, talking to someone on his mobile, his voice filtered, muffledly calm. I wipe the steam from the mirror above the sink, still somehow amazed that there's a mirror here, that a squat has a washbasin that works. Under this bare electric bulb I look as white and unforgiving as a suicide. My boobs seem to be giving up the struggle, but my legs are OK. I must be eight years older than Bridge. That's a lifetime in the history of a woman's body. I'm pretty sure they used to have a thing together. Perhaps he's talking to her now, getting the report on today's protest, telling her he's got his tutor just where he wants her in the bathroom across the corridor. Correction. I'm quitting, aren't I? I *was* his tutor. He *was* my student.

The voice stops, and I freeze. There's no lock on the door. I hear movement on the boards outside, and then his voice through the thin panelled woodwork, telling me about a towel. His weight creaks off the boards and there's just the sound of a tank filling. I climb into the bath through a fug of my own smell, sink into the hot greenish water with a gasp, and with someone else's soap I wash away the last of America.

The only clean thing in my flightcase is a black long-sleeved top which comes down to the tops of my thighs. I put it on, and cross the corridor.

*

The slideshow has ended. There's firelight, then just the glow of a terminal screen. James is watching something on his computer. It's a video file, shot in a hurry and without the luxury of lighting. It starts with a rectangle of pure black, unscrolled by a blurry band of light when he presses PLAY. Some sort of lantern splashes light into deep space, and you can make out the pitted back wall of a low-ceilinged room. Figures jut out of the shadows and shuffle towards the source of the glow. Almost human faces, but not human. The light is turquoise. As I watch, the figures on the screen jerk and stumble over a few scraps of food. Some cower in the middle distance, hugging their knees and rocking on their heels. One flaps half-paralysed away, twisted and antic as a shell-shock victim.

'These are the videos that were smuggled out of Sansom?'

'Yeah. They were shot in the mines. Trouble is, Sansom's PR team have got hold of them and they've already countered. They say they're fakes. The kind of "evidence" that any half-intelligent twelve-year-old could fabricate using MovieStar 5.0 and a reasonably powerful laptop. What do you think? Do you think someone's just mashed these together from old footage?'

I see a bonobo grabbing at the camera, knocking it out of focus then scurrying away into darkness. In the next shot, three juveniles are being hauled into daylight, screaming.

'They're not fakes. Mateus believes in this, and he used to work there.'

In this shot the camera is trawling along a row of cages, each of which holds a stunned bonobo. The scene cuts to the sign outside Sansom's ultra-modern forest HQ. I feel the heat of James' body just in front of me, the sweet pressure of his breath reflecting back at me.

'OK,' he says, 'I can see what we're looking at now. We're going to have to do what Mateus said. We have to get down there, and be very persuasive when we get there.'

A bottle smashes into the recycling pod in the street below.

'Into the mines?'

'Yeah. It's the only way.'

He closes the viewer. The blue desktop spreads an aqueous light. It's a fullness to his cheeks, I think, which makes him look so young. He gazes at the screen, calling up a blank document, not yet ready to look at me. His breathing is deep and audible. I feel that if I spoke now, said a single word, this would all go wrong. He's wearing a brushed cotton shirt with several buttons undone. I can see the gleaming dip of skin behind the collarbone and, lower, a thread of dark chest-hair.

'Good bath?' he asks.

'Yeah. Nothing on me now.'

He's still not looking. His hand moves to the keyboard, little-fingers ⇧ and presses a single key.

?

A spurt of heat breaks across my face. It's happened. I've crashed in flames.

He waits, still turned to the screen, and taps ↵. I reach over and press a key.

y

He takes my hand and holds it there, his fingers hard on my knuckles, his thumb burrowing into my palm. My heart sucks on its drug. The key stays down and I can see its endless reaffirmation spreading out across the screen: **yyyyyyyyyyyyyyy**. Yes, yes, yes. Slowly, firmly, he fucks my hand with his thumb, digging deep into the soft nerve-lines, itemising each knuckle and tendon. I kiss his smoky mouth, and he twists around for me with all the grace of a boy dancer, opening his mouth for a song. I feel his hands lift the hem of my top, raising it an inch or two, then hesitating, uncertain. I laugh and tear at the buttons of his shirt, and he shifts up and lets me work at his buckle, ease down his jeans. He's not hard; I haven't given him time. I hook up my arms and let him lift my top away, and then he reaches around and pulls the wet bobble from my hair, only now registering my nakedness. I kiss him again and feel his filling cock cranking up against my knee, and I bring my foot up to play with his balls and I feel my wetness breaking, shivers up my back, desire roaring in my brain. I try to pull him onto the bed but he resists, and for a moment we're at cross-purposes. It seems like failure, and my heart starts to fall.

'Wait,' he says, and for a moment I think he wants to leave it there.

His thighs unlock from mine. He swivels back to the computer and jerks the mouse over the dock. Our bodies explode into brightness. The projector whirrs into life and sprays colour over every inch of skin, just random patternings at first, and then the brain gets to work and picks out fragments of medieval art, snippets of childish handwriting, colour stills of household objects, magnificent trees. Each second the slide-show clicks forward one frame, and I can just make out the fine micro-scopy of a botanical histograph, the hugely-magnified honeycomb of phloem and xylem. Next he's an eighteenth-century world-map, covered with the watercolour bruisings of continents and seas. The shapes slip and warp, stretching in and out of meaning, looming large and shrinking away. I look down at my own body, adorned for a moment with black-hearted sunflowers, and he laughs at the gift he has given me. He rears up on me, tattooed with light, his body a fresco, his hard cock veined with the obscure gradients of human portraiture, and I lie back and spread my pages wide, let him taste my illustrated skin, read my tangled arguments with his tongue.

In the morning he is gone. The window is open and I can feel the faint otherworldliness of fresh air. Sunlight tingles on my bare arm. March has turned warm in my absence, and it looks like staying that way.

The house is quiet. There's a demo at Sansom and they're all going. I put my glasses on and smile briefly at the note James has left me. I pull on the shirt I pulled off him last night and pad gently down the stairway of death. The hall is full of sunlight. There's a pile of mail on the bare tiles, but it won't be for me. I go into the kitchen and switch on the kettle, hallucinating the buzz as the power surges into it. I watch the water boil, mesmerised by the play of bubbles in the clear filling-strip. The slightest details waylay me, as though there's a question about every minuscule fact of existence and I need answers to each one. I pour water on a tea bag and look out onto the yard, where a kid's trike has been abandoned to a creeping tide of rain-grime. Did David Overstrand have children? I've never seen any here.

I was wrong about the mail. There is something for me.

As I bend down I feel it again, this faint dizziness, an empty-headed tingling like a virus starting to prickle at my insides. I have to put a hand down to steady myself. The pattern of the tiles stills into a yellow after-image, which shifts with my eyes and nets out across the floor, overwriting the reality beneath. The package is light, and I cling to the airy certainty of it. As I stand up again the warmth shivers across my shoulder-blades. Is this how it feels? Is this the stir of a body forming inside you? It couldn't be gentler, I think, or less frightening. And then, when you do the test and it's all confirmed, does the body whisper: I told you so? You thought you knew your own heart, but life knew it better. It gave you what you wanted, when you didn't know you wanted anything at all.

That tingling again. I lean back against the wall with the package clasped across my chest. I can see my face in the oval mirror on the other wall. I look young, unready, scared. Jetlag and breathless sex have cut holes out of me. I can't be pregnant. This is all a bizarre daydream, the wrecking telepathy of a child who wants to be born.

The package is marked Yvonne Churcher, 76 St. Lawrence Road. The postmark is Fulling. I know it's strange, but I'm too far gone to question it. I start to pick at the tape. Inside the padded envelope is a shallow rectangular tin, decorated with Chinese enamelling. There's a golden wire latch making an airtight seal. It smells of incense. It hardly weighs anything. Frail, full of air, like the thoughts that would interpret it. The envelope I'm dropping to the floor had more substance to it.

Open it, says James' child.

I lift the latch. The breath rises from my lungs and bursts. All the light of the universe is in this box: all the stars, planets, streetlights, computer screens. It's like that dream of wakefulness, the light of God shining into my soul. Then darkness, as the whole brilliant universe shrinks to a dot of pain. There's a smell of gas and burning. Is there a way out of this? I ask, as the blackness fills up with tears. Follow your nose, replies the unborn child. Love my father. Don't wait for the truth to come to you. Go after it now, or it'll be gone.

CHAPTER THIRTEEN

Are You Going With Me?

◉

A voice reels me in.

'Yvonne…'

For hours I've been dodging the light, clinging to pre-conscious shadows. Even in that airy darkness I was physically joined to something, a metallic edge of pain which meant that I was never quite asleep, never quite cut free of my body. It was cold, dull, peripheral, like a handrail in a cave, something for me to cling to and haul on. Now the light finds me out, seeps into my sleep with gauzy clarity, and shows me the unplugged clutter of a hospital ward.

'You've got visitors, Yvonne.'

'Oh, good,' I murmur, trying to hitch my way back into a dream.

The light stands its ground. I can see the folds of a hospital sheet, a big bunch of flowers, a plastic water jug with a blue lid. Since I last opened my eyes, someone has ignored my need for chocolate and brought me some magazines. Dad has turned up in his vicar's jeans and home-knitted jumper. His dog collar is a wonky Möbius strip. The news must have caught him on his way somewhere.

'Is this business or pleasure?' I ask him.

'You've no need for a priest yet,' he says. 'You're going to be fine.'

'My poor sweet girl…'

Mum breaks away and comes over to hug me. She's been crying, probably since Gloucestershire. Her neat auburn bob is wisped with silver. Her eyes seem crowded with worries about what she's left untended, an oven left on, a bill not paid, as though something worse than parcel bombs might be happening elsewhere.

'You got here quick,' I say.

She looks puzzled. The last few hours don't seem to have passed quickly for her. That's the least of her troubles, though, and she blinks it away.

'Yvonne, do you understand what happened to you?'

'I don't know. Someone wants me dead?'

I sense her tender impatience. Her face has that puffed-up gleam of certain-aged womanhood. I sometimes wish age didn't have to come upon her so slowly; I wish it would do its work and move on.

'We spoke to a policeman. He said you were probably targeted for being... because of what you do. The research. You know, the animals. Apparently they were expecting that one of the groups was going to declare a new campaign. They've been tracking one lot in particular, called Aslan's Law. A really nasty militant splinter group. They think it was they who sent you the ...'

She can't say it. There's something missing from this family scene, but even if I could explain it to her, I'm not sure she'd understand.

'That makes sense. I screw up animals' brains and then laugh at them. I'm one of the people they're trying to punish.'

I look down at the burn on my arms. My body and legs feel fine. There's a buzz in me, a need to get going.

'You were lucky,' Dad says. 'The bomb seems to have been intended to scare you as much as anything.'

'I smelt gas...'

'They were trying to knock you out. That's why your injuries are only light.'

I remember the moments before the explosion, my own face looking in on itself in the oval mirror. I'm thirty, I was telling myself; old enough for this. That feeling of completeness. The voice in the hallway, urging me on.

'Who are the flowers from?'

Tiny wings flutter in my womb, zygotic echoes.

'Gillian. We didn't get a chance to talk to her. James did, though.'

'You've spoken to James?'

'It's been hard to avoid him. He's been phoning non-stop. Your dad had a long talk with him. James says it was his house you were staying at. He feels responsible, daftly enough. He's says you've got to call him when you're feeling better.'

'Did he say anything about Gareth?'

She hesitates, grappling with the facts she's been entrusted with.

'He says Gareth didn't show up when he was supposed to. He says you'll understand.'

He's heard nothing, then. Gareth will still be out there somewhere, trying to talk his way into the Echofield mines.

'Whoever Gareth is,' Dad says, 'he's not your concern right now. We're going to take you back home and get you fixed up. You can worry about Gareth later.'

By the window next to my bed, his beard and trendy vicar's jeans, the tank of his body blocking out the light. I have a sudden, vivid memory of us in my childhood lab at the vicarage, his weight creaking on the stool, the dregs of my chemistry experiments cracked and whitened in the test-tubes. I used to make myself cry, thinking about him dying. In some weird way I wanted the proof of the pain; I wanted to put my fingers in the wound, feel the huge torn-out imprint of my love.

'Who found me?'

'One of your friends. Bridget, I think she's called. She discovered you in the hallway. Thank goodness she turned up when she did.'

Of course: Bridge. I remember her taut, thin face, swimming inches from mine. I wondered if I'd dragged her down with me, whether we were fighting underwater, or whether she had dived in here to save me. *We need to know, Yvonne. We've got to find the people who did this to you.*

'Someone sent me a parcel bomb. I've got to find out why.'

'You can let the police do that. They'll catch these people.'

'How did they know where I was staying?'

'They think you must have been followed. These people are determined. It would have been pretty easy for them to track you down.'

I push myself up on my elbows and look around. The ward is empty. There was a crowd in here last time I looked. Everyone gets better, it seems. Nothing wrong with us that a good night's sleep can't fix.

'When do I get out?'

'The doctors are happy with you. You recovered consciousness quickly and you had a comfortable night. You've had a lucky escape. You can come back with us as soon as you feel ready.'

I swing my feet onto the floor and test them with my weight. The bed is firm behind me, and I can stand without holding it.

'What time do you want to go?'

'If we get an early start tomorrow we can be home by lunchtime.'

I stare up at the curtain with my one good eye, pulling the rustling plastic shut in my mind. I need to be alone with these thoughts.

'Give me a moment,' I say.

I tell them I'm going to have a bath. I go out into the corridor and call James from the card-phone. I tell him to pick me up from the hospital entrance in an hour. He sounds surprised when I explain where we're headed.

'I thought you weren't going back there. I thought you'd quit.'

'Yes, but that was before someone tried to maim me with home-made explosive. Have you heard anything? Did you know that Aslan's Law were going to start attacking people?'

'No, I didn't, Yvonne, and they're nothing to do with me. What are you going to tell your folks? They seem convinced that they're taking you back to Gloucestershire.'

'I'll think of something. I'm not going back with them. There are things I need to do.'

'Jesus, Yvonne, I'm so sorry.'

'It's not your fault. It's a risk you take, doing this kind of research. Look, they've checked into a hotel in Fulling. I've persuaded them to put their rescue mission off till tomorrow.'

'Great. I can come back to your treehouse and play doctors.'

I stand in the bathroom and pull at the neck of my nightie. There's a cut on my collarbone where I fell on the metal box. I can feel the sting of the wound on the right-hand side of my skull. I peel back the tape on my left arm and see how my skin has become a blistered smear of Pyronox. I feel different, light-headed, strangely restored. Whoever has tried to hurt me has only made me stronger. Out to destroy me, they might just have made me more the person I am.

◉

PART THREE

The Moor

CHAPTER FOURTEEN

Avatar

◉

Somehow I'm expecting to find my treehouse ransacked, the stove kicked in, all my drawers and cupboards tipped out onto the floor. But my only visitor has been the runaway chimp, McQueen, who has climbed up onto my balcony and eaten all the banana chips I left out before I went to Florida. For all I know, the security man is still roaming the forest with his rifle, his bloodlust no weaker for his now having officially changed his allegiances.

'Christ,' James says. 'You really do live in a treehouse.'

'I used to. Once I get sacked from my job I'll be living *under* a tree.'

'They won't sack an innocent victim of terrorism,' he says, dumping his rucksack on the balcony table. 'They'll let you get better first. Hey, wasn't I going to help you change that dressing?'

He stands at the rail and looks out over the distant sprawl of Sansom. I fill a hot-water bottle and lay it on the sofa in the living room. I unstick the tape on my arm and check on the glistening, meat-smelling wound. There's a message on the machine from Daren, saying that Effi was discharged yesterday and is now safely back in front of her TV at Millennium Heights. The world moves on without me. I hold the hot-water bottle to my stomach and feel the pain easing, the bloody forgetfulness of my loss.

'How are you doing?' comes his voice from outside.

I go back out onto the balcony, where he's reading something at the table. I notice the cover of my old science notebook, the moth-death crush of dried flowers under sticky-backed plastic, and my heart makes a fist.

'You could have asked…'

He frowns, not even the forethought of an apology, and keeps turning the pages of the notebook. I unearthed it at the vicarage last Christmas, and found it so grimly fascinating that I had to bring it back here with me. My fastidious teenage-girly handwriting, neat little haloes crowning the *is*. How carefully I set them down, these naïve scratchings at all the impossible questions of my childhood. I was barely into my teens when I started writing it, on holiday from my boarding school in Suffolk. A geeky, tallish thirteen-year-old, sprouting in all the awkward places, not even remotely interested in boys. Even then, curiosity was like an itch in my brain, and the only things that could scratch it were hard, bright, indisputable facts.

'*I want to understand how conscious humanity could arise from blind evolution…*'

'I wrote that a long time ago.'

He runs his finger down to the bottom of the page. 'Wait, I like this bit. *The only way of answering this question is by Science. All we have to go on is the evidence of our senses. It is thoroughly perilous to forget this lesson.*'

I'm hot. I feel like the burn on my arm is fermenting. But I can't have a shower because of the dressing they taped to me before I left the hospital. All I can do is sit down.

'You believed that, even back then?'

I can't tell if he's serious. He's worked up about something, but he won't tell me what it is, and his deflections are so scattergun that I can't even tell if it's a good thing or a bad thing that's happened. He seems to be acting this part, like he acts them all, playing hide-and-seek with the very idea of himself. It's as though he wants to show off the layers of artifice that shroud a person, to prove the trueness of the self below. If that's his game, he's wasting his time. I'm too tired to be convinced of anything.

'I still believe in it, James. It's because I believe in it that this has happened to me.'

'Sometimes you have to give up on what you've always believed in, if you know it's wrong.'

'What do you mean?'

'I mean, maybe we're not going to make any progress until you start believing in something else.'

'Stories, you mean? David Overstrand's fairy tales? Look, Gareth's life is in danger. Someone's just sent me a home-made bomb. I haven't actually got time for any more stories.'

He doesn't answer. He seems caught up in a thought, anxious about where this attack has taken things. His knowing smile has gone. Perhaps it's his own beliefs that are being threatened here, as much as mine. He looks up, squinting at the sunset further up the dale. April is carrying on where March left off: with radiant sunlight and the scent of resin blurring the air.

'Where did they find me?' I ask him.

'In the hallway, when they got back from the demo.'

'Were you there?'

'No. They'd gone on ahead. I was staying behind to film the clean-up.'

'And what time was that? How long was I lying there?'

'I don't know. What do you remember?'

I see Bridge's face again, staring into mine. The Lorenzo Circuit gets to work, knitting together its fragments of imagery. Her face coming out of the shadows and blurring in a bar of sunlight. I don't know if it happened. I don't know if I'm the same person who opened that box and exploded in pain. But the Circuit convinces me that I am, weaves the connections at the very moment I most need them. Consciousness is a confection, the fantasy of a brain obsessed with finding coherence, and I've been trained not to trust it. I remember waking up in hospital; I remember the soft slide of him into me. But maybe they were stories too.

'I can see myself opening the box. I can't believe I was so stupid. You get trained on this stuff, how to deal with suspect packages. But a bomb would have weighed something. This just seemed to be made of air. I was too out of it. Distracted ... '

The child in the hallway, crying for a way into the light.

'You can't have been expecting that, Yvonne. No way. You feel safe with us, don't you? You're one of us now.'

It's funny: I don't remember making that choice.

'Where did they take me?'

'To the Royal Infirmary.' He sounds as though he is trying to convince himself of something.

'Straightaway?'

'I don't know. Bridge called the ambulance.'

He slides the notebook down onto the table and stretches back, closing his eyes. There's something vulnerable about the gesture, this cautious determination to make himself at home. It's not arrogance, for once, but an appeal for protection. It's as though he's now ready to say sorry, but the object of his apology keeps leaping out of view. Instead he reaches down to the belt of his jeans and unbuckles it absent-mindedly, then tightens it again. His skin above his waistband is coppery in the sunset.

'We need to get going,' he says. 'You ready?'

'I just got out of hospital ... '

'You're fine. The doctors wouldn't have discharged you if they didn't think you were fit to go.'

'I don't know if you've noticed, James, but somebody's already trying to kill me.'

'They're trying to scare you. If they were trying to kill you you wouldn't have just walked out of hospital. The police said it was twenty-five grammes. That's tiny. That's why the package was so light. It seems to have released some kind of gas which knocked you out. They want you to promise never to work with animals again. They don't want a dead vivisectionist. They just want a retired one.'

'Why are they attacking me now? I've been working with animals my whole career. Nothing like this has ever happened before.'

'Well, maybe things have finally caught up with you.'

His fingers make a tense claw on the corner of the notebook. He flips it up and grins at the dried-flower pattern on the cover. I want to believe that this nonchalance is all a show, a sign of how much he's been scared by this. But I'm not sure. I can't make sense of him today.

'I need to go online. I've got to find out who did this to me ... '

My FireBook clicks out of sleep. The lilac interface of Des✶re blooms from the dock. He reaches across and pushes the laptop shut.

'No, Yvonne. You're not going to learn anything from a networking game. Trading webcams with your secret admirers is not going to tell you who sent you that bomb, any more than it's going to help you to find Gaz. When he vanishes, he really vanishes. He's done it before. We've got to work this out for ourselves now. You have to try and remember what he said to you.'

'I've told you. He didn't say anything.'

'He must have said something. You're the only person he trusts. You're the only one who's got the information we need to find him.'

Memory again, overpowering me in a flood. Gareth in the shell of the

Memory Centre, staring up through the girders at life forms that could not be seen. Wishing the birds into existence.

'He wants to stimulate people's memory. He's got some idea that it's the secret of human happiness. He's interested in the technology that Sansom have been working on. I just wish I could see how it fits together...'

'OK, so we have to get into the mines. Find out what this technology is that he's talking about. We have to go down there and see for ourselves what's going on. That's the only way we're going to find Gareth.'

'Why can't we just go to the police?'

'And tell them what? The bit about you helping Gaz to lay a sniffer on the Lycee's top-secret system? Or the bit about you rolling up to Sansom in the dead of night and trying to persuade their security men that you're royalty?'

I catch him looking at the Chinese amulet. I haven't taken it off since he gave it to me, the night before everything changed.

'Why are you being like this?'

'I'm not being like anything. I'm the way I am.'

'You're the way you choose to be.'

He stares out at the ruins of the sky. There's a bruised looseness under his eyes, signs of sleeplessness. Sometimes he has the face of a hassled executive, a kind of clammy, bloated frazzlement. I wonder what happened to the face he deserves.

'Things happened to me. They shaped the way I am. The way I *am*, not the way I choose to be.'

'Your true self?'

'Yeah. OK.'

'Is this about David?'

He sighs. 'Everything is about David.'

'Can you tell me about it? Those things that shaped you? Your story?'

He yawns. 'What do *you* think?'

That haunted look. It's as though the things that have hurt him were re-running their effects on his face, like those time-lapse photographs where someone speeds towards death in front of your eyes.

'You told David.'

'David told me. *I* didn't know what this Bankstown Underpass stuff was all about. I needed him to see it.'

'What happened at Bankstown Underpass?'

'Everything.'

'What kind of everything?'

I give him a moment, hoping that he'll snap back into this reality we used to share. He gets up suddenly, tossing the notebook onto the table.

'Where are you going?'

'I'm going down to the Peer Review. See if anyone wants to get steaming.'

He doesn't know the code. He stands at the door, waiting, till I go over and key in the unfunny joke of Mateus' birth-date. Even with the stairwell open in front of him, he doesn't move.

'Your problem, Yvonne, is that you can only work at one level of explanation. The rational mind is always trying to take things to pieces and find evidence of its own works. The heart watches, and laughs.'

'So observed David Overstrand?'

'Exactly.'

He stares into the depth of the stairwell and sways forward alarmingly. You'd think his body was just a way of getting down there, out of here, like a weight a diver might throw to drag himself to record-breaking depths. He puts one hand up on the frame of the door and starts to descend the rough larch steps. At the first landing he pauses briefly, and I think he's going to throw a glance back at me. But if he did he'd see nothing but the daylight at the top of the stairs. I'm gone, invisible, the floor the lift doesn't stop at. Whatever he struggled with at Bankstown Underpass, he'll have to deal with it alone.

There's a myth about Des*re. When you reach a certain level of connectivity, the experience changes. The blocky, low-res interface of a computer game is lifted away. The virtual takes on the shimmer of the real. It's a moment of intense, vertiginous consciousness, the boost of hereness and nowness that can finally link up all your disconnected moments. I always thought it would happen gradually: a slow awaken-ing, the faders of sensation creeping up so minutely that you don't even notice the reality you're coming round to. But this is nothing like what I knew before. I've made it through to the next level, and it's a different world.

There's no interface, for a start. No lilac banner, no welcome page. As soon as I'm logged on I'm actually there, impossibly in the scene. Somewhere in the hyperlinked world I'm standing in a wet car park on a dreary afternoon. A squally breeze is blowing across the asphalt. I recognise the domed austerity of Sansom's European headquarters, the lights of the atrium with the insect-black figures of the guards inside. Behind it is the lift housing that Gareth showed me on the camcorder. There's a red sports car, parked with its passenger door ajar.

`Try your cursor keys.`

The message scrolls up at the bottom of the screen. This hunch that he's out there. Now. Online.

I press on the forward arrow. The car comes closer. Surprised at this new responsiveness, I edge forward again. This shouldn't be happening, but somehow I'm moving through the scene. My visual field is no longer tied to fixed surveillance-cam angles. I've become a hand-held consciousness, controlled by cursor keys. Is there someone out there too, a robot Yvonne whose eyes I'm seeing through? Some kick of rationality wants to deny that this is possible, and yet it's happening: I'm walking towards the car and angling in towards the open door. Beads of rain glisten on the smooth metal of the roof. Inside there's the silhouette of a man.

`Get in.`

I cursor forward some more. I reach into the drawer, pull out my virtual lights and tug them carefully over my ears. There's a moment of blankness while the lights connect wirelessly, and then I'm back inside this startling new vividness. In another nudge of the cursor, I'm in the passenger seat of the car. Next to me, with his hands resting on the wheel, is Gareth. He's sitting, staring out at the building with an ironic, movie-star squint. He's an avatar, his features smoothed out by computer graphics. Half man, half cartoon. But it's him.

`You took your time.`

A bored elevator-voice repeats his words back at me through the rain.

`You didn't make it easy for me,` I type. `Where are you?`

`Come on, Miss. You don't really think I'm going to trust that information to an internet connection?`

The goggles are like a vice behind my ears. I push my fingers up under the arms and feel the pressure ease on my temples.

You're in danger. You have to help us to find you.

I've already told you, Miss. I've told you everything I know.

I wait for him to look at me, but the lights of Sansom have him
hypnotised.

Is this safe? I thought you were trying to hide
away.

Don't worry. We're not in the real world. They can't
find us here.

I look over at the guards in the atrium. They don't seem to have
noticed the people in the parked car.

How have you done this?

I haven't done it. *You've* done it. We're in a
scene from your memory, Miss. You're telling this
story, not me.

He looks at me through the gloom. His eyes are blue and shining.

Really? Since when could you hack into my memory?

I always said I'd turn up when you were least
expecting it. You have to go and find the Saxons.
They'll show you how to get down there. Without anyone noticing, that is.

Into the mines? Have you been there?

I'm in too much danger. They're making things very
difficult for me. They're ruthless. I turned down
their money, and that made them angry. I need you to
do this for me. I think I know what they're doing,
but we've got to know for sure.

And then you'll tell me where you are?

You'll know. If you've understood any of this.

He reaches forward and twiddles the dial of the radio. There's music,
something sawn, something set gently ringing.

You were hoping I'd have guessed already?

You need more help. You've got to prove to me that
you remember what I told you.

You didn't tell me anything, Gareth.

He looks at me. I've taken a risk in typing his name. His raytraced eyes have thickened into two fat exclamation marks. Then the blueness returns, and he gives a slow digital smile.

Listen, I have to go. Send me a signal when you've worked it out. Change your icon. I've told you everything. I let you into a secret no one else could understand. Not James, not anyone. And now I need you to show me that you care about that. I've done my bit, Miss. The rest is up to you.

CHAPTER FIFTEEN

The Saxon Kingdom

◎

I wake up crying. Sunlight answers, tells me I haven't been to bed. It picks out the scalloping of my laptop keys, skids off the white ceramic of the stove. Reality is here now, and it disappoints. The wallscreen is winter-pale. The sleep light on my FireBook pulses gently. This body I'm stashed in feels soft and heavy, yet somehow veined with fire. It is an awakening so intimate and reliable that I can't ignore its message: I've been dreaming. What I saw back there was all vivid distraction. There's no getting back to it, knowing what I know.

James is on the balcony, composing messages on his phone.

'Sleepyhead...'

In my dream, Gareth was not Gareth any more. The form he'd left behind was a magnificent long-necked bird, purple plumage soaked black with rain. I held its beautiful curved head and cried for its strangeness, its shabby iridescence. It was a joke played on nature, a proof of what could not survive.

'It was Gareth,' I tell him.

James stands in the doorway, uncertain about entering this aftermath.

'What was Gareth?'

'I've found him,' I say.

The connection timed out hours ago. The lilac banner flickers across the wall of my living room, awaiting my username and password.

'You had a rough night,' he says.

'Where were you?'

'I went for a long walk. Just me, my self, and this atmosphere there is between us. It was pretty illuminating.'

I ease the virtual lights down over my ears and hit LOGON. The galaxy of people I've been trading with flickers up in front of me. There's nothing new, no friendly icon sparking recognition. I follow the warmest links, the paths I've trodden most recently. There's a cam of the West Gate of Sansom, where the Conscience protestors gather on Saturday mornings. The dome of the main building is a distant smear. I try to move towards it, like I was moving last night, but the cursor keys are dead. The surge of memory that first tipped me over into that new consciousness has faded back to nothing. I'm back where I started: a newcomer, dreaming of what lies beyond.

'So where did you get to? On your long walk?'

He sighs. 'Bankstown Underpass, as usual.'

'You walked a long way. Bankstown Underpass is in Pelton.'

'No,' he says, touching his chest. 'It's in here.'

I take the lights off and look up at him. I'm touched by how he can cling on to sincerity, push himself beyond self-consciousness through sheer force of will. He really believes in what David Overstrand has taught him, and it's a belief he wants to shout about. I can argue about his grounds, but that's all.

'So this true self of yours. Is it still a crazy mixed-up kid?'

He sits down on the other sofa and looks at what he has thumbed into his phone.

'I had a good look at it. I didn't like what I saw. I saw something way down, underneath all the layers of fear and pretence, a fact about me which is absolutely true. I can't let anyone else see it. But I can't hide it, so I have to push people away.'

He's trying to say sorry. Whatever happened to him at Bankstown Underpass, I'm going to have to wait until he's ready to tell me. If you ask me, it's so much simpler being an empty network of connections. You can save yourself so much heartache.

'Come here,' I say.

But it's me who's moving. I snib the FireBook shut and go over to where he's sitting. There's a funny plumpness in his white, unshaven cheeks, the ghost of puppy fat. A bitter, disappointed frown. He takes my hands and holds them, not looking at me but cellularly aware of me, stricken by my closeness. He opens his thighs, thick inside his jeans, and I move in between them and wait for him to bring me into this, give up whatever it is he's circling around.

'Are you pushing *me* away?' I ask him.

'We all hurt the ones we care for most, Yvonne.'

'Are you trying to tell me that you care for me?'

I touch the amulet on my chest, just to give him the courage to look at me.

'That I love you,' his quiet voice says.

The amazing hangover cure of hills in sunlight.

We're in Grandstand's car, high on the ridge that runs under Torn Cloud. James hasn't been out of third since we left Scarf, half an hour ago. What we've left behind is now below us as well. To the south and left, the land drops steeply towards the coal-bright Churl, the lush grasslands of the river plain. To the right it's sheer rock, opportunistic grasses, protective netting that's torn and useless against an endless drift of scree. Long-haired sheep with shitty dags drift across the road between bristly pads of turf. If you looked back now you'd see the forest spread across one wall of the valley, with the plasma-gleam of Sansom in the far distance. Today you can see all the way to the spires of Fulling.

'Gaz wants us to go into the mines. He says he needs us to see what they're doing down there. He said we should talk to the Saxons to find out how to get down there without anyone noticing. So that's where we're going.'

He loves me. He said he loves me.

The road levels out onto high moorland, crumbling to asphalt gravel at its edges. Pipe-cleaner lambs spring away from under our heels. Their mothers stare, desolate. The road tips away into a shallower valley, lined with faded rugs of purple-brown heather. Curlews rise as we pass. At a bend in the road below us, a sealed track splits away towards a modern one-storey building set apart from a group of thatched huts. A few tourist buses nuzzle in at the end of an empty car park. A steady breeze sweeps wood smoke from the scene.

'The Saxons?'

'Welcome to the ancient Kingdom of Esha,' he says.

*

The girl on the turnstile seems to know him.

'Brunhild,' he barks. 'Do you wear pants under that?'

She tugs at the bit of sackcloth she's dressed in and fakes a smile.

'Get lost,' she says. 'It's closing time.'

Her voice has a buzzy looseness to it. She's small, blush-flecked, with a tender, bruisy colouring. I wouldn't have thought she was James' type. She stares at the dressing on my arm, probably wondering the same thing.

'How's uni?' she says, pressing the button to let us through.

'Jacked it in. Couldn't stand the teachers.'

He squeezes my hand secretly and pushes me forward onto the approach path. The sunlight hits me like laughter.

'Brunhild used to work in a call centre. Found the people a bit too modern.'

We cross a drawbridge over a moat and climb to the top of a ring of earthworks. From the rampart you can see the reconstruction of a Saxon farm, dotted with livestock specially bred for authenticity. Everything looks windswept, battened-down. I'd want to be battened down up here. I count five thatched huts, outhouses to the larger hall in the middle. Beyond them are the watchtowers of a Saxon fort. Cagouled time travellers are wandering from one numbered feature to the next, listening to the commentary on rented headphones. Brash modern children are petting eighth-century ducklings. Some Korean students are being taught to operate longbows by a thegn in a leather tunic. To the left of the fort, a boarded-up area leaks the sounds of construction.

At the doorway to the Great Hall, a blond-bearded Saxon is talking to a tourist in a faded red anorak. The Saxon sounds Australian. He tells the tourist that his name is Aelfric, that he lives here with his wife and daughters, and that he is the thegn of this burgh. He recognises James and waves us inside. After the sunlight the gloom is blinding. Aelfric is just a voice.

'Fucking prick,' he says to the anorak receding into daylight. 'Of course Aelfric's a Saxon name.'

'But you're from Coff's Harbour,' James says. 'That's what he was quibbling.'

The Saxon's dark-adapting eyes pick out the dressing on my arm.

'You've met with the Norsemen, my child.'

'Aslan's Law,' James says. 'I reckon she got off lightly. Have you heard anything?'

The Saxon shakes his head.

'They were making noises about starting a new campaign. Looks like you were an unlucky bystander.'

He grins. It's stifling in here. My burnt arm is a salty, blistered agony.

'Come over to IT Support,' he tells James. 'They've got information for you.'

He leads us through a low doorway at the back of the hut and across a paddock scattered with straw. The sound of hammering echoes across the valley.

'Making your schedule?' James asks, looking across at the taped-up construction site.

'We don't do schedules. We finish it when it's ready.'

Another busload of visitors is queueing to get past the security checks at the entrance to the Fort. With the thegn of the burgh leading us, we're waved through. Inside it's cinema-dark, blue with VR ghosts. Full-sized holograms of instances of the Saxon populace move slowly through a dry-ice mist, rehearsing their tasks in perfect historical detail. Several VR booths have schoolkids enthralled behind virtual lights. A display describes the harsh realities of life in Saxon Northumbria. There's a showcase of real-life treasures from the original eighth-century burgh. Some kids are engrossed in a themed Des✶re play via a link-up to another faux-Saxon community in Germany. After the Sansom car park, it looks dull.

Aelfric taps a code into a door at the back. Beyond it there's a dim stairwell, a narrow descent. At the bottom of the stairs is another doorway. A casing mounted to the woodwork holds an old cathode-ray tube, scribbled on in wipeable pen. *Back in a Viking's heartbeat*, the message says. We wait. Saxon time drags on. Aelfric has to go and see a man about a horse.

'He was here,' says the Saxon in the chain-mail vest. 'He wanted to know where all the shafts were. He looked pretty serious about getting down there.'

The basement buzzes with tube-light. A shoal of delicate blue fish circles around a fish tank constructed from a gutted iMac. The Saxon's face is arctic, leonine, grooved with deep folds and framed with premature white.

'He didn't manage it,' James says. 'Too many people trying to hurt him.'

'How did he seem?' I ask the Saxon.

'Exhausted. He'd walked here from the twenty-first century.'

'When was this?'

'A couple of weeks ago.'

James sits down on a chair woven from the tails of computer mice. 'So it must have been before the news about the data broke. I think that means he could be anywhere.'

'Why do you think he's in danger?' the Saxon asks.

'He's got something other people want. People who don't ask nicely.'

'He was known to us. He was here last year, wanting to know where he could pick up several thousand second-hand laptops. He wanted to connect them all up. Get them talking to each other at the same time. Kept saying something about the possibility of an artificial consciousness...'

'That sounds like Gaz,' James says.

The Saxon looks mournful. I can see that his chain mail is woven of thousands of electronic components: brightly ringed resistors, thick blue-and-white capacitors, the tiny grey leaf-buds of old-style transistors.

'Did he look as if anyone had tried to hurt him?'

'He was walking with a limp. Could have twisted it in a badger hole. He'd walked a long way.'

The Saxon goes over to his workbench and comes back with a bright thread pincered between finger and thumb. It's a bracelet. He's taken the beads from scores of disused optical drives and soldered them together on a chain of blue and green resistors. It's beautiful. He takes my hand and fastens the bracelet around the bit of pale skin between my dressing and the back of my hand. I can feel his quiet satisfaction.

'Where are our cathedrals?' the Saxon says. 'They gave us football stadiums. Retail pavilions.'

'Go on,' I can hear James urging him. 'Show her.'

At the far end of the basement are some wooden steps leading up to a hatch door. Outside, the sun is setting over the half-finished shell of a Saxon church. We climb over a nave wall made of polyurethane CPU housings, Dells and Compaqs and Packard Bells, glued and bolted onto a framework of server-cabinet girders. The banging I heard earlier was the sound of circuit boards being smashed with a hammer. On the nave floor, a girl in a hair shirt is sorting the fragments and adding them to a huge floor-mosaic depicting the Passion of Christ. Shards of printed circuitry craze in the beery evening light. The face they've made for the Christ figure reminds me of something, an obscure benevolence, a connection I can only grasp at. I feel a dull ache, the memory of a not-happy, not-sad childhood.

'Yvonne? Are you OK?'

I finger the warm metal of the amulet, grateful for its intimate weight, the feel of its solidity amid this dizzying strangeness. There's something loose on the top of it, like the winder of a watch, and I realise that I'm twiddling it nervously, hanging on the routine of it. From my stand-point in the nave, I can see someone soldering microchips onto a rood screen made of upright nineteen-inch racks. A weaver is making an altar cloth from coloured cables, the veins and arteries of thousands of obsolete machines. The facts are known to me before I can even process them. It seems impossible, but this place is not new to me. Then another memory comes in, and I'm powerfully conscious that I am alive in this moment, as though a lens were turning and bringing everything into focus, lifting me into clarity. Dad, in the doorway of my childhood lab, talking to me about science and faith. That warm, agonising premonition of him dying. Suddenly my legs won't hold me any more.

'Should she be doing this?' the Saxon is saying. 'There's no shelter up there.'

The warning snaps me back. 'I'm OK. I'm fine.'

The tourists have gone. The Saxon Kingdom winds down. In the lee of the half-built church, people in rough jerkins are making prepara-tions for a feast. A pig turns slowly above a pit of charcoal.

'Did Gareth see this?' I ask.

The basement Saxon nods, his concern turning slowly to satisfaction.

'He had an eye for crazy dreams. He was desperate to know what they were doing down there. Go down there and find your destiny: it's up to you. First you need to find the Broken Twins. You can stay here tonight and get going in the morning. It's a day's journey across the top.'

'By car?'

He smiles and points to his leather-strapped feet.

'Welcome to the Dark Ages, baby.'

CHAPTER SIXTEEN

Whole-World Window

◉

Up here, the view is hills within hills. From this first rise your brain is stretched by nested horizons, purple-brown landscapes fanned out across a clear midday sky. Ten miles away, as sure as geometry, there's a valley floor and an old drover's hut by a burn. Make yourselves at home, the Saxons said; you'll be in the mines tomorrow afternoon. We've brought sleeping bags, a primus, some dry pasta and a chunk of cold pig roast wrapped in computer foil. James and I lug it all, plus the mining gear we borrowed from Aelfric, in a couple of rucksacks our bodies hardly feel. We're high on sleep and sunshine and the whole-body aftermath of a night of starry love. The Pennine permagale has dropped to a heathery breeze. In weather like this you could trust the land, give yourself to its slopes like a ball on a pinball machine, and let its massive embedded energies pull you down along lines of least resistance, placing your feet for you, making decisions that you thought would be your own.

'Tell me about David,' I say.

He stops, scanning distant layers of haze.

'David gave me this …'

'Really?' I follow his gaze over the treeless scene. 'I always thought it was four billion years of planetary cooling.'

'He didn't *make* the world. He showed me how to see it.'

'He was your god?'

He denies it impatiently. 'Gods aren't human beings. The thing that blew you away about David was his humanity. He had so much compassion. He filled us with love.'

'I know who to thank, then.'

The wind mutters in our ears. I remember how he found me, in the light of the Saxons' fire. Just the two of us, prickling with the static of sleeping bags, tipsy and joyous under a star-creamed moorland sky.

'Get one thing straight, Yvonne. The guy with the insatiable lust for you: that was me.'

I laugh, showing my true vicar's-daughter colours. I know he's putting it on, trying to shock me. Perhaps this too will turn out to be a pretence, like the Fred Flintstone mask he used to wear to tutorials, or his offended denial that he was ever a Conscience activist. Or maybe his love of play-acting is part of something more interesting, a genuine vulnerability that will betray itself in a million slow ways. As he starts laying out the threads of another story, I realise that he's proving me right. It's not what's beneath the layers, it's the fact that the layers are there at all. He's like me, in that respect. The layers are what he is.

'David told me I needed to see the big picture. He said I was like a man trying to read a book one letter at a time. I was puzzling over these individual shapes and wondering why they didn't make any sense. The first thing I had to do was stand back and read the whole page. When I'd done that, I could put the story together.'

'What if we haven't got a story, though, James? What if we're just molecules?'

'We see the world in different ways, babe. You're a materialist. You want to believe that there's nothing more to us than networks of nerve cells. But if you want to do that, you've got to explain how you're going to live your life. Where does your moral sense come from? What are you going to do about love, and compassion, and humanity? Or are they just molecules as well?'

'I don't believe that because I *want* to believe it. I've got no choice. I believe it because the evidence proves it.'

'Your "evidence" is a fairy tale, Yvonne. There's a deeper truth about this world of ours, if you only want to let yourself see it.'

I'm trying to rise above this, but still it's getting to me. 'You might not have noticed, James, but my evidence matches up with the way things actually are.'

He sets off up the slope, strenuously dismissing me. 'There is no "way things are". There are just people who get attached to their stories.'

'So what are you, then? A storyteller, like David?'

'I'm somebody who's looking for the truth about himself. Things have happened to make me the way I am. That's what I've got to try to understand.'

'That's Freudian mumbo-jumbo, James. You can't reduce me to what happened to me as a child. You can't rewind a tape and show me where each little bit of my character was formed. I'm so much more than that, and I'm so much *less* than that.'

'I'm not trying to reduce you to anything. I'm trying to show you the truth about yourself.'

'So you know the truth about me, do you?'

'I know you're hiding behind a whole lot of masks. I know you're trying to find the answer in science, because of things that have happened to you.'

'What are you talking about?'

'You became a scientist because your dad gave up on science. He was a vet first, wasn't he? When he became a vicar you felt betrayed. He wasn't talking to the animals any more, so you thought you should.'

'That's such crap, James. You don't know the first thing about me.'

'Sometimes we're blind to our own stories. We don't even know that we're telling them. Listen, your science is telling you the same thing. That network in the brain that you're obsessed about? The Lorenzo Circuit. You told us it's constantly spinning new stories out of the bits of information it's got stored away. I sat there in your office and I wrote that down. Our brains are at it all the time, making order out of chaos, stitching together patterns of meaning. All those different bits of the brain working in synchrony, knitting it all together. I don't know, maybe that's what Gaz has got obsessed about as well. Maybe that's why he thinks you're the only person who can help him.'

Suddenly I'm back in the lab, with Gareth's cortex projected onto the twilight in front of me. Again, this queasy sense that I'm recalling things I haven't yet lived through, that I am no longer the facts I thought I remembered. The Lorenzo Circuit spins its web.

'Anyway, that's what David was trying to show us. We're blind to our own stories. We need someone else to help us to see them. That's what we never finished. He had to leave us, just as I was starting to get there.'

'And your story is Bankstown Underpass? Something happened there that changed the way you are, for ever?'

He stops, hugging himself inside his fleece.

'I nearly died there. In a way, I *did* die.'

'You look pretty alive to me.'

166

He sighs a deep breath onto the breeze. A mile to the north, two huge Chinook helicopters swing low over the valley, heavy gods on the move.

'David used to say to me, Bankstown Underpass, you can't get bigger than this. You can't get bigger than your own story.'

'Bankstown Underpass? Is that what he called you?'

He narrows his eyes, as though the thought were causing him pain. 'We all had names. It was part of the way we tried to make ourselves real to each other. Except David. He was always just himself.'

We sit down on a rock to spare our knees. Our rucksacks stand back to back on the hillside, reluctant duellers. I hold my head in my hands and feel this weight I'm carrying, the heft of myself.

'But why all parts of the city? Bankstown Underpass, Grandstand...'

'Because they're the places where David found us.'

'I don't get it.'

He starts picking at a clump of heather, stripping the brown flower-buds with his fingers.

'You remember the woman on the Half-Span Bridge? So thin that she could have dropped through the railings like a set of car keys...?'

Now I see it, in all its obvious colour.

'Bridge isn't short for Bridget, is it? It's short for Half-Span Bridge.'

He looks disappointed that it's taken me so long to make the connection. 'Her real name's Stephanie. Needless to say, she hates her real name.'

'And when David found her... she was really about to throw herself off?'

He shrugs. 'That makes it sound pretty dramatic. But that's Bridge. She's a drama queen. David talked her out of it. He worked out what was happening for her, and he made her see it.'

'And the others?'

'They all needed him. He found them when they were at their weakest, and he didn't let them down. Level Ten was at the top of the Byggate multi-storey. Grandstand was at the stadium.'

I think of the faces I know from the squat. If what James is saying is true, they came close to not being there at all.

'So that's what your storytelling game is all about? Celebrating the fact that you'd been saved?'

'We never wanted to forget what David had given us. We'd been blessed. Skipped the fake brain doctors and their happiness drugs. We'd had a lucky escape.'

'Isn't it a bit creepy that you rejoice in it like that? All the myth-making, the storytelling: isn't it a bit weird?'

'It's our truth, Yvonne. David saved us by showing us our own stories. That's why I sent you the soundpod. Because I wanted David to save you too.'

I remember the child's trike in the back yard.

'What was he like? There aren't any pictures of him at the squat.'

'David didn't believe in cameras. He didn't want us living our lives through a viewfinder. He wanted to show us the world as it really is. Anyway, we remember him in our stories. He had such an amazing presence. He had this aura; you always knew when he was in a room. Trying to take a photograph of him would have been like pointing a camera at the sun.'

'You're talking about him as though he's dead. He is coming back, isn't he?'

The view blurs up with mist. I don't know if we've climbed up into the cloud or if the cloud, tired of flight, has sunk down onto us. We sat down here in bright sunshine, but now the air is vaporous and grey. You remember how the land can catch you out, send your thoughts twittering off in one direction and then say: look, fool, the truth is over here. How it can even get you doubting your own memory of the sunshine, of ever having believed that there was a star out there.

'I don't know. We hear rumours, stories of sightings, but no one really knows. He was trying to stop a dam being built in India. He'd got into Tibet and was trying to blow the fascists apart. He moves among the people who believe in him. No one else can see him. There's not one thing you can say about him that won't be contradicted by someone else. He's become his own shadow, and that makes him hard to find. We just have to stay here, and keep believing. Wherever David is, he's a long way away.'

*

Then the sky suddenly opens and you're higher than you ever thought possible, and the land ahead of you becomes the land below you, shining with the green-hued opulence of sunlight on rain. The river, the furrow it ploughs through the hillside, the tiny ruin of the drover's hut detailed in broken lumps of sandstone, like an abandoned game of mah-jong. And a sob in your throat that this beauty could have crept up on you like this, that you watched for it at every possible entrance and yet never saw it coming, it's had you, you've been caught out again.

It's pushing night by the time we reach the hut. All that's left of the sunset is a lemony afterglow, a layer of clear spirit under the night. The earth has shape again, contours you can get your bearings by, black solidity. Behind us, the fellside we've climbed down is roofed by girders of cloud. Under our torchlight the hut is psychoactively vivid. Going in there is a battle of curiosity and disgust, as compelling as a roadkill. Actually, it feels quite homely. The roof has been shucked off in slabs of broken pantile, but the half that remains is shelter enough. Whoever was here last has even left a pile of firewood, which James quickly gets going. I watch him crouch by the newborn flame, feeding it scraps: prehistoric man at his life-or-death task. I want to ask more about David, but this secret of his is so big, such a huge dead-weight of fact, that manoeuvring it into an attackable position is more than I have strength for. When I go outside for more firewood I see lights on the other side of the valley, several miles away, maybe lampers looking for rabbits. They're a long way out to be lamping. I wait for the gunshots but there's only the spook-show of owl-talk, the cluck of burn-water on rocks. I watch the flickering lights for a while, eventually judging that they're moving away from us, with the jerky pace of human walking. We got this far without seeing a soul. It never occurred to me that we might not be alone up here.

When I go back inside the fire is blazing. James is still crouching, his arms outstretched for balance, the hood of his fleece pulled up around his face. He stares into the flame with a kind of flustered intent, as though he'd only built this thing to hypnotise himself, and the magic wasn't working. Or maybe it's just another way of shutting me out, another party I'm not invited to.

'What happened at Bankstown Underpass?'

'I walked out into the traffic. I was seventeen years old. David was there, watching. It's like he knew it was going to happen. He healed me. He made me understand why I'd done it. Why I had tried to do it, and also why I had failed.'

He's laid our sleeping bags out under the bit of roof. I go over to mine and sit down.

'And now you feel like you owe him everything?'

'Of course I do. But I can't repay that debt. Other people keep getting in the way.'

'What others?'

Then I realise. He's still thinking about his friends. Bridge, Grandstand, Level Ten. They're the only others that matter.

'I've been watching them, Yvonne. I've seen what motivates them. I've seen why they're doing this, and it's not for the reasons it was supposed to be. This was meant to be about me and David. It wasn't meant to be about them.'

'I don't get it. This afternoon you told me that you were all in this together. Bonded by what David meant to you.'

He shakes his head, mourning a reality in which that might have been true.

'I told you part of it. The whole thing is more complicated.'

'Try me.'

He scrapes at the dirt floor with a piece of bark, and then flicks it into the fire.

'David gave us tasks. Things we had to try and achieve while he was away. The Atrocity Exhibition. The campaign against Sansom. That's what we were supposed to be focusing on. But we've been getting distracted. Level Ten has been trying to sell a book made out of our games. Bridge has been talking to TV people, for God's sake. They're making a lot of noise, but it's the wrong kind of noise. When David gets back ... I don't want to think about that.'

'Have you told them this?'

'While you were in Florida. We had a ... situation. A frank exchange of views. I didn't like what I heard, and I told them so. It's over. I'm not going back there. I'm finished with them.'

I stare at his hunched-up form, trying to judge this new information. I remember the phone call I overheard in the bathroom the other night. It didn't sound like an argument, but it could have been the aftermath of one. Sometimes, when I see him together with them, he has the appeasing smile of an unwilling participant, caught up in something out of habit or a greater dedication. Now I can see the extent of what he has been trying to hide. I can't say that it disappoints me. I've always hated the thought of the hold they have over him. While someone else has got him, he can't be completely mine.

'What about *your* tasks? The things that matter to you?'

'I can't make them happen without David. I realise that now. I haven't got the fire in me that he had. There are moments when I look around and I doubt everything.'

'Everything? Including me?'

He puffs out contempt. 'What are you? Just another story I tell myself.'

'So what can you rely on, then? Bankstown Underpass? Isn't that just another story?'

'It's the truth that makes the stories true.'

I'm irritated now. 'You know, *I* think there's a truth that makes the stories true. The difference is that I go out and try and prove it.'

'Yvonne.' He's quieter now, as though my anger were the excuse he needed to cool his own. 'You doubt your own existence. The continuity of your own self. You've read some stuff about diffuse neuronal systems and now you don't even think there's a person called Yvonne Churcher.'

'But I don't doubt her nervous system. I don't doubt that she's made of chemicals and blood vessels and a heart and some fucking painful *burns* …'

He swings around on his heels. His two-day-old stubble glints silverishly in the firelight.

'Is that it? Is that what your faith amounts to?'

'It's not faith, James. I don't need a faith. I look for evidence. *Then* I believe.'

'Sure,' he says. 'The evidence of a few tortured monkeys. I'll stick with the mumbo-jumbo.'

The gash on my scalp is stinging. I put my hands up and clasp my neck from behind, pulling my elbows forward till they touch, blocking out the fire, James, everything. My own private gesture of doubt.

When I look up again, James is crying.

I touch his cheek in the firelight and he flinches, caught out by his own irritability. What a soft-triggered gadget is a man. Always wired for action, reacting to an imagined threat, even if it's just the comforting hand of a girl. I pull him into me, feel his head surge up against my ribcage, signalling an intent, if only to show that we're equals in this. We kiss. He tastes of tears and cigarettes. I break off and start unbuttoning his shirt, aware that I'm being rough with him, dimly convinced that I can manhandle him out of his grief. I yank at his jeans and his full cock twitches up into view. I trace its taut underseam with a finger, a line of frail abalone. Now listen. In the silence of the hut you can actually hear it pulsing, retwitching up into hardness with an infinitesimal kissing sound. I open my mouth and swallow it whole. It tastes like a lost part of you, something you thought you could never live without, as salty and tragic as a missing tooth.

We go up and we go down. We scale a peak and find it's only a sub-peak, the start of something bigger. There's a straight path to the sky, and then the horizon turns into another embedded hillside, the pattern within the pattern. The air is clear, the sky rigged with fake azure, and the feeling is one of total abandonment, of being lost on top of the world. The Saxons' map seems more and more irrelevant. By noon on the second day we've reached Mickelhope Ridge. The forest they told us about is supposed to be visible from here. But all we can see is moorland, abandoned stonework, an occasional white farmhouse hinting at human occupancy, like a star you know to be a sun, but whose glow never reaches you, never quite confirms your faith in its warmth.

'There's a road,' I say, eyes watery with wind. 'It must be five miles away.'

He checks the map again. They've scratched it with a goose quill on a sheet of rolled-up cartridge paper, and he's fed up with having to furl and unfurl it all the time.

'They haven't marked any roads. Not even the one we drove down.'

I look over his shoulder at the map. The Kingdom of Esha stands in splendid isolation. There's no access road, nothing to drive along in any direction. A showy medieval banner in the top right-hand corner states Here Be Dragons.

'You know what this is,' he says, wiping a hand impatiently over his hair. 'It's a Saxon map. It's how this place looked in the eighth century.'

The forest, the one we should have come across by now, has been etched on in a wide cloud formation, detailed with neatly individuated trees. We've tried the GPS on his ancient phone, but the tiny screen shows nothing but fields of brown heather. And I left my own phone behind in Florida.

'But then again, unless we find the forest we won't find this stupid Broken Twins thing. Which means Sansom get to Gaz before we do.'

He crumples the map and tosses it westwards, or possibly southwards, into the heather. A curlew whirrs up without a cry.

'They were right about the hut,' I say.

'We found *a* hut. Surely not the only drover's hut on Mickelhope Moor.'

He stands there, tasting something he's not sure about. Maybe it's the total emptiness of this horizon.

'You don't think we should go back? I could go online. Try to get back into the car park. See if he's still there.'

'Yvonne, Gaz has gone missing in the real world. You don't think he's actually going to be sitting in some computer game version of the Sansom car park, waiting for you?'

'It was different. I got through onto a totally new level. I could move. I could see him.'

'You dreamed that stuff, Yvonne. You fell asleep on the sofa. The whole point of Des✳re is that it's reality-based. You're hooked into a network of fixed webcams. You've got people sending you bits of their lives: home movies, messages, scenes they want you to see. That's fun, because real people can appear in the game and truth blurs into fiction and all the rest of it. And it's self-regulating, so you don't need game-masters or a wizardry. But it can only go so far.'

He reaches for me, putting his arms round me from behind. He's gentle, knowing where my wounds are. I feel him reaching for the amulet and fingering it uncertainly, twiddling the knob at its ear, winding it up and then letting the spring uncoil between his fingers, as though he were trying to work out some detail of its mechanism. I lean back into him, wanting him but wishing I didn't, wishing this could be simpler.

'You weren't there. You didn't see it.'

'Your dreams are your own business, babe. He sent you some really good graphics. You saw a bird with amazing feathers. He did it all on the computer. He's playing with you. He's fucking with your mind.'

'He was talking to me. If I could just keep him talking, he might tell us where he is.'

'He's *not* going to tell you where he is.' He drops the amulet and pulls away. 'Don't you understand? He's a hacker. He's going to be paranoid about any internet connection. As far as he's concerned, he's already told you everything he's going to tell you. It's up to you now to put it all together.'

'So why can't he just give me a clue? Whatever it is I'm supposed to be remembering, it's not happening.'

'He *is* giving you a clue. He's just doing it as quietly as he can.'

It's one thing getting lost in the fog. But getting lost on a clear blue day, when you can see for twenty miles and still have no idea where you're going — that's a whole different kind of lostness.

Every copse might be the start of it. A stand of firs in a half-occluded dip gets our hearts racing. But then we're high enough to see how the blank grass on one side joins up with the blank grass on the other, and this is just an island when we're looking for a continent, and there's nothing above waist-height between here and the next bit of sky.

Some time in the afternoon we hear gunshots. It's too early for grouse-shooting. It might be the lampers I saw last night. But lampers don't hunt by daylight. The rabbits see them coming. The quarry gets wise.

Even lost, I never feel completely alone.

I wish we hadn't thrown the map away. A half-right map is better than no map at all. Or does the bit that's right make you more likely to trust the bit that's wrong? The road has vanished, anyway.

The sun goes down on our left. We eat the last of the pig roast on a wooded bank above a stream, and stumble into the forest at nightfall.

Mateus used to try to explain to me what was frightening about a forest at night.

'It's not what's *there*,' he said, playing up the hot intelligence a bit. 'It's what *isn't* there. Every terrifying thing you can possibly imagine can take shape in that darkness. The brain works overtime, making its hypotheses, and they're never proved wrong. And forests are noisy places. Your brain is tacking every kind of scary meaning onto each sound and sending it out into your body as a full-scale alarm. No rest from it, because nothing to disprove the fear.'

So the forest is the terror that can't be consoled. It's the absence that can morph into the thing you fear most. James' darkness, he wants to tell me, is Bankstown Underpass. His darkness is locked away in memory. In which case, I'm following his deepest terror into an even greater darkness. And someone is following me.

The moon stalks us through the trees.

'James?'

He can't hear me. I turn back and look at the lights on the hillside, the same lights I saw last night, except this time coming this way.

We come to a burn running through a clearing in the trees. The water is fast and shallow, easily fordable. There's a strip of sandy earth where we can light a fire, a hollow under a stand of beeches for shelter. The wood is dry and lights quickly. I lay the sleeping bags out and tend to the fire, getting up a blaze with dry beech leaves, hearing pine cones crack and sizzle. James rummages in his rucksack and pulls out two mining helmets.

'You stay here,' he says, putting one on and handing me the other. 'I'll have a look around.'

'You're not going to see anything now.'

He twists a knob on his forehead and a brilliant beam jerks like a good joke across the beech trunks.

'The map said there was a burn. We cross the burn and follow it out the other side of the forest. Then we'll see this Broken Twins thing.'

'How long are you going to be?'

I'm whispering. Why?

'Not long. We stick to the edge of the forest. Give me half an hour.'

He hands me his phone. There's no signal: we're too far out. The clock on the display says 20:09.

'Then what?'

He grins. 'Start without me.'

I watch him ford the burn, doing ballet moves with his arms as he fights for balance on slippery river stones. He rests on something steadier and watches the beam of his lamp pierce the water, lighting possible paths through the swirl. A last leap gets him to the other bank, and I think he glances back, to see if I'm following him. Then he's just a cone of yellow light, the height and pace of a man, barcoding across the trunks of black trees.

By 20:14 he's afterglow, the scatterings of an unseen sun, only visible in what reflects him.

I look back the way we came. To start with I'm blind, retinas still bleached by the firelight. Gradually there are trees, bronzed and dancing closer in, and then dimly silvered by moonlight.

The lights that were following us have gone out, for now.

An owl shrieks. I hear something rustling just beyond the firelight. The brain makes its hypotheses. I'm frazzled, asphyxiated by fear.

'James?'

There's no answer. Then cognition: harsh rationality.

We're after Gareth. Sansom are after Gareth. Along the way, they might just come across me and James.

Which is why I'm filling our water bottles at the stream, trying to douse the fire.

*

At 21:48 he's still not here. The dead fire hoists smokescreens in the moonlight. A few embers still glow among the wet ashes. The signal meter on his phone now shows one bar. I could phone for help, maybe. Hunger slowly takes me apart, unscrews each limb and empties it, leaving a dull nausea. I still believe he's coming back, but how will he find me? The smoke scrolls palely to the sky.

A branch cracks in the blackness. My hand goes to the other helmet. There's a shadow where there wasn't a shadow. Someone is standing in the space between two trees.

The phone shimmers into life. It takes me a moment to realise that it's ringing. The caller's number is recognised, and the display flashes up the ID.

DAVID.

'Don't answer it,' James says.

I answer it. I can hear the hubbub of a bar, but no one answers my hello. There's an impatient sigh, and the line clicks into silence.

'Who was it?' he says.

'I don't know,' I say, killing it with my thumb. 'He didn't feel like leaving a message.'

'He never does.'

'Do you reckon he could get to a phone?'

'Who?'

'David. Wherever it is that he's vanished to.'

He says nothing. I can't see him yet, but I think he's in a worse state than I am. Every breath seems to hurt him. He puts a hand against a tree and leans there in obvious pain.

'I doubt it.'

'Oh. Must have been another David.'

He calls out, a hurt shout of denial. I clench my fists, ready to fight him, absurdly ready to finish this somehow.

'No.' He's quieter now. 'It would have been him.'

'So why didn't he want to talk to me?'

'I don't know.'

'I can't see you,' I say. 'Can you put your lamp on?'

'It's broken.'

'How?'

'I dropped it.'

'You dropped your helmet? Was your head in it at the time?'

He limps over to where I'm sitting. I reach for the other helmet, switch the lamp on and hold it so it picks him out. His face is dark with dirt or bruises or both. There's a bad cut under one eye.

'What happened to the fire?'

'I put it out. I thought we were being followed.'

I see him staring at my chest, at the amulet that hangs in the space between my breasts. It seems to be bothering him.

'No one's following us. I saw some kids with torches. Lampers. That's all.'

'Did the kids beat you up?'

'No one beat me up. I fell down a fucking ravine.'

'The shaft? The entrance to the mines?'

He doesn't answer. I watch him stretch out awkwardly on my sleeping bag. His body shudders violently and then is still. The thought flits across my mind that he might be dying. But I'm sure the dying don't snore.

I'm attuned to the forest. I answer its alarms. At five the blackbirds start twittering, and then a woodpigeon bows a bass note and wakes up the mistle thrushes. By the time the ring ouzels get going, at six by James' phone, the trees already have a spectral blue sheen.

I get up and splash my face in the stream. I haven't fallen asleep so much as climbed up onto it, meticulously, after hours of muscle-pulling effort. The air up there was suffocatingly thin. Hunger had already dismembered me, laid my bones out to be picked clean. I dreamed I was awake and trying to dream. Then pain woke me, a sudden all-over pain that told of falling from a great height, in my back, my neck, my ribcage. I couldn't sleep through that. So I got up and thought about food. We should have been in the mines yesterday afternoon. We finished off the pig roast last night, and I poured the last of our drinking water onto the fire. If we don't find something soon, we're going to die up here. Just seeing the problem clearly: it's a comfort, somehow.

James, too, looks like he's fallen down a mountain. His cheeks are black. His upper lip is swollen.

'We've got to find your mineshaft,' I say.

When he wakes, he can only open one eye.

We're supposed to have pinpoint memory for pain. When you shock a rat in a T-maze, it remembers where it got hurt. But after an hour and a half James still can't find the hole he fell down.

'I came out of the forest. I followed the burn, just like the Saxons said. The forest is narrow. I was out in the open in no time.'

'We've done that. Both sides of the burn. Are you sure it was near the forest?'

In the sunshine I'm even weaker. Lush grass climbs to the sky. There are sheep now, watching us, strutting off hippily and then turning back to be curious again. One seems stuck in a collapse of barbed wire.

'It was dark,' James says, striding off towards the caught sheep.

'It was moonlight.' I sit down.

He reaches the sheep and starts unpicking it from the wire.

'What are you doing?'

'I don't know about you, Yvonne, but I can't walk past an animal in trouble.'

'This is not about Gareth any more,' I yell after him. 'This is about me getting home. You can come or you can stay here.'

I lie back on the grass and close my eyes. Getting tough has exhausted me. The heat of the sun scans my image onto the grass. It's over. I'm a trick of the light, lost in the brightness of day.

Gareth is trying to explain something to me.

'You can't implant a memory, Miss. You can only enhance what's already there.'

'Are you trying to tell me that I already know where you are?'

'That's right. All the information is in there. The birds are packed in and they are impatient. You've just got to make them come to you.'

'But I don't remember. I don't understand all these clues you've been giving me.'

'Your memories are not *you*. They're electrical activity in a physical system. You just have to take control of the system.'

'How do I do that?'

The brilliant bird-eye gleams.

'You know that feeling you've been having? Where you sense these fizzing connections running right through your body and you feel like you're about to remember everything? That's what I mean.'

'Gareth, stop fucking with my mind.'

'You don't have a mind, Miss. You have a network of bioelectrical systems which has somehow managed to convince itself that it is conscious. You've been careless of late. You're beginning to believe in the illusion.'

I can see his real face now. His ears stick out more than ever. He seems to be all rubber. His eyes make their own glow.

'Am I dying?' I say.

'No. You're about a hundred yards from safety.'

'Thanks,' I say, sinking into sleep.

CHAPTER SEVENTEEN

The Broken Twin

◉

They're walking, dressed for any weather, an energetic stride-past of Gore-Tex and conspicuous synthetics: lost-in-fog red, hypothermia blue. They march down the hillside, making dainty runs down steep banks of scree, braking with their telescopic graphite walking sticks, an adult education class on the move. The bearded one in front has a waterproof map-wallet hung like a sales tag around his neck. He fords the burn on heavy tiptoes, offering a helping hand to women. The wind preserves them in a jelly of silence. They carry all they need in emergency-colour daysacks they never open. They run on fine weather and oxygen. Their faces look hale and hearty, and a little hot.

I lie where I woke up, tipped out on my side with my ear pressed into a folded jumper. A reef of heather flinches at my every breath. I feel psychotic with untimetabled sleep. James is on his feet, facing the way of the walkers but having second thoughts about calling out. Instead his eyes are staring northwards, to the cheerful cabin the walkers have just emerged from. It must be the loneliest tea-shop in England, with only a dirt track to feed it: miles from anywhere, in the middle of the moor.

The sign says BROKEN TWIN TEA ROOM. The missing S is betrayed by the stubs of snapped fixings. Inside is a mid-afternoon gloom, through which I can make out trestle tables overlaid with blue-and-white chequered cloths. Home-made cakes glisten under glass. Whatever the walkers had, it has vanished. Newspaper cuttings and wall-mounted black-and-white photographs give the place an atmosphere of quiet commemoration. It's as dark as a museum, and as empty.

'Where are the Broken Twins?'

I can't see who James is talking to at first.

'Twin,' comes a voice from behind the counter. 'Only one left now.'

'What happened to the other one?'

'Dust,' says the voice. 'Silicosis. Twenty-three year.'

I can see him now, perched on a wooden stool behind the counter. A weather-beaten old man, licking at a rollie. The sight of the cakes compels me. But there's a warm feeling too, at the thought that they're all this old guy's work.

'From the mines?' James is asking.

'Aye. Cut his lungs to pieces.'

'So the Broken Twins aren't some kind of rock formation?'

'Near enough.' The old man nods slowly. 'Amount of that muck we inhaled.'

I catch him staring at the grubby dressing on my arm. He has a way of being utterly, unbreathingly still. His crow's feet are so deep they look like gills. For a moment I wonder if that's how he breathes.

We order all-day breakfasts. The proprietor gets to work with painful slowness. The first whiff of frying almost finishes me. He comes in with long oval plates on which slabs of bacon are skating about in a yellow grease. I consume it like a shredder. When it's gone, I feel even fainter than before.

'So there were mines around here?' James asks, getting started on the toast and jam.

The old man points to the floor.

'Underneath here? Can you go down?'

'Keep walking,' the man says. 'You'll fall down one soon enough.'

'Is the main shaft nearby?'

'There's a shaft,' he says. 'The cage still works.'

'Can you get us down there?'

The old man nods. 'Take you down meself, if it weren't for this knee.'

He finishes clearing our table, and then pulls a chair over and sits down, breathing hard.

'So tell me who's asking.'

James frowns briefly, dramatically. 'The grandson of a very brave man.'

I stare at his bruised, animated face, dismayed by a premonition of the bullshit that's to come. But if it helped us to find Gareth, I'd believe it was Christmas Day.

*

We're looking at a map of the Mickelhope mines. It's a roll of ancient architect's paper, which the old man has pinned to the table with four sugar-sprinklers. At first it looks like a basic Ordnance Survey, stretching from Fulling all the way up to the head of the Churl. Then you notice that the entire area is criss-crossed by the pencilled ghosts of mine-workings.

'Echofield,' James says, pointing to a network of lines away to the right. He traces a main drive along the length of the paper, underneath where Wenderley Forest would be, to an area that has been ringed in red pencil.

'That's us,' the old man says. 'That's where your grandad would have worked.'

'It all connects. It's a continuous network of tunnels from here to right back down the dale.'

'Aye. Bit of a walk, like. Echofield must be fifteen mile.'

'So you could go down here and come out underneath ...' He pauses, deciding against something. 'Underneath what used to be Echofield.'

'You could walk it, aye. Your grandad probably did, a few times.'

'They don't walk it, though, do they? They've got roads down there. They get around in Land Cruisers.'

The old man shrugs. 'So I've heard. They say a company has got it. You hear a rumble or two from down there.'

'Are the actual workings still safe?'

'They cut them buggers from granite. The supports are three-hundred-year old oak. They haven't shifted since your grandad were working down there.'

With each mention of James' imaginary grandad, I squirm a little less.

'The company is called Sansom,' James explains. 'They're a biotech. What used to be Echofield is now their European headquarters. They've taken over the old mines and set up a research station down there. They're doing experiments they don't want anyone to know about, playing around with the brain function of chimpanzees. We think they're using some kind of neural implants to control their nervous systems by computer. They're using a light railway to get the chimps into the mines and right on up the dale. Up here, in other words. That rumbling sound is probably the trains.'

The old man closes his eyes, as though on a headache. He seems to know what we're asking.

'It's a squeeze, like.' He looks up at the map again, sketching out an area with his finger. 'Your Sansom lot have got all this. They think that's as far as the workings go. They should have done their homework, talked to some of the people as knew. Them buggers were chasing the seam through nothing. You were down there on your side, swinging an eight-pound hammer on a tap you couldn't even see. Didn't waste time digging it out to make it comfortable. Just wanted to get the lead out. They were ferrets. The gaps they crawled through. You wouldn't find them if you weren't looking.'

'So who's got a copy of this map?'

He shakes his head. 'This one's ninety year old. Drawn by hand. They didn't make copies.'

'You mean there's a way into Sansom's mines that Sansom don't know about?'

'And a way out, too,' says the Broken Twin.

The battery pack buckles around your waist. The wire clips on behind and the lamp slots into runners on the front of your helmet. James switches his on, testing the power of the borrowed lamp, as the old miner slam-slides the gate shut on the cage. I can no longer see the tea-shop, the gantry or the pile of rucksacks we've left behind for safe-keeping. It's just me, James and this red iron elevator.

'Call us when you reach the first phone,' the old man shouts over the noise of the winder. 'I'll pick it up in the shop.'

A bell rings, and there's a rattling as the winder lets us down. Daylight scrolls up into the vanishing overworld, dimly replaced by the yellow light from James' helmet. The cage percusses on its runners. We're on an ancient hell-train, lowering on a straight track into the earth. I reach up and turn the knob on my lamp to the second stop. The timbered shaft wall flies up in a grey blur. We haven't been told how far down this thing goes. I start counting the seconds and give up when I get to thirty. James' eyes are fixed on the chink of daylight that's slowly fading above the top of the cage door. I touch his arm, in a wasted gesture of reassurance. It's me who needs reassuring. I keep telling myself that no one else knows we're down here. I'll be fine, as long as we can keep it that way.

The cage slows, halted by complaining frictions. James slides the gate open on a tunnel that just clears his head. Our lamps make the only light, the pale glow and shadow of rough-hewn rock.

'Come on,' he says. 'Let's make some cooped-up chimps really happy.'

'James, we're not here on a rescue mission. We're going to see what they're doing down here and then we're heading straight back the way we came.'

He sets off along the drive. Underfoot are the wet rails of an ore-cart system, half-buried in solidified dust. The granite shines with sparkles of mica. James' helmet scrapes the roof. A grey gleam of daylight from a vent far above our heads scuds past like a dream. Crosscuts are pitch black until you angle your light into them, and even then you can only see a few feet into the gloom. Men worked in these holes by candlelight, chasing the body of ore through cracks a half-metre wide. Struts and old ropes lie scattered around, pale with dust. A pile of rubble stands abandoned at the entrance to a crosscut, backfill that never went back in. The roof bows down further and James is crouching, and then even I'm ducking under a huge uncut mass of rock that swells down from the hillside. I can feel the Chinese amulet bouncing around inside my fleece. James is bent double up ahead, his head and upper body swung out awkwardly to one side. The beam of his lamp leaps and warps, shattering into nothingness in crosscuts, breaking into stripes of reflection and shadow.

Then, unexpectedly, we can stand up. The stope caverns out on either side. A grey plastic telephone hangs in a bracket on a timber. It's huge and toy-like, as though moulded for giants. James picks up and waits. He shrugs, hearing reasonable advice, okays and hangs up.

'Our friend says to keep going. When we get to the fifth of these phones, he'll tell us what to do.'

The second drive is timbered in receding frame-squares like the hold of a ship. My beam splits on the cross-struts and falls away into blackness. I'm in front now, bent double, feet slipping on rust-red tramlines. There's running water here, forming black rivulets on either side of the rails. A ladderway descends to another level, an unguessable distance below. A passing stope is fenced off with thick wire mesh. Hammers and taps lie abandoned where they were last used. This is the grave of an industry, and we're robbing it. What I need to know is whether the industry has ghosts. Whether anyone else is breathing this graveyard air.

At the second phone the old man doesn't answer. By the time we reach the third, my battery has started to dim. Still the darkness reels us in.

The drive stops above a ladderway. I can't see its bottom. Holstered on a timber above us is the fourth grey telephone. James listens, laughs quietly and hangs up.

'Down,' he says.

It wasn't the fear of collapse that was bothering me. It's when the weight of rock above me concedes to empty space: that's when I really start getting scared.

I hang in darkness from the ladder, all my weight suspended above James' plastic-hatted head. The beam of my dying lamp spatters against limestone a few inches from my face. Black stringy plant-matter hangs down from an unspeakable crevice. Ferric stains like prehistoric cave-paintings slide upwards into shadow. With each rung of descent my coccyx is bashed by rock. I couldn't fall: I'm jammed in too tight. Every step I take hurts me, but going back without James is not an option. There's a moment of sheer panic, the rehearsed nightmare of being trapped underground, and then this pressure is eased from my spine and my lamp picks out the walls of a decent-sized stope. I can hear water running through the drive below me. I look up into the hole I've just crawled through, and judge about ten metres. We've made it. This is the level below.

James is waiting at the foot of the ladder.

'That's the fifth phone,' he says, fixing it with his beam.

He calls up to the surface while I investigate the drive. There are cross-cuts, no more than two feet high, running off either way from where the phone is mounted. They both end in solid plugs of backfill. Further down, the floor of the main level is slurried with red ooze.

He hangs up, and then reaches up to flick off his lamp. I can't see his face.

'Turn your light off.'

He's whispering.

'Why?'

'Just do it.'

I reach up and toggle the lamp to off. The darkness is total. But the silence is not. There's a roaring sound, like industrial machinery, muffled by layers of limestone. The pitch is high, like a jet engine. Something that can make fire, endlessly, two hundred metres beneath the earth.

A flame sparks up in the darkness. James' face shows up in its coppery light. You can't read a face by matchlight: you can only trust its sulphurous glows. The flame splits, passing its light to a candle that he's holding in his other hand. The match flame goes out. He drips wax onto a rock and glues the candle there inside the leftwards crosscut. The roar pulses in and out of phase. James climbs up onto the pile of backfill and seems to be waiting for me.

'In there?' I ask him.

Then he's turning, crawling through the earth.

CHAPTER EIGHTEEN

At The New Hsi K'an Hotel

◉

Water. We're swallowed up in the roar. A darkness so total you start to synaesthetise, see things with your hands, feel these immeasurable rock-masses in blobs of colour. Blood shades: yellows and oranges. This cut of granite I'm jammed into squeezes the breath from my ribcage. The roar is a sucking gravity, like the turbine of a jet plane. Then a dim refracted blueness, and a feeling of breaking through a flaw in the earth to a place that has been tropical and sunkissed all along. The din is staggering. James is turned to me and shouting, but his voice doesn't even shade the whiteness of the noise. I reach the shelf he balances on and look out through a steaming curtain of water. My eyes ache with the brightness of blue sky. On slopes to either side, brilliant flecks of plumage flit through a canopy of rainforest green. Hundreds of feet below, the waterfall crashes into a pool of unreal emerald, raising a mist we feel as high up as here, the palpable breath-fug of a daydream.

Down to one side of this outcrop of rock, a torrent of holographic fall-water rages through the foyer of a five-star hotel.

The style is Modern Asian opulent. Everything that could be gold-plated has been; the rest is upholstered in synthetic leather. We're standing on a ledge above a little seating area off the main foyer, with the artificial waterfall to our backs. The only person down there is a young woman, in slimline virtual lights wired up to a FireBook. She looks Chinese. I can see the glow of some visual presentation spilling out from behind her goggles. Her head is tipped back against the sofa, as though she'd been put to sleep by TV.

I watch James climb down onto a broad stepped terrace. At the bottom of the steps there's a picket fence and a gate that opens inwards. Imaginary plesiosaurs splash softly in the pool beside him. I look over into the main foyer, wondering about following him. There's no one else around.

The woman smiles dreamily at something her virtual lights are showing her. The screen of her laptop flickers, reflected in the grey casing of her goggles.

I follow James down into the alcove. The blue-glass shelves of the foyer bar are stocked with alcopops and malt whiskies. I wonder how long it would take to get served. The waterfall goes into a quieter cycle and I can begin to hear shopping music, piped in with the authentically humidified air.

We sit down on another sofa with our backs to the waterfall. The Chinese woman doesn't look up. A play of reflections on the outsides of her goggles suggests that some kind of film is showing. From this distance I'm certain that she's asleep. But then she smiles at something behind her virtual lights and a hand goes up to her neck. Her fingers become busy. She seems to be adjusting something obscured beneath her white top.

I look around. The footage of the chimps was shot in a rough-hewn cave. There must be more to this place than the glitzy foyer. I wonder if this is one of the researchers. She looks mid-twenties, the right age for a post-doc, but with the slightly hassled look of a young mother. I try to judge her eyes from the frame of them, and imagine them crinkling in teary laughter. But what could the eyes tell me? They're puppets, like all the other parts on show. Some neural cluster buzzes some other neural cluster, and another deluded meat-machine reads it as joy or despair.

'I haven't finished,' she tells us.

We've said nothing. The backs of her goggles are opaque grey plastic. I don't see how she can know we're here.

'You always were impatient,' she says. 'My hot-headed little brother. You never could wait for anything.'

On the coffee table beside her is a neoprene drinks holder sheathing a plastic sports-drink bottle. She reaches for it and sips at it through its integral straw.

'Do you remember when we were children in Anhui province? We received a parcel that time. You wanted to open it straightaway. But it was a gift for Dong Zhi, and Mother said you had to wait until the winter solstice. See, I've gone right back to our childhood in Anhui province! That has to be encouraging.'

She breaks off to concentrate on something on the screen. Her hands hover above the keyboard then come down on a fluent string of characters. She sighs. One hand goes up to her neck again and reaches inside the white cotton. She smiles, as though hearing satisfying news.

'Does that feel good?' James says.

I watch him, wondering what stunt he's planning now. His black hair is plastered wetly onto his head. Four days of stubble have grown into a patchy beard, through which I can see the doughy swell of a double chin.

'I'm remembering,' she tells us. 'That means it's working.'

'It's all in there,' James says. 'Everything that ever happened to you is tucked away somewhere. We're just helping you to recover it. You're amazing. You're a treasure trove. We want you to reclaim your own story. That's why we're here.'

I wait for him to remember my presence. But something has taken him over, something that hasn't heard about our love affair. I'm excludable, the girlfriend who doesn't need to know. Then all at once it's clear to me: the tone of quiet encouragement, the persistent quest for the truth about the soul. The reassuring voice of David Overstrand, scraping away at the layers.

'Are you a doctor?' the woman says, looking blindly our way.

'Yes.'

I worry about this. We should be seeing what we need to see and getting out of here. But David Overstrand's grip is sure.

'Have you come for my responses?'

'I don't need them. I can see for myself that it's working. You're doing so *well*.'

She applies her mouth to the sports drink. There's a label on the bottle that I can't read from here. With a lurch of pity I realise that she's not a researcher on the experiment at all. She's taking the instructions, not giving them. She's one of the pale apes Sansom's scientists are experimenting on.

'They've given me this movie to watch. It's supposed to be all about me. Some people are travelling a long way. They're speaking to each other in Cantonese. I'm supposed to type my responses in here. But I've forgotten what the story is about. That's my problem. I don't remember what this has got to do with me.'

'You understood it once. All the knowledge is in you. Somewhere, deep down.'

'James,' I whisper, 'I need to talk to you.'

He turns to me, distracted. To my dismay, he starts briefing me at the same volume as before.

'They've fucked up her memory. Don't ask me how. They're showing her films from her past and looking to see if she's going to remember. It's what we thought they were doing with the chimps. Now we know what they're really up to.'

The woman turns her head, sensing for the first time that James is not alone. We need to get out of here before the bar-staff return. I nudge him with my elbow, and he finally seems to acknowledge the urgency.

'Give me your key,' he says.

She hesitates, unplugs a smartcard from the port in her FireBook and holds it out to him. Various access privileges are listed on a crystal display. James pockets the card, satisfied.

'Don't feed the dinosaurs,' he tells me.

'Don't give me time.'

I watch him heading towards a glass door at the back of the alcove, where the smartcard swishes him through. I can see him on a CCTV monitor above the door, foreshortened by the pitch of the camera, just a random hotel guest headed for his minibar. The image switches to another sweep of discreetly numbered doors, another empty maroon-plush corridor.

The rainforest blinks out. The water is now flowing into a shady rockpool flanked by endless white beach.

'That's better,' the woman says. 'The birds spook me.'

She puts out a tentative hand, feeling at the dampness of my clothes.

'Where is everyone?' I ask her.

'They are working. We are all working hard.'

'Are there animals here?'

'No. They were taken away. They used to make so much noise.'

So McQueen wasn't the only chimp to have escaped from the mines. But this can't be what Gareth wanted me to see. His plan was to create a system that could talk directly to the Lorenzo Circuit. There must be more.

'How did you get here?'

'We came in a lorry.'

I reach for her sports drink. There's some Chinese writing, a picture of a smiling face, and the legend AMYL-7.

'We?'

'All of us. Three families.'

'From the same village?'

'Yes.'

I look at her. My questions are just noises, strings of characters in a language she no longer understands. It's the same blind, confused doubt that I see in Effi's face. Was this girl's memory destroyed before she came here? I can't see how else to explain it. A woman in her mid-twenties doesn't just come down with Alzheimer's.

'Did you have to pay?'

She grins. 'Look around. The five-star treatment. They've arranged everything. We can leave here any time we want. As soon as our documents are ready we can look for work.'

'Work? What are you going to do?'

Her pride is evident. 'I trained as a communications manager. But there are no jobs for communications managers in Anhui province. So I have to come here.'

I glance up at the CCTV monitor again, which is still showing the ghosted efficiency of mid-afternoon in a luxury hotel. I remember what James told me about the light railway carrying secret deliveries into Sansom. The lorries discharging their cargoes under cover of darkness. Now I understand the detail that was eluding him. It wasn't chimps they were shipping in here in the dead of night. It was people.

'Who are you communicating with? Who's asking you these questions?'

'The doctors, mostly.'

'There are doctors here?'

'Some. And some up above, too.'

I see her pulling at the cotton around her neck. It's just nervousness now, a scrabbling for an escape from her forgetfulness. Then the poignancy of her silence seems to hit her, and she starts sobbing quietly.

I go over to her sofa. I ease the lights from her face and she curls into my arms. On the FireBook's screen, a lorry is cruising down a motorway. The spotlights in the ceiling of the lounge mist the screen with white reflections. She's wearing a white top and pale blue hipsters. The skin on her neck is like halva. There's a fine gold chain around her neck, bearing something of weight. Inside her top I can see the glow of metal. I reach my finger under the chain and pull up a gold amulet. A sick recognition sets my hand shaking, sending the charm flapping against the woman's exposed clavicle, where the thread of a long scar runs between the top of her ribcage and the fine hairs behind her ear. I lift the girl's amulet in my fingers and feel the looseness in one of its golden ears, the same sprung rotation that James was so interested in. The exaggerated Chinese eyelids, peering out at the room. I twist the ear in my fingers, charged by the body-warm gold, an energy that's infecting me. I put my other hand to my own neck and feel the weight of the goddess' twin hanging there. The woman is saying something to me, but I can't shift my tongue or force my breath out into a reply. I'm back in the shell of the Saxons' church, assailed by alien feelings of remembering, my only certainty this little nub of metal in my hand. The Lorenzo Circuit pulls me into its story. And if something tampers with the circuit, the story is changed. A spreading heat begins to creep up along my spine. My stomach muscles start to tighten, sensing a weather my brain has not yet caught up with. Whatever this woman has had done to her, it has also been done to me.

PART FOUR

◎

The City

CHAPTER NINETEEN

Hostage

◉

I'm running, strobed by a broken beam of lamplight. Every breath of this black air burns my lungs. James is behind me, urging me back towards the ladder. After the brilliance of the hotel, seeing is guesswork, fleeting obscurities briefly illuminated, too fast for thought to catch up.

'They didn't see us.' His voice echoes nightmarishly around the drive. 'I got back just in time. I'm pretty sure we've got away with it.'

'Who?'

'Their security people. I could see them on the cameras, heading towards the foyer. They weren't expecting visitors. We're OK.'

I pull up, crippled by doubt.

'Yvonne, what's the matter with you?'

I feel him taking hold of me, trying to push me on. But the amulet drags me down. I put my fingers to it and its warm density compels me again. The Chinese girl was playing with hers, twisting and pressing on its golden ear. When I did the same, it affected me. I was part of it. I was wired into it. The thought knots me up with fear.

'That woman. Did you know her? Have you ever seen her before?'

'Of course not. Why?'

I reach back, trying to unclip the amulet, but I can't make my cold fingers respond.

'What is this thing, James? What have you given me?'

'It's nothing. I've got a friend who makes jewellery. I thought you'd like it.'

'But that girl back there . . . She was wearing the same thing.'

He looks surprised. He didn't see what I saw hanging around the woman's neck, and it's bothering him. I can see him muttering to an invisible adversary. He reaches the fifth phone and rattles the holster furiously. I hear him talking to the old guy, forcing himself to sound calm. He hangs up, looking back along the drive.

'He's sending the cage for us. Now we have to get back up that ladder.'

'What did you see, James? What was going on back there?'

'Nothing. I saw a load of empty corridors.'

'She told me the other guests were all working. She said they'd cleared the animals away.'

'And now they've got some new animals. Chinese migrants, here in the belief that they're going to get work. That's almost as bad as doing this stuff on chimps.'

'*Almost* as bad?'

'Those people made a choice about coming here. The chimps didn't.'

He turns away, testing the stability of the ladder. He drags himself onto the first rung and beckons me after. I dither, wondering what it would take to make him listen to me. I could slip away from him now, while he's not watching, and he might never know what had happened. But I stay where I am. When it comes to the important things, I never can decide. I'm torn in the most obvious ways, between doing a thing and holding back, between saying no with my mouth and yes with every other part of me. I want to tell him what happened back there, and I want to keep it to myself. I'm half a person, ruled by linkages I have no map for. I'm a passenger in my own life, a hostage in a runaway car.

I watch him driving. It's been raining steadily ever since the old man dropped us back at the Saxon Kingdom. We hang on the brake-lights of a queue of executive cars, watching lorries do-si-doing on the inside lanes. I could probably have got back to Fulling without him, but then I would never have had a chance to find out what he knows. Even if it risks playing into his hands, I need to keep him close, for now.

I finger the amulet, conscious of James' presence in the corner of my eye. I don't know what's harder to believe: the idea that he could have knowingly done this to me, or that he could have given me this gift without realising what it was. At least I understand now why I've been feeling different since I got out of hospital. The thoughts that weren't my own. The memories that came unbidden, made me a stranger to my own mind. The birds control this, not me. Whatever I do next, deciding is not part of it. The birds will have their say.

His phone rings. He tosses it across to me, gesturing for me to answer it. The number isn't recognised.

'Yvonne?'

It's Bridge. I remember her peering at me through the shattered light of the hallway, telling me that everything would be all right. I haven't spoken to her since she swam into my unconsciousness and seemed to leave something there: an idea, the shell of a terrifying thought.

I hand the phone to James. He clamps it to his ear, gripping it with his chin, and listens. I suppose I should have said something to Bridge, thanked her for getting me to hospital, but the irony would probably have killed me. Should I take the phone back from him now, corral her mermaid attention and force her to explain what they did to me in the hallway? But James looks as though he were hearing bad news. He needs to mind the road; for once, he can't avert his eyes. I wish I'd offered to drive for him. Let him fight his own fight, without the distractions of traffic.

He lowers the phone, weighing it in one hand. I get the impression that Bridge has just hung up on him.

'What did she want?'

'She says we need to talk.'

'Is she still jealous?'

'It's gone beyond that, Yvonne. She's angry. They all are. I'll drop you back at the forest and then I'll get over there.'

The rain gets heavier. I've managed to change my clothes and the worst of the dressings, but still I'm cold and shaken. The wound on my scalp is fizzing. The suspension on this old hydrogen-cell conversion makes my Santana a memory of luxury.

'Did Bridge call the ambulance?'

'Yes. I told you. She went with you to the hospital.'

'And what happened before that? While I was lying there?'

'Nothing happened. Why?'

I could tell him. I could explain that I've worked out what this amulet means. But I want to find out what he knows.

'Can you take this thing off me?' I tug on the figurine with my still-numb fingers, feeling the chain cut into my neck. 'I'm sick of it.'

'You know what? So am I.'

He thuds his hand on the wheel helplessly. He's eyeing the junction signs, calculating how much further we have to go. I fix my eyes on the smoky fringes of the forest, forcing my imagination on to the scene that lies beyond. The bright, clinical order of the Forest Campus. The shocked hush that will confront me at the Institute. I don't how this plan came to me, and I probably never will. I'm the hostage in this scenario. I'm the decided, not the decider. But I know where I'm going. I'm going back to my lab, right now, to try to explain all this to Gillian. A train of lorries peels away in the slow lane, and the skyline of the medieval city reels into view. Then James says:

'Well, I guess we're going to find out how ruthless these people really are.'

A cold weight falls through me. 'Really?'

'Yeah. Tonight. Bridge just told me. Seems there's going to be a bit of a confrontation. I want you to see it.'

'Who's going to be the winner?'

'We are. You and me.'

'What about David?'

'I'll worry about David later. I'll talk to him. I'll have to.'

His face is still flushed from the phone call. Whatever Bridge has just said to him, it's put the fear of God into him. He told me, that afternoon on the moors, that he and the others had had a falling-out. A frank exchange, he called it, in that deafening euphemism. Bridge, Grandstand, Level Ten: they were losing their focus, branching out into places where they shouldn't be going. They asked him to do something that he didn't want to do. And now there's going to be a showdown, and we're going to find out whose side James is really on. I know he's lying about David, like he's been lying to me from the moment he walked into my lab. The trouble is, I prefer the lie to the alternative. Which is that David Overstrand is not as far away as James has been making out, and finding Gareth might mean finding him as well.

CHAPTER TWENTY

The Scan

◉

The mouse feels almost weightless. He has died in a shrug, eyes shut in a final gesture of relinquishment, his feet clawed into little bony burrs. I could hang him from my top like a brooch, my own version of the Conscience green ribbon, telling the world *A vivisectionist lives here*. A vivisectionist who doesn't use a knife, perhaps, but guilty all the same. The fact is, I didn't need to tamper with their brains when I was wreaking such spectacular havoc with their DNA. This little guy had his fate decided before he even made it to embryo. He was programmed to fail, and he's followed his genetic instructions to the letter. I count four dead bodies in all. A luckier transgenic is scurrying around his maisonette in a perfect wall-hugging rectangle, as baffled by his suffering as I am.

I give up on trying to count the survivors and cross the corridor to the lab. Here, the evidence of my neglect shows in a sort of exaggerated stillness, as in a busy house suddenly abandoned, things sealed off for weeks in silence and eddyless air. The new infrared motion tracker, bought with the remnants of our grant money in January, stands blind and useless next to the drained water maze. I'm not sure that even Gillian has been in here. The bin has been emptied, and a few weeks of mail, journals, late essays and stuff stand piled up on my desk. I tear the plastic off last week's *Nature* and glance at the job ads. The thought of having to find something else to do is a low-level terror, lurking around the corners of my gut, ready to spring. If I lose this, I'm fucked. This is all I know how to do.

'How's the patient?'

I didn't hear her come in.

'You look in better shape than you did when I last saw you. How are those wounds healing up?'

I peel back the dressing on my arm and show her the fierce smear of Pyronox. But the damage to my scalp interests her more. She's a couple of inches taller than I am, and she has no trouble lifting herself on tiptoe to inspect the wound on the right-hand side of my skull. The dressing is a pad of soft plastic, taped to a small circle of skin where my hair has been cut away. Above it, closer to the crown, are two tender bumps like scabbed insect bites. The pain there is different, the placing uneasily regular. Gillian looks as though she wants to touch them, but she stops herself.

'Thanks for the flowers,' I say.

She shakes her head, dismissing it.

'This mystery package you had. Has anyone claimed responsibility?'

'I don't know. How do they do that?'

'They send you a badly-spelled death threat. My laundry room is plastered with them.'

'Nothing's come,' I say. 'But then I haven't been home ...'

She starts unpacking the helmet. It took a twenty-minute phone call to convince her that I was serious, but now she's all busy efficiency.

'And it was this James fellow who took you to hospital? You're still together with him?'

I recognise the aluminium casing of the headcoil, the grey visor, the tail of cables hanging down. The moment becomes transparent, and I can see this other reality behind it, swelling to fill it. Gareth in his nun's costume, sitting in that same chair, convinced that he could see his own thoughts. James, hiding his avoidant eyes behind his Flintstone mask. The amulet commands my gaze from the corner of the desk, safely distant from whatever it is that it's controlling. I can trust this memory. It is mine.

'I was staying at his house. I don't imagine he was expecting an animal rights attack. One of his friends found me. I woke up in the Royal Infirmary.'

'They didn't scan you there?'

'Why should they? They wouldn't even have thought of it. They'd have found it as far-fetched as you did.'

'OK, let's get this thing going. Find out whether that bomb shook anything loose.'

'Don't I need an MRI? A big magnet, high res?'

'We're not going to find an MRI tech on a Saturday. Anyway, we don't need an MRI. If there's anything there, we'll see it with this.'

I take the helmet from her and put it on. It's heavy, and the still-new padding scratches my cheeks. There's a smell of acetone. I push the visor up and notice that Gillian has dimmed the lights and blinded the windows. The projectors spark up, and I can see the clenched gloves of two cortical hemispheres taking shape in the air between us.

'Like you said, we're not getting good resolution with this. It's going to be hit and miss. What worries me is where they could have put it. They'll have entered the brain through that wound on your scalp. That's how they could do this without attracting any attention at the hospital. Those little bumps are from the fiducials. Positioning devices, fixed by tiny screws to your skull. They'll have used a stereotactic column, and they were probably also scanning you as they went in. If they were heading for where I think they were heading, there are going to be some pretty important homeostatic pathways running close by. I'm praying that these jokers have been careful.'

I can hardly process her words. 'Could they really have gone into my skull while I was lying there in the hallway?'

'It was reckless. This is not open-brain surgery, but it's a serious procedure. Implants for deep brain stimulation tend to go in when the patient is conscious. That way you know straightaway whether you're straying. You keep the patient talking, see if there's anything weird going on. Your patient isn't feeling anything, of course: no pain receptors up there. You just watch for whether they start talking Japanese or breathing too fast. It's a valuable safety check.'

'But … because I was unconscious, they could have screwed up badly?'

'They could have done. The fact that you're still here suggests that they didn't.'

She moves around the hologram, studying it like a sculpture.

'So someone knew what they were doing?'

'Thankfully, yes. In the right hands, this is a half-hour operation. For Sansom, that's the appeal. They can sell this technology as only minimally invasive. People will be having it done in their lunch hours. That's why Sansom want the mapping data, so that their techs can be putting these things in blindfold. The good news, though, is that it will take only slightly longer than half an hour to reverse it. You'll be back to your old unenhanced self in no time.'

I feel a swell of panic. They did this for a reason, whoever it was.

There's an order to this. A logic that needs following through.

'We're not going to find a technician to do *that* today, are we?'

My voice breaks up. Gillian pushes out a little squeezed-lip smile of solidarity. I can't help liking her, for all the bullshit, for all the mannered Leichhardt High sassiness. I'm glad she's on my side.

'Before we get you booked in for that, let's see if you've really got this thing inside you. Until we actually see something, we're still guessing.'

She plays with the remote, rotating the image and zooming in. The lines of circuitry are pale blue. My cortex is a cavernous space, a tunnel lit by tiny lights. It's as I imagined it, the last time we sat in the presence of this thing, those few short weeks ago. The brisk efficiency of life-or-death routines, but no shape to those connections, no focus that could correspond to a soul. If I weren't so terrified by what might show up here, I'd be disappointed that my own nervous system looked so dull.

'This is a structural image,' she says. 'We need a functional one. We need to see your brain actually working.'

She types some commands into my terminal. The shimmering cerebrum explodes into colour. I see a throb of activity, reaching from way back in the visual cortex right up to the frontal lobes, a self gathering itself, the exquisitely complex matrices of the Lorenzo Circuit swirling into action. The connections come alive. The past takes shape. I'm remembering.

'Now where is this widget you thought was controlling it?'

I point to the amulet on the desk next to her. She picks it up and inspects it, shakes it at her ear.

'I'd say this was a remote control device. The power supply for the electrodes is inside you. They've probably buried a small pulse generator under your collarbone. Hence that delicate little wound on your neck. The doctors probably thought it was caused by the bomb. The actual wires run subcutaneously.'

'OK.' My voice is thin. I put my hand up to touch the cut, tracing its familiar shape with a new buzz of horror.

'You can thank Mateus for that particular scientific breakthrough.'

I give a cynical laugh. 'He's a bastard, but he didn't do this.'

'He gave the world the Pereira Effect, though. And his old employers have made dramatic use of it. Their research is about stimulating memory. These implants give them a new way of doing this. Spreading an electrical charge across different areas of the brain, and so triggering the crucial parts of the mechanism.'

'And that woman I saw in the mines ... She was testing out the technology.'

Gillian moves away from the desk and approaches the ghost brain.

'Exactly. If what you told me on the phone is true, Sansom created the problem before they solved it. The idea was to model Alzheimer's in healthy individuals. That was what the amyloid suspension was for. I'm guessing that they didn't want to use real dementia patients — too many other problems, mainly associated with ageing, which could confound the results. So they found some healthy "volunteers". Migrants looking for help with their asylum applications. People who could be relied on not to understand the consent forms. Sansom made them comfortable and started feeding them this amyloid smoothie. Tangled their brains up with plaques, just like what happens in the real dementia. Next, they used the implants to try to stimulate their subjects' circuits again. Sansom want a therapy for dementia. Grandma's magical box of memories. That's what this is really about.'

I say nothing. There's a tiny, embarrassed flame inside me. I'm remembering what Gareth said to me when we sat here in this room, about making the birds come when you call.

'Yvonne?'

She turns back to me. The birds startle and scatter.

'What are you thinking?'

I glance at the hologram. 'Can't you tell?'

She laughs and gestures vigorously with the amulet.

'This light-show gives us patterns of bioelectrical activity. You know as well as I do that it doesn't show us thoughts. How many times have I had to set students straight about ... ?'

I gasp, my whole body jerking. 'Jesus. Do that again.'

She pulls back from the hologram, tucking the amulet out of range behind her back. She looks at me, ablaze with curiosity.

'Do it again ...'

I see her twisting at the figurine's ear. A spurt of activity yellows in the cleft between the hemispheres.

'There it is,' she whispers. 'There she blows.'

Gareth. In this room, right here. The vision hits me with such force that I have to glance over to the door, to prove to myself that he hasn't just walked in.

'I saw him.'

'Who?'

'Gareth.'

'You didn't see him. You remembered him. There's a difference.'

Those hooded, thyroid eyes. His scarecrow ears, turned towards me. A weird yellowness to his skin, as though his natural colour were green and this were the effect of years without daylight. The face of a less complicated time, looming into my derailed here-and-now.

'So where is he?' Gillian says. 'Where did he put our data?'

'He was talking about an aviary. Materialism. Thoughts that have nothing to do with *you*... Wait. It's gone. Press it again. Do what you were doing.'

'I do pity your boyfriend.'

She is quiet, her fingers busy with the thumbwheel. I hold my eyes closed tight, but nothing happens.

'Yvonne...'

I'm losing it. There's a flood of raw emotion, a swell of directionless sadness. My eyes are wet with tears.

'What have they done to me?'

'Come on.' Her voice is firm. I can hear a printer working above the hum of the projector. 'Let's get you out of there.'

'No. I'm just... You must have hit something. All these pathways are woven together, thoughts and feelings, rationality and emotion. But how did I see Gareth? It was like a new memory. But it was real.'

'It came from you, Yvonne. This implant can't give you memories you haven't had. It can only give a nudge to what's already there.'

'But memory's a fiction. That's what I tell the students. It's hashed together from bits of knowledge, sensory impressions, all stitched together in a hurry. It's not what actually happened. It might be, but I can't rely on it. That's my problem.'

'OK, so you've finally joined us in the real world. That's how the Circuit works, Yvonne. None of us can rely on it. The brain has to impose order on whatever information it has available. That information gets lost, overwritten, degraded, you name it. Your cortex has only got a part-time interest in the truth. For the rest of the time it's a deceitful egotist, just wanting to suit its own needs.'

'Tell a story that fits...?'

'Exactly.'

'I could go to therapy if I wanted that.'

'You got anyone in mind? I need a good shrink, what with everything that's been happening here.'

'There's a guy called David Overstrand.' I wipe my eyes, smiling bitterly. 'But I don't like what he charges.'

'You don't need a therapist, Yvonne. You need to find out who did this, and why. Or rather, you need to let the police worry about it.'

I flip the visor shut. I'm getting used to the weight of this thing. Perhaps it's just the force of my determination. I want to see this through.

'Someone has had the bright idea of fucking with my memory. I need to understand that before I do anything else.'

'Yvonne, we have to get this thing out of you. If that implant slips, it could kill you. I know someone who can get rid of it. I'm not saying they won't ask questions, but it's not going to be like rocking up to A&E with a bust of Beethoven up your arse.'

I flip up the visor and watch the hologram rotating slowly. The swirling has subsided. The scattered empire of the Lorenzo Circuit is almost calm.

'I don't want it taken out. Not yet.'

I stare at the yellow ember in the fold between the two hemispheres. For the moment, this implant is part of me. The gleaming ghost in the machine. Without it, I'd be less than I am.

'Are you serious? You're going to keep that thing inside you?'

'Until I've remembered what I'm supposed to remember,' I say.

CHAPTER TWENTY-ONE

Fulling Flames

◉

James said he would wait for me at the station. The medieval streets are busy with Southside supporters, arrived on special trains for tonight's relegation play-off with Pelton. They seem eerily clean, unweathered, sleep-shiny aliens with brand-new human bodies, still learning how to walk right, carry the weight of all this unwrapped flesh. At the new riverside development they crash into bars for last pints before kick-off. Others, dizzy red-and-purple blobs, are crossing the footbridge by the arts centre, their swagger checked by the gravity of the water-mass below them. James ignores them warily, his changing colour registering the threat. He seems anxious, gripping his phone in his hand, checking the screen constantly. Out west, the sun is taking on bloody colours, and its heat on my skin is a weird, amnestic violation. There's an epic feel about these crowds, a sense that whole peoples are on the move. For the moment, at least, I can blend in with them. No one will have to know I'm here.

I can hear his phone ringing.

'Aren't you going to answer it?'

He pulls it out and looks down at it. He presses down on the power button, blanking the screen.

'Well?'

I stop walking. He stands looking at the stock prices in the window of the Imperial Bank. Sansom shares are moving up again.

'Who was it?'

'No one.'

'He makes a lot of phone calls.'

I finger the amulet in the pocket of my satchel. I guess he's seen that I'm not wearing it, but he hasn't asked why.

'Come on,' he says. 'I'm starving.'

The Magic of Asia Food Court. You could lose yourself in there.

✳

'I went to see Gillian. I told her about what we saw in the hotel.'

'Yeah? What did she say?'

He slides his tray down opposite mine and sits down. A gull flaps off the embankment wall, dives in under the tarpaulin after a discarded fortune cookie, and screeches away over the river.

'She said it was ethically abhorrent, but scientifically possible. That Chinese woman had been implanted with a set of cortical electrodes. The thumbwheel on her amulet was allowing her to tune them in, spread the charge across them in different ways. They weren't just showing her films, trying to get her to remember. They were controlling her memory.'

'That sounds like something out of a movie, Yvonne.'

'I said to Gillian, "That sounds pretty far-fetched." And then I said: "So is it significant that I'm wearing the same amulet?"'

His bruise-yellowed face wears a look of dismay.

'And then Gillian said that the only way to answer that question would be to give me a brain scan. So that's what she did.'

I take the envelope from my satchel and show him the printout. He studies it, puzzled.

'And this shows … what?'

'This shows my limbic system. Part of my entorhinal cortex. Some frontal and occipital regions, and some cortical midline structures. Oh, and there's a bit of parietal in there as well. Pretty much the whole Lorenzo Circuit.'

I touch at the scab on my collar bone. It's too tender to press on it, to feel what's concealed under there. The wound on my scalp throbs, more deeply than before, but its dressing is discreet.

'And what did she find?'

'I've had a little cluster of electrodes implanted next to my hypothalamus. That necklace you gave me was controlling the current to them.'

'Hang on, have I just woken up in an episode of Doctor Who?'

'It sounds bizarre to me too, James. Your friend obviously makes some powerful jewellery.'

'I didn't know about this.'

'Should you have done?'

He shakes his head.

'You must have known about it. This scar on my neck is not from a parcel bomb. It's from the power supply for a cortical implant.'

'That's ridiculous, Yvonne.'

'Is it? Is this just something else I imagined?'

He sits with his eyes closed, the blue swirls of my cortex laid out before him. He has his head forward and he's pinching the bridge of his nose. I can't listen to any more of this, the posture says. Take your truth elsewhere.

'Wouldn't you have known if you'd had this thing inside you? Wouldn't you have, I don't know, felt different?'

'James, the brain has no pain receptors. It can't feel anything. People walk around for years with chunks of metal in their cortex. Bullets, nails... they never know they're there.'

'Well.' He sits up, gathering himself, and flashes his indestructible smile. 'I like a woman who's been enhanced.'

The joke crashes. Chastened, he picks up the printout again, trying to catch up on this information he's been missing.

'The question is, who did it?'

I see Bridge's face floating through the streaked light of the hallway. *We need to know, Yvonne. We've got to find the people who did this to you.*

'Bridge called the ambulance. She went with me to hospital. Whoever it was who put that thing inside me, Bridge must have known about it.'

'Why Bridge? Come on, Yvonne.'

His scepticism sounds lame. He knows there's something going on here, and that he doesn't know as much about it as he would like.

'She was there, in the hallway. She was talking to me.'

'You *remember* her talking to you. If Gillian has got her facts right, you're not going to know what you're remembering. You might be getting it wrong. That little widget in there might be tricking you.'

Gillian told me that they try to keep an implant patient conscious. Perhaps that's what I'm remembering. Maybe Bridge was spreading her fake reassurances at the very moment that they were inside me.

'I know she was there.' I push the scan back towards him. 'That thing can't make me remember things that didn't happen.'

'But it can make you put the pieces back together differently. The brain is a storyteller. It cobbles together a narrative from whatever information it's got available. That's what you keep telling us.'

I wipe my eyes. Somewhere, deep inside, I'm still crying.

'So when are they taking it out?' he says.

'They're not. I don't want them to.'

I stare at him, attacking every shadow of emotion. I need to find out what he knows. He smiles uncertainly and reaches for my hand across the table.

'That's your choice, I guess. Does it change anything? You're still *you*, aren't you?'

'There isn't a *me*, James. There's just a bunch of neural systems doing their own thing. A billion little cortical implants, each as mindless as each other.'

A roar from the stadium tells us that someone's gone one down. At the table just behind James, a fan is clearing a space for himself amid the debris. He doesn't seem to be going to the game. I notice the Pelton FC tattoos, the purple-and-red stripes of this year's home strip, and I blank him out as another stray Northsider, a rare loner in this land of gangs. He pulls out a card-thin phone and starts texting. It's the phone my eyes get stuck on.

'At least we know now what Gaz was interested in.'

James sounds distracted. He's frowning, looking out at the river, as though understanding something for the first time. Behind him, the Pelton fan is still busy with his phone.

'So when I see him,' I say, 'I'll tell him he was right about what Sansom were doing.'

'The trouble is, Gaz has lost touch with reality. His brain is doing a ton in the fast lane. He's making connections that don't always make sense to us. I told you about the semester he went manic. He was obsessed with these thought experiments. How the brain is a biological machine, all that jazz. These implants would have turned him on. You know, twist a thumbwheel and a person has an actual subjective, conscious *experience*. He'd have loved that.'

The Pelton fan is looking this way. He's talking into his phone, not taking his eyes off me. Then I remember where I've seen him before. The stranger in the forest. The negligent menace of his rifle. It's the security man.

'Anyway,' James says, 'we have to be patient. Remember what I said about Gaz reappearing in this, in some form no one can recognise?

Well, that's what I mean. From here on, things are going to look different to how they're used to looking.'

He grins suddenly, and jerks around to look at the brightly lit coffee stalls.

'Cappuccino?'

Before I can respond, he's scraping his chair back and heading off towards the shop-fronts. The security man catches my eye and glances away. He's texting again, tapping out his orders with a practised thumb. Last time I saw him he was already spying for Sansom. He was out there hunting the runaway chimp with a rifle because the biotech were paying him to. The pits under my toes start to burn. It seems that the Lycee's old head of security has found someone else to hunt. He's trying not to make it obvious, but he's watching me.

I look over the way James went. He's switched his phone back on and he's standing there with two mugs resting on a ledge, reading a message. He doesn't know I'm watching him. He's looking puzzled, as though getting instructions he doesn't like. I feel a moment of cold satisfaction at catching him off guard, even if I hate the thought of who's checking up on him. He told me he was going back to the squat after dropping me off this afternoon. The thought of St. Lawrence Road is a new kind of fear, smelling of burnt plastic and Pyronox. What I need to know is whether James is as sick of David Overstrand's disciples as he has been making out. If he's really finished with them, perhaps I can start believing him again. If not, then I'm going to have to find out the truth about this on my own.

Then I realise who James is looking at. He's glancing across at the security man, who is reading a message on his own phone. I tell myself that it's just coincidence, two men texting in public at the same time, but my heart has already made the connection. When the big stuff happens you feel it directly in your body, opening taps and setting hormonal fires, squeezing the gut like nicotine. James and the Sansom security man are exchanging messages. I catch myself in the moment before realisation, wishing I could be wrong. But I can see it too clearly, the way James has been seeing it all along. He's putting his phone down and looking over at his contact, who's angrily avoiding his gaze. James is not even trying to pretend. I trusted him with everything I had, but still he's found time for secrets like this. If James is in touch with

Sansom, then he's in touch with the people who mean me the most harm.

A police helicopter hangs over the river, balanced on a thin beam of searchlight. Below us, men are running for the bridges. Across the river something is burning: a car, maybe, parked where you should never park a car. The noise of the riot reaches us thinly, like the goals did, muffled in blankets of night. James watches it all with quietness and a strange tension in his shoulders, sizing up the violence as though he knows he'll soon be part of it, he won't get through this without skin being broken. He has that bigness about him, the bones in his face almost comically swollen, a physicality that asks to be confronted. The thought that he might be killed out there struts coolly through my brain. Fuck him. I've been lied to for too long.

I haven't said a word.

He's still looking at his messages. I've a feeling that he wanted me to see him doing this, but I cannot raise the mental energy to work out why. I thought it might be a weird kind of thrill, the realisation that the person you've given your life to is not the person you thought he was. But it's not. It's draining, a slow enervation. It crushes you like flu.

I stare at the neat trim of his neckline, the black hairs already sprigged with grey. What is it that I should have noticed? The lies, maybe. The lies should have done it for me. It should have been obvious that he was hiding something the moment he started denying his involvement with Conscience. But even that was an invention. James' career as an animal rights activist was only ever a show. I swallowed his protests about the suffering of my experimental mice, the whole sick prank of the Atrocity Exhibition, as if I were being paid for it. He'd say it was the unfaceable reality, the truth that makes the stories true. But things are different now. Someone has hurt me, and someone will still be trying to hurt Gareth. That's not a story. It doesn't need any help in becoming true.

He starts down the steps. A couple of Pelton fans tear down past us, laughing and whooping. They'll be killed if they stay here. They crash to the bottom of the steps and out into the road, making a taxi swerve and blare. The security man is behind us, keeping to the shadows. In a car park across the road I see a white van, night-windowed and inscrutable.

A police van rips past full of cops in riot gear. At the bottom of the steps we turn left towards the river. The helicopter has moved on, and for a moment the riot is all distance. Under the streetlights the road is the colour of putty. The Memory Centre gleams behind shadowed hoardings on the other bank, a bright thought throbbing in the night.

Now the road goes two ways. We could follow the slip road up to the bridge, or we could stay in the left lane and join the road that runs west along the river. For the moment we're fudging it: we're actually walking along the raised central reservation, cars trying to shave bits off us on either side. Close up, the traffic feels as warm and intimate as the crowds did. When I glance back, the security man is just climbing into the white van. I hear a petrol engine starting, the sound of a gear being found.

'He's coming after us,' I say.

'Who is?'

'The bloke from the food court. The only Pelton fan who wasn't at the match or glued to a wide-screen.'

'Oh yeah.' He glances back, not even far enough to take in the van. 'I'm supposed to give him a signal.'

My heart sinks. It's like a sudden fatal sadness, chilling me to the bone. It takes an effort, but I try to sound calm.

'What sort of signal?'

'To say I'm ready.'

The concrete peters out into a single raised line of kerbstones. We're balancing now, tightrope-walking.

'Ready for what?'

'To tell him where Gaz is.'

He's walking ahead of me again. He has to step around a railing, and a passing car full of victorious Pelton supporters misses him by inches. The backdraught pulls him around.

'So you know that, do you?'

'No. But you were supposed to. You haven't delivered. So I'm now going to be in a bit of shit.'

'I'm sorry, James. I don't follow.'

'That's what all this was about. You're the key. You're the one Gaz confided in. I was just meant to pass on the information, as and when it came back to you.'

The van pulls out from the car park and moves into the lane for the bridge slip road. I think of James' tales of demonstrations at the West Gate of Sansom, the Flintstone mask which, it now appears, hid nothing.

'You're working for Sansom, aren't you?'

'I *was*.'

He raises a hand at the van, hailing it like a taxi. It slows at his signal and pulls up alongside the kerb.

'So when did you stop?'

'About five minutes ago.'

I'm sick of his lies. I'd walk away now, if I knew where to walk to. I see him step out into the road and stroll back towards the van. He's working for Sansom. This is his contact. The window on the passenger side is down. James leans on the sill and says something to the driver, who shakes his head and revs the engine. James tries again. I can see the security man behind the seal of the windscreen, staring down the prospect of an unwanted fight. Then James is reaching in through the open window and trying to grab something, the handbrake, maybe, trying to stop the van from pulling away. The security man has a hand in James' face and is bending it backwards with sickening force. The engine finds its gear and the van jerks forward with James still hanging from the window, and then it brakes with squealing fierceness, throwing him forward over the bonnet and down onto the kerb. The front wheel clips his trainer as the van pulls away towards the bridge road. Already James is on his feet, running a few steps then stopping to pick up the vacant light-box of a kicked-in bollard. He looks exhilarated, as though violence were a joy he was rediscovering in random outbursts, at night, with people whose names he'll never know. I watch him raise the bollard high and hurl it in a heavy, twisting arc at the van, just missing the brake-light as it blinks out and accelerates away.

His tee-shirt's almost off his shoulder. He's breathing so hard.

'I'm supposed to tell him when you remember.'

'When *I* remember? What's this got to do with me?'

'That thing you've got in your head. Sansom put it there.'

I know he's right, but this is like learning it all over again. The shaking spreads downwards, wrecks me at the knees.

'Why?'

'So you'd remember. The clue Gareth gave you. They didn't want to leave it to chance, so they thought they'd make sure. Give your memory system a nudge in the right direction, with the help of their new technology. I thought that necklace thing was a tracking device. I was supposed to give it to you so they'd know where you were, and they could keep an eye on you. I had no idea it was connected to anything. They didn't get round to telling me that bit. I thought I was just meant to be hanging around, ready to pass on the information, hoping that you'd remember naturally.'

I can't believe I'm hearing this. 'What information? I don't know anything…'

'You're the only one who can find Gareth. You're the only one he confided in.'

'And you told them that?'

He says nothing.

'So that's why you were hanging around with me? So you could find Gareth for the people who are paying you?'

'No. I was hanging around with you because I'm fucking crazy about you.'

I feel like crying. There's a judder of panic in my voice.

'So you were never part of Conscience? You never actually went on all those actions?'

He finds bitter delight in the idea. 'Sure I used to go on the actions. I got started on that when I was fifteen. It made me feel powerful. The demos at Sansom: get to know the guards, have a bit of a laugh. Most of the time I was doing it, I believed in it. Then one day it went too far. High spirits, a bit of material damage. They dragged us in for a bollocking, then they called Fred Flintstone back for a little chat. Bought me a drink in the directors' bar and made me an offer. That's when David got interested.'

'David? What's he got to do with this?'

'He set it up. He saw that we could help them, and get some help from them in return.'

'Help them? What, by spying on our work at the Lycee?'

He nods. 'We were going to help them to get their hands on the mapping data. I didn't even know what neuroscience was. But I was in

216

your group. I was coming to the Institute every week. David thought I might as well make myself useful.'

I start walking.

'Yvonne . . .'

'It's funny, James. I never saw you as being motivated by money.'

He catches up in a couple of strides. This angry pace seems to expose him, shake him out of his complacency. He seems like just another guy who could trip and fall.

'It wasn't about the money. It was about what we could have done with it. What we could have achieved.'

'The Atrocity Exhibition? Your big statement against science?'

'Our big statement about truth. We needed Sansom's cash to make it bigger. To have some real impact. It costs money to make the kind of splash we wanted to make.'

We're on to the approach to the bridge. The river is a celluloid print of the night. There seems to be nothing around.

'So how long have Sansom known that Gareth has got the data?'

'Since the news broke that a Lycee student had hacked your top-secret server. Sansom went to him, offering him a deal, and he turned them down. He didn't want their money. He wanted you. He was trying to tell you something. He took the data so that you would listen to him. I don't think he realised how much trouble it was going to get him in.'

'And you told Sansom all this? You were going to find him for them?'

'Yeah. With your help.'

He smiles. He has the security man's claw-marks on his cheek. His eye is starting to blacken where he was hit. I could almost feel sorry for him.

'I can't believe you're working for Sansom.'

'Like I say, I *was*.'

'Why should I trust you?'

'Yvonne, you saw what happened back there. The guy was supposed to be my contact. I think I've just pissed on my job, don't you?'

There's going to be a confrontation, he told me. And the winners will be me and him.

'Is that why you wanted me to see you talking to him?'

'I've had enough,' he says, slowing to light a cigarette. 'I want out.

When you remember what Gaz told you, you'll know where he is. That's as far as this will go.'

'And how exactly do you get out of this?'

'I'm going to find Gaz. Get him to unscramble the mess he left on your computers.'

I pull on his jacket for a cigarette for myself. He shows me the empty packet, and crushes it apologetically.

'I don't believe you, James. I don't believe a word you say.'

'That's why I knew I had to show you. Take that guy on. Make a clear statement. I knew you wouldn't have believed me otherwise. Look, you're right. The Lycee should have that data. If Sansom get hold of it they'll clean up. It should be in the public domain, not making the world's third biggest biotech even richer.'

'So why didn't you tell them that you didn't know where Gareth was? It would have been true. Oh, I forgot. You do stories, don't you? You don't do truth.'

'I tried. That night on Mickelhope Moor. I told them I wanted out. They weren't very receptive.'

I remember how he walked out of the forest, his lamp broken, his face a joined-up bruise. The torch-lights on the hillside. They weren't lampers. They were the people Sansom had sent to check up on us. And then the phone call he wouldn't answer, the elusive voice of David Overstrand. I get it now. It's not just Sansom he has betrayed.

'You didn't fall down a mineshaft. They kicked the shit out of you.'

'They were trying to improve my concentration. Keep me focused on the task.'

'So how come you feel you can double-cross Sansom now?'

'Because I've seen what they were prepared to do to you, and I can't stand it.'

We reach the bridge. He stands there, looking out across the empty road. I'm angry, staring around for things to blame, and I don't see what he sees.

'Why should I believe that, James?'

He seems to know that he's lost the argument. 'I don't know. Because it's true.'

I turn the way he's looking. The bridge is deserted. They must have sealed off the entire city centre. Halfway across the bridge the van stands with its driver's door asplay. There's no one at the wheel. Before I can say anything James is walking, he's on the road and circling the van, sizing up a way in. I want to stop him but he's already climbing up into the driver's seat, starting the engine and revving it experimentally.

'Get in!' He's holding the passenger door open.

'Are you crazy?'

'It's OK. He wants us to lead him to Gaz. We may as well oblige.'

I've nowhere else to go. I climb up through the passenger door, grimly curious about how it is that I came to be doing favours for Sansom. The cab is a litter of fast-food wrappers and sports drinks, the tat of single-manhood. I look for cigarettes, but find none.

'Here,' James says, tossing me a blue plastic folder.

He eases out the clutch and we pull away. The end of the bridge is blocked by a police motorbike and a cop in biking gear who's directing traffic down along the embankment road. As James pulls up and winds the window down, I can see a bunch of Pelton fans gathered behind the cop, cheering him on.

'Who won?' James asks.

'Why, it's Southside's star striker Zazou Jordan who'll be selling lighters on the Byggate next season!'

The Pelton fans cheer this. The policeman peers in through the window, seeming not to notice James' blackening eye. I make myself busy with the plastic folder. We're waved down a slip road marked out with traffic cones. Then there's nothing ahead of us, nothing behind.

The medieval town slides by. It's quiet here, apart from the occasional police siren curling off towards a flashpoint somewhere near the riverside developments. The streetlights fill the cab with shifting slabs of steel-blue light, which give you enough time to get an initial fix on what you're reading, and then snatch it away before it can mean anything. There are photographs: holiday snaps, plundered from a profile page somewhere; security camera printouts of the three of us sipping coffee in the atrium of the Institute; James and Gareth as a pantomime horse, somewhere in an academic interior. A hard copy of Gareth's essay, with key phrases highlighted. Mobile phone logs, credit card transactions. There's a long rambling letter to the acting head of Sansom R&D, in which Gareth sets out his plan for a non-invasive human–computer interface, allowing meaningful signals to be patched directly into the individual's nervous system without any harm to their biology. Sansom approached Gareth, offering money for the data, because he had previously approached them. But it wasn't money that he wanted. He knew Sansom would be back, and this time they would make an offer he couldn't refuse. And that left him no option but to disappear, as thoroughly as it's possible for a person to do.

The last thing in the folder is a birdspotter's inventory in a pocket-sized grey plastic binder. Gareth has made handwritten notes next to some of the entries. *A morning spent in calm reflection. A day of slightly nihilistic thrill-seeking.* The words drop into their slots, neatly familiar. Perfect fits to memory.

'Do you know what this is?'

James glances at the inventory, squinting to see.

'Gaz bought a load of birds. It was part of his manic plan for world domination. He gave them all names. Well, they weren't really names. They were more like … *ideas*.'

'He bought birds?' My heart is thumping. 'Where from?'

'I don't know. Some warehouse in Pelton.'

'Why didn't you ever tell me this?'

'I don't know. Is it relevant?'

The birds are memories. Memories are bioelectrical events. If you can learn to speak their language, you can make them come when you call …

'What happened to them? All these birds?'

'I let them go.'

'How?'

'I unclipped their cages. Their unquenchable thirst for freedom did the rest.'

'Why did you do that?'

'I told you. I can't walk past a caged animal.'

'Was he pissed off?'

'Immensely. But he was so hyper, he just immediately started hatching a plan to replace them. He said he was going to get some more, and do it better this time.'

'Is that what he was up to? Before he disappeared?'

'I don't know. I think he was busy hacking your priceless data, wasn't he? He wouldn't have had time for a whole lot else.'

He goes quiet, watching the road. In my door-mirror I can see the twin headlights of a hydrogen-celled Mercedes.

'Nice car,' he says. 'Shall we take him on?'

'I've got to get out of here, James. You've got to help me get away from this guy…'

'Yvonne, we have to stick together. Sansom are going to be making life hard for both of us now.'

'Let me out. If I'm the one who's key to all this, then you've got to cover me.'

'Where will you go?'

'I'll go back to Effi's. I'll call you.'

'I'm not going back to the squat, Yvonne. I'm finished with them.'

'And are they finished with you?'

'What do you mean?'

'David's coming back, isn't he?'

'Yeah. He's coming. We're expecting him any day.'

'You failed in your task. The one thing he asked you to do. You were supposed to find the mapping data for Sansom, and you haven't done it. What's David going to say when he finds out you've double-crossed the people you're supposed to be working for?'

'I don't know.' He glances anxiously into the rearview mirror. 'He's got a temper on him.'

I stare at the streaming light-show of his profile, the fleeting Jameses that take on human form and then blink out. The blood on his face has been smeared into pale brown mascara-tears. It's not his blood; I don't know if they're his tears.

'Well, I'm sure you can talk to him about it. You talked to him about all your other traumas. All those things that made you what you are.'

He jerks his head away, denying me. The Mercedes is still on our tail.

'David is a terrorist. His understanding only goes so far.'

'A freedom-fighter.' I find the energy for a bitter smile. 'The truth that makes the stories true. I know all about that now.'

But there's something I'm not getting. He's having to repeat it, just for me.

'A terrorist, Yvonne. The real sort. The sort that kidnaps an animal lab technician on his way home from work, drives him to a remote spot on the Eskdale moors and burns a cattle-mark onto his skin with a branding iron. A really bad guy, if you're into animal research. To others, a hero. It was him who sent you the bomb.'

The blood on his face starts to flow. Like in some animated nightmare the scars come to life, the bloodstains thicken and bloom. Sticky masses of it well up in his tear-ducts, run from his nostrils, squeeze out horribly from the cuts on his cheeks. Soon it's running off him, obliterating his face, a fountain of blood pouring from his mouth, his ears, his eyes.

'He tried to kill me?'

He shakes his head, scattering the hallucination. 'No. He had a deal with Sansom. They gave you the implant, but he arranged the anaesthetic.'

'Why?'

'That's what I didn't understand. Now I can see that it was because they had to get that thing into you. The bomb was just meant to knock you out. I knew nothing about it. I was just meant to be sticking with you.'

I close my eyes. The tin box in my hands. The Chinese enamellings. Open it, says the unborn child.

'Why? Why did they do this to me?'

'Because you're a scientist. You want to know how it all works. In David's view, that's a crime against Nature. Nature is a fluffy animal, in case you didn't know.'

And then all those hours of blackness. An empty box. An emergency exit left open to the wind. All the birds flown away.

'And after they'd put this thing in? Where did they take me?'

'To the Royal Infirmary. You were in Room 6, Armstrong Ward, all that time.'

I shouldn't be surprised. Vivisectionists are targeted all the time. Theirs is a Conscience household. You have to expect them to keep their hell-fires burning.

'That's why I didn't question it. I assumed it was Aslan's Law who'd attacked me, like everyone was telling me. So you knew nothing about it?'

'Of course not, Yvonne. I went back there and I screamed at them. They'd hurt the person I cared for most. You have no idea how much this destroyed me.'

I look out through the beginnings of drizzle. We've circled the town and are now coming back in on the ring road. The abbey smokes distantly in an amber mist.

'You've lied to me from the start, James. Why should I start trusting you now?'

'Don't shout...'

I grab the door handle. 'Let me out.'

The van thuds to a halt. I can hear the Mercedes braking violently behind us.

'We need to stick together. You'll never find him on your own.'

'But it's *not* just me, is it?'

I pull the amulet from its pocket in my satchel and hold it up to the light from the windscreen. He stares at it, weighing its significance, wondering what space it leaves him for more pretending.

'OK. I'll hold him off. You just get out of here.'

He gets down from the van and starts walking back towards the Mercedes. I hear shouting, and then I'm running as fast as I can.

CHAPTER TWENTY-TWO

The Memory Centre

◉

I crash through the foliage onto the road. Up at the top of the bank, I can hear the skids and scrapes of their fighting. Neither of them can have seen me go. I slipped down behind the van, blindsiding them. Then I was just falling through the undergrowth, ground alder and ivy ripping at my bare ankles. The riot is a dull roar over the town. I start walking, fast, along the road leading back towards the abbey. The moment I realise that I've stopped crying is the moment I become that new thing, whatever version of me lives through this. I've evolved into an exotic organism, with a dry-weather metabolism, re-using water from the inside. Like those mice in the desert that never need to drink. Subsisting on their own tears.

James seems to have stuck to his word. He knows that I'm the one who needs to get away. He's fixed the security guy, somehow, and no one's coming after me. If I can get a taxi, I can get back to Effi's place in Southside. Usually I would head for the taxi rank in the market square, but no one will be picking up fares from the old town tonight. A siren pedals across an intersection ahead of me. I can see a parade of burnt-out cars, steaming in the fine drizzle coming out of the sky.

I see a taxi approaching. It has its light on, although it's travelling fast and the driver looks in no mood to stop. I put out my arm, hailing it, and it speeds by in a throttling squeal. I'm wet, and the scratches on my ankles have started to fizz and sting. Even with this thin cardigan to cover my burnt arm, I'm a late-night fright, conspicuously damaged.

I keep walking along the road towards the abbey. The rain is getting heavier, and the soles of my sandals are slippery under my toes. There's no traffic coming this way, which makes me think they must be sending cars out onto the main ring road, bypassing the town centre. I glance back. There's no sign of the white van. To my left, the townhouses are ranked in terraces down to the river. The abbey is floodlit on the other bank. There's no one on the footbridge. They seem to have shut down the entire city centre, and somehow spirited the rioters away, those that aren't still fighting in the market square.

I hear laughter up ahead. Some Pelton fans are walking up the hill towards me, high on drunken swagger. I pull out of view behind a yellow hoarding panel, and find myself stumbling over the rubble of a building site. Wet dust grits my foot-soles. I sigh and shiver, feeling the unpleasantness of this night on every inch of my skin. I look up at the shell of a building. There's a sign bearing a mission statement and the logos of the investing partners. *Celebrating the Lycee's contribution to the neuroscience of memory*. I can't suppress a bitter laugh. I've come round the back of the building, which is why I didn't recognise it at first. I follow the hoarding panels round to the south side, high above the river. They're building a concourse that will link up to the riverside walkways, knitting this grand statement of the Lycee's achievements into the fabric of the ancient town. They've had no time to adjust to the fact that, thanks to my carelessness, they've lost the very thing they were supposed to be celebrating. The map is in pieces, scrambled on a server no one can unlock. The secrets of the Lorenzo Circuit are in the pockets of a madman. Even in its unfinished state, the Memory Centre draws the eye to the Lycee's ambitions, but also to its loss.

The door in the hoardings is still unlocked. I duck into the darkness between the scaffolding, half-expecting Gareth to step out of the shadows. In a moment I'm inside the circular shell of the Centre, looking up at the metal skeleton of the building. The floodlights are bathing the outer shell in light, but in here it's twilight. It's the light for seeing ghosts in, for seeing the reflections of things, if not the things themselves.

I look up into the roof space. They don't seem to have added much since I was last here. The girders still jut into nothingness. A tarpaulin flaps, straightened by the wind.

But Gareth could see something. He stood here next to me, his face a silhouette. Watching something moving in the space above our heads.

I pull the amulet from the pocket of my satchel and turn it in my hands. In the dim light, the almond eyes of the figurine peer back at me. The warm metal holds a gleam of firelight. My fingertips are cold, but I can just manage to unclasp the chain and fix it around my neck. I'm aware of nothing except the weight of expectation. My fingernails sting where I've prised the clasp apart. Apart from that, I don't feel any different. That's Gareth's point. My consciousness is a blind machine. Any cog will fit. I could have been wearing this all my life, and I wouldn't have known.

I look up again. I still can't see what Gareth saw. The cables hang down idly in their insulating sheaths. The building forgets. But the building never had memories in the first place. I made sure of that.

The thoughts crowd and scatter. I'm waiting, patient for the end of this.

The birds flew away. That's what James told me. He let them go, and Gareth said he was going to get some more. He was going to do it better this time.

I'm tired. I don't know what I'm remembering, but knowledge here is pure sick hunch and I have to follow it wherever it takes me. My fingers wander up to the ear of the figurine. I catch myself, alarmed. I'm falling into their trap. I'm going to end up doing exactly what they wanted me to do. And yet I have to find him. I'm the only one who can do it. No one else has forgotten what I've forgotten.

I twist the thumbwheel. I have that image again of Gareth in my office, talking about his imaginary aviary. Each bird is a thought, a memory. That's the point of materialism. Everything Gareth has told me comes back to this. Wisdom is getting to know your birds, finding a way to make them come to you. I twist the wheel again, feeling the facts morph together, the dizzy tilt of understanding on the move, shifting, breaking away, starting to slide. Bridge's face in the hallway. Something moving deep inside me, like butterflies, a tiny beating of wings.

Then the space is empty again. I like it that way. An exit kept clear for an emergency. So, when the thought hops up for attention, it might catch my eye.

A bird comes to me. I don't have thoughts; they have me. Processes you don't understand, shaping a consciousness, making the flesh-and-blood machine think and feel, billions of numb reflexes fashioning a mind out of data.

The bird is behind me. I don't turn around; I don't want to scare it away. It says, If you turn around you will understand everything.

'Go on, then,' I say. 'Tell me what it is that I'm supposed to remember.'

My fingers touch the amulet. Their tips are numb, and I can hardly feel what they're pressing on.

'You know it already,' the bird says. 'It's all in there. You just have to catch it.'

There's a stinging across the back of my neck. The amulet is in my hands. The chain is broken, snapped by the force of my anger. I drop the figurine to the concrete, my insides lurching. The figurine gleams in the darkness, and then vanishes under the heel of my sandal. I stamp on it with all my weight, feeling the shell crack, grinding the entrails with my heel. It can't control me. There is no 'me' to control. I don't have thoughts, I have wildlife. I live through the wildlife, discrete pointless happenings beyond my control. I stand straight, breathing hard, and stare at the lights outside. I hear them chirping, all the unconscious decisions that I am.

Where did Gareth see the birds in their cages? What did he tell me that time, when he came alone to my lab?

A haze of tears clears slowly. I have a sense of being suddenly lifted into consciousness, of watching automatic routines from the inside, of *being* those routines, all the trillions of reflexes that make up me. Sparks of ghostly activity in systems that act without knowing, siren warnings from a storytelling machine.

I know where he is. That's the point. I have always known.

PART FIVE

◎

James

CHAPTER TWENTY-THREE

All'estero

◉

I am wearing sunglasses. The train is rattling through brilliant daylight. The sunlight hits me side on, making the insides of my sunglasses reflective. I can see this nameless part of my face, the patch of skin on the outside of the eye, where you tell a woman's age. The skin there is slack and wizened, and squirms in constant motion. In the little smoked-glass mirrors of my sunglasses, the sunlight picks out a curve of wet flesh inside my lower eyelid, the part that betrays that you've been crying. Next to that, a rounded darkness, with a faintly windowed gleam of sky. My own eye, looking in on itself.

I think about what Gareth told me. It was the clue that would explain everything, although I didn't realise it at the time. The innocuous story from his childhood; the birds in their cages, stacked high above his ten-year-old eye-line. He wanted me to remember. He was telling me where he would be. But it took me this long to understand it. I knew it, but I couldn't make sense of it. I couldn't do that until I'd seen what he wanted me to see.

I think about what I said to James. I told him that I had to leave, that we should travel separately. He knows where to meet me, but he doesn't know that it's hundreds of miles from where Gareth actually is. The wound on my skull tingles. Have I told him too much? I don't know. But I realise that I've stopped checking the face of everyone who passes. I look out of the window at the ghosts of mountains. I pretend to read.

*

At two in the afternoon we reach Rosenheim.

'Allo? Oui. Non. Je suis dans le train. Non. Personne. Personne ne sait.'

No one. No one knows but me.

Forests brush by. The woodlands of Bavaria rise to the pined slopes of the Tirol. Every time the train stops I fear the new influx. I fear it, but I stay on the train.

The forces that carry you resist understanding. The things you want are things you don't even know about. But now and then the light is reconfigured by a hurtling copse of trees, and you catch a glimpse of how the facts are truly aligned. It's like that breathless moment when you've almost understood a problem, and you pray that the world will freeze the way it is, with everything fixed in that arrangement: the phone won't ring, the letterbox won't go. You know no more of this train than the length of this carriage. You could go the whole journey without knowing more. But then the tracks swing around a curve and you see the yellow locomotive, the car transporters and freight trucks way out ahead, all the baggage you've been hauling through space, oblivious, all this time.

I'm on a long subway. The walls are yellow with painted-tile motifs. I hear the drone of a didgeridoo. A considerate neohippy has turned his instrument parallel to the wall so that people won't trip over it. There's another sound, a tiny harp played by a young conservatoire type. The miniature strings sound like the soundtrack to wizardry. As I walk between them, one instrument slowly fades into the other, with people's voices on either side, echoing off the curved walls. Then the didgeridoo stops and it's just the sound of the young woman's harp, brittle and exquisite, like the tinkling of the fairy orchestra at the end of the story.

The station concourse is a hive of taxis. I climb into one and dump my rucksack on the floor. My satchel feels almost weightless without my FireBook. I am in Vienna.

*

The hotel reception is full of luggage. A queue rope steers a line of beardy youngsters towards the plastic counter. I await my turn, reeling with sleep deprivation. I show them my passport and tell them that I'm cancelling my reservation. I ask if there are any messages for me. There's a letter from James. He used to word-process all his essays. Amazing how close you can get to someone without ever seeing their handwriting.

'Tell him I had to check out early,' I say.

I read the last paragraph in the taxi to the Südbahnhof. James says he'll meet me in Vienna. He'll be at the hotel on Wednesday afternoon. Today's Tuesday. He says to wait for him there. He warns me not to phone anyone, not to go out, not to answer the door.

He's written eight, nine pages. I know half of it is lies, but I don't know which half. Faced with uncertainty, all a scientist can do is test her hypotheses. Make a risky guess, and see if it's proved true.

There's a short wait at the ticket counter. The woman in front of me is arguing with the ticket officer about her reservation for the overnight train. She's been given a berth on Romulus when she asked for Remus. The ticket man is shrugging it all away. I read James' last paragraph again. Stay in Vienna. Don't move. Wait until you know where he is, then call. When I look up I'm at the front of the queue. Stay in Vienna. Do not depart immediately for any Italian city.

The expressionless ticket officer is waiting for me. I have to tell him something.

'Verona,' I say.

CHAPTER TWENTY-FOUR

Bigger Than Your Heart

◎

Yvonne,

Stay in Vienna. I mean it. Don't move. Wait till you know exactly where he is, then call.

Babe, if you can actually read what I'm saying then I'm better at doing this handwriting shit than I remember.

There's stuff I haven't told you. There are things I <u>couldn't</u> tell you. I've thought of you all the way. I didn't want you to be hurt, and this would have hurt you. It's up to you. If you decide you don't want to hear all this about me, you don't have to. You can tear this letter up. You know where Gaz is. You don't have to call.

I've been playing a game, Yvonne. Not with you: with me. Hide-and-seek, if you like, with the real James. Sometimes you can get a better idea of who you are by being someone else. The gods have always known that. The avatars, the incarnations: anyone but who they really are. But the soul underneath doesn't change. The thing that makes you what you are stays the same. I wanted you to find yourself. It would have been enough if I'd got you just to ask the question. Challenge a few of those assumptions you've been basing all that arrogant certainty on. You could do that. It's not too late. If you can only open your heart and be honest, you can get there. But honesty's hard. Honesty has to be fought for. Not everyone has the strength for that kind of battle.

I tried to kill myself, Yvonne. I was seventeen and I couldn't see any way through this emptiness. I couldn't see any <u>meaning</u>. I was still living at home. My parents couldn't think beyond their next executive holiday. I wanted them to see what they were doing to me; I wanted them to feel the pain and fury I was feeling. They'd done this to me, with their dinner parties and the whole sick rigmarole of suburban fakery; they'd made it so that being alive was no different to not being alive. At least I could make that call. I went down to Bankstown Underpass on a Saturday night, emptied everything out of my pockets and walked out into the traffic. David saved me. He was driving one of the cars I was trying to get hit by. But it was like he knew this was going to happen, and he was ready. He was like a god in that sense. Clairvoyant. Attuned to the amazing story that's unfolding around us. He didn't say anything; he didn't ask any questions. I just sat in his car and watched his reflection in the windscreen, the lights on the dashboard, the needles going up and down, the whole beautiful secret regularity of it. People were coming out of the pubs, caught up in the relentless chaos of being alive, and I suddenly understood what was happening for them, how they all fitted together. Reality hit me with such force it made me cry. I knew I was here. I knew I was part of this crazy privilege that is life.

You're here too, Yvonne. That's what I keep trying to tell you.

He took me back to the squat. He gave me a room. I had a bath and a smoke. I met Bridge. She winds you up, I know, but she gave me love like it was falling out of the sky. Grandstand was there. Level Ten came later. David found him on top of the Byggate multi-storey, about to do a birdman stunt. He was dressed up for it. He wanted to die fully feathered.

We were all suicides, more or less. People who'd given up, and then found hope in despair. David was like that angel on the bridge, you know, who's supposed to stop you jumping? He always left it a bit late. He wanted us to taste the fear. He thought it was good that we got so close, because it gave us a chance we wouldn't have got otherwise. We could be born again as someone else. That's what it felt like. When I opened my eyes from the lies I'd been living through, everything was different. I felt I could make anything happen. We all did. We wanted to share that feeling around. We wanted people to see the truth in front of their faces, the possibility of happiness. The possibility of love.

They were already big on the actions. Saturday mornings, down at the West Gate. Level Ten was Barney Rubble to my Fred Flintstone. It was a laugh. A real thrill, you know? When Level Ten joined, things really got going. He was smart, he had loads of ideas. How to keep the protest peaceful, mainly: we were never into people getting hurt. But then things started going too far. One minute we were going into shops and switching small bits of merchandise around, and the next it was the sound of ambulances. Looking back, I think maybe they were trying to test my loyalty. I went along with it because I owed David so much. And you get caught up in things. I'm the proof of that. Take your eye off the ball, and things get so much bigger than you. You can hardly find yourself amid all the shit you've made happen.

That's why David had to go away. It tore him apart. He loved this place, loved what he'd achieved here. But the pressure was too much. The constant scrutiny. Trying to keep it all quiet. For months we weren't doing anything, just lying low. Pretending he was dead. We wanted to get the attention off him completely, and it seemed the best way. That was a real headache, trying to pretend that he'd died. We actually drove his car up to Holy Island and left it on the causeway, waited for the tide to come in. They found his clothes on the beach and they thought he'd walked out into the water. But the myth didn't die that easily. People swore that they'd seen him. People <u>wanted</u> him to be alive. They couldn't face the reality that there could ever be a world in which his presence wasn't shining out.

Finally we had the idea of sending him away, for his own safety. Seems hard to believe it now, but it was actually my idea. The plan was for him to go out and bring the message to the world, trying to keep himself safe as he did it. Hugging the shadows. You can imagine how that made me feel. He'd already saved my life, and I'd repaid him with this. The thing was, he just came at me with mercy and forgiveness. All he gave back to me was love. So when he came to see me just before he left, saying he needed me, there was something only I could help him with, I had no choice. I had to go along with it. I had the connections. I could pass as a student. I owed David everything. It was time I started repaying.

I have to tell you the truth about that now. Me working for Sansom was all part of David's plan. He arranged the whole thing. I'm sorry, but knowing all this would have put you in danger. Better that you got the wrong idea about it than get mixed up in something that could hurt you.

You already know the bit about David doing a deal with Sansom. He would get them the mapping data so that they could develop their Alzheimer's therapy. If they knew exactly where the circuits ran, they could use their implants to reverse the effects of the disease. In return, they would give him the money he needed to take the protest to a new level. Sansom wouldn't know it, but their cash would bring the sordid business of science to its knees. All I had to do was go to Sansom and offer to spy on the Lycee. The thing is, it wasn't any coincidence that Sansom security called me in and bought me a drink. I volunteered. I was doing it because David wanted me to.

Well, that was the plan, anyway. Trouble is, we didn't count on our little manic friend. Just as we're rooting around, trying to find a way onto Ermintrude, we find out that Gaz has beaten us to it. He'd already got hold of your precious mapping data, posted it to an obscure server somewhere and probably buried it under some decent security. When Sansom got wind of this, suddenly I was in a whole different situation. Finding the data meant finding Gaz. I knew he trusted you. He'd talked to you about what he was planning to do. I knew that if anyone could find him, you could.

I realise I had to keep a lot from you. That hurt me more than you can imagine. Sansom said I should stay with you, so I could pick up the information when it came out. I thought that simply meant waiting for you to remember in your own sweet time. I could not have imagined what they really had planned for you.

You know the reason for the bomb now, anyway. David didn't send it to you because you were a vivisectionist. He sent you the bomb because he wanted Sansom to get this implant into you. It wasn't enough for them to wait until you remembered Gareth's clue naturally. They had to bring their new technology into it. Apparently his idea was to send it to you at the squat, so you couldn't possibly have thought it was him. Who the hell would bomb their own house? He knew we'd all be out on an action. I thought that bit was pretty smart.

But that was the end of it for me. I knew nothing about the bomb, I swear to you. He'd made it tiny, 25g of potassium chlorate mixed with aluminium powder, just to knock you out. That stuff you could smell was an anaesthetic gas. They only needed half an hour to get that electrode into you. It was all part of the deal. You'd blame Aslan's Law, and you wouldn't ask any questions. Your burns were supposed to be acceptable damage. I hated him for that. But he had so much power over me. I went to tell the others I'd had enough, that I couldn't stand what they were doing. They denied everything. We had a screaming row. I just wanted out. I tried to get out, that night on the moors, and those thugs from Sansom nearly killed me. Now I've betrayed them all. Maybe I've just finished what I didn't finish that night in the Underpass. Or maybe we can get through this. Maybe, if we stick together, we can find a way.

We've got to find Gaz. For a while I didn't want to; I'd had it with him. But it's the only way. We've got to get the data back to the Lycee. Finish it, right now. So there's no more race. So Sansom are <u>out</u> of it. David is coming after me, I'm sure of it. I know he's already in the country. He's got a bad temper, and I've fucked up his plan. I've blown my cover with Sansom, and he staked a lot on that. No one's ever done this to him and got away with it. You've seen what he's prepared to do. Human life is just a detail to him. That's why we have to travel alone. I don't want him on your back as well. And that's why I'm handwriting this. No one writes letters any more. He'll be checking the computers, looking for a message. He's probably in your treehouse now, going through your stuff.

I didn't tell you this before because I didn't want you to know how much danger I was in. But you know now. I'm afraid you had to know.

I wish I knew how it came to this. When this started, you and me, I was full of dreams. I really thought we could find a way to be together. But too much has happened. Too much life. At first I thought I could deny its influence on me; I thought I could be bigger than it. But David taught me that you can't deny it. You can't be bigger than your own story. We can't help the things that make us what we are. But we can try and face them. We can be brave enough to realise how they're affecting us, the things we do, the decisions we make. Whatever David thinks of me now, nothing can change the reality he helped me to see. I am like I am because of what happened to me. Simple. That's me. That's my truth.

I love you, Yvonne. I love you because of who I am. I love you <u>in spite</u> of who I am. Look at me, I'm shaking. I'm still afraid.

Stay in Vienna. Don't move until you've heard from Gaz. I've no idea how you know he's there, and I can see you don't really want to tell me. I'll be at the hotel on Wednesday afternoon. Don't phone anyone. Don't go out. Don't answer the door. Just wait, and keep your head down.

Fucking huge amounts of love,

James.

CHAPTER TWENTY-FIVE

At The Antica Porta Leone

◉

I get in to Verona in the early morning. On the Corso Porta Nuova, businessmen are walking slowly to work through liquid sunshine. After a sleepless night in my seated accommodation, the night sky unreeling at high speed, the built-up world looks distorted, skewed by impossible depths, as though I'd put my contact lenses in the wrong eyes. I feel I could slip off the pavement at any moment, stretch out in the gutter in a thin hallucinating line. The municipal trolleybins are painted with scenes from civic life. The businessmen are talking into their palms. He'll be headed for Vienna. I'm in Verona. Easy cities to get confused.

I step into a café and order a cappuccino and a custard cornetto. The morning sunlight basks at the bar, plays jazz on the chroming of the Gaggia. I sit at a table on the pavement, smoking something that tastes petrochemical, and watch the girl clear away cups and plates. I wonder how life looks from where she guards it. I wonder how much I could change. Across the street is a convent, a jumble of dark medieval doorways from which six nuns are unspooling silkily. The girl watches the nuns. I witness her dreaming, feel every pang of life-envy. A sign inside the doorway gives opening hours.

The Hotel Antica Porta Leone lies at the end of a cobbled alleyway. I'm shown upstairs by a pale-stockinged widow with a bitter smell. From the window I can see a telecoms booth, a square parking area and the corner of a department store. As the proprietress leaves, I ask whether there have been any messages. She shrugs, in that devastating Italian way. No one. No one knows I'm here.

I leave my rucksack on the bed and stare at the walnut dressing table, the cheerful clock radio, the little brown bakelite telephone. I feel the agony of a soul that needs to be online. But I left my FireBook behind at Millennium Heights, with a freezer full of food for Effi. And my phone is still in the lost-and-found at the Marriott Waterside. I look out of the window at the telecoms booth, wondering whether to call his mobile. He'll be in Vienna in a few hours, booking us in for dinner at the hotel restaurant, waiting for me to ring. I need to call him soon if he's going to make it. What I want to do needs his company. Finding the truth about a person: it's not a game you can play alone.

But if I phone him now, I lay myself open. I go back to being Sansom's experimental monkey, controlled by contingencies someone else is dreaming up. This way, I stay in control.

I don't call.

The image of a church. The cam is mounted high, foreshortening the ancient façade. The refresh schedule is fast, maybe three seconds. Blink and the picture will have changed, a subtle reconfiguration of mottlings that tests the limits of what you can notice. The pavement is bleached by sunlight. There are people on the street, cars. The white minibus that was parked at one side has moved off in a succession of blurry snapshots. It's a dull stretch of mid-morning, slowed by late spring heat, and this is my reward for remembering Gareth's story. This shabby medieval building is where he will keep his side of the bargain. The church on the cam is somewhere in Verona. I just don't yet know where.

Someone is talking. I set the image printing and click back to the anonymity of the lilac welcome banner. There's no sign of Gareth's icon. When I first went online and changed my icon to two fat exclamation marks — my signal that I'd worked out what he'd been trying to tell me — I knew it would only be a matter of time before he made himself visible. His return to the public gaze was brief, but it lasted long enough for him to use the cam feed function to show me what I was looking for in Verona. The counter at the bottom of the screen tells me that sixteen million people are currently living the narrative of Des*re. He's given me a time and a date — tomorrow — but no other information apart from this webcam. I still have work to do. An old bloke at the table behind me is working on a puzzle book with the aid of a large dictionary. A young man sits on a high stool behind the information desk, gazing at a screen. A colleague in a blue floral sundress is telling him the latest instalment of some ongoing saga, as loudly as only library workers know how. The young man seems to want to get back to his catalogue.

He glances up and notices me watching him, then speaks impatiently to the young woman, who drifts aimlessly back to her own station.

I go over and pick up my printout. The brains keep working.

The home screen on my workstation is a search page. Every terminal in this row shouts back the same invitation: `Cerca!` It's safe: I'm in a public library. No one can trace me here. I type in his name, with the same sick trepidation as if I were saying it out loud, somehow afraid of who might answer. But no one answers. The net comes back empty. `Non sono stati trovati risultati per "james bonham".`

I google `"david overstrand"`. Nothing. I try it without the double quotes. Two hundred and thirty-six items are returned. Overstrand, Norfolk. Overstrand Cricket Club. It's a place, not a person. Finding nothing proves nothing, except that I'm not looking hard enough. I go over to the information desk, my mouth set in a hyphen of determination. The young man looks alarmed.

'Per favore. *Corriere?*'

I write some dates on a piece of paper and hand it to him. He goes to a drawer behind him and turns back holding a stack of CDs. I take them over to my workstation and flick through them. I choose the year that James started getting involved with the protests, the year he turned fifteen. Two years before he met David in the traffic at Bankstown Underpass. I'll start at the beginning, and see what unfolds.

I choose the search option and enter `david overstrand inghil-terra`. The arriving truth is measured off at the bottom of the screen, in the progress of a blue status bar. `Pelton, Inghilterra, 17 Agosto. Animalista militante David Overstrand, 19, è stato lasciato ammazzato secco dall'incidente...` I dredge up some holiday Italian and try to guess the rest. Animal rights militant David Overstrand, 19, was... But the last phrase beats me. There's something about a shipment of livestock, an aeroplane. `È stato lasciato ammazzato secco dall'incidente.` The auto-translate function is returning gibberish. I set the article printing and take the discs back to the desk. I need a cappuccino. I need to think.

*

I stick to the back streets. The tourist areas feel too exposed. I won't see the Arena on this trip, or meet my lover at the fountain in the Piazza dell'Erbe. My wanderings are centrifugal. I'm interested in the outskirts, the life that clings to the periphery, the short cuts out of town. Deserted piazzas, balcony-crowded alleyways. Places where people live, where cars are parked impossibly on corners, as though fork-lift-trucked into place. Churches I notice more than anything. I'm churching. I'm a churcher. But all of them let me down: they're too tall, too white, too new. None of them matches this printout I'm holding. Gareth is keeping me guessing. And while I'm guessing, I can't call James.

I stop at a café on a tiny piazza, in the shadow of the wrong church. I order a whole half-litre of red and watch the waiter's expression. There's a phone booth nearby. I could call James now, ask him what *è stato lasciato ammazzato secco* means. But I'm not sure I'm ready for any more of James' truth. Lunchtime slides slowly into siesta, and the wine seeps into my blood. At a table opposite me, a man and a woman are breaking up in Italian. Love can't survive even these perfect afternoons. I'm killing time, killing my one chance to gain control. The facts are still out of whack. Whatever I want to say, I could just as easily say the opposite. He loves me. He loves me not.

I know the convent re-opens at four. I wait.

'Per favore. Questa chiesa. Dove?'

The nun takes the printout from me and peers at it. The band of her wimple is like a weather stripe on a cosmic TV, interference from another universe. She bends closer, trying to focus, and I wonder if she can smell the booze on my breath. The cam printout is pale and bubble-jet pointilliste, not much better than an old newspaper. My heart sinks. I'm asking too much.

She shakes her head and disappears through a door into the back. I'm left alone in this dark ante-room to salvation. A plaque on the wall gives the history of the convent in English. I sit in a black wooden chair with my pale legs and wonky eyes and think about taking the veil. I wonder how desperate you have to get before you give it all up for the peace of a clear conscience. I have no job. Everything I've worked for is in tatters. But even as the thought goes through me, some fleeting heart's protest tells me that I still belong to the world of colour. The nuns must have had lives before this. I'm not yet ready to give up on mine.

The nun returns with a map and spreads it out on the counter. She points to a spot on the north-western outskirts, across the Adige. She writes the name down in careful lettering. S. Maria della Concezione.

'Finita,' she says. 'Sconsacrata.'

'Non chiesa allora?'

'Si. Si. Non chiesa.'

'Per favore. Questa?'

I hand her the clipping from the *Corriere della Sera*. She reads it with little devotional lip-gestures.

'Animals rights,' she says, in strikingly clear English. 'They are flying cows, for food. Veal. The militanti try to stop the aeroplane...'

'This bit,' I say, pointing to the phrase about David Overstrand. 'Lasciato ammazzato secco. Che volere dire?'

She looks up at the history plaque, trying to convert my Italian into hers.

'Killed instantly.'

The wound on my scalp begins to burn. I feel the jolt of understanding. So David Overstrand didn't save James' life at Bankstown Underpass. By the time of James' suicide attempt, the animal rights campaigner had already been dead for two years. He died at nineteen, no terrorist mastermind, just an ordinary sleek-skinned teenager who thought he could change the world. He never kidnapped unsuspecting vivisectionists, or firebombed remote biotech units, or went roaming the earth in self-imposed exile. Whoever sent me twenty-five grammes of home-made explosive, it wasn't him. James' myth of David Overstrand, his own reason for existing, is just a fairy tale. And if the truth about James is a fiction, what's left? Only he can tell me that.

If I call him now, he can be on the train from Vienna tonight. I could meet him at the station in the morning. But I know what James will be like in the morning. He'll be tetchy, hurt that his own inner struggle has not stopped me wanting breakfast. I could call him now, to ask whether he's changed. I wonder how his voice would sound. He'll be in the hotel in Vienna, mobile in one hand and dick in the other, watching strangers fuck on cable TV. Sweetly, endearingly offhand with himself, even when he's most convinced that he rules the world. Checking his belly in the mirror, bowing to the glass in search of grey hairs. Dimly aware that he's alone, invincible, and staying that way.

I call James.

CHAPTER TWENTY-SIX

Finding James

◉

As I sleep, the camera keeps filming the building. The night is picked apart frame by frame. Most of it is shadow, blotches of oversaturated darkness that seem to rotate, as though a dirty lens were turning, as the street updates itself on a three-second refresh schedule. The ground is wet with metallic streetlight. Where the cam catches the source of the light, a ray of it stretches upwards to form another star. The church is grey, a human face in moonlight, detailed in lines of shadow. The solid blue-blackness of total video darkness spreads to another part of the screen. The blotches swirl and reconfigure. Maybe one of them turns into a man.

I don't sleep, actually. Thoughts go by, vengeful and slightly crazed. I keep still while time moves past me. I'm a camera, filming a locked door.

I get up and sit in the window. The piazza is an empty inbox, downloading loneliness with the sound of taxi brakes. His train gets in at 8:30. I told him to be down there at nine, outside the department store. I said I wanted to talk to him first, in private. When he comes, I'll watch him standing by the phone booth for a while, until he starts to need me more than I need him. Then I'll go down the back stairs and jump into the first taxi that goes by.

At 8:30 Via Leone is busy with office workers. I told James the name of the church, but I kept the directions quiet. He doesn't know it's on the other side of the Adige. I've still told him too much. I forgot about his ego, his need to be there first and leave his mark, scratch his name on anything of value. At 8:40 it dawns on me that he's not coming. It's a relief, in a way, not to have to walk there next to him, wondering which lie he's telling now.

I leave the hotel, alone, at a quarter to nine. A few minutes later I'm in a taxi.

It takes twenty minutes to get from Porta Leone to the north-western suburbs of Verona. James is in every car. I see his silhouette in the window and a spurt of fear breaks through me. When we stop at traffic lights I'm strangely glad for the automatic locks on the doors. I don't know why I think he'll hurt me. His cruelty has always been a hands-off sport. All he's ever wanted is to spare me the facts, knowing that I need confirmed knowledge like some people need holidays. Cutting me off from certainty: that's hurt enough for me.

Via della Concezione is deserted. The church soars silently from behind a parade of half-parked, half-crashed cars. I stand in the road and look up at the buildings opposite, trying to guess the point to which my image is being gathered. I'm a blur on a webcam, a character trying to understand her place in a video game. They say that you only start understanding who you are when you see yourself as others see you. Maybe James is right about that. Sometimes you can get a better idea about yourself by being someone else.

The door is heavy, enough to make me think it's locked. There's a porch, filled with polish smells and a distilled blackness. Then another door. I hesitate, feeling its wooden weight pushing back at me. I don't need to be doing this. I could walk away, right now. But then I'd never get to know Gareth's big plan. And James would never get to know mine.

I push on the door. Wings in my face. Dark bodies startling against walls. A feeling of the most intense exhaustion, a delirium of sleeplessness turned outwards into scattered energies. The roar of them. Their chatter and whirr.

The church is full of birds. After the glare of daylight I'm fully blinded, and it feels as though I could only have come to this greenish, suboceanic realm through gravity, in a descent from somewhere. As my eyes adjust, I can see that the light is mostly coming from above, from a few chinks of sky between shrugged-off roof tiles, and a stained-glass window above the altar. The reflected light strengthens and clarifies, and the walls resonate with a faint blurred restlessness, the muted twitter of hundreds of trapped lives. Cages, stacked high in unstable towers, ranged in rows along stone windowsills and smashed, dust-logged pews. Some lay fallen and broken, their occupants flown. Others hold a moving body, silvered and quickened by the strengthening twilight. There is a design here, connections I don't understand. That's all we are: connections. I realise with a pang that Gareth meant every word.

The roof of the aviary is coarse netting, held up on scaffolding poles. The church has a second skeleton within its shell, as though in preparation for a renovation. I walk along the nave and stop at the altar. Feathered weights blunder against me. I'm a life form that evades their radar, turns bird grace into clumsiness. There's a distant percussive sound, like an intercom coming on but no one speaking, echoing in the high corners of the building. A thrush thuds past me in the gloom. The hubbub throbs and then quietens again. I can see some of the birds settling on ledges, folding effortlessly into inscrutable poses, preening themselves as they settle down to wait.

Then the ringtone of a mobile phone, patiently rising above the murmur of the aviary.

'Better get that,' a voice behind me says.

I don't look around. If I look around, I might change my mind.

A display screen flashes on the seat of a pew in one of the front rows. I hear James behind me, getting up and shuffling across to the aisle. I go over to the phone and pick it up. The caller ID is flashing: ANSWER ME.

I press the touchscreen and put its glow to my ear.

'Miss?'

I never guessed how much the sound of his voice would affect me. After all this, he still won't call me by my first name.

'Gareth? Where are you?'

'I'll tell you later. Is he there?'

I turn to look. James is watching from the gloom of the nave.

'He's here.'

'I might have known he'd try to spoil everything.' I hear Gareth hesitating, suppressing a tremor in his voice. 'Still, you're going to learn the truth about him pretty soon.'

'Don't worry. I'm working James out.'

Gareth's breath rasps at my ear. I imagine him looking around his place of safety, his big eyes scanning the corners for danger. I once thought that I could never properly earn the trust he wanted to place in me. But perhaps that's changed now.

'Why did you take the data?'

'Because I wanted you to understand. I wanted you to listen to me. You were the only person who seemed to care about this.'

'This wasn't worth it, Gareth. The problem of materialism is not worth risking your life for.'

'It's everything, Miss. It's how the ghost gets into the machine. It's how a dumb lump of flesh can inherit a soul.'

James hasn't moved. Keeping track of him means risking him over-hearing. I turn my back on him, cupping the phone in my hand, and move closer to the altar.

'Where are the data now?'

'They're all around you.'

I look up. I can see boarded-up windows where before there was just blackness. Tiny ledges that would once have held shrines. Every surface is a perch for something feathered, something flickering.

'The birds are the data?'

'*Kyrie eleison*, Miss. You *have* learned something from all this. Listen, I have to go. Watch carefully. I've put on a show for you. Try to understand. Take this phone with you when you go. I'll call you. And don't tell James anything. Let him talk. Find out what he knows.'

There's a thud, like a microphone being dropped, and then music starts. I pocket the dead phone.

'I get it now,' James says. 'He's here, but he's not here. Trust Gaz to always want to be one step ahead.'

I feel him move in beside me. We left each other five days ago, at the roadside in the rain. There wasn't time for long goodbyes. He had his unfinished business with the security man, and I had to get away. What did we not say then that we should have said? I glance at him, hating my weakness. His eyes make stained-glass reflections. Whoosh. Just whoosh.

'I know how you know now,' he says. 'I saw the bird market. Piazza dell'Erbe. Gaz must have spent a bit of money there.'

I could have guessed that he would get there before me. It seems odd, after all this, that I came to Verona and I never even went to look at the bird market.

'He told me about it. Before Easter, when he came up to my lab. He came here with his family as a kid. He was giving me a clue, even back then.' I glance at the pews behind, suddenly anxious that James might not have come alone. 'That's how I knew he was here. That was what I was supposed to remember.'

'Verona,' he says. 'Sounds a bit like Vienna.'

Maybe we can both see the funny side.

'Where's David?' I say.

'He's coming.'

I start shaking, quietly, like a timer going off.

'Does he know?'

'He knows everything.'

The nave behind us is empty. The music has stopped, and a voice is speaking from the dark corners of the church. It's Gareth. He seems to be reading aloud. *May not a man 'possess' and yet not 'have' knowledge in the sense of which I am speaking? As you may suppose a man to have caught wild birds — doves or any other birds — and to be keeping them in an aviary which he has constructed at home; we might say of him in one sense, that he always has them because he possesses them, might we not?*

'Plato's aviary.' My voice is drowned out by a spasm of flapping. 'That's the point of all this. How a system that is purely physical can become conscious, aware of its own workings, its own past.'

'That's it. He's created one big feathery mind. All you have to do is jog its memory!'

He runs at the cages, shouting. The flapping of wings clatters around the church. Through the stained-glass window above the altar, the sun prints him with a stencil of colours.

'OK, so I got the wrong city.' He turns back to me, breathing hard. 'But still. I thought you were going to wait for me.'

I put a hand in my jeans pocket. The cutting from the *Corriere* is still there. But I don't think I need it now. Just keep him talking. Let the lies prove themselves.

'I said I was going to call you. If you had other ideas, then that's your look-out.'

The music starts up again. If Gareth is controlling this, he must be listening.

'What are you, James? What am I dealing with?'

The question pleases him. That's what all this has been about: finding James.

'I'm this idiot who's in love with you. I can't help it.'

'You can't help what you are?'

He shrugs, enjoying himself.

'This stuff that happened to you. Is there no way you can beat it? Is there no way you can get bigger than it? I mean, I don't understand therapy or whatever, but people go through all sorts of traumas and they get over them. Why not you?'

'It's a process. It takes time.'

'How much time? A lifetime? Could you die not knowing?'

I feel his hand on my arm. He knows I know something. He wanted me to know. The letter, the excessive detail about David Overstrand: it was all there to ram the point home. That Bankstown Underpass is a fairy tale. Not the truth that makes the stories true. The lie that reveals nothing but lies.

'I'm learning,' he says. 'I'm learning all the time.'

'So these fads. All the gods you've prayed to in the search for yourself. Which of them is right? Which of them is the truth?'

'The method is not the truth. The method is the method. Science is a philosophy which holds that a certain method is privileged above all others.'

'You believe that? Still?'

'I won't judge you, Yvonne. You want me to judge you, but I won't. I love you. I trust my emotions on this. I want you to find out who you are.'

I pull my arm away. I never imagined what it would be like, today, to have him touch me.

'I know who I am, James. I'm a person who refuses to find herself. Because I don't believe there's anything worth looking for.'

He shakes his head. 'You're kidding yourself. You disprove it every time you use the word *I*.'

I slap his face, as hard as I can. My fingers come away stinging.

'There. That's all I am, James. Flesh and blood and chemical reactions. There's nothing more.'

'No.' He dabs at his cheek, gorgeously aroused. 'I think you know who you are. Why would you do anything if you didn't have a self? Why did you come here today, if there wasn't a *you* to want it?'

'I came here because you said you loved me. I want to know what love is.'

'Love is a story,' he says. 'The funniest one of all.'

He goes over to a cage and peers in. He has his back to me, crouching. Telling the truth about a man: it's not like shooting him. You don't have to look him in the eye.

'*I'll* tell you a story, James. It's about a boy who realised he had nothing inside. So he went out to try and find some meaning for his life. He thought he would do whatever it took to find himself a story.'

'I know that one. It's not funny at all.'

I wait, wondering how to say it.

'You lied to me about Bankstown Underpass. David Overstrand didn't pull up out of the traffic and save your life. He'd already been dead for two years.'

He still has his back to me. When he speaks it's quietly, to the bird.

'I know my truth, Yvonne. I know my story.'

'But it isn't true. You made the whole thing up.'

He coughs out a laugh. 'Now why would I want to lie about that?'

'Because it made you. It gave you something to be. The failed suicide. The guy with the guilt. The man with the trauma he can't speak about. Without it you were empty. Like me: an empty box.'

He reaches for the latch of the cage. The door swings open. He crouches back on his heels and watches the bird hop onto the sill, and then, with a final vigilant head-twitch, take flight.

'I feel sorry for you, Yvonne. You can't help trying to rationalise. You're given a choice between thinking and feeling and you choose brainpower every time.' He looks up at the broken ceiling, tracing the bird's trajectory beneath the rafters with a kind of pride, as if he himself had given it the gift of flight. 'I know what the truth is. I can feel it. My whole body tells me. Your trouble is, you won't trust your feelings. You won't trust your love.'

He turns to me. His smile breaks my heart. My voice is firm, fighting to be strong. I want him to tell me that he's not been lying. I'd believe him, even now. But he says nothing. He won't even answer the charge.

'You've lied to me from the start, James. You've lied to yourself. Not about what you've done or where you've been or who you've been sleeping with. You've been lying about the big stuff. About the one thing you could supposedly only tell the truth about. About who you are.'

He reaches for my hand again. I let him. It's the last time.

'You love me, Yvonne, but you won't trust that love. You feel it in your heart, in your body. But your cortex throws it out. It doesn't make sense. It won't compute.'

'Don't try and tell me what I feel. You've had me, but you've never known me.'

Now he pulls me closer, tries to hold me. I'm losing it. It's all I want him to do.

'You've never loved anyone, Yvonne, because you've never let go. Your head runs the show. Your heart never gets a look-in.'

'Well, maybe,' I'm crying now, not trying to hide it, 'I'm happy with that.'

'You're fooling yourself.'

'No. I'm just waking up.'

There's a crash from high up in front of us. A bird has struggled so hard against its bars that it and the cage below have toppled over. The music has stopped, and Gareth's voice is speaking again.

And yet, in another sense, he has none of them; but they are in his power, and he has got them under his hand in an enclosure of his own, and can take and have them whenever he likes — he can catch any which he likes, and let the bird go again, and he may do so as often as he pleases.

'Listen to what he's saying, James. Isn't it time you took what you came here for?'

'I didn't come here for the data. I came here for you.'

'Well, David wants the data. What time is he coming?'

The bluff surprises him. He seems to stiffen.

'I don't know.'

So let us now suppose that in the mind of each man there is an aviary of all sorts of birds — some flocking together apart from the rest, others in small groups, others solitary, flying anywhere and everywhere.

I smile at the words. 'Are you going to let him find you here?'

'I don't give a fuck about the data. I don't give a fuck about David. I want *you*. I love *you*.'

'Is he coming?'

'Who?'

'David. Is David coming?'

We may suppose that the birds are kinds of knowledge, and that whenever a man has detained in the enclosure a kind of knowledge, he may be said to have learned or discovered the thing which is the subject of the knowledge.

'What do *you* think?' he says, staring in irritation at the broken cage.

And thus, when a man has learned and known something long ago, he may resume and get hold of the knowledge which he has long possessed. Shall we say that he comes back to himself to learn what he already knows?

To learn what he already knows. But that's it. I already know.

'We're not waiting for David at all, are we? We don't need to.'

'What are you talking about?'

He seems caught out. I can see him forcing himself to enjoy something which, in the end, leaves a bitter taste.

'Gareth wanted me to find out something about you. Is this it?'

'I don't know what you mean.'

'You're David Overstrand?'

He laughs. It's funny how I never had an image of what the mythical terrorist looked like. It's because he wasn't a person at all.

'We all are. It's a code word. Our name for each other.'

'You took his name? That kid who was killed by the plane?'

'He was a friend of mine, Yvonne. I was there when he was killed. I saw him carted off in an ambulance. It was the first action I'd ever been on. I was fifteen.'

'That's why there were no photos of him ...'

I feel the blast again, burning my face, filling my cortex with light. The silent outrage of the unborn.

'You put that thing into me ...'

'No. I told you, I didn't know about the bomb. I didn't know about the implant. That was all Sansom. I wasn't involved.'

A pale face above me in the hallway. Bridge's pinched sincerity, shimmering through my pain. We seemed to be fighting underwater, trying to turn each other in a direction we didn't want to go. *We need to know, Yvonne. We've got to find the people who did this to you.* She was there. She was David Overstrand, the terrorist. They all were.

'What did you know about, then? The other animal rights attacks? All those lab workers who got tortured? Or was Conscience just another way of forgetting how empty you were?'

'They're my friends, Yvonne. They saved my life. They stuck with me through everything. Until this happened, they'd never let me down.'

'So when were you planning to tell me? After I'd agreed to join you?'

He goes over to the fallen cage and unpicks the wire latch. Inside there is a frightened brown bird. It has something on its leg, a tiny grey tag like an electronic monitoring device. The bird stays hunched in its corner, not as convinced by the promise of freedom as we are.

'It didn't have to go as far as it did. If you'd only trusted your feelings. Done some thinking with your heart for once.'

'You wanted me to find myself? You wanted to make up a story for me too?'

He unpins another cage and watches the bird lift off into a gap between the rafters. Look after the birds, the wise men tell us. For James, that always meant letting them go.

'You could have joined us. They wouldn't have hurt someone who was helping them. You could have been part of it. But you chose reason. You chose to be right, all the fucking time.'

'There's nothing wrong with being right.'

'But you weren't right. You took it to pieces to find out how it worked. Then you didn't know what to do with the pieces. They didn't fit back together. You'd lost the very thing that made them what they were.'

'No, James. There's nothing else. The pieces are all there is.'

Ghosts look strange in the flesh. Familiar. But then they were alive once. In your arms. Inside you.

'You're empty, aren't you, James? There's nothing inside. Not even Bankstown Underpass. Not even a story.'

A hassled frown dents the space between his eyes. This is not how he wanted this to go. He stands there, patiently curving his hand over one side of his hair.

'I'm yours, Yvonne. I'm your puzzle.'

'And I was always one to fall for a challenge, wasn't I?'

His eyes react, as though something brilliant had just started up behind me.

'Come with me. We can get through this.'

'No, James. It's too late.'

The sound of a motor makes him turn. I look up to see a jet of light shoot out over our heads into the boarded-up gloom at the end of the nave. The whirr of a data projector. There's a spell of darkness, and then Gareth's face looms up against the ruined wall, a pulsing hologram, bright as a dream in the ruins. His eyes are closed. I wonder if he could have fallen asleep so quickly. I watch, not breathing, as the projector adjusts its rotation slightly and then magnifies it so that the image of Gareth fills the space between the two central columns. His eyes behind their closed lids seem more sunken than ever. His face has the angular severity of an old man's.

'Where is he? How's he doing this?'

'He's connected. He's rigged himself up to this entire aviary. He's feeling it, breathing it. It's become his consciousness.'

'How?'

'I don't know. He believed it was possible. And maybe that's made it come true.'

Gareth stirs, his restlessness blurring the hologram. His eyes are moving under their lids.

'He's dreaming,' James says.

'No. The birds are dreaming. There are only birds.'

The beam catches on the side of James' face, lighting him up like we were lit up for each other, long ago, when I was his cinema.

'You'd better go.'

'No hurry. They don't know about this place. They'll have seen the cam, but they can't know it's in Verona. Gaz did a good job of hiding that.'

'They? You mean Sansom?'

'The people who work for them. The Chinese gangs who arrange the stowaways. They've left me alone so far because they wanted me to find the data for them. Shame they can't be here to see it.'

'What do you mean?'

He unclips another cage and gently removes its occupant. He holds the bird towards me, lifting the grey tag in his fingers.

'It's here. Look. Every bird has got one. It has to be the mapping data. Gaz would never have trusted it to a computer. He's put it into thousands of these little data chips, and he's attached each one to a bird. They're yours. If you can catch them.'

I look at the other cages. Each bird has a similar grey tag. Those that have been freed are also carrying tiny data chips. The data are all around you, Gareth told me. James is opening more cages and shooing their inhabitants out into the air. The data scatter noisily around us, colonizing different corners of the church.

'So this is how he disguises them from Sansom?'

'You said the data were in pieces. Each bit was on a different account on Ermintrude. They weren't going to put them together until all the pieces were ready.'

More startled birds flutter up from his hands.

'What are you going to do?'

'I don't know. Report back to Sansom. Tell them they're not getting their precious mapping data.'

'And what about your friends?'

'I walk out of here. I make myself disappear.'

He tightens his cheeks, creaselessly betraying his youth.

'Are you scared?'

'Not for me. Like you say, I'm empty. What's an empty box going to feel?'

I shiver, feeling everything. 'What about me?'

'It's not your problem, Yvonne. Sansom know who double-crossed them. They know who didn't deliver on the deal. Go ahead and live your life. Go to Effi. She needs you. She's not part of this.'

He seems to be waiting. Tears blur the lights of the cages, brilliantly swollen. I'm frightened and cold.

'Do one good thing,' I say. 'Pretend you got what you came here for. Make out that Gareth told you where the data were. Lead them off on a really long wild goose chase. Keep them away from this place.'

He grins. 'Since when have I ever done anything for anyone?'

'Maybe no one's ever really needed you before.'

The idea flows into him silently. He goes to pick up his bag, and then stands there before me, sunglasses hooked onto his shirt pocket, the white threads of his headphones tangled around his jacket buttons.

'What will they do to you?'

'Nothing. The gangs have their methods for settling things. They'll wait until I have a son. That's the Chinese way. The son pays.'

'He already has.'

'What?'

I feel the blast again, the quiet voice in the hallway. I can't tell him. It was a feeling. It wasn't truth.

'James...'

He's on me now. Something's wrong. I tense, ready to fight him. Our sudden movements startle the birds, and they flap up towards the light, deflected by the netting above the aviary. James' arms close across my back and I feel the strength he pins into me, a grip that is too strong for love. He rocks with strange upheavals, feelings you could never name. There's a white stain on the shoulder of his jacket. His voice is thick in my ear.

'They can't hurt me, Yvonne. They can tear me to pieces, but they can't do what you're doing...'

He's sobbing. I let him hold me until it stops.

'You nearly died once, James. Do what David was supposed to have done for you. Take the chance you wouldn't otherwise have had.'

He stands back, unsteady on his feet. I feel a pinch of pity, watching him. What's left of a man, after you take away his stories?

'All right. I'll do it. Sansom aren't going to get the data.'

He looks at me for the last time. His eye contact is uncertain, as though he'd not quite decided that, after all this, I was the person he really wanted to be talking to. The hurt of a moment ago has flowed right through him. He's a boy again, with the world at his feet, a whole lifetime in brilliant view. He looks as fresh as the day he first walked into my lab, bristling for a fight. He got his fight. He got his story. I watch him swing his bag up onto his shoulder, his fist gripping the strap up by the neck of his polo shirt. He starts down the aisle, and I think he's going to head out through the same door I came through. But then he stops and turns towards the scaffolding that holds the netting in place. There are some feed bins there.

'Where are you going?'

'There's another way out of this. For both of us.'

He upends a feed bin and climbs up onto it. From there he can grip the edge of the scaffolding and clamber up. The poles are wet, and he's wiping bird-slime from his fingers. He holds one shit-streaked hand out for me.

'Come with me. There's a door leading onto a balcony. Rooftops. Ways out of here.'

'No, James. You're on your own.'

He retracts his hand and stays there on his hunkers, watching me. After a moment he stands up and starts pulling himself up onto the scaffolding platform that runs around the upper part of the church. I see him bathed in light from above, unbending from a crouch and scrolling through a menu on his phone. Then, finding no one he can think of calling, he puts the phone away and continues climbing, grabbing handfuls of netting and pulling himself up towards the stone ledge that marks the upper limit of the aviary. I realise now that it conceals a door. Gareth's face hangs below him, brilliant in its sleeping stillness. The projector whirrs. When I look back James is gone, like the memory of the thing that woke you, vanished before you can work out what it was.

◉

PART SIX

Millennium Heights

CHAPTER TWENTY-SEVEN

A Box Of Birds

◉

The nurse comes in the mornings. He makes himself breakfast, spends an hour playing backgammon on the computer, and then remembers that he's supposed to help me wash Effi. I hear him thumping around in the kitchen, then mumbling my name around my bedroom door, wondering whether I'm decent. I come out in my dressing gown and follow him into the living room, where we've set up Effi's bed. I can sense the heat in his dark skin, the nervousness behind his big brown irises. Effi greets him with a fart and bathes in his shadow as he leans over the bed to strap the pressure gauge to her arm. She loves that silhouette of him against the daylight, the tang of his breath as he separates a finger or finds a vein.

'My dishy nurse,' she whispers, scanning his face then trying to refocus on the TV in the corner. 'Thank God for you.'

He switches on the blood-sugar meter and waves it playfully under her nose. He finds a fat brown finger and she says 'Ouch' though he hasn't done anything yet, and he says 'Now for the icepick in the forehead' and she says 'Will you be so clumsy when I finally expire?' He punches the needle into the flesh and peers down at the readout, and we stand there, the unlikely family, waiting for the numbers to settle.

'And I reckon your mum could lay off them jelly babies,' he says, showing me her latest blood-sugar outrage.

His colour fascinates me. I want to examine him close up, work out exactly how that face is put together. I imagine his lips on my shoulder, the scrape of his stubble on my bare skin. I wait for another track to start up in his earphones before mouthing a sexual invitation whose exoticism surprises even me; he finally clicks off his soundpod and stares.

'Well, Yvonne? Are you going to help me bath this fat pig or not?'

The traffic roars through the half-drawn curtains. I go into the kitchen, which still reeks of the full English breakfast he's just cooked himself, and flick the kettle on for tea. Daren stands at the end of the bed and lifts his arms like a Scooby Doo monster. Effi doesn't move. He finds a big toe under the sheet and gives it a squeeze. The sensory jolt sends a flood of power rising through her brainstem, sifting her dreams like stones on a beach. She hears the bark of a chai-wallah on a rocking jetty. The slap of ocean against the pier. She feels a hand squeezing her, pushing the sari between her legs, the first man that ever touched her, faceless and lost in the pre-dawn crowds. The stain of Bombay washed out by a curve of sea. Then her cortex crackles back to life and she stares out dully at her two torturers, the blue rubber lifting-straps, the soap and flannels and towels. 'Christ,' she says. 'Am I dirty again already?'

'You stink,' Daren says. 'You are absolutely minging.'

'That's because it's so bloody hot in here.'

'It's summertime. And the people what own this building haven't worked out how to turn the heating off. Don't worry. You're paying for it.'

'Can't you open a window?'

'The windows *are* open. Can't you hear the motorway?'

I'm off with the traffic, racing my own souped-up demons.

'Come on, Yvonne. Let's get this big fat minger sitting up against the pillow.'

We drag one thick arm around each of our necks and get the straps under her. Then one two three and she's upright on the pillows, panting from the heat and the insult of displacement. The nurse gets busy with the flannel. I like watching him work. He keeps pursing and softening his lips as the task gets tricky and then easy again, as crises of gravity and access arise and are deftly handled, threaded knots of concentration unravelling and pulling free. His arms are bare, and you can see the dry skin on his shoulders, the oil-black hair in his armpits. He tosses me the flannel to wash her down below, and then he squeezes some toothpaste onto her brush and tells her to open wide. She sits through it obediently, grinning like a lunatic while I hold up her lacey orange nightdress and dab her dry with the towel. He gets her to spit into a bowl then stands over her, brushing her silver-lined tresses and asking about her holidays, playing the hairdresser game, the not-dying game, until they're both thick with smiles.

'Swimming,' she yawns. 'I want to go swimming.'

I put the tea down by her bed and perch on the edge. I pick up the old Bombay street map, unfold it along its familiar lines of softness, and start tracing a path between the beaches.

'OK. You get off the train at Victoria Terminus.'

It's like a gift of oxygen. I hear her dry cough, then her sigh, her grateful release from this world.

'You can see the top of the GPO like a great big onion. Dabawallahs are everywhere. You come down through the main concourse and you're on to Bori Bunder. You go up Cruickshank Road towards Dhobi Talao. A little side-street gets you onto Queen's Road. From here you can hear the sound of boats and seagulls and everything.'

She listens, breathing heavily. There's an abrasion in her lungs, a waking snore. A tentacle of neural activity reaches far across her cortex, links up with a flicker of sensory memory and claims it for her life story. All the while her cortex drifts into slow synchrony, out of the rolling foothills of the alpha wave and into the greater ruggedness of theta and delta. The smell of Crawford Market. The shouts of children on Chowpatty Beach. Sometimes her ancient eyelids flicker, jolting over some feature of Bombay's topography, and I wonder how much is getting through. Daren insists that she can't hear me, but that's just medical bombast, the unwarranted certainty of nurses' training. I'd rather believe that consciousness was a luxury Effi had learned to live without, that she'd moved on to a thriftier place where the body operates without knowing. Maybe it always did, and a graceful dying is just the proof of it. She's going out as she came in, a bundle of automatic routines that can cope perfectly well without the buzz of being here.

'Don't stop,' she murmurs, from somewhere on the edge of sleep.

I keep reading, tracing the route from Opera House Junction, cutting careful shapes out of post-war Bombay. Her forehead is soft and elastic, like the skin on hot chocolate. There's a pale blue cross from radiotherapy. Several more on her abdomen, if I were to lift the sheet and look. Cancer has joined her up, bowel to lungs to liver, made her whole. It's the strokes, the sudden blood starvations, that we're afraid of now. I fold the old map, taking care with its yellowing creases, and try to make out the sound of her breathing over the steady tear of the dual carriageway.

'Ninety over sixty,' Daren says. 'Getting better all the time.'

He coils up his blood-pressure meter and stows it in his bag. He surfaces with a tube of paper strips. He stabs a finger with a lance, dabs the paper in the blood and carries it over to the window. For a moment he conducts the roaring stillness with gentle hand-gestures, fixing her sweet blood in the overheated air.

'All these cars,' he says, holding the curtain aside with his other hand. 'Where they all going? On such a hot September day.'

Bright sunlight blazes on the carpet where he's standing. In the corner, the TV shows a bleached, dusty screen.

'What's this you're watching?' I ask.

He lets the curtain drop to frame a strip of brightness. He grabs the remote and thumbs the volume higher. Dim sleeping figures are visible, the ghostly denizens of a twenty-four hour reality show.

'This is brilliant. It's called *The Retreat*, right? They're on this healing retreat halfway up the highest mountain in New Zealand. They sit around all day shouting at each other and once a week someone gets voted off. The thing is, there's a storm going on and they're running out of supplies. The camp's completely cut off. The rescue services can't get to them because the weather's so bad. They reckon they might die up there. It's a real bummer because someone just got voted off. He can't leave because of the weather.'

I don't know why I want to know more.

'What's his name?'

'David. His name's David.'

I stare at the blackness. My heart knells strangely. It's a feeling. It isn't truth.

'What really gets me,' Daren is saying, 'is that about a hundred million people are watching this, worldwide. Would you really want to be so famous that even your own death is on the telly?'

I wonder if James would see the irony. He would find a way out of it, another mask of deceptions to hide behind. Unless, this time, reality has finally caught up with him. The stories bought him time, but in the end they simply stopped being true.

'I don't know. If you've got people coming after you, this might actually be the best place to hide away.'

He thumbs it off. The screen returns to a purer sunlit blackness, mottled with fingermarks. He pulls the curtain wide and looks out.

'It's a beautiful day, Yvonne. Effi's asleep. You've been cooped up in this place too long. What you need is a swing on the swings. What you need is a bit of sun on them lovely legs.'

'I...'

'Come on. Feel the fear and do it anyway.'

He stands there, holding imaginary swing-chains, pushing himself back and forwards in the middle of Effi's curtained sitting-room. Forward, back, forward, back. I can't help laughing. He's actually swinging, pushing, pulling, shuffling his feet on the carpet as he goes. I laugh until the incubated air makes me giddy; I laugh until I can almost hear the person I used to be. He's swinging, on the swings, on the carpet, on the eighth floor. It's easy, when you know how.

We wait for a gap in the traffic and run across the road. I'm wearing a yellow sleeveless sundress cut above the knee. Daren has taken off his smock and is displaying a red basketball vest with a huge question-mark where the player's number should be.

'See?' he says, opening the gate to the playground. 'No ten-year-old drug-pushers with baseball bats. They're all at school.'

There are two swings in the one frame. We sit down, dipping backwards side by side. The rubber is hot against my thighs. My skin fizzes with the unfamiliar prodigy of sunshine. Daren stretches his hands high up the chains and tries to pull himself up through brute strength.

'So this memory place you're taking me to. That's where they've put all the data?'

I cling on to the chain-linked steel. So many people in the world I could have confided in, and I go and spill my secrets to Effi's nurse. But we've been spending a lot of time together, staying up late with Effi, hiding out like gangsters while the summer motors by without us. It's time to face the world again. The launch of the Memory Centre was always going to be the most convincing statement of the Lycee's success in mapping the Lorenzo Circuit. So Daren and I are calling in a night nurse for Effi, getting dressed up and going along to the grand opening. I haven't seen Gillian since she arranged for my operation. She wore the transcendent tiredness of someone who had won a long victory. She was surrounded by her trophies: the treasured special issue of *Nature*, hot off the press, with its three back-to-back papers on the structure of the Lorenzo Circuit. Big fold-out colour plates showing the material basis of memory in three-dimensional glamour. Three meticulously detailed articles that would change the world, with Gillian's name taking pride of place at the end of each long list of authors. The wonderful back-to-frontness of it all: the woman whose vision had made it possible tacked on at the end like an afterthought. She made the calls quietly, fingering the toned bicep of the arm that held the phone, warding off a few awkward questions with her stay-where-you-are smile. Later, when it was done, she left me alone with it, sensing my need to say goodbye. It was a tangle of platinum–iridium wires, insulated in polyurethane. The pulse generator was as discreet as a hearing aid. The thorn in my soul had been excised and rinsed clean. I thought of Mateus, whose research had made it possible. He still had his hooks in me. It had been part of me without my knowing, and then eventually with my consent. I tried to remember how it had felt, to have that secret buried in my cortex. But it hadn't felt like anything. It was me, and it wasn't me. That was exactly what Gareth had been trying to say.

'So your people haven't lost anything?' Daren says.

'Gareth didn't actually steal the data. He copied it. We thought he was going to hand it over to Sansom. Or we thought that they would force him to. It was still there on Ermintrude, the Lycee's server, but he'd encrypted it. He'd locked it away, surrounded it with weird firewalls, so that no one could get at it without his help. They were working on reconstructing the fragments from their back-ups, but it was taking too long. He talked to Gillian. As soon as he knew that I'd seen what he wanted me to see, he got in touch with her. She persuaded him that he'd made his point, and he agreed to cooperate. He reversed the mess he had made, they pulled the data off the servers, and they were ready to publish.'

Brown eyes hang on my words.

'And what happened to Sansom? Their experiment in the mines?'

'Gillian needed no persuading to take on that particular cause. It's proving to be a complex investigation. Sansom have the muscle to cover their traces. They're claiming that the only people they ever had working up in the dale were some visiting scientists manning a research lab, under perfectly ordinary levels of industrial security. I still don't know if I'm going to have to testify. They'll have moved them out by now, anyway. In the meantime, they've got a renewed terrorism campaign to deal with. Aslan's Law have taken a particular interest in their activities.'

I think of the woman with the amulet, hurriedly released from underground into a new life as a hyper-promoted researcher. I've had my tangle of wires removed, but she's stuck with hers. There's no doubting the power of Sansom's technology, even to reverse the damage that she has had done to her. Perhaps that gives her some hope, that she might find her past again, like she found the new life she thought she wanted. Whatever happens, Sansom will have to keep promoting her.

'So what about your job?' Daren says. 'Are you going back there?'

I look at the yellowing trees that screen off the park from the dual carriageway. Mid-September. Fulling will be full of betas in four-wheel-drives, unloading duvets and home cinema systems for a new university year.

'What, to cause more animals unnecessary suffering in the pursuit of some half-baked theory? I never wanted it, Daren. I had no more choice about it than the mice whose genes I tampered with. I thought I was experimenting on them. Actually, I think they were experimenting on me.'

'You've grown a conscience.' He sounds pleased to have made the connection. 'Con-Science. That's a good joke, isn't it, Yvonne?'

'They're not against science. They're against its dominance as a way of knowing. They think there are other ways of getting at the truth.'

There's music in that smile, music for driving to.

'But you weren't a bad person to be doing that research. That work does a lot of good. That drug we're giving Effi, to help her breathing? She's already had four months' more life than she would have had otherwise. Think of all the fun we've had in four months.'

'So are you saying that they ran their mazes for a reason? All those mice in all those experiments that never led anywhere?'

'I'm saying Effi's drugs were tested on animals. The people who test them do everything to make sure the animals don't feel pain. I see the good this stuff does. I care for you, Yvonne. I'm not going to let you beat yourself up over this.'

I manage a jaded smile.

'Come on, Daren. You know what would have happened if Sansom had got the Lorenzo Circuit data. They would have patented them. No one would have been able to use that mapping information, to develop treatments or whatever, without paying a licence fee. We wanted it to stay in the public domain. That's what Gareth risked his life for.'

'He wasn't doing it for the data, though, was he? He was doing it for you.'

I shrug, acknowledging the baffling wisdom in his words. I feel the tug of another sleepless night, and let my arms drape forward around the chains.

'The data on Ermintrude had only been encrypted. They hadn't been destroyed. As long as he was prepared to help us out, we could unscramble everything. I went to see him in hospital. I had his phone, of course, so he knew how to contact me. Getting himself admitted was his idea. He said he had his own data to unscramble. I saw his face light up and I think I finally understood. He wanted *me* to come after him. It had to be me. He said I was the only one who appreciated what he'd been trying to say.'

'Why birds, though? What's that all about?'

'The birds are your thoughts. Electrochemical processes you can have no knowledge of. You have to look after them. You have a duty of care towards them. Otherwise, what does it matter what you do? That's all he was trying to tell us.'

'Oh, yeah.' He frowns, showing flex-points in his face that I never knew were there.

'That's why he stole the data. He didn't want Sansom's money. He wanted my attention. Never mind that he got everyone else's attention too. This was all about me proving how much I cared for him. He made me remember. Me finding him, in his eyes, was a proof of how much he meant to me.'

'The poor boy was in love with you!'

'What does it say, Daren, that all these young men keep falling for me?'

'It says, Yvonne, that you have an interesting personality. And you're not wearing anything under that dress.'

I hide my blushes in the sky. As I incline my face I feel hair sliding down my back, a wave of spangling softnesses. The sky is blue. The sunlight passes right through me.

'That's what I don't understand,' Daren is saying. 'It was just you and James in that church. How did you stop Sansom getting their nasty hands on the data?'

I close my eyes on the light. I push back with my feet and let go. The breeze on my skin, my whole body moving. At the centre of it all, this flicker of knowing.

I'm here.

The birds startle and clatter around us. They mob him, high on the scaffolding that lines the church, and he's having to flap his hands to keep them away.

'Yvonne. Come on. We can get through this.'

'No, James.'

His face is stretched by tiredness. That stubble looks rough. It's his moment to stand straight and tell the world that he denies every shred of its reality, but he looks embarrassed, caught out in front of a crowd. I still don't know who he is. Behind all the lies there must be something that doesn't trip itself up, make a joke out of its own self-contradiction. Or did I fall in love with the contradictions, the supreme confidence that couldn't look you in the eye, the militant truth-seeker who hid himself in stories? He wanted the sleepwalking masses to wake up, but all he had to give them was another fairy tale. Surely a man's lies will always lead back somewhere, to the facts of his character that are bio-logically true: the thing itself, not the thing's invention? If he could have been honest about that, we might have got on. But he couldn't find it. He tried to make it up, and he fell apart. In the end, I was happy with the contradictions. I could have loved them, if he'd given us a chance.

'There's too many,' he yells. 'They're crammed in too tight. We'll have to let them go.'

He starts pulling at the netting, ripping a long tear in the fabric.

'What are you doing?'

'Yvonne, I can't walk past a caged animal. I couldn't do it before and I can't do it now.'

269

I watch him climbing again, reaching for a girder that juts out from the stonework, from which he can reach the mesh above his head. He starts tearing at it with both hands until the whole of this side has come away. A few of Gareth's birds flap flatly into freedom. But James wants them all set free, and he keeps tearing at the netting with all his weight until two edges of the rectangle have come down, freeing a sagging triangle of sky. He runs around the ledge at the top of the church, whooping out his satisfaction. Columns of light from the strengthening sun are melting the darkness of the nave. The birds startle at James' noise and begin to rise in shoaly layers through the hole in the mesh, yellows and greens and browns, with dazzling wing-flashes and staring, sky-struck eyes. I can see the grey tags on their legs, each bearing a nugget of data. I stand on the midden floor of the aviary and watch the treasure of the Lorenzo Circuit take off through the gaps in the roof-tiles, rising past me in a flock of separate happenings, thoughts that cannot know themselves, the scattered wisdom of the morning.

SUBSCRIBERS

⊙

Unbound is a new kind of publishing house. Our books are funded directly by readers. This was a very popular idea during the late eighteenth and early nineteenth century. Now we have revived it for the internet age. It allows authors to write the books they really want to write and readers to support the writing they would most like to see published.

The names listed below are of readers who have pledged their support and made this book happen. If you'd like to join them, visit: www.unbound.co.uk.

Stan Abbott
Jad Abumrad
David Adger
Jessica Adkins
José Ignacio Alcántara
Andre Aleman
Richard Allen
Ian Apperly
Kelvin Arellano
Helen Armour
Marc Armsby
Jill Ashby
Lane Ashfeldt
Michael Atkins
Anthony Atkinson
Steve Back
Sara Bailey
Charles Bamlett

Natalie Banner
David Barker
Susan Barrett
Elizabeth Barry
Cat Barton
Rachael Beale
Michael Bearpark
Nick Bedford
Vaughan Bell
Richard Bentall
Kinga Bisits
Jonathan Blackie
Anthony Blackmore
Andrew Booker
Karl Bovenizer
Alan Bowden
Tim Bowness
Alan Braid

Don Brechin

Heather Briggs

Patricia Brindley

Lee Broadley

Jon Brock

Matthew Broome

Karl Brown

Gareth Buchaillard-Davies

John Budgick

Jonathan Bullock

Marcus Butcher

Felicity Callard

Xander Cansell

Jane Cantellow

Sarah and Stephen Caro

Bernise Carolino

Gianfranco Cecconi

Kayo Chang

Dave Chantrey

Lynne Chellingworth

Harry S. Chima

Ian Clarkson

Emma Cleasby

Kenny Clements

Tim Closs

Stevyn Colgan

Annabel Connor

Clare Connor

Lucy Connor

Stephen Connor

Ben Cons

Joy Conway

Maddy Cook

Tristan James Cook

Ann Cooper

Nick Cottam

Robyn Cowan

Nik Cox

Eleanor Crawford

Caroline Cresswell

Molly Crockett

Kate Cross

Lisa Crozier

Chris Currie

Jennifer Curtis

Nija Dalal

Valerie Daly

John Danaher

Gillian Darley

David Darmon

Ian Davidson

Peter Davidson

Carrie Davies

Buff Davis

Jane Davis

Ian Davison

Jonathan Davison

Jim Demetre

Marc de Rosnay

J F Derry

Lee de-Wit

Sarah Dilnot

Andy Ditchfield

Mark D'Mello

Ann D'Mello

Jenny Doughty

Rebecca Doyle

Catherine Dyer

Christine Dyer

Nicola Dyer

Sara Dyer

Colin Edgar

Len Edgerly

Caroline Edmonds

Kay Elliott

Gabriel Engel

Martyn Evans

Florian Feder

Athena Fernyhough

Isaac Fernyhough

Justine Fieth

John Findlay

Iain Finlayson

Philip Fiuza

Steve Fleming

Jo Fowler

Mya Frazier

John Frewin

Uta Frith

Valere Fry

David Fuller

Harry Galina

Hilary Gallo

Gill Garratt

Jane Garrison

Wendy Gayler

Lisa Gee

Trevor Gentry

David George

Kenneth Gilhooly

David Gill

Sophie Goldsworthy

Helen Gordon

Terence Gould

Neil Graham

Voula Grand

Siobhán Greaney

James Greaves

Johnny Grey

Rhett Griffiths

Viv Groskop

David Grossman

Sam Guglani

Joey Haban

Alys Hale

Melanie Hancox

Graham Handscomb

Tom Hartley

Stacy Hartung

Caitlin Harvey

George Hawthorne

Jonathan Heawood

Bill Herbert

Vincent Hevern

E O Higgins

Jonathan Hoare

Jessica Hobson

Ala Hola

Helen Holmes

Bruce Hood

Aidan Horner

Sophie Howarth

Philip Huebner

Robin Humphrey

Shona Illingworth

Sue Ireland

Mags Irwin

Majeed Jabbar

Fadi Jameel

Emma James

Simon James

Simon J. James

Julia Jary

Simon Jary

Karine Jegard

Lyndsey Jenkins

Mikael Johansson

Sholeh Johnston

Alice Jones
David Jones
Gail Jones
Jessica Jones
Nick Jones
Avril Joy
Peter Jukes
Vassiliki Karapapa
Laura Karnath
Alex Kaula
Philomena Keane
Andrew Kelly
John Kent
Rachael Kerr
Jan Kewley
Dan Kieran
Maree Kimberley
Sally King
David Knell
Lynsay Kobelis
Sreenivas Koka
Peter Kollarik
Roman Krznaric
Lia Kvavilashvili
Suzanne Laizik
Keith Laws
Jimmy Leach
Jonathan Lee
Mary and Paul Lewis
Sai Li
Jane Lidstone
Caroline Lien
Catherine Lloyd
Robert Loch
Catherine Loveday
Simon McCarthy-Jones
Emma McCartney

Kyle McCreary
Loren MccRory
Rod McDonald
Mo McFarland
Anthony McGregor
Ewa Maciejewski
Catherine McMahon
Paul McMahon
Dominic McMullan
Jane Macnaughton
Sara Maitland
Claire Malcolm
Tom Manly
Laura Marcus
Caroline Martin
Tracey Martin
Sarah Massey
Ryan Matthews
Laura Mazzoli Smith
Joel Meadows
Alan Meins
Elizabeth Meins
Kathleen Meins
Christopher Middleton
Margo Milne
Patrick Mineault
John Mitchinson
Sascha Moege
Victor Montori
Alice Moody
Chris Moore
Frank Moore
Julia Morris
Michael Mortensen
Peter Moseley
Marianna Murin
Tiffany Murray

Gordon Mutch
Malin Nilsson
Beate Nolan
Courtenay Norbury
Greg Norman
Richard Northover
Lauren O'Connell
Joseph O'Dea
Trevor O'Gorman
Susan Oke
Allen O'Leary
Kathleen O'Neill
Yang-May Ooi
Silvia Orr
Richard Osbourne
Clare Overton
Patricio Pagani
Mike Page
Raquel Pais
Kevin Parr
Mike Pearce
Jonathan Peelle
Orit Peleg
Philippa Perry
Michael Kai Petersen
Freddie Phillips
Helen Phillips
Edward Platt
Ingrid Plowman
Justin Pollard
Ulrich Pontes
Liz Power
Marianne Preece
Alex Preston
Kate Pullinger
Jackie Quang
Tom Quick

Brady Rafuse
Ben Ralph
Dineshi Ramesh
Varpu Rantala
Matthew Ratcliffe
Katherine Ray
Primula Rayner
Colin Read
Dr Jeremy Rees,
    Consultant Neurologist
Nic Regan
Stephen Regan
Vincent Reid
Mark ZaaZ Richards
Graeme Rigby
Tim Ringrose
Heleen Riper
Jeanette Roberts MBE
Wendy Robertson
Mary Robson
Harriet Rosenthal
Sue Ross
James Russell
Amanda Sander
Lisa Sargood
Andrea Sarner
Corinne Saunders
Anthony Scholfield
Tom Shakespeare
Sharad Sharma
Jon Simons
Ross Sleight
David Smailes
Marc Smith
James Smythe
Beverley Snape
Frank Spencer

Manuel Sprung
Katie Stamas
Vanessa St Clair
David Stevens
Jessica Stevenson
Laurence Stevenson
Karen Stott
Alison Summers
Mark Sundaram
Jon Sutton
Melissa Terras
Stephen Thompson
Sarah Thwaites
David Tubby
Luca Tummolini
James Tunnicliffe
Michelle Turner
Jon Turney
Richard Vahrman
Mark Vent
Essi Viding
Belle Wallace

Judi Walsh
Jürgen Walter
Miranda Ward
James Watts
Patricia Waugh
Grace Webb
Martin Webb
Valerie Webb
Susanne Weis
Zena West
Angie Wheeler
David Williams
Hilery Williams
Julia Wilson
Ashley Wolke
Angela Woods
Erica Woods
Steve Woodward
David Yaden
Sophie Yauner
Marc Zeller

ACKNOWLEDGEMENTS

◉

This book was made possible by the generosity of more than three hundred subscribers; I am very grateful to everyone who supported the project. Special thanks to John Mitchinson, Rachael Kerr, Cathy Hurren, Xander Cansell, Matt Railton, Dan Mogford, Justin Pollard, Jimmy Leach and everyone at Unbound; to Richard Bentall, Sarah Caro, Cristiana Cavina-Pratesi, David Chalmers, Andrew Crumey, Christine Dyer, John Findlay, Rhett Griffiths, Claudia Hammond, Simon James, Bella Lacey, Jonah Lehrer, Anthony McGregor, Sara Maitland, Gill Norman, Richard Osbourne, Edward Platt, Eleanor Rees, Nic Regan, Trevor Robbins, Jon Simons, Hugo Spiers, Angela Tagini, Pat Waugh, Valerie Webb, Susanne Weis and Angela Woods. As ever, I owe a huge debt of gratitude to my agent, David Grossman, and to Lizzie, Athena and Isaac for their patience and support. A version of the first chapter appeared in *New Writing 14* (Granta/British Council). I received assistance at critical points from a Time to Write award from the Northern Writers' Awards and an Arts Council of England Grant for the Arts. The quotations from Plato's *Theaetetus* in Chapter 26 are from Benjamin Jowett's nineteenth-century translation.

A NOTE ABOUT THE TYPEFACES

◉

The typeface used in this book is Minion, designed by Robert Slimbach for Adobe Systems, California, in 1989. Inspired by the timeless beauty of types of the late Renaissance, Minion was digitally created primarily as a traditional text face whose name comes from the archaic naming system for type sizes, in which minion is between *nonpareil* and *brevier*.

Chapter headings are set in Futura Medium, designed in 1927 by German designer Paul Renner. Futura is based on the geometric shapes representative of the Bauhaus design style of the 1920s.